BLACK SHEEP

Feathers and Fire Book 6

SHAYNE SILVERS

CONTENTS

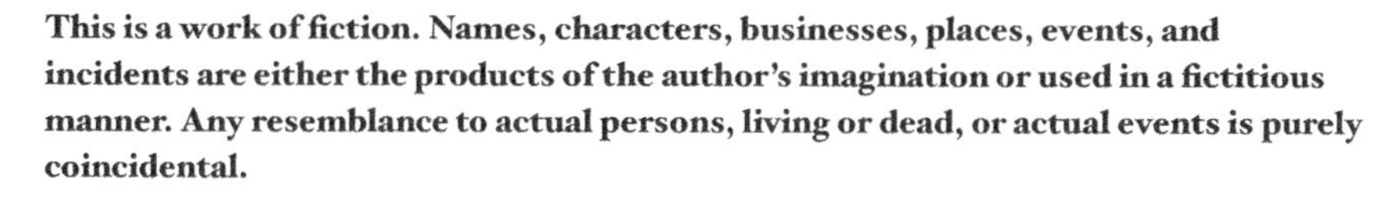

Shayne Silvers

Black Sheep

Feathers and Fire Book 6

A TempleVerse Series

ISBN 13: **978-1-947709-23-2**

info@shaynesilvers.com

THE WHITE ROSE IS DEAD...

Callie Penrose returns home to find a year has passed, and that everyone believes her long dead.

Roland Haviar, once her mentor and now a Master Vampire, has become a bloodthirsty tyrant, fulfilling his vow to bathe the City of Fountains in blood until he avenges her death. And the Vatican Shepherds, once his brothers, stand in his way.

In his quest for closure, Roland surrounds the city in a magical barrier that blocks all methods of escape—or help—giving him time to seek out an ancient artifact powerful enough to put an end to everyone and everything once and for all...

In honor of Callie Penrose.

But when Callie is mysteriously cursed to appear as a demon, she finds herself hunted by the very people she wants to protect. Her only hope is to forge new alliances—make deals with devils—to stop the man she once loved as a father.

And all the while, the devil laughs in delight, naming Callie friend as he waits with bated breath for the world to end...

Shayne Silvers
WORDSLINGER AUTHOR

DON'T FORGET! VIP's get early access to all sorts of Temple-Verse goodies, including signed copies, private giveaways, and advance notice of future projects. AND A FREE NOVELLA! Click the image or join here: www.shaynesilvers.com/l/219800

FOLLOW and LIKE:

Shayne's FACEBOOK PAGE

www.shaynesilvers.com/l/38602

I try my best to respond to all messages, so don't hesitate to drop me a line. Not interacting with readers is the biggest travesty that most authors can make. Let me fix that.

I

Cain stepped up beside me as I stared down from the expansive marble balcony of the fabled Solomon's Temple to the spread of green gardens below. From this vantage, they resembled a patchwork quilt of new life—in a vast array of green shades. Plants, flowers, and fruits that shouldn't have been able to grow beside each other were thriving in perfect harmony, despite all odds. New buds of color peppered the green quilt—flowers being born in a kaleidoscope of beauty that made any words obsolete. This scene demanded silence. Respectful admiration. Awe—

"It stinks here," Cain grumbled, pinching his nose.

I elbowed him in the ribs, smiling in spite of myself. It smelled beautiful and earthy; the humid, warm air was pregnant with life.

"You ready?" Cain asked.

My heart fluttered slightly at the question. Phix had only just told us about how long I had actually been gone during my trip through the Doors—a quest I had undertaken in order to gain access to Solomon's Temple. My ancestral home.

It still felt surreal to be standing here, like I was standing in the heart of the Renaissance—back when all the now-famous art was first being painted or architecture being erected. Like I was the first person to see it all and know what it would one day become.

I had, quite literally, only seen the balcony where we now stood—a massive structure overlooking the gardens. The balcony stretched for over a hundred yards and was filled with all manner of furniture, art, sculptures, and plants; the roof soared high above our heads, supported by gargantuan marble columns.

And this was only one *side* of the *outside* of the vast Temple.

I considered Cain's question pensively, thinking back on my city. Before I had left on my quest, Roland had warned Fabrizio—the First Shepherd—that if anything happened to me, he would drown Kansas City in rivers of blood. He had also sworn that he would hunt Fabrizio down like a dog, turn him into a vampire, and only *then* kill him—just to be sure Fabrizio's eternal soul was damned and black-listed from Heaven. He had warned Fabrizio that only the entire might of the Vatican Conclave and its Shepherds would be able to save Kansas City from his wrath.

Even though Fabrizio was entirely innocent of any guilt—I had just learned that my trip through the Doors had lasted for one year and that most everyone thought me dead.

If one thing could be said about Roland, it was that he was a man of his word. There was a chance that he was still waiting for me, but the more I thought about it, remembering the look I'd seen in those eyes, and his promise to Fabrizio...I didn't have high hopes.

I let out a breath, rolling my shoulders. "We will handle it," I said, more confidently than I felt. I almost didn't want to go back myself. Not because I was scared of what Roland had done.

No.

It was because I was terrified to see what his *actions* had done to *him*—a man of the cloth resorting to violence of the sort that he had previously only reserved for monsters. Except...now *he* was one of those monsters. And the only thing he still seemed to care about was my safety. So I feared that, if he had given up on my return and thought me dead, his actions may have broken something inside him—something he might never be able to recover. In that case, I was the only one who stood a chance of providing any possibility of his redemption—or saving Kansas City.

He needed to see me alive and well, unharmed and whole.

In my journey through the Doors, I had seen a stained-glass window on a church. In fact, that window had been what let me escape the Doors to earn the right to enter Solomon's Temple.

And in that window had been a depiction of Roland and a childlike version of me, holding hands before a burning cross, with Heaven above, Hell below, and four haunting figures at the darkened corners of the glass. One of those figures had resembled Nate, I was sure of it, but the others had been only vague silhouettes. Terrifying, frightening silhouettes astride wicked winged beasts of nightmares.

Nate Temple's new gang of Horsemen to balance the Biblical Four Horsemen.

But that was a problem for another day.

Roland, figuratively speaking, had rescued me from the Doors. Now, it was my turn to rescue him—from himself.

Solomon cleared his throat behind us and I turned to face him. He was a roguishly handsome older man with shoulder-length white hair and a well-groomed white beard. His tan skin was a sharp contrast to his white linen pants and shirt, and his green eyes held all the colors of his gardens below the balcony—brimming with life just as vibrant. The one majorly noticeable aspect of Solomon was that a good portion of his veins were black—looking like a root system beneath his skin. Everyone's veins looked that way—you just couldn't normally see them. He didn't seem particularly affected by the veins, so I was assuming they didn't bother him much. Or he had a high pain tolerance.

Richard—or Last Breath when in his lion form—stood in his human form at Solomon's side, hands clasped behind his back. He currently looked like a tall Asian man, heavily corded with muscle and sporting short, black, spiked hair in a messy look. He had the ability to shapeshift entirely into any look he wanted but seemed to prefer this look so far as I had seen.

"Richard will go with you," Solomon said.

I opened my mouth to argue, knowing that having any new faces at my side when I returned to Kansas City might only make matters worse—let alone if Richard shifted into his lion form and was recognized as Last Breath—the creature that everyone had heard so much about when I was last in town. The one everyone had thought to be hunting me.

Richard must have read the uncertainty on my face because he suddenly stepped forward in an almost aggressive manner, causing Cain to growl in warning as he set his feet and his hand shot to his hip where his bone dagger was tucked into his belt.

The dagger he'd used to kill his brother, Abel, so long ago. I placed a hand on his forearm.

Richard lowered his eyes in a submissive gesture, but his voice was anything but as he raised his eyes to meet mine. "I will simply stalk you from the shadows if you deny my aid. My purpose is to keep the Solomon bloodline safe, and thanks to your mother's schemes—hiding your very existence from me since your birth—I have so far failed you in that capacity. I will not let my honor be discarded so easily now that I have finally found you."

My mouth clicked shut, seeing the raw pain dancing in his eyes. He had a point. My parents had concealed my identity with a powerful ward so that those hunting me couldn't find me when they left me on the steps of Abundant Angel Catholic Church as a baby. My mother had fled Solomon's Temple, taking the ancient Seal of Solomon with her, before anyone even discovered she was pregnant, and hadn't been seen since that fateful day at the church where they said their final goodbyes to me.

By coincidence or design—I wasn't entirely sure which—I had discovered the Seal of Solomon in an underground vault in Kansas City. Using it had essentially turned my GPS signal back on, and Solomon and Last Breath had wasted no time in answering the call—in sending me on the traditional quest of searching out the infamous Solomon's Temple, my apparent birthright as his only surviving heir.

A birthright that I had just earned, only to discover Kansas City was tearing itself apart in my absence, and that I didn't have time to explore these halls, get answers to questions about my parents and possibly learn why they had seen the need to hide me from Solomon and Richard, giving me up to be raised by strangers rather than these two.

My mother's actions led a very loud part of me to hold a certain amount of caution when dealing with Richard and Solomon. She must have had a reason to keep me from them. If a magical fortress on a different plane of existence wasn't safe enough to raise me, how could an orphanage or adopted family be any safer?

So...

Part of me wanted answers from these two. Part of me wanted to keep my distance.

"You are our family, Callie," Richard added, in a much gentler tone this time, reading the hesitation on my face.

"She already has a guardian," Cain said, pointing at Phix. The legendary Sphinx—who had been lounging on a nearby fur carpet, cleaning her wickedly long claws with her teeth—paused to look up at us, blinking lazily...lethally.

2

Phix could moderate her size to some extent, because I'd seen her the size of a horse and other times the size of a large lion. Somewhat like a centaur, she was a cross between a stunningly beautiful exotic woman from the belly button up and a feline murder machine from that merging point to her tail. White, feathered wings arched from her back, but they were currently tucked in close, surprisingly compact. She was curvaceous to a level that proved I could be envious across different species, and she both knew and relished the jab to my ego, never bothering to wear a shirt. Her thick, long, ebony hair hung down her back, and her purple eyes were like pools of eternal dreams that just might be able to hypnotize you. She loved riddles—primarily making you look a fool—and murdering pretty much anything.

She was also my friend and self-proclaimed Guardian—capital G, in her opinion.

Richard dipped his head respectfully at Phix. She watched him with her mercurial eyes, not responding. Phix was what one might call territorial—entirely comfortable with eviscerating, dismembering, and then feasting on the still-steaming flesh of anyone who stood between her and her toys. I, in this example, was one of her toys. At least that's the way she saw it—I still wasn't entirely sure why.

I also had uncomfortable suspicions about her self-proclaimed role as my ally, and not because I knew so little about her. No. It was something else entirely. Something I didn't want to even consider thinking about at the moment.

Richard turned back to Cain. "Phix is her companion. Perhaps even a guardian as well. But I am *family*. Much like you, Cain." He smiled faintly at the world's first murderer. "Technically, I was family first. You should call me big brother," he added, the corner of his lips curling up into a smile.

Cain's hand actually gripped the bone dagger this time, and his smile was as sharp as a scalpel. "Come closer for a second so I can whisper a secret in your ear, Dick Breath."

Cain thought it was amusing to combine variants of Richard and Last Breath in truly creative ways—as if he'd spent years doing it rather than the brief time they had known each other.

Richard's shoulders tightened and his eyes narrowed dangerously. Phix's purr was suddenly audible, even from this distance, like a small generator had just fired up. I flung up a hand, forestalling them. I rounded on Cain with a stern glare. "Richard or Last Breath. None of this mix-and-match crap, Cain. Save that for our enemies."

Cain continued glaring at Richard over my shoulder. Finally, he turned to me with an ingratiating smile. "I'm just trying to teach him about brotherly love," he said innocently. "I guess I can meet you in the middle, Dick."

"Whatever you say, Abel," Richard said through his teeth.

Cain and Richard both lunged at the same time, but I had been waiting for it. I swept Cain's legs out from under him so hard that he landed flat on his back, knocking the air from his lungs. I spun and struck Richard three times in a rapid, calculated series, targeting specific points across his torso like Roland had long ago taught me. He grunted with each strike, his eyes shooting wide open at the second blow, and then my third strike locked his body into a rigid paralysis. Unbalanced and unable to move, he toppled over like a falling tree, unable to use his arms, or anything else, to break his fall.

Which was just awful.

Cats didn't always land on their feet. Sometimes they landed on their face.

Specifically, Richard landed on his nose with a sickening crunch. Phix's purr was like a tiny diesel engine now, so obvious she may as well have been clapping. "Oh, yes. Let's take them with us for their propensity to provide endless entertainment."

Cain was staring at Richard from about a foot away, struggling to catch his breath. He managed to painstakingly reach out his hand to flick Richard in the nose. "Bad kitty—Gah!—" he gasped as I used my magic to yank him back to his feet. I redirected that magic to instantly grasp his finger and bend it backwards at a ninety-degree angle, tight enough to strain his ligaments and tendons. Cain gritted his teeth, hopping desperately as I tugged him left to right, not letting him find a comfortable posture.

"Are you two quite finished?" I asked. Cain nodded eagerly. Richard jerked his eyes up and down—the only part of his body he was able to move.

"Say sorry to Dick—Richard," I corrected myself too late, and Cain let out a big old grin despite his pain.

"Sorry, Dick. Won't happen again, Dick. Just a little brotherly love, Dick."

I rolled my eyes, pinching the bridge of my nose. "Cain..." I warned in my best mom voice.

Solomon was watching us with both awe and amusement, unsure which of the two reactions to settle on. Then again, he had been cooped up in his house for the better part of a millennium or two and was very likely severely lacking entertainment or social interaction. It didn't matter how fancy his digs were, his life had awkward parallels to Howard Hughes, milk jugs and all.

I finally released Cain and pointed at Richard. "Help him up. Say even *one* rude comment and I'll allow Richard to give you a free, undefended, full-armed slap to the face, even if I have to hold you down myself."

Cain's mouth snapped closed and he blinked a few times, weighing the punishment with the satisfaction of the crime. Richard was a big guy—even when he wasn't in his lion form—so Cain didn't think too long on it. He helped him up.

"Hold him upright for a second," I said, walking up and striking Richard three more times to unlock the pressure points I had frozen across his body. He let out a relieved gasp and immediately shoved Cain back. Then he began patting his chest where I had hit him, looking incredulous.

"What was that?" he finally asked, meeting my eyes.

Instead of answering, I furrowed my brows, folding my arms. "Listen up, you two. You might both be family, and we might all fight like family, but for this trip I'm playing mommy. You guys may be badass warriors and hold the equivalent of black belts in forms of martial arts the world no longer even remembers," I said, complimenting their prowess in battle. Then I stepped forward, my face growing harder. "But no black belt is higher than the *mom* belt."

There was a tense silence and then the two of them grinned from ear to ear. In unison, they nodded. Then they shot each other dark looks as if it was the other's fault they had nodded at the same time.

I sighed, shaking my head. "We have enough to worry about without you two getting in pissing matches every two minutes. If either of you annoys me with your brotherly love, I'm granting the less-guilty party the right to give the other a full-bodied, unobstructed slap to the face."

Then I turned away, satisfied by their shocked silence. Not only would this hopefully keep them in line, but it worked on multiple levels. They would keep pestering each other and feel each other out—kind of like tough love in the military. But also, whenever a punishment slap was administered, it would be humiliating. That alone—their pride—should keep them in line for the most part.

Solomon and Phix met my eyes. Phix was silent, but Solomon was chuckling openly. "Well done, Callie."

"Thanks. Despite how amazing all this is," I said, gesturing at the Temple around us, "I think I need to figure out what's going on in Kansas City as soon as possible. I'd love nothing more than to explore this place and pick your brain over about a million things, but I need to make sure my friends are okay."

Solomon nodded. "Now that you've earned your place here, I can show you how to use the Seal to return," he said, smiling. The Seal of Solomon was a heavy silver ring to all outward appearances, but it was also a prison for a surprising number of demons. And I wore it on a finger. Solomon had just put Nameless inside the ring, relieving me of the shadow ring that had lived on my thumb for a while.

Still, having demons wrapped around your finger wasn't as cool as it sounded. I could hear them sometimes, if I tried hard enough.

I had chosen to wear it on my right ring finger in case I wanted to punch someone in the face in the near future. It had slipped over my finger like warm oil—a perfect fit, even though I'd worn it on a different finger a few times. The Seal formed itself to me, no matter where I wanted to wear it, and I knew it couldn't just fall off on its own.

Solomon smiled at it wistfully. "Just kiss it to come back home—or to leave the Temple. It is very similar to Shadow Walking in that regard, although Shadow Walking won't allow you to enter the Temple or leave it. Consider it a private elevator with keycard access. Just imagine where you want to be and kiss your ring."

I stared down at it, shaking my head. It was still a large ring—looking too large for a woman's finger—but it also looked...right. "Will that let me bring others back with me?" I asked, thinking of Cain.

Solomon nodded. "Like Shadow Walking, just maintain contact with them. Though I advise you not to bring too many people here. The fewer who know of this place, the safer you are..." he said soberly. Not warning me against the prospect of inviting my friends over for a sleepover, but a literal warning that if people knew I had access to the Temple, I would likely become a target.

I nodded. "I understand."

"I shall make you a Gateway out," he said, motioning for me to follow him. I turned to see Richard and Cain immediately stiffen beside each other—as if I had caught them in the middle of something they weren't supposed to be doing. "Boys," I said, motioning for them to follow.

Richard cast a meaningful look at Solomon. "You need to tell her—"

Phix hissed loud enough for me to flinch. "No," she snapped. "She needs to go home first. The rest can wait. She can't afford the distraction. She needs to see for herself."

Solomon nodded his agreement. "She is right. Nothing has changed. What will be, will be." I frowned at them, turning from one to the other. Solomon held up a hand, forestalling me. "It can wait," he said firmly.

Richard didn't look the least bit pleased, but he also seemed to accept Solomon's decision. He just didn't look happy about it. Maybe I would pester him about it on our travels.

This was going to be a long day. But I anticipated needing all the help I could get, depending on how close Roland had stuck to his promise. And hearing Phix say I needed to see for myself was not even remotely reassuring.

3

Cain and I stepped through Solomon's Gateway—his magic seemed entirely different than mine. His Gateway crackled strangely, as if fighting itself. I turned back to examine it and saw veins of black webbed throughout the orange sparks—as if it was protesting his command—and it seemed to hum with a grating squeal like feedback on a radio. Solomon stared through the Gateway at us, wincing as if in pain. He saw the look of concern on my face and held up a hand in answer. Seeing the black veins on his forearms and the strain on his face wasn't a good combination, only serving to increase my alarm. "Don't worry about me. When you're ready to return, just use your ring like I showed you."

I glanced down at the Seal of Solomon on my finger, nodding. I wondered if his ability to make his own Gateway was something that came with age or if it was a result of him being the patriarch of our bloodline. I also wondered if my ability to use the Silvers—that mysterious magic that I could tap into but didn't entirely understand—was some extension of my ties to Solomon or something else my parents had done.

I'd heard answers, but I was hesitant to believe everything I'd been told.

It had been one of the many things I had wanted to talk to Solomon about, but Kansas City needed me now. Personal questions could wait.

The Gateway winked shut, but not before Richard and Phix stepped through after us. We stood in the warm Kansas City night, the air pregnant with humidity, letting me know we had missed a heavy rain. Luckily, we hadn't appeared in the middle of a busy intersection or anything. In fact, we were in an alley a block away from Roland's church. I set my feet and began walking, eyes alert for any sign of danger. I realized I was smiling absently as Phix hissed and snarled about the moist air matting her fur. Cats.

Cain abruptly flung out a hand, halting my advance. I met his eyes, not bothering to hide my impatience. "A lot can happen in a year," he said gently. "We need to be careful."

Phix was eerily silent in the darkness. So silent that she may as well have been shouting. She pointed a paw ahead, silently repeating that I needed to see for myself.

Cain nodded at her and then turned to me. "Fabrizio was the last one to see us. And Roland sent us to Fabrizio, warning what he would do if anything happened to you..."

He obviously had an inkling of what was going on but was choosing not to share details. He knew me well enough to know I was a firm believer in seeing things for myself so why was he offering commentary without substance? Was he trying to justify things? Or maybe come to grips with whatever Phix had obviously told him. Either way, it wasn't good.

I shook my head stubbornly. "I know what Roland promised, but I just can't imagine him following through with it. Going to war? And all his talk about terrorizing the city? That's just...*insane*. Fabrizio had to have told him about us leaving through the Doors."

Cain gave me a very significant look. "You mean that Last Breath *chased* us into the Doors," he said, pointing his thumb at Richard. I grimaced, having forgotten that small detail. To Fabrizio's recollection, we had been chased into the Doors by Last Breath. If Fabrizio or Roland saw Last Breath, they wouldn't bother asking questions. They would kill on sight.

"Damn it," I cursed, kicking an empty beer can behind a dumpster. At least Richard wasn't recognizable in his current form. I hoped.

"You saw the changes in Roland, Callie," Cain continued. "You...might have been the only one holding him together after his...change."

I sighed. "I know. Which is why we need to show him that I'm alive and well. Any fights he has picked in my absence can be resolved like that," I said, snapping my fingers.

Phix snorted. "The Red Pastor has done quite a bit more than picking fights, Callie. Why do you think I went looking for you in the first place?"

she asked. She glanced up at the night sky and actually shuddered ever so slightly. I realized her fur was slightly raised, as if someone had rubbed it the wrong way and she wasn't remotely pleased.

I met her gaze, not liking the nickname she had so casually tossed out. The Red Pastor. "How bad is it, Phix?"

She regarded me thoughtfully and finally licked her lips with a yawn. "Listen to the air. Can you not hear the fear? Taste the anguish? The tension practically tickles my tongue." Everyone shot her various flavors of disgusted looks until she finally lifted a paw and pointed towards the alley opening. "See for yourself. Carefully. Unseen eyes watch the streets these days..."

Without further ado, I crept closer to the end of the alley, keeping close to the wall. As I moved, I began to pick up on what Phix was referring to. It did feel tense. Like the city was holding her breath. I'd been at a music concert once when someone had called in a credible bomb threat. I had been stuck inside the building for hours. The level of paranoia and fear had increased to a palpable scent and sensation with each passing minute as we awaited status updates on the threat.

Or, one final update heralded by an explosion.

The air felt exactly like I remembered from the concert—a calm before the storm. Or...the fear of attracting the attention of those who had brought on the *last* storm. Phix was right. Whatever had happened in Kansas City had not been pleasant.

I took a calming breath, trying to find my center. I remembered the epiphany I had learned from my journey through the Doors. I had entered in search of answers—about my past, but also about my future. About what kind of person I wanted to become. I had been involved, or loosely affiliated, with many groups and causes over the years, but none had ever truly felt like I could permanently rally behind them.

I had always felt like an outsider. A very angry, unstable outsider—especially recently.

I'd earned a reputation for stalking the streets in the night and killing bad guys. That reputation had grown like wildfire through the supernatural community, primarily *because* I was untethered to a specific cause or group. I quite literally had played judge, jury, and executioner for Kansas City. Answerable to no one and held accountable by no one.

The fact that I hadn't shared my manifesto with anyone had only terrified them further. The creed, rules, or laws that defined what I deemed a crime had never been shared, and since no one knew who I might possibly be working with, they had simply avoided me like the plague.

It wasn't exactly difficult to realize what I found right and wrong, punishable and forgivable. Well, not to me. Then again, these Freaks often played on somewhat grayer fields, the line between right and wrong more a suggestion rather than a law of nature.

They were, after all, monsters.

My journey through the Doors had taught me that I was done playing games, picking sides, being angry. That I simply wanted to do good by my city. To keep those who couldn't protect themselves safe. To be...well, not to get too ironic, but a Shepherd. Not for the *Vatican*, but for my *city*.

Like most governments, I felt the Conclave and Shepherds had gotten too political over the years. Political might not have been the correct word, but it was a close synonym. Large groups with power often adopted ulterior motives and objectives as time stretched on. I felt that the Vatican Shepherds, somewhere over the years, had lost their way. Forgotten their true purpose—to look after the weak.

Of course, the parties involved in a war often grew jaded, and it wasn't a stretch to consider the Vatican Shepherds as an army in a millennia long war. It wasn't necessarily *their* fault, but it was *a* fault. Their creed was tarnished or possibly long lost and forgotten on some past battlefield.

But I was done with group-think. I was going to form my own family and, if nothing else, be a thorn in the side of anyone who wanted to bring trouble to Kansas City.

Even if that trouble was brought on by Roland, my old mentor.

Cain rested a hand on my shoulder and I almost jumped out of my skin. "Jesus!" I snapped in a hissing sputter.

Cain cocked his head. "Sorry. You were just standing there, staring at nothing. Roland's church is right around the corner. Maybe you should try calling him before you consider waltzing up to the front door. Seeing you alive and in person when he thinks you're dead might be a little too much for the old boy to handle," he said meaningfully.

I took a calming breath. "No. He's old school. He wouldn't trust a phone call. He would demand a meet and then arrive with his guard and suspicion up, likely with Paradise and Lost, assuming it's a trap. Surprise is best. That moment of confusion will be our friend. Our best chance to get through to him."

Cain raised one eyebrow in a doubtful rictus but finally sighed. He checked the dagger in his belt and shot Richard a meaningful look, silently encouraging him to look alert. Richard's eyes flickered with blue flame in the dark alley and he grew unnaturally still.

I held out a hand, stalling them. "We're not an invading army. Cain and I will get a good look at the church. You two keep an eye out behind us. We don't want anyone sneaking up on us from behind."

Cain followed my lead to the edge of the alley as Phix and Richard turned to watch back the way we had come.

I took cover behind a dumpster and peered out.

Roland's church—the one I had bought for him—looked very different than I remembered. It wasn't necessarily physically different, but it had an... aura about it that was new. It stood out like a fistful of wicked daggers stabbing up at the heavens. The old gothic structure was adorned with crenellations, tall stone spires, and it was replete with gargoyles, angels, and other mythological creatures perched on the roof. Light bloomed inside the building, but the windows had all been replaced with crimson glass. Or perhaps there was a crimson light within. Roland's magic seemed to be tainted crimson after he became a vampire, but to have that much red illumination within meant he was currently using a hellish amount of power.

Except...I didn't necessarily feel a storm of power within.

As I scanned the nightscape, I realized that the moon in the sky also seemed to have a faint reddish hue to it, as if the sky itself was tinted.

Like a snow globe of red glass. Just without the snow.

And vampires were everywhere. I saw them leaning against the low wall surrounding the church property, standing in a huddle smoking near the newspaper stand across the street, under the awning of a bar around the corner, all in groups of two or three within easy sight of the church—covering all angles. None of them looked particularly secretive, as if not bothering to hide their natures. I caught the reflections of light in their eyes and noticed many had a crimson glow to them—which was very strange. That had been a very uncommon feature about Roland—his crimson eyes.

Paradise and Lost—his adopted werewolves—had formed a bond with him, and as a result also had crimson eyes, so did that mean all these vampires were bonded to Roland in a similar fashion? Why would Haven, the Master Vampire of Kansas City, allow that?

And what were all these vampires doing *here*? Hanging out in the open, obviously acting shady? What about the police? The locals? It wasn't late enough for the city to be quiet, but I didn't see a single car on the streets. At least none that were moving.

I ducked lower as I realized that silhouettes also lined the roof on the building across from the church—sentinels keeping an eye on everything from a higher vantage point. And they had rifles that they weren't bothering to hide.

I slowly looked back at Cain, feeling stunned. "What the hell is going on here?" I asked hoarsely. "Shouldn't these guys all be at Haven's compound? Keeping the Master of Kansas City safe?"

Cain cast me a sickly look, eyes flicking to Phix as if for backup, but she didn't offer aid. He winced. "Haven...is dead, Callie. Roland is the Master of Kansas City, now..."

I blinked stupidly, wondering if I'd heard—

My world suddenly flashed white and my body locked up in pain. I stared up at the sky, confused by the ringing in my ears. I groaned, my hands shaking as I blinked rapidly, trying to roll over or climb to my feet. Why was no one standing over me, trying to help me to my feet like the overprotective mother hens they all usually were?

I felt hungover—dazed—but not necessarily injured. Cain had said something...but my head felt stuffed with wool. My arms shook as I managed to prop myself up. I saw a figure walking away from the outside of the alley, heading in the direction of Roland's church. I narrowed my eyes, not recalling having seen him a moment ago. Why did he look vaguely familiar? "Take care of the demon," he said over his shoulder before disappearing from view.

4

A *whooshing*, *whipping* sound abruptly zipped just over my face, trailed by a crackling current of electricity that made my hair rise up on end. Phix let out a shockingly loud yowl and I heard the crackling hiss of live current and the smell of singed hair. Adrenaline suddenly roared through my veins at the near miss, snapping me out of my daze. I scrambled to my feet to see Phix trapped under a web of snapping electricity, a menacing black spear embedded in her side. What the hell? An ambush? How had none of us noticed a scent?

How long had I been knocked down?

Phix was coated with blood and her eyes were rolled back in her head as she scraped and scratched at the concrete, rapidly losing strength. My heart was beating wildly, both in stunned shock that I hadn't anticipated the attack and shaking with fear to see someone as formidable as Phix so easily taken down.

Before I had time to jump up and free her, six figures dropped from the fire escape above, blocking me from Phix, and laughing loudly. Two of them peeled off to fight Richard—still in his human form but his eyes glowing fiery blue—and two peeled off to fight Cain—who seemed to be struggling to get back to his feet as well. What the hell had knocked us all down? That flash of white light. That faintly familiar man who had left us for his men to clean up like we were trash.

I narrowed my eyes murderously at the remaining balance of the six-pack of attackers, deciding they had insufficient funds for the transaction. "Let go of my friend and I won't feed you to her," I warned, my voice quivering with uncontrollable rage. I was still slightly dazed from whatever had hit me in the head, but it was masked by my bubbling fury.

I briefly wondered why Cain hadn't made short work of his two before diving in to steal mine. I glanced back to see him lying on the ground about ten feet away, struggling to regain his feet as more than the two men I had seen took turns kicking at him while he was down—four on one. And in full view of the vampires we had seen guarding the church.

I slowly turned back to the three—wait, there had been *two* a moment ago!—men in front of me. Richard also had more than two to contend with, now, but he looked to be holding his own for the moment. Where the fuck were they all coming from?

"What's the meaning of this?" I snarled, my skin practically vibrating with the need for violence. Especially as I saw the pool of blood spreading beneath Phix and her efforts at struggling growing weaker and weaker, like a fish too long out of water.

Two of my attackers leaned down over Phix, laughing at her agony. "Look at the tits on this one! She might be a *furry*, but I bet she knows how to be *friendly*, eh?" one snickered, revealing the long fangs of a vampire.

Then he reached out through the electrified netting, grabbed a handful of her breasts and squeezed hard enough to make Phix whimper, her eyes dancing in a wild daze. He and his pal burst out laughing, an undercurrent of malevolent glee dancing in their eyes. "I've wanted to do that for months after she ripped Brian's face off."

His pal nodded darkly, licking his lips. "Yeah, but what's she doing here now?"

The first man shrugged dismissively. "You take a whirl, Charlie," he urged.

Charlie, the sick son-of-a-bitch, obliged, fangs protruding from his lips as he grinned.

My vision pulsed red and wavered before me as if I was standing before an open oven. I couldn't actually process that this was happening right now. Phix wasn't some human girl they could dominate and terrorize—no matter what she had done to their friend months ago. She was obviously a non-human and an extremely powerful monster. I'd seen her utterly decimate squads of killers with an almost lazy, feline grace. Which meant it wasn't just about revenge or sex to these guys. They were predators of the worst kind—not just of the hunt, but of the supreme dominance of their victims. And one look in their eyes told me this was only the beginning of what they intended for the Sphinx.

They saw breasts and had the misconception that those breasts were specifically designed to please them—regardless of consent. No, they hungered for it *because* there was no consent.

Roland—no matter how he had changed—would rip their faces off for even *talking* to a woman like this, even if the woman was an enemy. Luckily for the good pastor, I would teach them a very clear lesson in the birds and the bees.

Namely, that some of those cute little birds liked to rend flesh from bone with their bare beaks and loved nothing more than ripping wings off the buzzing little bumblebee.

This, I decided, would require a very...*personal* touch.

Three other men dropped down from the fire escape above, joining the lone man who hadn't moved to torment Phix with Charlie and his pal, keeping his eyes locked on me. The four of them slowly advanced, stepping into the light enough for me to make them out. They were all young, and their eyes glowed crimson.

As did the tips of their fangs.

"Not a sheep, and not a furry," the man who hadn't opted to fondle Phix—the apparent leader—said, though he eyed me up and down with a similar, perhaps even darker, intent. "But I bet she still tastes like a succulent little lamb, lads."

"I've been dying for a bite to eat," another, larger vampire agreed, licking his lips with a leering grin even more scandalous than his associate. "And I've never tasted a demon before..."

"The forbidden fruit," another agreed, panting with open lust. His eyes held not even a flicker of fear or consequence. As if he knew beyond a shadow of a doubt there would be no repercussions for their actions.

I wasn't sure what they meant by calling me a demon, but I intended to be overly demonic in my upcoming lesson.

Time to show these little fangers what fear tasted like.

To remind them who the fucking White Rose was and what she did to naughty little boys who tried to trample the flower gardens she called home.

5

I felt a cool, merciless wind rip through my soul at hearing more sounds of Phix's torment from Charlie and his pal as they continued pawing her breasts, slapping her cheek violently when she didn't cooperate with their sick game. Whatever had been strong enough to knock me down and incapacitate her should have terrified me. But instead, I found myself growing frigid and unyielding. The maestro—that strangely familiar man—in this attack would pay, but right now...

Slap. Laugh. Whimper.

Slap. Laugh. Whimper.

Each sound was like a gunshot to my ears, and I could hear nothing else as I slowly lifted my gaze to the appetizers laid out before me.

There would be no wave of my magic hand to decapitate them all on the spot.

Each of these men were as guilty as the two manhandling Phix. Because not a single one of them had told the other two to stop. Hadn't even cast a disgusted look over a shoulder. They had just laughed. And then cast that same hungry, feral, possessive look at me.

I promised myself I would give them something to laugh at.

I slowly lifted my hand to reveal Silver claws from between my knuckles. They weren't a set of blades that I actually held, but a manifestation of that alien magic I didn't quite yet understand. But I knew a few things they were capable of. And they were very, *very* personal.

The vampires' crimson eyes locked onto the obvious threat with a look of anticipation that let me know they were pleased that I was going to make their conquest fun. Which meant they didn't see the trash can I'd lifted with my magic hurtling toward their backs, knocking them straight at me. I buried my claws into the soft flesh beneath the first vampire's chin so hard that the tips came out the top of his skull.

"Bah," I bleated at him, staring straight into his dying eyes as I licked my lips.

Two others turned their momentum into a blurring attack, hands outstretched to show me claws of their own. I spun to the side, dropping the sack of meat from my claws and swung downward in a violent motion, amputating both attackers at the wrists. They struck the brick wall face-first, followed by their fresh stumps punching the wall, and they crumpled to a heap before they could cry out about the blow to the face or the hands I had removed.

The last vampire was staring at his two downed friends in flat disbelief. I sprinted at him while he was distracted and drove my claws straight into his groin at an upward angle, hard enough to lift him off his feet a few inches. He attempted to slash his claws at me from above, so I shifted slightly as I squatted and stabbed my other hand into his throat, exploding upward, and lifted him overhead like a bale of hay.

That's when I saw Charlie and his pal running for their lives down the alley past Richard.

"Not so fast, Charlie!" I yelled. "I wanted you to grab my tits!"

And I hurled the bale of vampire at them, using magic to make sure I threw far enough to knock them down. Before it even hit them, I was running. I scooped up a discarded wooden broom leaning beside a door, snapped it over his back as he attempted to rise, and then stabbed him in the chest with it at an upward angle hard enough to prop him upright on his knees in a mockery of supplication, pleading for absolution to a demonic White Rose who only knew Old Testament love.

Then I bent over and grabbed the other vampire by the legs and began dragging him back towards Phix so his face scraped across the dirty asphalt the entire way. I think he was screaming but I couldn't have been sure.

Richard and Cain had finally managed to take care of their own attackers—just not as creatively as I had.

Cain stared at me, his lips set in a grim, tired line. He nodded one time. That was all. Richard, on the other hand, was staring at me as if he'd never seen me before, his mouth opening wordlessly. I dismissed them both.

I dropped the vampire and immediately stomped down—hard—onto his balls, pinning him to the alley floor as he grunted so deep that I thought even Roland, his Master, might feel it from within his church.

I hoped he did. Like me flicking the porchlight on outside to let him know I was home.

The vampire continued to gasp breathlessly as I used my claws to slash the electric web covering Phix. I yanked it off her by the handle they had used to throw it at her—a rubber grip so they didn't electrocute themselves.

Then I very slowly and very meticulously wrapped the last vampire up in it, smiling and humming to myself as his screams grew louder and less coherent. I crouched down in front of him, smiling at his agony. Then I carefully sliced an opening in the web, grabbed a fistful of his shirt, and ripped it open. I grinned, licked my lips, and squeezed his chest hard enough to physically tear skin. I didn't let go. I just stared into his eyes until he was drooling and about to pass out.

Then I spat in his face and decapitated him with a single swipe of my claws. I stood there, panting raggedly, trying to get my thoughts back under my control.

Cain gently cleared his throat. "Callie." I looked up at the tone in his voice. "There are about a hundred more of these guys running over here right now. They must have heard the commotion."

"Good," I snarled, turning to face them.

"Too many," he urged. "We need to get out of here."

Richard had stopped staring at me so strangely and was now leaning over Phix. "She's not going to make it without medical attention."

I gritted my teeth, still not able to process the fact that such a dangerous creature as the Sphinx had gone down so easily. Hospitals were out for obvious reasons. "What about Darling and D—"

Phix's eyes suddenly shot wide open, and I had never seen her look more terrified. "NO! Anywhere but there! Please!" Then she promptly passed out as if she had used the last of her energy to plead her case.

I shared a long look with Cain, momentarily at a loss for words at her reaction. "Aren't...they her friends?" I asked, wondering for the hundredth time just exactly who Darling and Dear really were.

He was studying Phix, looking troubled. "We've been gone a long time, Callie. Who knows?" he all but whispered.

Richard heaved Phix onto his shoulders with ease, reminding me of his ridiculous strength. "I can take her back to Solomon. We grow some healing ointments in the garden. I'll watch over her until she recovers." He didn't look pleased with that, but he could tell by the look in my eyes that I would have told him to do so anyway rather than have him tagalong with me. His presence was too much of a liability—especially after witnessing what Roland looked for in his vampires.

His vampires...

Because Haven had been killed. I didn't have time to think about that—I could hear the vampires drawing closer.

I nodded at Richard. "Hurry."

He shifted into a white fog, making it look like Phix was hovering on a cloud, and then they simply disappeared. It made sense that Richard could also enter and leave Solomon's Temple at will. He was the guardian.

I turned to Cain, my heart beginning to race at the sounds of the hunting party not far away—screams that coordinated an attacking pack. Attracting the ire of Roland's vampires had definitely not been how I wanted to return to Kansas City. "We need to run. Now."

Cain grabbed me by the arm and shoved me ahead of him towards the back of the alley.

"You need to step up your game, Cain. I took down six."

He grunted. "Trash talking while running for our lives is kind of oxymoronic, you know."

6

Cain and I dashed down the dank alley, avoiding puddles as best we could—both to avoid making noise and not to get our shoes soaked. The night was warm and running in wet shoes was a great way to acquire blisters.

We rounded a corner into an adjacent alley and I skidded to a halt to try ripping open a Gateway to escape the vampires. I felt a strong resistance like I had thrown a ball at a wall and it bounced back at my face, making me stumble. I shot Cain a sharp look. "I can't make a Gateway..." I told him incredulously, frowning as I resumed running more desperately than before. Vampires were fast.

Cain grunted, nonplussed. But he seemed like the kind of guy to expect the worst of any situation and roll with the punches. "What about Shadow Walking?" he asked, barely breathing hard.

I could hear the vampires a few alleys behind us. They sounded busy with the remains of their brethren rather than deciding to pursue us. That wouldn't last long. At least I didn't think so. I figured they would be more interested in finding the group who had just dispatched a dozen of their comrades.

I grabbed Cain's shoulder and tried Shadow Walking. My magic slapped back at me like a reproachful ruler from a Sister during Bible Study. What the hell? Richard hadn't seemed to have any trouble using his magic to leave.

I momentarily debated kissing my ring to head back to Solomon's Temple—just to verify that I still could. But another part of me knew if I did that, I would convince myself to stay until Phix healed, and I couldn't let myself do that. The fight with the vampires had my skin crawling. And whatever that man—likely their leader—had done to momentarily incapacitate me had been powerful, so why hadn't he simply killed me? To consider that the vampire rapists might actually work with Roland and have his blessing...

That meant Roland had indeed changed. And absolutely not for the better.

"Let's head to my apartment. It's not far," I growled. "We can get a quick look at the rest of the city as we do. See if anything else has changed," I said, glancing nervously back up at the sky to see the faintly red glow. Cain grunted his agreement, his eyes dancing both up and out, checking for any surprise attacks—not wanting another gang of vampires to drop from a fire escape and catch us unawares. We reached the mouth of the alley and slowed, glancing out first. We were all alone, but I sensed eyes out there somewhere, watching, waiting. Phix had mentioned something about unseen eyes watching the streets, and she'd sounded troubled by it. The very shadows seemed to be alive, watching us with predatory instinct—like a pride of lions warily watching another pair of lions run through their territory.

Not aggressive and not afraid, but not necessarily friendly either. Just hyperaware.

I motioned for Cain to enter an adjacent alley to conceal our movements as long as possible. He did so without a word, leading the way. After a few minutes of stealthy running, he glanced back at me meaningfully. "They called you a demon."

I gritted my teeth, nodding in response but letting him know with a look that I had no idea why. "Maybe it's the White Rose thing?" I suggested.

Cain shook his head. "It didn't sound specific or they would have just called you White Rose. And what the fuck did that guy do to us? I thought he was dead."

I frowned at Cain. "I thought he looked familiar, but I didn't get a look at his face."

Cain looked troubled. "Le Bone. The vampire who came to Kansas City on behalf of Henri Bellerose—the Master Vampire of Paris." He turned to look at me.

I blinked a few times. "Le Bone? Are you sure?" I asked in disbelief. But...I was almost certain he was right, now that I thought about it.

Cain nodded. "I know faces."

I shook my head in confusion. "Le Bone...Roland and Henri were taking turns torturing the bastard when we left. How in the hell is he still alive?"

"Exactly," Cain growled. "Makes you wonder who is running things back there."

Which was something I hadn't anticipated. Haven was apparently dead, but why would he release Le Bone? Even if Henri was still in Kansas City—which seemed unlikely—he had wanted Le Bone dead more than even Roland or Haven.

What was going on here? I really wished I had pressed Phix on the matter. I turned to Cain, controlling my breathing as we ran. "The attack caught me off guard. I don't even know what happened. Just a flash of light and then him walking away," I admitted. "And I don't remember Le Bone having powers like that before."

Cain nodded stiffly, his eyes still flicking here and there, watching the shadows like I was, obviously feeling the same attention on our backs. "Same here. A flash of light and then I was being kicked by about six pairs of boots."

"What did Phix tell you?" I demanded. "What did she see in Kansas City that concerned her enough to find me in the Doors?"

Cain gritted his teeth in frustration. "That Kansas City rained enough blood to remind her of the old days back in Egypt. She didn't give any specifics, just that you needed to come home. That there had been many...changes."

I shuddered, ignoring the sensation of those eyes suddenly seeming to stare at the two of us even more intently—as if they had heard Cain and wanted to silence him. I let my claws out as I ran, pumping my legs as fast as I could maintain for our run back to my apartment. Cain noticed and gripped his dagger in a fist, eyes alert.

"It didn't look like those vampires knew who or what you were. Not even gloating at the fact that they had the White Rose dead to rights. And they *definitely* seemed to know Phix. Not many know about her affiliation with you, but enough for me to expect at least *some* kind of association with you."

I narrowed my eyes, pondering that. It had only been a year. Granted, that was a long time on the streets, but not enough time to completely forget about Callie Penrose or the White Rose. And all the vampire power players who might be in town knew of me—so their acolytes should have at least heard about me. Long white hair and silver claws were not typical attributes. I had expected all vampires to recognize me on sight. Especially since I was assumedly the reason Roland had snapped in the first place. Their initial jobs had probably been to scour the city looking for me, which meant everyone should have a very good idea what I looked like.

None of those vampires had known me.

Whatever was going on, it didn't bode well.

"You sure your apartment is safe?" Cain asked after a few minutes and a few more alleys—angling our path to simply get as far from any vampires as possible. They, surprisingly, hadn't given chase. Maybe they had gotten the message that we weren't easy prey.

I thought about Cain's question. We could go to Abundant Angel Catholic Church. I knew Fabrizio, the First Shepherd. And I had found a crucifix on my trip through the Doors—one belonging to his old friend, Anthony—that I wanted to give to him as a memento. I'd also introduced a homeless man named Arthur to Fabrizio, and last time I'd checked he had been in training to become a full-fledged Shepherd. An acronym suddenly popped into my mind.

Shepherd in training...SHIT?

Yeah. That was sticking. I had been one once, what seemed eons ago, so I had the right.

Arthur had been a SHIT for a year now. With the increased vampire presence, maybe he'd been promoted.

And Father David was there. The man who had first found me as a child. I wanted to speak with him, anyway, ask him some questions about the day he'd found me. When he'd heard a demon outside the church, clawing to get her hands on the child.

That demon had been me. I didn't quite understand how that was possible—that I had somehow gone back in time to revisit that fateful night on my journey through the Doors—let alone that I had only succeeded in making Father David think I was a demon intent upon killing the child.

All I had wanted to do was to give the child a little love. To tell her that everything would end up alright. That that little child would one day find herself running down an alley from a coven of vampires with the world's first murderer at her side, and that everything would be peachy.

I scowled at the dark thought. Regardless, Abundant Angel seemed like a good place to go. Anthony's crucifix necklace would prove to Fabrizio that it was really me and that I wasn't some shapeshifter playing games. It would prove that I wasn't an enemy.

Because if Roland's original threat was to be believed, Fabrizio was most likely his number one enemy. If anyone had answers to what had happened in my city, Fabrizio would.

I told Cain my idea.

He took one look at me and snorted. "You look like a drowned rat and you're drenched in blood. No way anyone at the church is going to let you in. In the middle of the night, I might add. And especially not if they're at war with Roland and his vampires. Having the world's first murderer at your side probably won't help your chances either. You need to make yourself presentable, sis."

I found myself smiling at the last sentence. Sis. Because Cain had adopted me as his family, his sister. I had done the same—not in any mystical, magical, supernatural ritual or anything. But in our hearts.

Which was the only way that really mattered, in my opinion. Screw blood. Real family was made, not inherited.

For Cain—the man who had murdered his first sibling, Abel—adopting me as his sister was a big freaking leap of faith, an extension of trust neither of us had known he would ever be able to make.

It was the primary reason Cain had even survived our journey through the Doors. His test had been to prove that he loved something more than himself—that he was willing to open up his heart and offer up his life to protect someone he saw as a sister. Absolving him of his past crime.

Blood or not, we were brother and sister. And with each step Cain took, I could sense that deep well of pride that it gave him—like an added reservoir of power. Not a magical power, but a power of the soul. An inner, personal strength he hadn't had for quite some time.

That someone in this crazy world loved him. Hadn't given up on him. Hadn't condemned him for his past.

"Right," I agreed with a sigh. "Let's stick to the original plan. Head back to my place. Get cleaned up. Hit up the church after sunrise when the vampires are napping."

Cain changed direction slightly, knowing where I lived, but his face looked troubled. "If the vampires nap during the day..."

I frowned at him. "Of course they do."

Cain shot me a look. "One of the vampires Richard and I fought was strong. If Richard hadn't stepped in to help me...well, I'll just say that Phix might not have been the only one heading back to Solomon's Temple," he admitted meaningfully. I frowned in disbelief. Cain was a killing machine—one of the scariest men I had ever met. He was absolutely merciless in the art of combat.

He was a one-man symphony in the orchestra of delicious death. A Maestro.

For him to say one of the vampires was *strong*...

"Oh."

He nodded soberly. "No way to tell how old he was, but he took a licking and kept on ticking. Some of the old vampires can tolerate sunlight to an extent. Luckily, Richard found an opening and managed to tear his head off. But it didn't look easy." He paused, letting out a grunt. "Richard took a beating, too."

That stopped me short. Richard took a beating. The guy was a mountain of power. As Last Breath—his white lion form—he was a literal specter of death, able to kill indiscriminately like a wraith in fog, but even as a man, he was a veritable titan of destruction. And I hadn't even noticed he was injured. Last Breath was so horrifying that even the monsters spoke of him like the boogeyman.

The fact that he hadn't used a funny nickname for Richard only backed up his claim.

"What the hell kind of power did Le Bone throw at us?" I cursed, my mind running wild with fears, ideas, or any semblance of a logical explanation. "How long were we down?"

Cain grimaced, wiping rain from his forehead. "I have no idea. One second you were standing there snarling at the church, and the next thing I saw was a flash of light. That was some Dracula-level shit, Callie. Seriously." He met my eyes meaningfully, letting me know it wasn't hyperbole. "I've never seen vampiric power like that, but it was definitely Le Bone. Maybe the new Master of Kansas City has been using that magic of his to beef up his army. You saw how many vampires were there. That church is a fortress, and Roland runs it."

I nodded grimly. The crimson eyes had been a dead giveaway, too.

Roland...

He now had his own army of killers and judging by their intended methods...Roland was not the man I had once trained with. The Shepherd who had once taught me magic. The man who had taught me the difference between right and wrong. Roland had become a monster. Even hiring monsters to do his dirty work was out of character for the once pious man. The Roland I knew would have hired dangerous men, sure, but never men without morals. They should have had very strict rules on how to treat women, at the very least.

If the vampires had simply attacked with excessive violence, that would have been different. But they had done things to Phix that would have never been approved by Roland.

Never.

We used the dark alleys to make the rest of the trip to my apartment in silence. It wasn't close, but it wasn't too far. It was a stressful jog through the deceptively quiet alleys, constantly checking over our shoulders for signs of pursuit, glancing up at fire escapes for aerial assaults, and generally waiting for a gang of monsters to jump out at us from behind a trashcan with the intent to see our insides up close and personal.

You know, a typical late-night jog.

I almost wished for an attack. Anything to get me out of my own head and away from thoughts of Roland.

It sure felt like Phix's description of Egypt...

Because each step I took was like wading through the unrelenting current of denial.

☙ 7 ❧

I stared at my apartment door, grinding my teeth. First, I had felt surprise.

Then understanding.

And then my old neighbor, blind, incoherent rage.

I didn't have a key, but that wasn't what had me ready to commit arson.

The bright orange eviction notice sticker was enough to make my blood boil. It had been there for some time, because it said I had only one more day to vacate my apartment.

Someone had helpfully written in permanent marker *dead chicks pay no rent*.

Incredibly insightful, my neighbors.

But none of it made any sense to me. The Vatican paid my rent. I had been gone for a year, but...Fabrizio knew about my trip through the Doors. Had Meatball even given up on my return after being missing for a year? I didn't necessarily blame him, but to see that sticker on my door—the place I called home...

It made me angry. Cain silently picked the lock with his bone dagger, simply jamming it into the slot for the keyhole and twisting it like a key. Surprisingly, it worked, and didn't shatter his bone dagger. Then again, I was betting it wasn't simply bone. It was the same knife he had used to kill his brother, Abel. And I'd seen him use it to stab several flavors of monster—all with thick, tough skin and bone. The dagger hadn't grown dull or ever snapped, and no hide had seemed impervious to its edge.

It did, however, shatter my lock. I kicked the door in, scanning the interior warily just in case any vampires or other nefarious types had decided to lie in wait for twelve months to pull off the ultimate granddaddy of all surprise attacks—ever.

I needn't have bothered. I took a few steps past the threshold, alert for surprises, but I quickly noticed that dust lay heavy on everything. Not a ton, but enough to be easily noticeable. And when I say everything...

I meant what hadn't been *stolen*.

I stood there, panting, as I scanned from left to right, able to only pick up on the absence of things—the empty space where things should have been. The place wasn't damaged or destroyed, but more meticulously robbed. As if the thief had obsessive compulsive disorder. Everyday things like appliances, pots and pans still on the drying rack, a basket of laundry, some department store art and décor on the walls, and random knick-knacks were all in their usual places.

But anything of a more...personal nature was missing. Every single one of my weapons that usually hung on the wall, any of the picture frames with family and friends, and—I stormed into my room, breathing heavier as I absently catalogued more and more missing items, desperate to find a specific one left behind.

But it was also gone—the stuffed unicorn and magical book Nate Temple had given me so long ago. The one I hadn't even finished reading.

I wanted to scream. I wanted to burn it all down. Someone had robbed me.

Me. The White Rose. Who would dare rob *me*?

Cain settled a comforting hand on my shoulder. "This wasn't a robbery..." he said quietly.

I snorted angrily. "I didn't have anything worth stealing."

Cain studied me compassionately—rare for him—and then glanced back at the bedroom before he pointed at an empty picture frame. "They took anything that identified you. It would have been easier to take the frame with the picture." He reached over and scooped it up, checking the back of the standing frame. Then he showed it to me. It was neatly clasped closed as if someone had just put a cherished picture inside it and set it up for display.

Cain was right. Someone had entered my home to take anything that identified me and then very neatly set everything back up so that it didn't look suspicious to the landlord.

The question was *why?* I did a mental inventory of anything I might have had lying around last time I was here. Weapons. They weren't anything magical, but they were strong, functioning blades, kept to a professional standard, but none were worth stealing. And why take my pictures? I shook my head, taking in a deep breath.

It had either been a friend or an enemy, and I wasn't sure which was worse. Because it signified finality. That they had no hope of my return.

"I'm taking a shower," I announced loudly. "If I come out and find the creep also stole my panties or towels, I'll finish destroying Kansas City myself."

And I strode into the bathroom, slamming the door behind me. I heard Cain mumble something about coffee, but I ignored him. I leaned my forehead against the mirror, closing my eyes as I counted to one hundred, focusing on my meditation totem.

It had always calmed me. Something Roland had taught me when first teaching me weapons—and ultimately, magic. A way to center one's self to focus on the important things rather than be buried under the noise of everyday life.

My constant meditation symbol hadn't been so constant recently. It had started out as a single feather I placed on a plain background. I would imagine the gentle breeze blowing against it, ruffling it slightly. Each sensation, thought, and fear would be fed into that wind and ultimately against the feather until all was calm in my mind—just me and the feather.

When I had gone through the Doors with Cain, though, that symbol had undergone a significant modification. It had struggled against me, fighting me until I finally submitted and relinquished the internal battle. Now, it was a white rose, a feather, and a pair of wings slowly sweeping back and forth over a black background as if hovering in place.

Much more complicated than my original symbol.

But at the same time, it felt more...genuine. A better definition of myself. Because I had changed quite a bit in my journey through the Doors. Initially, for the better. Towards the end, for the absolute worst—hungry only for power.

Solomon and Last Breath had ultimately helped guide me back, forcing me to make a decision—to come back to myself for the chance to make a real difference in my world rather than pursue only Samael, a greater demon who seemed wholly intent upon battling me one-on-one.

Coming back would give me the opportunity to fight not only him, but potentially the demon he worked for—and any number of other demons. It would also give me a purpose other than power and vengeance.

It had been a very tough decision—because I had been cloaked with unimaginable, god-level power when they confronted me. I don't know how they managed to get through to me—if it was a display of their ability to reason or if it was that inner desire for me to make an impact in this world. A meaningful, beneficial impact.

Like I had failed to do in Kansas City.

I released the symbol, opening my eyes as I leaned away from the mirror. I didn't want to get too close to my thoughts at the moment. I wanted to get cleaned up and clear my head in a less Zen way.

A bloody demon of a woman stared back at me. Thick gobs of crimson glistening on my long hair. It was normally thicker and wavier, but now it just looked greasy and bloody, plastered close to my scalp. My face was a mask of blood spatter, as were my clothes. I hoped none of it was mine from whatever Le Bone had done to me. I didn't feel any pain, though.

With a sigh, I stripped down and turned on the shower, breathing in the thick steam with a sigh of relief. The water struck my head and shoulders with an almost sexual sensation. I shuddered, relishing it for a few moments as I let the water wash away the pints of blood. I waited until the runoff in the base of the shower was clear before soaping up and getting to work. As I went through the familiar motions, the analytical part of my brain kicked on, digesting the facts of the day so far.

I spent longer in the shower than necessary. It had been twelve months, but thankfully, my legs didn't look like I'd turned into a shifter or as if I was fishing for furries. Still, when a girl is about to go out on the town and murder and maim to her heart's content, she needed to shave.

Murder and mayhem always come after the shave, gentlemen.

I toweled off and was putting on my robe as I opened the door to go see what was left of my wardrobe, hoping that the thief hadn't robbed me of my favorite killing outfits.

That's when I noticed the pungent smell of recreational smoke.

It's also when a mountain of white fur tried to murder me.

8

I ducked at the last moment and dove past the giant shifter polar bear, shouting out in both surprise and instinctive anger. I couldn't even get a minute to get dressed?

The bear roared loud enough for my untied robe to billow open, splattering me with shifter drool.

"Claire!" I shouted in relief.

But my best friend was having none of it. She swatted at my face with her big meaty paw, annihilating my bedroom television in an explosion of plastic and glass. I sprinted out of the bedroom, my robe catching on the handle and stopping me short. Valuing my immediate future over decency, I wiggled out of the robe and dove again right as Claire punched through the door frame, aiming for the back of my head. Wood splintered behind me, peppering my back as I shoved my hand into a potted plant to grab a rock I had placed there long ago.

I spun and flung the rock right at the furious polar bear just as she was roaring again. The rock slammed into the back of her throat and abruptly changed her roar to a choking cough. Claire bear began gagging and hacking before finally spitting up the rock, and as she did, she instantly shifted into her human form, naked as the day is long.

Because I had thrown a *moonstone* at her—a rock that prevented shifters from shifting. I'd kept it in the flower pot, masked by a discreet spell so that it could only be used when removed—so that any of my shifter friends weren't prevented from shifting if we were attacked while sitting on the couch watching *The Notebook* or a *Kung Fu Theatre* marathon for girls' night.

I'd never anticipated having to use the rock on my best friend to save my own life.

"Claire! What the hell is wrong with you?" I demanded, quickly scanning the apartment to make sure there weren't any other bears about to pummel me to death.

Claire looked dazed at the sudden transformation back to her human form, shaking her head back and forth as she hunched low, trying to shift back to her bear form. But the moonstone was preventing her.

I picked back up on the smoke smell again and glanced behind me to see a familiar face sitting in my recliner. Starlight—the shifter bear who seemed to be some kind of wise man or Shaman of the Kansas City Cave of Bears. He was powerful on a level I hadn't ever been able to quantify, even though he was as tiny as a bear cub.

Regardless, the most powerful bears I had ever seen gave him a very wide berth, and when he spoke, they listened to the little teddy bear with respect.

I stared at him in disbelief, momentarily forgetting the angry Claire behind me.

Bubble-bubble-bubble...

Like the sound one makes when exhaling a breath underwater.

Because he was currently taking a massive hit from a bong as long as his torso. It was cradled between his legs like he was fixing to climb it.

The words *Bear Necessity* were etched into the glass in ornate script down the side.

He wasn't looking at me, too intent on his task. Claire hit me like a truck from behind, slamming me into—and through—my coffee table. I snarled as the glass sliced into my hands and I spun as I kicked out with both feet, launching Claire up and over me to slam into the wall, knocking one of my paintings down. She left a solid dent in the drywall but landed safely on the couch as I struggled to scramble free of the remnants of my table.

I held out my hands, talking in a soothing tone despite my anger. "Claire! It's me—gah!"

She hit me with hands outstretched, grabbing hold of the towel I had wrapped around my head, yanking it down and to the side where her knee was waiting to say hello to my face. I slapped my palms down to block the strike and immediately counter-punched her in the hoo-ha, really putting my shoulders into it.

She gasped in both pain and astonishment, hopping on both feet for a moment.

I elbowed her in the ribs to get some distance. Then I jumped, spun in the air and flung out a back-kick as hard as I could, focusing more on the speed of my spin than the aerial nature to deliver the most force. It struck her hard enough to double her over before she flew into my television.

She went *through* my television—as in her ass got stuck in the center, momentarily trapping her long enough for me to get a breath of fresh air. I wheezed, feeling slightly light-headed because the living room was one thick cloud of noxious smoke as if the building was on fire.

Bubble-bubble-bubble...

"Starlight!" I snapped. "Quit toking and start helping! She's fucking feral or something!"

He didn't answer, but the bubbling did cease as he removed the bowl and took another giant puff. He finally glanced up at me with his eyelids partially closed as he held his breath for a few seconds, and then he finally let it out in another thick, noxious cloud that obstructed my view of him. He didn't cough. Not even once. Like a champ.

I could sense him staring at me through the smoke, still not saying a word. But he did paw at the smoke in a playful manner.

"I don't know who the fuck you think you are, bitch," Claire snarled from behind me, finally extricating herself from my television, "but I'm going to rip the skin from your bones and make a rug for my cave."

I spun in disbelief—what the hell had she been smoking to not recognize me in my own apartment? She was scratched up and bloody, and I noticed several pieces of glass or plastic from my television embedded in her flesh. Her body was heavily corded with dense muscle, but not enough to look like a powerlifter or CrossFit junkie—just enough for other elite athletes to take notice and deliver a respectful nod.

I'd busted up her nose at some point and it was a bleeder, fanning down across her full lips and chest, shining in the minimal moonlight that pierced the cracks between the partially closed wooden blinds covering the window. She looked more pissed than I had ever seen her, and that was saying something.

I yanked off the towel on my head and pointed at my white hair. "It's me, you moron!"

She took slow, deliberate steps my way, baring her teeth at me. "And who, the fuck, is *me*?" she spat, not seeming to care one way or the other.

I rapidly rolled up the towel, ready to whip the nipples right off her tits if she didn't calm the fuck down.

Cain coughed out a surprised sound and we both spun to see him standing in the doorway with two cups of steaming coffee in his hands. "Um...what did I miss?" he asked lamely. "Hi, Claire."

Claire took the moment of confusion as an opportunity and lunged at me again. I jumped laterally and whipped her knuckles with my wet towel, then again on the ass as she barreled past me. She yelped in both surprise and anger as I hit her right at the bottom of her ridiculously fit ass where it met her thigh, already producing a red welt.

She snarled, spinning and grabbing at her ass for a second. Then she dove at me again, this time a full-bodied swing with her right fist as if hoping to end the world with a single punch.

I dropped the towel and rode the punch, rolling my shoulders and twisting slightly so that her fist sailed past my head. Then I pivoted, wrapped my arm around her waist, and flung her up and over me to slam into the dresser in a hip toss. I used every ounce of strength I had, knowing she was a shifter. The only way I was going to knock any sense into her was to literally knock her out or incapacitate her. Shifters could take a beating.

The dresser splintered but didn't break entirely.

So I picked up a vase, lifted it over my head, and began hammering it into her back, breaking the dresser further with each blow.

I heard Cain creep past us like one would at a baseball game when returning to one's seat—not wanting to knock over the drinks of the people sitting next to him that he had to pass on his journey.

"Hey, Starlight. What, um, exactly is going on? And why are they both naked?" he asked, sounding baffled.

Starlight grunted. "I think it's a friend thing. Then again, it could be because she doesn't look like Callie."

☙ 9 ❧

I flinched, glancing back at Starlight sharply. "What—"

Claire kicked me in the stomach, knocking me on my ass and causing me to drop the somehow still unbroken vase directly onto my shinbone in a Fatality Move.

My vision flared white as God Himself stabbed my soul in the region that my shin encased. I'm sure everyone has experienced a solid shin strike before—on a coffee table at three in the morning when trying to get a drink of water or use the restroom.

In that moment, it felt like the most painful thing I had ever experienced, but it rapidly dulled to merely a fiery throb and I scrambled backwards on my ass, ignoring the shards of glass and wooden splinters decorating my carpet—and now slicing into my flesh. Claire stormed closer, twisting her neck from left to right and cracking the bones as if just warming up.

"What have you done to my friend, demon?" she snarled. "I will rip that black hair right out of your scalp so hard you'll feel it in your toes. I knew one of your kind would eventually come here. You didn't even sense the alarm I set up..." she growled smugly.

"Did you pick up anything to eat, Piglet?" I heard Starlight ask Cain. I couldn't quite make out Cain's response as I continued scooting back away from Claire. "Oh, bother. I'm starving."

"This is like Pay-Per-View material," Cain murmured conversationally. "Why can't she see it's Callie?"

I saw Claire hesitate, momentarily picking up on the conversation behind her, but she didn't let up her pursuit of me. I finally scrambled back to my feet, picking up the only immediately available weapon. A magazine. I rolled it up like I was drawing a sword for a duel, narrowing my eyes at Claire.

"Claire's been rather...on edge lately," Starlight explained. "Savage is probably accurate. And she doesn't look like Callie. Either that, or I'm way higher than I thought." They were silent for a few moments before Starlight spoke again. "I'm glad Callie made it out of the Doors."

"How did you know about that?" Cain asked in disbelief—as if it was the most interesting thing happening in the room. Not the two naked chicks wildly fighting to the death in a *Listed Sisters* behind the scenes episode.

But for whatever reason, Claire had halted, and I could tell the majority of her attention was on the conversation behind her. She kept her eyes locked on me with an intensity that let me know if I moved even one step from where I stood, she would do everything in her power to end me. That look was a warning. And since I didn't want to use magic on my friend, I waited to see how this played out. Was Starlight doing this on purpose? Kind of like that whisper game—that people will try harder to hear a whisper than they would a shout?

And in the middle of a fight, shouting was only so much white noise.

I was also damned interested and surprised to hear Starlight mention the Doors, because I hadn't been entirely sure that seeing him inside them had been real. Some of the visions I had gone through had been real, others more like a dream of the future. A possibility.

"I showed her some things there," Starlight said.

"Some things I would like to hear and some things I would not," I said softly, using his exact phrasing from when we had spoken within the Doors.

Starlight—for the first time—shot me a look that was more personal than observing. A look that acknowledged me, even though I was confident he had recognized me from the start, letting Claire go beast on me for whatever damned reason he had. Maybe he knew she had needed to get whatever it was out of her system.

I lowered my magazine very slowly and relaxed my shoulders.

Claire narrowed her eyes suspiciously but didn't attack.

"You were actually there?" Cain asked, still sounding confused.

Claire and I were both staring at Starlight now, but I knew Claire had me locked firmly in her peripheral vision in the event I tried to attack her.

Starlight nodded, holding his breath for a moment. "Sure I was," he said in a tight voice, slowly exhaling more thick smoke. "You just need to know where to place your feet. What to smoke. How much. You can get anywhere on a cloud," he explained with a chuckle that sounded frighteningly similar to that dryer sheet teddy bear in the *Snuggle* television commercials. He locked eyes with me, suddenly looking entirely serious. "I'm glad she snapped out of it. She was a force to be reckoned with over there. Almost no humanity left at all."

I nodded soberly—both aware of Claire's tension and Starlight's warning.

"Did you want some?" Starlight asked, angling his bong towards Cain with his tiny, soft paws.

Cain eyed it warily. "Where will it take me?"

Starlight glanced down at his bong thoughtfully. "No idea, man. I haven't left yet. This mixture is experimental. Sometimes you gain things, sometimes you lose things." He looked up at Cain again, a fiery twinkle in his eyes. "You can't ride the cosmos without a little risk, right? Want to go on a fucking adventure, or what?" he asked almost aggressively excited.

Cain leaned away quickly. "No, thanks. I need to help Callie figure some stuff out."

Then the two of them looked directly at me.

"Oh, look. They stopped fighting," Starlight mused, lightly clapping his soft paws as he hugged the bong to his chest.

Claire was quivering as if in the process of being electrocuted. She slowly turned to me, narrowing her eyes doubtfully.

I didn't understand exactly what was going on, but Starlight was obviously right about something. Claire couldn't see me. Couldn't sense me. Even now, when her mind and her friends were telling her the truth. Whatever she saw before her was not her best friend, Callie Penrose. I needed to prove myself somehow.

And I knew I had a very small window in which to convince her.

I thought back, shuffling through memories, trying to think of something that would stand out as entirely unique and private. Recalling events from the alley only an hour ago, I looked up at her, my smile gentle and soft.

"I molested some vampires in an alley tonight. Because they were trying to molest my friend. An old cat lady..." I said, hoping she would get the reference to Phix—because I didn't want to name drop. "They...hurt her, and when she was lying in a puddle of her own blood, they...took liberties with their hands, and promised to do much, much worse...I took their hands. Among other things."

I said this very gently, very softly, my voice hoarse.

"What..." Claire began in a dry rasp, then cleared her throat. "What did you do to them?" Her fingers were clenched in tight, shaking fists at her sides.

Because Claire and I had experienced a very similar assault the first night we had met Roland. A group of vampires had thought they could take us in an alley, and they had seemed more than willing to sample more than just our blood when Claire had lost her top in the skirmish.

She hadn't been a shifter then, and I hadn't been a wizard. Just two frightened teenaged girls riding our bicycles after a day of swimming and tanning.

"I did what I wished I could have done that night years ago after we went swimming. Because..." I trailed off, my eyes growing misty at a new thought. "I didn't have a Shepherd to help me this time, and my friend was hurting. In fact, I'm pretty sure the Shepherd was the bad guy this time..." I said, letting out a pained sob, even though I had tried to keep it locked down.

Because that night so long ago, Roland had *saved* us from the vampires. It had been the first night I accidentally used magic to harm another life, even though I had no knowledge of how. I had seen them circling Claire like a pack of predators and I had reacted. Without Roland's intervention, the remaining vampires might have even done worse to us—extracting vengeance in addition to their other desires.

Except...now Roland was apparently *leading* the monsters. The same kind of monsters he used to fight. The same kind of monsters he had once saved two innocent little girls from.

Tears brimmed up from Claire's eyes, streaking down her cheeks and parting the blood coating her face like Moses splitting the Red Sea. And then my best friend crashed down to her knees, her shoulders hunched as she wept.

I felt a flash of heat on my scalp and almost jumped out of my skin. I patted my head anxiously, wondering if we had accidentally started a fire in our fight and a spark had hit my hair. If that was the case, friendship or not, Claire had to die. It was in the rulebook.

But I felt nothing else. It hadn't exactly been pain, just a sharp, noticeable sensation of heat. Claire was staring up at me, now, her eyes as wide as teacups.

"Callie?" she whispered, looking at me in startled disbelief.

I nodded, raising up my arms to welcome her into a hug. She sat entirely motionless, staring up at me. "Get over here, Clairebear," I pressed. "Before I tell Kenai you're being a bitch."

Claire leapt to her feet in one smooth motion and grabbed onto me like a life preserver, squeezing every inch of her body as close to mine as she could possibly get, even tucking her chin into and around my neck as she squeezed tight enough to almost cause pain.

She was sobbing inconsolably, unable to even speak. Her hands ran repeatedly down my hair in shaking, desperate motions as if trying to calm me down or convince herself I was real.

I cried back just as hard, having no idea what was going on, but the sensation of that much love hitting you at one time was powerful enough to break anyone.

I had my best friend back. And my brother.

And that distant stoner friend who always seemed to linger on the edges of social groups.

"I'm going to need another shower, thunder-twat," I muttered.

Her body shook with laughter and I heard her whisper something back in a very fragile voice. "I thought...I lost you," she sobbed. "Don't *ever* do that to me again..." It sounded like she had a lot more to say, but then she was shoving me away, back in the direction of the bedroom. "Hurry up. You're a mess."

I smiled, wiping at my eyes and readied myself for another shower.

I chose to grab a fresh towel rather than shake the glass out of the one I had just worn.

10

I sat on my couch, having shoved some of the detritus aside to make room for everyone. While I had been showering, Cain had left to get another coffee for Claire and some pastries for Starlight—which he had instantly devoured, complaining that Cain hadn't bothered to buy any Cheetos. The tiny bear seemed genuinely upset about the lack of chips, clutching his bong lovingly and muttering about needing both salty *and* sweet to truly ride his high out.

I'd caught them up on my trip through the Doors and meeting my ancestor, King Solomon, knowing I wouldn't be able to get anything useful out of Claire until she knew all the pertinent details of my absence. Then I told her about the welcome party outside Roland's church and how Phix was injured but hopefully okay. Claire had grunted at that part, but still seemed awed about my trip through the Doors. She'd also punched Starlight in the muzzle upon hearing he had seen and spoken with me inside the Doors. He hadn't told her, apparently. In all fairness, he'd been gobbling mushrooms like they were skittles, so it wasn't beyond the realm of possibility that *he* had thought it was a hallucination at first.

Claire stared off at nothing, shaking her head at my story, struggling to process it all.

"I don't understand why you look different, though. If this Le Boner guy zapped you, why would his next plan of action be to send his vampire goons after you? Kind of a waste of effort, isn't it?" I was smirking at her moniker for the French vampire, but I didn't have an answer to her question as I stared down at my hands hanging over my knees. "And if the zombie wizard vampire boner hit both of you with this magic, why doesn't he look different?" Claire asked, jerking her chin towards Cain.

He shot me a silent look, as if asking if I'd come to any conclusion on the matter. I shook my head and he sighed, obviously frustrated. "No idea. Maybe Le Bone had nothing to do with..." he trailed off, waving a hand in my general direction, "whatever it is you think you sense on Callie. But we haven't run into anyone else, so it's an educated guess."

Claire narrowed her eyes challengingly. "You think I'm *imagining* this? Look at her! She's taller, fuller, and has black hair!"

Cain smirked mischievously. "To be honest, men don't often notice such subtle changes like that in a woman. We are crude, aloof creatures."

Claire didn't appreciate his teasing, jumping to her feet in frustration. Cain made a grumbling sound of appreciation, not bothering to hide his interest in the display Claire had given him. Because Claire, as usual, seemed allergic to clothing, and had chosen to remain naked for our conversation—dismissing my offer of a robe because "it looked itchy." The shards of glass and splinters on the couch hadn't seemed to bother her, though.

She walked over to the door where she had apparently left her belongings before preparing to ambush me as I came out of the shower. She squatted down to dig through the pile, and I found myself wondering about the ward she had mentioned placing around my apartment—the one we had unwittingly set off.

"She's right, you know," Starlight murmured, polishing his bong absently. "You look and feel different. Except for that white streak appearing after Claire recognized you."

I glanced at him thoughtfully, not understanding what these changes were. I had looked in the mirror before my second shower and I hadn't noticed any of the changes Claire had mentioned—just same old Callie. "You knew all along it was me, though," I accused.

He nodded. "I can see both." He glanced down at his bong. "Maybe this experimental mix improved my perceptions," he mused, scrunching up his nose pensively.

I narrowed my eyes at him. "Well, it sure hasn't improved your judgment. You could have just told Claire it was me."

Starlight shook his head. "She wouldn't have believed it. I think she needed to *see* it."

He had put special emphasis on the word *see*, as if it was some kind of power.

I caught Cain too-casually glancing over the back of the couch to see what Claire was up to as she crawled about on all fours, flinging items around wildly. Cain looked on the verge of dusting off his chivalry lance to ask if she needed assistance in any way whatsoever.

I lifted up a piece of wood that had broken off the frame of one of the paintings we had knocked off the wall and calmly broke it over the back of his head. Starlight burst out in a panting giggle.

"Ow!" Cain snapped, flinging up his hands in a protective gesture for a second swat, dropping the remnants of his coffee onto the floor in the process.

I brandished the jagged piece of wood trim at him in warning. "Class. Get some. Or whatever you were considering doing to her, I'll do to you. With *this*."

His eyes riveted on the wooden stake, an uneasy grimace plastering his face. "Just window shopping."

I hefted the stake in a threatening reminder, and he clammed up. "Clean up your mess," I told him, pointing at the spilled coffee.

"Why? You're being evicted tomorrow. Let's trash the place some more," he suggested, taking in the obvious damage from Claire and I duking it out earlier.

I gave him a level look, one my mom had given me many times over the years.

He grumbled something under his breath that sounded like he was reconsidering having a sister in his life. I let him continue to rant as Claire came bouncing back to the couch with her phone. Without explanation, she snapped a picture of me. Before I could speak, she held out the phone and showed me. My mouth fell open as I stared at...

A stranger. Long, dark hair hung down past my shoulders—except for a single white streak starting where I had felt the flash of heat upon Claire recognizing me—and my face was more of an apple shape with higher and broader cheekbones. My eyes were wider and darker, giving me an exotic flair. My skin was also a shade off-white, more bronze than normal. And I was indeed...fuller—broader shoulders, wider chest, and my torso did look longer—taller—than normal. Not significantly, but definitely enough to notice. It was downright eerie. I glanced down at myself, staring at my hand, trying to spot the changes with my own eyes.

Then I looked up at my friends, frowning. "I have no idea what that's all about. I still look like me in the mirror."

Cain piped up. "You still look like Callie to me," he said, leaning over to stare at the picture for himself. I studied the long white streak in the picture's hair, frowning.

Had Le Bone hit me with some magic power he had gained—or been given—in my absence? But Claire was right—it didn't make sense to send vampires after me immediately after casting such a spell, and Cain hadn't been physically altered. I snapped a picture of him with Claire's phone, just to be sure. He had managed to fling up a middle finger close enough to the camera that it dominated the shot, but in the background, Cain was unchanged.

I turned to Starlight, handing Claire her phone as I went over specific details of what I remembered from Le Bone's attack. Cain piped in with his experience, which was remarkably similar. Starlight listened raptly, nodding along thoughtfully.

Once I was finished speaking, he leaned in close to stare into my eyes, my face, even sniffing at my hair. "Not magic," he said, absently. "Not that I can sense, anyway. But Claire is right, you look and smell like a demon. It's unsettling to see both visions at the same time—Callie and not-Callie."

With that simple comment, a new thought suddenly struck me.

I couldn't simply walk up to Fabrizio or Roland anymore. Couldn't show them that Callie Penrose lived. They would see this new me—a demon. I realized I was grinding my teeth.

If Le Bone had been behind this, wouldn't that have gone against Master Roland's wishes? Because the only reason he would have invested the time and power to change me in this way was if he recognized who I truly was—which would have surely interested Roland. I doubted Le Bone just wandered around Kansas City, arbitrarily making people look like demons for entertainment.

Also, Le Bone was supposed to be dead. I hadn't checked with Phix or Richard, obviously, but from the fact that Cain still saw me clearly, I was betting they would have as well, or they would have demanded an explanation. Maybe they couldn't see the change because they had been beside me immediately prior to the attack. Hell, they could have been hit by the attack as well—just with different repercussions than I had suffered.

I knew it had to have happened before the vampire gang attacked, because the thugs had also called me demon a few times. Apparently, it hadn't been a casual comment. They saw me as Claire had initially seen me.

There had to be another way to convince people who I really was, because it wasn't conducive to a long life to challenge all my old friends to a fight in order to convince them who I really was.

"I need to go let the other bears know that you're alive and well," Starlight said.

I lifted a hand, stalling him. "I wasn't able to make Gateways earlier. Or Shadow Walk. What's up with that?"

Starlight nodded easily. "The red sky. The vampires have warded Kansas City from travel. No one in or out for the time being. We're stuck here," he said cheerfully. "Well, you are."

11

I almost fell out of my chair. That level of magic...the power needed to do such a thing on such a large scale...

I'd only seen one place with wards like that. The Vatican. And guess who used to work for those assholes? Roland—the new Master Vampire who had retained his wizard's powers. I leaned back into the couch, both disgusted and impressed, recalling the red haze to the sky I had noticed earlier tonight. No wonder my Shadow Walking and Gateway hadn't worked. Solomon's Temple was still online for some reason, though, which was a huge relief. Otherwise, we wouldn't have even been able to enter the city.

Claire piped up. "That's why we were concerned when Phix disappeared. She used to stalk the streets at night, killing indiscriminately in search of you. It's one reason for the intense security around the church. Well, both churches."

I frowned. Phix had been off on an errand for Darling and Dear when I entered the Doors. Remembering that made my stomach flutter queasily—recalling her newfound fear of Darling and Dear. Had she done something to upset them? And how had she found me at Solomon's Temple if traveling was currently on lockdown?

For that matter...

"If the city is warded, how do you plan on visiting the other bears? Are they here?"

He waved a hand dismissively. "I told them to stay in Alaska for the time being. And wards have never been much of a problem to me. I explore new galaxies on a regular basis," he said, caressing his bong adoringly, "so a ward is a little...juvenile to me."

I leaned forward abruptly. "Can you take others with you when you travel?"

He shook his head. "No can do, or I would have brought an army back."

I let out a frustrated sigh. "I think it's fairly obvious what you need to do next."

Cain gave him a very dry look, silently stating that it was not remotely obvious.

I agreed with Cain. "I was planning on visiting Fabrizio or Roland, but since I apparently look like a demon, I don't think that option is on the table anymore."

Starlight cocked his head, seeming disappointed in my lack of mental capacity. "No, silly. You need to go see the Black Warrior. I hope you like turtle-snakes. I'll let him know you're coming. Don't dawdle. He hates slow-pokes."

With that, Starlight simply vanished. Him and his magic bong and the last pastry. Maybe that bong really did let him travel unmolested through the cosmos—like Dr. Who and his Tardis. Starlight had visited me in the Doors, after all. One day I would get some answers on exactly what his story was. A wizard who chose to become a bear—permanently, rather than shifting back and forth like the others in his Cave.

Claire was strangely silent, not looking the least bit surprised at his departure. Or by his suggestion. I narrowed my eyes. "Who is the Black Warrior?" I demanded, fearing I wasn't going to like the answer one bit.

"Um..." Claire began, scrunching up her nose as if trying to figure out how to answer my question. "A lot has changed since you...left. Remember when you found that demon's secret office and all his notes about Missouri being important—how so many beings were trying to get here?"

I nodded, remembering Johnathan's office very well.

"I think he was right. Before Roland's ward went up, new...beings were moving here on a fairly regular basis. With the growing tension between the vampires and Shepherds, everyone was too preoccupied to notice them moving to town. I only picked up on it because I was practically knocking door-to-door to find anyone who might know anything about your disappearance since neither Fabrizio nor Roland had time to meet with me." She closed her eyes for a moment, realizing that had sounded like a guilt trip. It was, but an honest one. "I picked up a lot of useless information, heard about a lot of new people in town. For the most part, they've all kept a pretty low profile, not wanting to get involved in the obvious war between Roland and Fabrizio."

My mind raced with a dozen of the worst potential beings that might have moved here, wondering what kind of future problems they might create. That wouldn't really matter if Fabrizio and Roland's fight left Kansas City a pile of smoldering ashes, though. "And this Black Warrior is one of these new beings in town?" I asked, shrugging. "Who is he?"

"I'm pretty sure the Black Warrior brought ninjas to Kansas City. At least, I think that's what they are. No one ever sees them, but everyone senses them watching from the shadows. I don't think it's an official title or anything, but people have begun calling them the unseen eyes," she said, shivering.

Cain cursed, jumping to his feet at the mention of ninjas. "Motherfucking ninjas and a trouser-snake?!" he bellowed.

"*Turtle*-snake," Claire said, drawing out the first word. "And I think he's a god. Or the next best thing."

"Ninjas?" I demanded, in the exact same tone Cain had used.

Claire nodded with a sickly look on her face. "I guess we're about to find out."

Cain climbed to his feet, muttering under his breath. "No matter how much some people have changed, I trust Starlight. He helped you in the Doors. If he thinks we need to speak to the Black Warrior and his ninjas, we probably shouldn't keep him waiting."

I nodded in agreement. Starlight, as kooky as he was, often had a method to his madness.

Rather than wasting time talking, I headed to my room to salvage an outfit from what had been left behind in my closet. It looked like it was a jeans and tank-top kind of day. And my Darling and Dear jacket, of course. Before jumping into the shower, I had hastily scrubbed off the most noticeable bloodstains from my fight with the vampires. It would have to do.

I was dressed and hurriedly stuffing a duffel bag full of my other clothes when I heard Claire come up behind me to help. As she reached for a shirt, I noticed the band of creamy leather adorning her wrist, etched with dark, unknown symbols—courtesy of Darling and Dear—that allowed her to withstand bullets. A type of Aegis, like Zeus' shield.

Every item created by the pair of leather smiths was imbued with a magical property.

My boots could sense demons, tingling at the toes when facing one.

My coat could take a significant beating, protecting me like armor.

Both leather and boots could be modified in design and color with a simple thought.

After Phix's terrified outburst at us for suggesting we bring her to Darling and Dear while she recovered from her wounds, I wasn't entirely sure what to think of the self-proclaimed Armorers of the Apocalypse. I had thought they were friends of hers.

I had thought they were friends of mine.

I would continue using their gear for the time being, but Phix had some explaining to do when she woke. Right now, it was time to go see a ninja turtle-snake god and then find a way to wash off *eau de demon*.

My last experience with Ninja Turtles in Las Vegas had been...memorable.

12

We took an old Jeep Claire had borrowed from one of the other bears in her Cave. They were all out in Alaska anyway and agreed it was safer for her to switch cars often since she was being hunted as a known associate of me—by both the vampires and Shepherds.

She was living a life on the lam as a result of being my friend—coming home to check on me because I hadn't answered any of her calls. And then not being able to leave because the shield went up before she could get back out. Leaving her cut off from the other Kansas City bears, from Kenai. Which made me want to hit something.

Very, very hard.

Leaving my apartment, I kept getting the nagging suspicion that I was forgetting something vitally important, even after I'd searched every room three times. It finally hit me—after I had eventually given up and walked out the door—that it was my cell phone. I'd drowned it in a pond while fleeing from Last Breath the morning I had entered the Doors, but the act of leaving my apartment had jogged my muscle memory, even after spending so long without one.

It was oddly invigorating to be free of that tether, although I kept finding myself subconsciously reaching for a purse or checking my pocket for it. I'd tossed my single depressing duffel bag of possessions into the trunk, nodding woodenly when Claire told me she would call a moving company to get the rest of my stuff in the morning. It wasn't like I had anywhere for them to send my stuff, and any of the sentimental things had already been taken by someone. My money was on Roland, the creepy vampire overlord now known as the Red Pastor.

Just to be absolutely certain about at least one thing, before leaving my apartment I'd asked Claire to put on my boots and point the toes in my direction. When she admitted she didn't feel a tingle, I almost shouted out in relief. Because it confirmed that it really was an illusion I was dealing with—not that I had somehow, at some point, actually been infected with demonic blood or picked up a hitchhiking possession, or that the Seal of Solomon on my finger was leaking demons without my knowledge. Although all of those fears had been unlikely, it had removed at least one persistent stressor on my mind.

Cain sat in the backseat, glancing frequently behind us as if expecting a tail. Or maybe hoping to catch a glimpse of these unseen eyes—the ninjas—Claire and Phix had mentioned. I didn't blame him. Simply knowing they were out there made me feel like they were watching my every move.

Claire had told us that Starlight gave her the address to the Black Warriors home in the event she ever needed a place to lay low—a sanctuary if she was ever in danger—but that she'd never had the stones to visit a house full of ninjas.

So I let her do the driving. I stared out the window, taking in the familiar sights I used to drive past on a daily basis. But things were subtly...*different*. Buildings looked slightly under-maintained and there were a lot of *For Sale* signs staked in the wet grass—both commercial and residential. A lot of Regulars—even if they hadn't known why—had decided to leave Kansas City. It was also the middle of the night, so the moonlight shining down upon the deserted streets added to the haunted vibe. Even still, there should have been a lot more cars: ride-share drivers, teenagers screaming down the streets in embarrassing attempts at drag racing, adults coming home from the bars, or early shift people on their way to work.

Instead, we drove through very light traffic for a Kansas City evening.

I absently commented on the *For Sale* signs, still staring out the window.

Claire shrugged numbly. "Yeah. You get used to it."

Her hollow tone—coupled with the knowledge that I had been the reason she was forced to live like a fugitive on the run from the law the past year—made me want to reach out and wrap her up in a hug. "I should have called you..."

"Oh, god!" Cain gasped dramatically. "It's starting. I'm going to catch a virulent strain of estrogen, aren't I? I can feel it creeping into that crusted, hollow shell I once called my heart! What do I *do*?!"

Claire had stiffened at my words, her grip flexing on the steering wheel for a moment, but Cain's comment seemed to snap her out of it, a small smirk ghosting across her face as she loosened her shoulders and relaxed her fingers.

I clapped lightly at Cain's performance.

"Thank you."

Properly composed, Claire let out a forgiving sigh. "You told me about your quest, Callie. And everyone knows you can't turn down a *quest*," she said, a whisper of a grin making her dimples pop. "It's not like you knew you would be gone so long, or that any of this might happen. I really can't rationalize being angry at you. As much as I want to. And as much as I will still be angry with you anyway, in spite of logic."

I laughed, nodding. "Deal."

"I've had no one to bitch to for a long time. I try talking to Kenai about it all on the phone, but it's not like either of us can do anything with the barrier between us. I can't escape and he can't come join me." She wiped at her nose, blinking a few times. Finally, she shrugged. "It is what it is, you know? But you're back, now. And you're fucking *alive*, Callie. I hate to admit it, but even I began to doubt your return."

Hearing it laid out like that...was just so heartbreaking. But I smiled at her, wiping my own nose. It felt like the weight on my shoulders had lightened ever so slightly upon getting that poison spoken out loud before it had the chance to fester...well, to fester any longer than the year it already had. Because knowing Claire, she had likely beaten herself up with overwhelming guilt, shame, righteous anger at herself, and ultimately blind anger at me upon hearing about my disappearance and probable death.

I could tell her shoulders felt lighter as well. Cain could just suck a koala wang for trying to interrupt girl time—even if his banter had eased the tension somewhat. I silently told him this with a look, letting him know that *brothers should be seen and not heard* for the remainder of the adult conversation going on in the front seat. He grinned toothily, saluting me.

I rolled my eyes, turning back to Claire. "Now, tell me how it all went down on your end. Maybe the three of us can jog loose something important. Find a way to end this insanity," I said, gesturing at the window and beyond.

And she did—in very clinical, concise terms, not giving me the chance to interrupt.

"I wasn't here for all of it. I returned to Kansas City a few weeks after you apparently disappeared—coming home to see why you hadn't returned my calls. I heard about your disappearance, and that Roland went to Abundant Angel, demanding to see Fabrizio. Demanding to see you. Even Cain. Anyone who had been present at the church the day you disappeared. Fabrizio declined, probably expecting you to return soon, or not trusting a promise of safe conduct with Roland after all the threats he was making about going to war with the Shepherds if you didn't return in one week. That's about the time I showed up. I heard about many closed-door meetings taking place between Roland, Haven, and Henri Bellerose, a visiting Master from Paris."

I nodded, letting her know I was familiar with Bellerose.

"The Shepherds were uneasy about three Master Vampires plotting behind closed doors after making such brazen threats as Roland had. Everyone was walking on eggshells. Many of the supernatural factions you're familiar with fled in those early days, including the Nephilim, the Templars, and the Chancery. Then a few dozen men from Rome came to support Fabrizio, and when Roland heard about it, he declared for all to hear that it was a preemptive act of war—claiming that the Shepherds wouldn't have called in allies if you were safe and sound. And coming from an ex-Shepherd himself, many believed him. Who better to know the inner workings of the Vatican?"

She swallowed audibly, turning onto a side street.

"That's when Roland put the barrier up around the city—without warning anyone—preventing any more Shepherds from entering or any more supernatural factions from fleeing. Haven was furious with Roland for it, demanding he take it down—that he had no right to do such a thing, let alone threaten war with the Shepherds without the approval of the Sanguine Council. When Roland refused to listen, Haven tried to use his strength as Roland's maker to force him to submit, to cease his warmongering, and to make peace."

Cain was leaning forward, his ears practically twitching in anticipation.

In the back of my mind, I was wondering why Roland hadn't approached the Sanguine Council for support. They had seemed to see him as their poster child—asking him to take a hold of his powers and bring honor and respect to the council of Master Vampires. Which meant that either he feared how they would react, or he had become so wrapped up in his personal vendetta that he refused any outside help.

After all, the Shepherds had abandoned him, and then they dared to stand in his way, keeping him from me—the one person he seemed to care about most in this world. Maybe I really had been his moral compass, his lighthouse in a stormy, turbulent sea.

Claire grimaced before continuing, as if the words were particularly distasteful. "Roland not only withstood Haven's power...he managed to kill Haven right then and there."

Cain whistled. "That's impressive. Tough to stand up to your Master at all, let alone win. There's some kind of bond made between the two. Roland must have some crazy powers—or Haven was incredibly stupid to attempt turning a Shepherd in the first place. That's never been done before, right? Maybe there was a reason for that..."

I pointed a thumb blindly back at him. "That one. It was a gamble Roland was forced to take." I laughed bitterly at a new thought. "Ironically, he became a vampire to *prevent* a war between Shepherds and the Sanguine Council." I waved a hand towards the window. "Hashtag NailedIt," I muttered dryly.

13

Claire nodded, knowing full well how Roland's change had gone down—and how the Vatican had turned their backs on him so fast it was almost like they had never supported him in the first place—back when he was dutifully killing their enemies, hunting monsters for them, saving little orphan girls from vampires, and overall being a shining example of a pious man. I didn't condone his actions, but I couldn't dismiss his motivations.

"Following Haven's death, any vampires still loyal to him were promptly slaughtered, leaving the rest to wisely join Roland. He even scooped up Bellerose with little to no effort. It was either join or die, and without any means to leave the city, Henri chose life."

I nodded, idly studying the nice homes around us. There were less signs of disrepair here, but the homes still felt less vibrant—as if the neighborhood had grown reclusive.

"With so many new vampires under his command, Roland promoted Bellerose and some other vampire, who I haven't identified, to be his lieutenants, but rumor makes me wonder if Bellerose's promotion was more of a publicity stunt or ego boost than for any real need of assistance—to have the Master of Paris under his thumb where everyone could see. Just another tool in his work-belt to use when needed and put on a shelf when not."

Cain shook his head, his eyes distant, doing absolutely nothing for my confidence.

I ventured a question, not wanting to ask it but some small part of me hoping for a certain answer. "Any chance one of these lieutenants is really wearing the pants in the relationship? Or maybe both?" I asked. "Before this all began, Roland warned me that Henri Bellerose was incredibly old and very powerful."

Claire scoffed as if I'd told a joke. "Not a chance. Roland is *no one's* puppet. Trust me. If you'd been here, seen what I've seen..." she shuddered, shaking her head. "The Red Pastor owns this town. Period."

I saw it all unfolding before me, pieces of Claire's story clicking into place. "And with Roland's barrier up, the Sanguine Council had no idea what was going on or were too late to do anything about it if they did. Even now, they are helpless to interfere. Unless they *wanted* all of this to happen," I added, figuratively putting on my tinfoil hat.

Claire shrugged. "I'm just telling you what I know for certain. I'll leave speculation to you." She checked over her shoulder to switch lanes before entering a quiet, tree-filled neighborhood, driving beneath a tunnel of thick branches and leaves. "That's when Roland began recruiting, turning humans to build his army."

Cain and I sat in silence, wondering how much worse it could get.

"With his growing numbers, Roland then set his sights on Abundant Angel, letting them know that their allotted time to hand you over had expired. A few of the Conclave must have snuck in before the barrier went up, because I'm pretty sure they are the only reason the church still stands. They protect the property with a ward and their power, and the Shepherds—some little more than boys in training—do what little they can. There were a lot of fights in the beginning, and Roland soon put up a barrier around his own church like Abundant Angel's—one only Roland's minions could cross. A twist on the trope that vampires can't cross a threshold without being invited inside."

Cain let out a whistle, leaning back into his seat. "That's actually pretty clever," he mused, shaking his head. Clever wasn't the word I would have chosen, but it wasn't wrong.

Something Claire had said was nagging at me, though. "The vampire who attacked us tonight, Le Bone, was strong. And he used to work for Bellerose. Could he be Roland's second lieutenant?" I asked.

Claire shrugged. "No idea. I'd never heard his name before you said it back in the apartment. But if Le Boner worked for Bellerose, he now works for Roland. I've never been able to learn the second lieutenant's name. The vampires are close-knit. I only knew about Bellerose because he was one of three Master Vampires in town when I first arrived, and that seemed like two too many, in my opinion."

"And all this fighting has gone unnoticed by the Regulars? The police?" Cain cut in.

Claire grimaced. "Roland has the local government in his pocket. Somehow."

"He *turned* them?" I whispered, my eyebrows threatening to climb off my forehead.

Claire shrugged. "Whatever he did, they fell into line very quickly. They don't request support from outside of town and the news channels continue to act like nothing has changed. No one has any idea there is a new kingdom in Kansas City. It's unbelievable."

Cain let out a slow whistle. "That can't be sustainable. Sooner or later some Regular is going to leave town to visit a relative and spread some juicy details..."

Claire glanced at him in the rearview mirror. "Oh? And who's going to believe them? Especially when there is nothing official in the news. *Oh, Auntie May. Kansas City has just gone to hell lately. Trash in the streets, murders and abductions every day. Even the church seems to be fighting gangs of thugs,*" Claire said in a pantomime whine. "Then Auntie May turns on the television and sees nothing of the sort reported. Clearly, her niece is exaggerating, overstressed by the big city life and she decides to encourage her niece to move to a smaller town closer to home."

I sat back in my seat, thinking. Cain wasn't wrong. Neither was Claire. Eventually something would get out, but how long would it take? It had already been a year, lending credit to Claire's statement.

Controlling the media and the government meant he controlled the narrative in addition to having superior numbers. Which made an already powerful, dangerous man nigh untouchable. Even if someone managed to get the truth on recording or something, what was really happening in town, that person would likely be silenced by the very people who should have helped him expose the truth.

I brushed my fingers through my hair and thumped my head against the headrest. "Any demon activity in town?" I asked, closing my eyes. Because on top of all of this, Samael was still out there and, more than anything, he wanted to battle me, destroy me.

Claire shook her head. "None. Not since you ran into Samael the day you disappeared."

I drummed my fingers across the armrest, thinking over everything I had heard.

"If I can get in front of him, prove who I am, maybe I can get him to stop this insanity," I said, feeling as if I was trying to convince myself as much as the others.

Claire was staring at me, not bothering to watch the road, and I realized we had stopped at a stop sign on a quiet street. "No one sees Roland, Callie. And I mean that. No one."

I gritted my teeth. "He will see *me*."

"Technically, he will not see *you*," Cain growled, emphasizing the last word. Roland would see a demon. Not Callie. Right.

"I've been living—surviving—here like a refugee for a *year*, Callie. I've been hunted just for knowing you—hunted by both Shepherds *and* vampires." I felt like wilting under her glare. "So believe me when I say you can or cannot do something. If I knew a way to put an end to this, I would tell you. But it sure as hell won't be by storming the castle."

Still sensing my stubborn doubt, she held up a hand, ticking off fingers as she spoke.

"Considering Roland's army, you don't stand a chance," she said, holding up one finger. "No matter how badass you are, you can't take on that many vampires *and* his pack of werewolves—run by our dear old friends, Paradise and Lost, if you remember them."

I grimaced at that. They were formidable, ruthless, and their loyalty to Roland was unparalleled—possibly even magically bound.

"Secondly, you *don't look like Callie*. All he will see is what I see." My mouth clicked shut. "Thirdly, even *if* you made it past his army and his two lieutenants, and didn't look like a demon, you quite literally could not get past the ward protecting the church without Roland's express permission. The same goes for Fabrizio. Each one sits like a king in his castle, never daring to step foot outside these days, letting their serfs do the dirty work."

That was interesting. To hear they both locked themselves up inside their fortresses. I could understand Fabrizio doing so, but why would Roland hide if he had such superior numbers?

Claire's face looked haunted for a moment. "Back in the beginning, I saw Fabrizio himself railing against the doors, flinging around enough magic to destroy the Sprint Center—all to no avail. He and his Shepherds ended up fleeing before the vampires and werewolves could regroup and flank them. That's the closest I've seen anyone ever get, and they took a lot of casualties in their retreat."

I let out a breath of despair. I wasn't giving up, but she made good points. There was no denying that the Roland I once knew was now gone, and a bloodthirsty man of the cloth was all that remained. It didn't matter that he had done all this for my sake—he was a war criminal if even half of what Claire said was true. He needed to be put down like a rabid dog—no matter that the dog had once been man's best friend. Now he was a liability. A danger to all those around him—even those he had once loved most.

Execution was the only answer.

Because he had *taught* me the difference between right and wrong—and now he had perverted it. Justice demanded he die by his own hypocrisy.

There could be no absolution for Roland Haviar.

But I didn't have to worry about that yet, because even if I did look like myself, I stood no chance of getting close to the Master of the city. Or Fabrizio for that matter. I needed to find another way to end this.

"I think I'm ready to see the turtle-snake guy," I said in a hollow tone.

"Let's stick with calling him the Black Warrior," Claire said tightly. "I'm not sure how patient he is, and we already have enough enemies to worry about. We're looking for allies or answers, remember?"

"Got it," Cain piped in cheerfully. "Let's go see Mister Turtle-head."

Claire sighed in resignation, unable to draw up a smile.

I couldn't blame her. I bet humor had faded pretty fast when she saw everyone around her become the opposite of what they had once been.

When the good became the bad.

When the righteous became the wicked.

When all hope died and despair entered the world kicking and screaming.

Even Cain's mirth faded as Claire gripped the steering wheel, taking us through quiet neighborhood streets to meet a ninja god.

❧ 14 ☙

We parked outside a humbly quaint mansion near the plaza. The single-story home was tucked back from the road obscured by ancient trees with low, wide-reaching branches and thick foliage, but I sensed the building was just as large and costly as its neighboring homes. Three men in sharp, perfectly tailored suits stood on the porch before a tall set of double wooden doors. They watched us with dark eyes that glinted like obsidian gems in the glow from the mellow lamps lining the meandering, snake-like flagstone walkway that connected the front door to the drive where we had parked. No garage here.

"If I see one talking rat..." Cain murmured, "I'm out."

"Starlight would have said something about a talking rat," Claire said with absolutely zero confidence. "I think..." she added, letting out a breath.

I placed a comforting hand on hers, smiling faintly. "We need answers on how to deal with Roland without a full-frontal assault. Gods usually have them." Cain grunted but didn't offer any alternatives.

It was still late, but sunrise was only a couple of hours or so away, and the city was nestled in that darkest part of the night right before dawn. I let out a breath and opened my door, hopping out of the Jeep. I was so overcome with everything I had seen and heard that I realized I probably wouldn't have even cared if this meeting ended up being a trap orchestrated by Roland or Fabrizio.

I might have even welcomed it. Because each step I took led me closer to executing my mentor or confronting Fabrizio, giving me the chance to prove it was me, Callie.

Similar to Helen of Troy, I was the face that launched a thousand...freaks into war.

My feet had never felt so heavy. Cain seemed to sense this and squeezed my shoulder reassuringly. I gave him a faint smile for his effort and the look on his face let me know he understood my trepidation as clear as day.

The three Asian men stared at us as we approached, hands clasped behind their backs and feet set firmly at shoulder-width. I casually assessed the garden. It was meticulously kept with expensive trees placed in seemingly precise locations—as if every consideration had been taken before planting anything. The landscaping consisted entirely of exotic plants, flowers and bushes, and even though I knew next to nothing about such things, I knew beyond a shadow of a doubt that they were expensive. Great care had been taken in trimming the trees and bushes so that the walk felt more like I was traipsing through an outdoor art exhibit.

The varieties of shrubbery all had characteristics of Bonsai trees—plants that were maintained and cultivated as a form of active meditation that many Buddhists practiced. The older the plant, the more valuable they became. And each tree looked very, very old.

I knew the three men before us were dangerous because they looked entirely relaxed. They looked ready to move at even the faintest gesture of a threat, but they looked mellow and inviting doing it. Their stances reminded me of water.

These three men had that feeling about them...able to consume anything that stood in their way and then return to their natural, calm state.

Bruce Lee had once taught a lesson about that. No matter how hard you punched the water, it would instantly reform the second your fist was retracted. That it was impossible to *hurt* water with force. That the power of water lay in its depth and undercurrent, but that even the surface was impervious to harm. Air could move it for a time, fire could turn it into steam, and earthly elements were simply swallowed by it. In the end, water always returned to its natural state, relatively unaffected by any brief war with its fellow elements.

I paused before the three men and dipped my head in a respectful gesture, not entirely sure how to introduce myself. Apparently, introductions weren't necessary. As one, the guards stepped forward, their left hands drifting to their waists as if to hold scabbards, and they bowed respectfully, never entirely averting their eyes away from my shoulders.

Not only respect, but a warrior's respect. A worthy opponent.

A fourth man in bright orange robes stepped out from behind them where he had been standing so quietly that I hadn't even noticed him. He was a short, grinning, round man—seemingly forged in the fires of happiness. Having said that, he had hellacious scars on his knuckles, wrists, and forearms, and his nose had been broken several times over his life. Mr. Happy had spent his youth making others unhappy, possibly even beating them senseless during school lunch to steal their happy money. Cain studied him more intensely than the three guards, which was saying something.

Without a word, he held out a hand, indicating for us to follow him to the front double doors. His compatriots stepped to the side, clearing the way for us, and promptly returned their gazes to the streets, ever vigilant for inbound threats.

Cain arched a brow at me but said nothing. He looked surprised that the three of us were granted passage behind only a single monk—someone we could easily overwhelm if we meant harm. Not that we had sinister intentions, but it was startling to step into a world where silent respect was the nation's currency over words and reassurances. That it was expected without fanfare, a default starting point. Trust could be taken away, but it was always offered up front. Claire simply followed my lead, keeping her eyes on my shoulders when she wasn't scanning our surroundings for danger.

We approached the great wooden doors, and I realized that a weathered painted motif was carved into the wood. Three squares in a vertical column and one additional square on either side of the center square—so that it was a horizontal row. Like a compass on a map depicting the Cardinal Directions, or an addition symbol. And within each square was an animal carved into the wood. Sticking with the compass analogy, the topmost square represented North and was depicted by a large, ancient, black turtle standing amidst crashing waves.

The Southern square was occupied by a red bird that made me think of a phoenix, but that could have been all the carved flames surrounding the creature.

The left—Western—square showed a white tiger surrounded by spikes that may have been long blades of grass but looked more jagged and rough than foliage should.

The right—Eastern—square was a blue dragon standing in what looked like an enchanted forest.

The center square showed a faded yellow dragon standing on solid ground. Our happy host was facing us with a permanent, endearing smile, but he made no attempt to open the door. I realized he was giving us time to admire the carving—like a priest would in a church when approaching the altar.

"It's very pretty," Claire said hesitantly, as if made uneasy by the continued silence and the man's rapt attention on our reactions. He smiled wider in gratitude before turning to Cain.

Cain nodded, narrowing his eyes at it thoughtfully. "It's...very old but well-preserved."

The man, still smiling, dipped his head slightly, turning to me, his smile seeming to fade slightly into an expectant, demanding grin—like he had higher expectations from me. While the others had been commenting on the door, I had been watching our guard's face, trying to get a read on the man behind the smile while trying to recall anything from my martial arts training—or meditation training—that may or may not apply to my current situation. I had spent many years training in various martial arts with Roland and, as a result, had dipped my toes into Buddhist philosophy more than most Americans—which wasn't necessarily high praise on my part.

It just meant that I wasn't *entirely* ignorant. I had a better understanding of their culture, what they valued, and what they did not value.

So.

Against the instinctive screaming of my body's fight or flight mechanisms, I took a slow, thoughtful breath, squared my shoulders into a relaxed pose, and closed my eyes, forcing myself to ignore the intense observance of the secretly dangerous, outwardly ridiculously happy man before me.

I imagined my totem—that hot mess of symbols that I had chosen to portray the Tao of Callie.

My...Crest. My coat of arms. I hadn't ever considered it in such a way, but it was accurate. The feather, rose, and wings shimmered into existence within the black void of my mind, centering my thoughts. I fed all fears, concerns, and anxieties about Roland, Kansas City, Phix's injury, Solomon, and even Nate Temple into my totem, unburdening myself from the weights of the world. I would pick them back up later.

My senses spiked, picking up on the breathing of the bodies around me, the faint scent of juniper and sandalwood. I heard the slight breeze kissing the flowers before the guards nearest the garden behind us. And...

I felt an immense blanket of raw, unrelenting power humming all around me. The undeniable calm a mile below the crest of a tidal wave. I gasped, rocking back on my heels as I embraced it, feeling like it was about to bowl me over. Then my body relaxed, submitting to it, and the pressure ceased. You couldn't force water—not for any extended period of time.

You just sat back and enjoyed the gentle, rolling waves.

The entire property was deeply immersed in this tranquil power, and I distantly remembered we were dealing with a god somewhere beyond this door. How I hadn't managed to sense this power earlier, I couldn't explain. But it didn't need an explanation.

It. Just. Was.

Eyes still closed, I lifted my hand and slowly approached the door. I sensed a brittle, shocked silence from my friends but I didn't pick up on any danger or anger from the guard. In fact, I felt the warm skin of his forearm suddenly brush under the pads of my fingertips—as light as a feather—and I realized that he was offering to guide me closer to the object before me. I accepted with a faint nod and an even fainter smile. I felt him stop and gently lower his arm before stepping aside.

I didn't open my eyes as I trailed my fingertips across the wood, focusing entirely on my sense of touch. My fingers brushed against wood that had weathered the infinite sands of time. Wood that had cherished thousands of years of romantic embraces with the sweet kisses of decay without ever relinquishing its grip on life, to this world.

The unconditional love the wood felt for the source of its agony and ecstasy—both its executioner and greatest desire—time.

It was one with its enemy and loved that enemy as much as it hated it.

My fingers stopped moving of their own accord and I felt a sudden surge of warmth, like I had just touched a fresh cup of tea. But the heat was a living thing, not merely warmed wood.

No.

This was *fire*, pure and simple. The fire of life screaming forth into the world with the immortal laughter of one who hadn't yet learned the concept of pain or death—young enough to think it was invincible and impervious to harm—like every teenager everywhere, soaring out into the world on wings of endless ambitions.

"Bird..." I murmured confidently. "Fire. Summer."

The air grew noticeably tense, no one daring to speak, but I was only concerned with one opinion on my comment. "Yes," the guard finally said, sounding surprised.

I lifted my hand upward and to the right and felt myself instantly smiling as my fingers trailed over the next depiction—the blue dragon I had seen. Because it almost felt as if the wood was vibrating beneath my fingertips, struggling to shove out new life from an empty void of nothingness. Creating something from nothing. I gasped as I even felt what seemed to be fresh buds and leaves tickling the pads of my fingers.

"Blue dragon. Wood. Spring," I murmured.

"Yes," the guard said excitedly, this time sounding as if he was on the verge of laughter.

I licked my lips, already lifting my hand to touch the left square. My fingers suddenly tingled—not a mellow vibration in the wood like a moment ago but a physical jolt within my own fingertips. And I felt my Silver claws burst forth without consciously choosing to do so. They struck the wood with faint *clicks* and I realized I was panting—both in fear and relief. The speed at which they had erupted had made me fear they would tear through the ancient door but at the last moment, they had halted, resulting only in faint *clicks* on the door.

I shuddered in relief, tasting campfires and falling leaves on my tongue—an entirely mental sensation. "White tiger. Metal. Autumn," I said in a whisper, suddenly realizing why my claws had leapt out like that. The Tiger symbolized metal, not spiky grass like I had initially thought. I just knew it.

The guard also seemed to be breathing faster. "Yes."

I took a breath and drifted my hand back to the center towards the yellow dragon. I paused, focusing intently. Suddenly, it felt as if my fingertips had sunk into the surface a few centimeters, the wood crumbling beneath my touch. It took me a heartbeat to realize this was just a sensation and not that I had pulverized their door. The fresh scent of earth filled my nose, and I realized the sensation beneath my fingertips was of freshly turned soil.

"Earth," I said, unable to place a particular season to the yellow dragon.

The guard didn't bother answering and I didn't bother waiting. My fingers trailed the wooden surface to the Northern square—the black turtle. But...something was strange about it. This one felt more vibrant and complicated, although I couldn't place why.

The wood was icy cold, my fingers seeming to scrape through a thin layer of frost, and I could imagine frigid mist kissing my cheeks. "Black...not just a turtle, but something more..." I trailed off, unable to place the contradiction in my mind. The image I had seen with my eyes had definitely been a turtle, but it didn't sound right on my tongue. "Water and Winter," I finally said, opening my eyes.

The guard was studying me acutely, likely wondering if this was all some show—that I had actually done some research beforehand in an attempt to impress him. "It is the Black *Tortoise*," he finally said, attempting to conceal an amused grin. "Not a *turtle*. No matter what Starlight may or may not have told you. Some terms are meant only for close family and friends, not to be used by others..." he suggested in a careful yet amused tone. More like a subtle yet insistent recommendation than any kind of threat.

I dipped my chin, allowing my smile to fade as I studied the door. "It is as it should be, with nothing out of place. It is at peace with itself and perfectly balanced." I glanced back at my two friends to give them an appeasing grin. Then I turned back to the guard. "It is *also* ancient and beautiful."

A slow, approving smile crept over his face and he dipped his chin lower this time—even averting his eyes briefly to show me further respect and trust. Or that he simply had less fear of me now—which could be either good or bad.

"I will pass on your thoughts. My name is Yín. Please, follow me, White Rose. He's been expecting you for quite some time, now."

I almost gasped to see he recognized me rather than seeing a demon on his steps.

And then Yín pulled open both doors with handles I hadn't noticed carved into the wood, splitting the image down the center. He entered the house ahead of us, pausing after the threshold and holding out a hand in welcome. I glanced back at Cain and Claire, caught off guard by the last comment. Their eyes were wide, and they shook their heads, not having an answer or opinion.

I also noticed the other guards no longer watching the street but staring at me very, very thoughtfully. Not in any threatening manner but...judging by their previous lack of conversational ability, they were practically screaming incoherently and waving their hands in the air.

I wasn't sure if that was a good development or a very bad one.

A boo and a hiss or a hug and a kiss.

15

The house was exquisite yet sparse in every way. Each room featured only a handful of decorations or items to focus on rather than the typical walls covered in art, bookshelves stuffed full of tomes and artifacts, or tables laden with ivory, weapons, and a dozen other knick-knacks.

Instead, each room simply had a...well, a soothing, tranquil *vibe* to it. The first room was warm and inviting. All three walls were made of sliding rice paper partitions, and the room featured a single Bonsai tree held up on a pedestal and warmly illuminated from below like it was the featured piece in a museum. That was it. Nothing else in the room, not even chairs or a side table.

I instinctively began taking off my shoes, even though I wasn't quite sure I wanted to leave them behind. They were magic, and they were mine...and magic...and they were *mine*.

But when in Rome.

Yín cleared his throat. "That will not be necessary, but I appreciate the courtesy."

Inwardly, I let out a sigh of relief and followed Yín towards the opposite wall as he slid it open to reveal a dim, narrow chamber. A hallway of sorts. He backed into it first, holding out his hand for us to follow. I sucked in a shallow breath when I realized that the floor in this room was a bubbling pond and that stepping stones led across it to the far wall where there was another door. An old clay vase was propped up against a rock formation in the water, the top rising a few inches above the surface of the tranquil pool but angled slightly away from the stepping stone path. A dozen or so Koi fish swam lazily around the pond, even between the stepping stones, proving a misstep wouldn't just get your toes wet, but your entire leg. I let out a relaxed breath, the vibe in this room seeming more peaceful than even the entryway.

Yín led us across the stepping stones and slid the door open before backing through it first, again, to reveal a manicured lawn behind the home. Several robed figures sat in a row before a large gong hanging beneath ancient, red-painted timbers. The figures were chanting in a soothing, steady hum like a basso rumble of thunder on the distant horizon. I felt the hair on the back of my neck rising as I rolled my shoulders subconsciously.

My eyes scanned the lush green grass, the rock gardens, and the stone-tiled path leading through the center. I sucked in a surprised breath to see six cloaked men kneeling on either side of the path, hoods drawn up over their heads to conceal their features. They wore all black and I saw they were each armed with sheathed katanas and other matte black blades—throwing stars and daggers. As I stared at them, they seemed to waver back and forth like smoke, but I sensed no magic about them. Just that they seemed to be openly staring at us, observing us, assessing us for threat—even though they weren't even *looking* at us.

Ninjas. The unseen eyes.

Cain and Claire were also watching the ninjas suspiciously, wondering if this was an ambush. But the ninjas didn't move, and the harder I tried to focus on them, the more their forms seemed to shift and writhe—like snakes struggling to escape the grasp of my vision.

Despite not openly looking at us, they seemed to not only be aware of our every physical feature, but of our very existence—down to our scent, our breathing...perhaps even our thoughts.

Power radiated from them and I felt my pulse quicken in reaction.

These were very dangerous men. And I sensed absolutely zero magic from them...just an inner power I couldn't quantify or define in any tangible way. They were peacefully violent. Lethally gentle. They were death with an altruistic smile. Mercy with a cool breeze of nothingness.

Yín waited patiently beside us, granting us time to process the scene.

"This silence is resting before returning to their patrol." Sensing our confusion at his choice of words, he waved his hand in a lecturing gesture. "A group of ninjas is called a silence. They are only a danger to those who torment this city." He smiled suddenly. "And those who step on the grass," he teased. He extended his feet to hover over the grass and every single ninja—like a hive mind—looked up at him from within their hoods with the intensity of a cocked gun.

I didn't see any motion, though. One minute they'd been staring straight ahead, the next, staring straight at him.

Yín chuckled good-naturedly, withdrawing his foot as he glanced back at us. "I advise *against* stepping on the grass. They work very hard on maintaining its beauty when they aren't patrolling." I nodded numbly, realizing the...silence of ninjas was no longer looking at Yín or any of us. I hadn't noticed them avert their attention away, either.

With that, Yín continued on down the path, carefully placing a foot on each stone, taking great care not to step on the grass. The three of us wisely followed his advice, my shoulders tensing as we passed directly between the assassins. They didn't look up at us, but I suddenly recognized the sensation of their attention as the same one I had felt when running through the alleys with Cain earlier tonight. Danger in the shadows. Eyes watching me.

We had been running past ninjas and we hadn't even known! If they had wanted to kill us, they easily could have done so while we were distracted by the pursuing vampires. I let out a measured breath and continued on, eager to get past them.

We reached a set of wooden steps leading up a small hill. I was surprised to suddenly notice that I saw no other houses around us—none of the neighbors I should have been able to see, and the red haze to the sky was absent. Instead, I saw only mountains and apple blossom trees decorating a field of gently swaying, tall grass. I shot Claire and Cain a meaningful look—silently encouraging them not to freak the hell out when they noticed we apparently weren't in Kansas City anymore.

Or maybe this was some kind of glamour. Like a backdrop to remind them of home.

Because supposedly, traveling into and out of Kansas City was off limits right now.

Unless...you were a stoner bear or a ninja turtle god.

We climbed the steps and resumed our trek onto a path through a wooded forest that obscured the house behind us. I could still hear—and *feel*—the chanting monks but I could no longer see them. I suppressed a shudder, hoping this wasn't the equivalent of taking the family dog out back behind the shed for a final goodbye.

Yín rounded a corner and glided to a stop. I followed suit and found myself staring up at a large statue sitting within a tall, three-walled, clay tile roofed structure. The three walls protected the statue from the elements while granting the ability for his disciples to gaze upon the weathered-stone statue—a man with a long wispy beard and formal robes seated on a throne of sorts. He was surrounded by flickering candles, but the walls prevented much of the wind from snuffing them out.

The stone figure gripped an elegant, slightly curved sword in one fist, looking as if he would never let it go, and he had one boot rested on the back of a large tortoise before his throne. A huge serpent was coiled around his other leg, facing forwards as if protecting its master.

"Xuanwu," our guard said respectfully, bowing lower towards the statue than I'd seen him bow at any point so far tonight. "Or the Black Warrior, as he is often called. I will await you in the garden below when you are finished paying your respects."

Then he promptly walked backwards a few steps, bowed once more towards the statue, and finally spun on his heels to resume his walk back towards the house.

I frowned at Yín's back, not wanting to be disrespectful, but also not knowing exactly what he intended. Pay our respects? Maybe he thought we had come here to pray. After all, it wasn't like we had actually told him why we had come here. Maybe there was something to be said for actually *speaking*. Then again, he'd told us this Xuanwu had been expecting us. Had he meant that in some spiritual manner?

Cain grunted. "So..." he said, spinning in a slow circle, checking our surroundings. Boulders dotted the small enclosed clearing, large enough to create a wall of sorts, and looking as ancient and weathered as the statue.

Claire leaned forward, sniffing the statue warily.

"Do you know anything about...Xuanwu?" Cain asked me, trying to replicate Yin's pronunciation. "Ever heard of this *man with many names*? Xuanwu, Black Warrior, Black Tortoise..." he recited, trailing off.

I shook my head.

Cain was still scanning our surroundings, but he noticed my gesture and grunted. "I dated a Chinese girl once. That door reminded me of some of her constellation drawings."

"Like the Chinese zodiac?" Claire asked, frowning thoughtfully.

He shrugged, turning to me with a frown. "You hit it on the head when you deciphered the front door. Pretty much summed up what little I know, and you're sure you've never heard of him? Could have fooled me."

"I was just guessing on the door," I lied.

Cain snorted indelicately. "Right. Well, those four creatures are obviously well respected and worshipped, representing the elements, seasons, and probably a bunch of other stuff." He pointed at the sword. "I don't recognize any of those names, but I once heard a story about a warrior god with a magic sword that he couldn't let go of. That's all I've got." He flung up a hand after a second. "Oh, and in case you missed it, ninjas work for him. I'm very observant," he said dryly.

That didn't make me feel better. Especially the magic sword comment. I pointed at the statue of the very human king. "Except he isn't a tortoise or a snake. He's got the creatures *serving* him."

Cain shrugged. "No idea. Starlight must have been *really* high if he wanted us to talk to a statue. Will the real fat Xuanwu please stand up?" he asked, cupping his hands around his mouth belligerently.

Claire threw a rock at Cain, hitting him in the shoulder. "Unless you want pissy ninjas decorating you with shurikens for disrespecting their sacred statue, shut your mouth," she snapped. Cain rolled his eyes, folding his arms pointedly. Claire, satisfied, turned back to the statue thoughtfully. "Do you think he can hear us?" she asked, leaning even closer to the statue. "Maybe he'll come to life and grant us the power to break into churches," she said in a hopeful tone. She cleared her throat politely. "Good evening, Mr. Xuanwu," she said, doing her best not to butcher his name. "Your friend Starlight thought we should come to pay our respects and make your acquaintance. My name is Claire Stone."

She glanced back at Cain pointedly, gesturing aggressively at the ground beside her. Cain approached awkwardly, bowing his head to the statue. "My name is Cain. I'm here to babysit these two." Claire elbowed him gently in the ribs. "I really liked your door," he added, looking like he had no idea what else Claire wanted him to say and that he thought this was all a giant waste of time. "And your ninjas. They had really cool shoes." Claire let out an exasperated breath and turned to me, motioning me to introduce myself to the statue.

Something about this just didn't feel right, but I wasn't sure what else to do so I smiled at the statue, dipped my head, and began to speak. "My name is Call—"

"I know very well who *you* are, White Rose. Even if you do not," a low, grumbling voice said from directly behind us off in the thick trees. I spun in both surprise and fear, the baritone of the voice low enough for me to immediately assume death was breathing across my neck. It made Nate Temple's friend, the Minotaur, sound like he had just hit puberty and the heifer he fancied had just asked him to the annual school dance in the pasture. Asterion had one of the lowest voices I had ever heard up until this point.

I squinted in the direction of the voice, not seeing anyone, and I began to grow very uneasy. Why was he hiding if he was a friend?

A gleaming black sword sheath slammed into the rocky ground beside one of the massive boulders, and I jumped in alarm, following the sword upward to see a dark stone reptilian claw gripping the hilt—the flesh resembling scales rather than human skin like the statue we had just been stupidly introducing ourselves to. I also realized that the largest boulder before us, covered in lichen and tattooed by time, was *not* actually a boulder. It rose up from the ground, shaking free of the earth and snapping roots and vines that had grown over it during the passage of what had apparently been many, many years.

And we had woken him up.

16

I saw wide, tree-trunk thick stone legs supporting it. Not human legs, but reptilian, complete with long, razor-sharp claws that reminded me of a velociraptor—times five. Each claw was the size of a handheld sickle a farmer might use in the field to cut wheat or weeds.

"Damned thorns," the baritone voice grumbled at a particular thick set of brambles enshrouding one of his feet. "Without sunlight, they just fester and multiply." He lifted the foot with an explosion of snapping, cracking roots tearing free of the earth, seemingly without much effort on his part, just annoyance.

The rest of the creature was hidden by shadows and low hanging branches so I couldn't quite make out the source of the grumpy voice, but another claw slowly reached out from the trees—well above my head—and gently shifted a branch to the side as it stepped fully into the light cast by both the moon and candles.

A hulking warrior of a tortoise stood before us, his shell like jagged, obsidian armor that crested up behind his head to resemble a hood—the surface decorated with hundreds of scratches, dents, and other signs of past battles and close calls. He looked more like a living boulder than a tortoise—like a prehistoric statue come to life. The tortoise extended his head on an impossibly long neck, leaning down to sniff us, giving us a close look at his wickedly pointed beak of a mouth, easily long and sharp enough to rip us in half with a single bite. His eyes sunk deep within his hard face, and they were inky chips of smoldering glass as dark as a starless night sky. His face was covered in scratches and gouges, and he even sported a pair of thick rings pierced in his ear holes.

Only a hammer drill with a diamond bit and powered by an exploding star could have pierced those suckers.

As he moved, flakes of stone continued to fall free, dislodged from grinding against itself so that he was a walking cloud of dust and gravel—causing him to snort frequently, launching tiny stone shrapnel like shotgun blasts wherever his nostrils were directed. I realized he wore an actual fabric cloak or robe, but it was so brittle and frozen with time that pieces simply snapped off at his languid motions. He stared at me politely, lowering his head and blinking very slowly. He used the sword sheath like a cane to support his massive bulk, even though it was apparent that the sword was anything but a simple cane. It thrummed with a low, pulsing energy that made my toes tickle in my boots. Not in an alarming sensation like they would have if facing a demon, but just the raw power of either the tortoise or the sword making the very ground tingle.

The sheath seemed made of hoarfrost—ancient crystals stained the same color as the rock—as if ice had continually repeated to grow over older ice, again, and again, and again. Hundreds, if not thousands, of times.

The tortoise slowly turned to Cain, dislodging more gravel at the motion, and blinked slowly. "Well met, warrior. Your explanation was both correct, and glaringly incomplete."

Cain was staring back at him suspiciously, his fingers gripping the hilt of his dagger. "I've always been more of a hands-on learner," he said in a low, warning tone. "Friend or foe?"

"I have been both over my many, *many* years," the tortoise said calmly, his basso voice making my teeth rattle.

Cain drew his dagger outright this time, stepping protectively between the two of us. I opened my mouth to protest but the tortoise simply swiveled his head and long neck at a glacial speed to regard me over Cain's shoulder, and I knew the look in his eyes was a silent command for me to shut my mouth.

He slowly shifted his attention back to Cain, looking both disinterested and polite as his neck shortened by retreating back into his shell.

You know those ridiculously stereotypical movies where a scrawny

Chinese guy is picked on by a gang of loud-mouth, arrogant bullies? And how the Chinese kid—no matter how many cruel taunts, finger jabs to the shoulder, or other disrespectful acts the bullies hurl at him—simply smiles back, dips his head politely, and apologizes for offending them?

And how the bullies just keep on pressing him for a reaction...

Until the Chinese kid becomes a blur and suddenly all four or five of the bullies are lying on the ground, whimpering as they clutch their wounded limbs. And how the Chinese kid smiles and helps them back to their feet as if he was some kind of Good Samaritan who just wanted to help the poor boys?

Yeah. This felt like that. Cain apparently hadn't seen the same movies as I had.

The tortoise blinked lazily, staring right at Cain from only inches away. "Have at it, man-child," he said in a patient, almost bored, grandfatherly rumble.

Cain didn't even hesitate, lunging straight for the tortoise's face with his fist in a powerful blow. I heard a very faint *clicking* sound and thought I saw the tortoise shift slightly before Cain's fist struck his cheek. The impact created a shallow divot in the tortoise's face—looking like a crater from a small asteroid hitting earth. The tortoise dipped his head patiently. "Again, man-child," he rebuked.

Cain narrowed his eyes angrily—perhaps at the repeated nickname or the fact that his blow hadn't seemed to cause the tortoise any noticeable discomfort, despite the visible crater. Something else danced in the far depths of Cain's eyes, too—shock? Momentary hesitation?

Cain feigned a jab, and my ears caught that faint *clicking* sound before Cain pounded the tortoise's beak with a right cross even harder than the first strike, creating another, wider crater. Chips of stone and ice crumbled free this time, and I noticed the tortoise's robe had even shifted at the force of the blow.

The tortoise smiled—I think—at me obliquely. "Watch *closer*, White Rose. *See*, don't *look*." Then he turned back to his aggressor, Cain. "Best three out of five, man-child?"

Cain was staring at the tortoise in open disbelief. I'll admit, the tortoise's ability to withstand pain was astonishing, but I was missing something much more important here. What exactly did he want me to watch for? *See, don't look*, he had said.

Cain gritted his teeth and I stared intently, following the tortoise's suggestion. I heard another tiny *click* before Cain came in with two solid punches followed by a swipe of his dagger. The punches landed true, but the dagger kissed only air—the tortoise having moved a hair's width away from contact. Cain stepped back, panting loudly and looking furious. Even as I watched, the four impact craters on the tortoise's face had begun to ice back over, repairing themselves. The tortoise looked like he had just woken up from a long nap or was in the process of tolerating a toddler's temper tantrum. He blinked lazily, as if trying to see how slow he could do it. To me, it simply looked like he was constantly on the verge of falling asleep, his eyelids slowly drifting closed before he caught himself.

"There is always next time, man-child," the tortoise said gently, the corners of his beaked mouth crinkling with cracked ice at the motion. We stood in silence, frowning. Why did he look and sound victorious when we'd all just seen him get royally pummeled by the world's first murderer? And what had caused those *clicking* sounds? I shot Cain a curious glance, only to see him muttering darkly under his breath as he stared down at his own chest.

I gasped as I saw three neat slashes tearing entirely through the fabric of his shirt, revealing thin red lines on the skin beneath, as if Cain had been slapped with a willow branch.

Cain slowly lifted his head to stare at the tortoise in bewilderment. Claire stood entirely motionless, her mouth hanging open wide enough that I could have stuck an apple inside.

The tortoise chuckled good naturedly. "I'm faster than I appear," he explained, leaning back as if to stretch out his spine. I heard several loud cracks, sounding like calving icebergs as he moved. Then he regarded me pensively. "Go ahead, White Rose. You won't be satisfied until you make your own attempt, and I would rather you try sooner than later," he said with infinite patience.

I didn't waste time with words as I reared back and hit him in the chest with a blast of air strong enough to send anyone else flying a dozen yards. The moment before contact, I felt a cool breeze across my chest, followed by a relieved, almost relaxed sensation as if my motion had loosed up something in my muscles like a good stretch.

I hadn't used my magic in a while, and it felt good to let off some steam.

My blast of power landed true.

And the tortoise simply exploded like shattered glass. Both Claire and Cain let out a startled gasp. The shards of ice and stone exploded around us in a thick cloud and we turned our backs, forming a huddle to shield ourselves from being eviscerated by shell shrapnel.

"Yippee Ki-Yay, Splinterfucker," Cain chuckled gleefully as bits of ice and shell continued to rain down around us.

I punched him in the arm without looking at him, glancing left and right warily. No freaking way I'd killed him that easily...

17

The sound of falling ice and gravel soon faded and was then replaced by silence in our clearing, and I realized I could still hear the soothing chanting from the house—as if they hadn't heard the...bombshell.

Too soon.

Maybe the sound simply hadn't concerned them, so deep into their meditations. That was good. No inbound silence of ninjas. Then again, if they were coming to kill us, we probably wouldn't have heard them—

I heard a dry, wheezing chuckle from behind me and immediately twirled, my hands up defensively, fearing a silence of ninjas ready to descend upon us. My chest felt less constricted and cold at my movement, and I wondered if one of my jacket buckles had come loose in the explosion. I also hoped my coat was strong enough to deflect a swarm of matte-black blades.

Instead of ninjas or blades, I found the tortoise seated on the ground behind us, his back to the statue as he regarded us with a tranquil look on his face. He sat cross-legged with his sword rested across his lap. One hand still gripped the hilt, but the other was palm up supporting the sheathed blade between his claws.

"Damn it," Cain breathed unhappily.

The tortoise was alive, and none the worse for wear. I let out a breath of relief. Seeing him seated before us, I got a pretty clear look at him in full context. He embodied grace, wisdom, and patience...yet I thought I sensed an undercurrent of lethality in his posture. As if his natural calm state was always one heartbeat away from killing everyone around him. Not to imply that he looked like a serial killer lying in wait—but that he looked *ready* to unleash carnage at any moment.

I narrowed my eyes, wondering what the hell was going on, and how he intended to retaliate against my attack. Xuanwu slowly extended his neck—at least four or five feet—seeming to strain at the apex before languidly twisting his head. Then, with a quick jerk of his head, he cracked his neck as loud as a string of firecrackers, sending shards of frozen gravel off like shotgun pellets, peppering and damaging the statue. Cain cursed, covering his face as the tortoise cracked the other side of his neck and then let out a long, relieved sigh. "Ah. Much better. I should have stretched before sword fighting."

His neck looked long enough to almost seem serpentine as it slowly slithered back within his shell, and I found myself wondering about the serpent aspect of his being.

He chuckled louder upon seeing our startled reactions, then patted the ground beside him in an invitation to join him.

I did so warily, not sure what else to do. Sitting down before him reminded me just how large he was, towering over me by at least a few feet. Cain and Claire—equally uncertain—took places on either side of me, looking ready to grab me and run at even the slightest change of wind.

"That was well done, White Rose," the tortoise complimented me. "Much better than the man-child fared. But I still struck you first," he added, slowly lifting a massive claw to point at my shirt. I glanced down, knowing for certain that I hadn't seen him move before I made him explode into crushed ice. Sure enough, a single line had torn through the fabric of my shirt. And I suddenly realized what the relaxing sensation I had felt was all about.

It hadn't been because it felt good to use my magic...

The perverted bastard had sliced through my *bra*!

The two cups now hung loosely from the shoulder straps. Luckily, I hadn't worn a strapless bra, or that he hadn't sliced my shirt entirely off. I blinked rapidly, spotting a faint red line across my skin through the torn shirt. It didn't hurt, but I could see the raised welt clearly—like I had scraped myself on a thorn on a hike through the woods.

I slowly lifted my head to glare at the pervy tortoise, trying to comprehend how the hell he had managed to strike me without my knowing. I hadn't sensed magic—none at all.

And I was reminded of the stereotypical scrawny Asian kid and the arrogant bully.

The tortoise watched me in amusement. "Not magic. This," he said, and slowly—almost effortlessly—drew his magic sword two inches from the sheath to reveal a frosty blue blade. It didn't make a sound—the gesture as frictionless as sliding a dagger across velvet. But when he slid it back into the sheath, I heard the familiar whispered *click* I'd noticed earlier as it settled into place.

Thankfully, his sword hadn't shredded my magic jacket. Or...maybe his sword *couldn't*.

Claire gulped audibly, sniffing at the air with concern. She hadn't sensed him move either, and she was a shifter—much more perceptive than either of us.

"Man-child," Cain repeated darkly. "I *told* you he had a magic sword," he said, shifting that dark glare my way.

The tortoise shifted slightly in a humble gesture. "We all have our... crosses to bear, our swords to carry. Of course, you know all about that, Callie," he said, enunciating my name.

I narrowed my eyes at him suspiciously. "I'm sure I don't, as a matter of fact. I don't have a sword or a cross." I had recently learned I was the prophesied sheath for the Spear of Destiny, or Spear of Longinus as many called it.

But that wasn't a sword.

It was the spear that stabbed Jesus on the Cross. And it was currently in a rehab clinic located somewhere deep within my soul, supposedly repairing itself from damage received during my trip through the Doors.

And it wasn't a cross, either.

He shrugged apologetically. "As you wish."

I found myself smiling despite the cryptic comment. There was something about the tortoise that just oozed goodwill. I even empathized with him. Here he was, locked in a temple garden behind his house, all alone. And now he had guests! This was an exciting time for him, and he didn't want to waste it being rude. He was just out of practice with social interactions.

Granted, it seemed his only other recent experience with social interactions was a stoner bear, so...he deserved a little leeway.

"You're the Black Tortoise," I said, flicking my gaze up at the statue behind him—the one we had expected to be our appointment. The very *human* statue.

"Black Warrior, Black Tortoise, Genbu, Xuanwu," he recited in a bored tone. "Depends where you're coming from and where you're going to, but yes. I am. Call me Xuanwu."

I had never heard any of those names before tonight, and I couldn't recall any legend or story about a magic sword, a tortoise god or any specific Chinese constellation reference. What I did pick up on was that he had just used a Japanese name—Genbu—as well as a Chinese name—Xuanwu. I'd studied enough martial arts texts to at least be able to tie most names to their respective origins.

"Are you Chinese or Japanese?" I asked. "You used names from both languages."

The tortoise snorted in amusement, shooting some gravel out from his nostrils like a bullet that struck right between Cain's legs, making him flinch. Then he turned to me, cocking his head as if I had done something incredibly interesting. He must have had pretty low standards.

"How very observant of you to notice such a distinction between names," he said in a complimentary—and creepily intent—tone, like he was delivering secret advice or a warning. I shivered under the scrutiny of those glittering dark eyes. "But names can change as time slips by. They are ephemeral, tricky little things, to be picked up and abandoned as needed."

I frowned. Some names—True Names—were often really freaking important and couldn't be abandoned in a cardboard box along the side of the road like he was implying.

The intense look faded, and he shrugged in a glacially slow, nonchalant manner, his shell rising up slightly over his head with the motion. "I am more than just a name. I am all. And I am nothing. Just a piece of this world, riding out my part to play in life like any other."

I frowned thoughtfully, but I really hadn't expected anything less mysterious from a god.

I had spoken with very powerful beings before, and they all adored the use of cryptic comments and advice. Oftentimes, it was the only method they could use to pass on information—not being allowed to involve themselves too *directly* in mortal affairs. So riddles were their *#TotesFaves*.

While the mortals wailed and gnashed their teeth.

But *Buddhists*...I was beginning to think that they could make *everything* sound like some great epiphany or parable, hence their penchant for fortune cookies.

Looking at him with the statue just over his shoulder, I realized that the sword in the statue's hand and the one in the tortoise's claw was identical. So who was the guy in the statue with his foot resting atop the tortoise's shell and a snake wrapped around his leg? In fact...if this was the tortoise, where was the snake? Starlight had called him turtle-snake, but we'd only met this invincible turtle-cube.

The statue had led me to believe we were looking for a man with two creatures at his command—a tortoise and a snake. Much like Roland had Paradise and Lost—as familiars, or maybe oath-maidens. So to be talking to the tortoise with no snake in sight...

As much as I wanted to ask that obvious question, it was equally obvious that Xuanwu meant us no harm—he could have sliced our noses off without us noticing—so I didn't anticipate a serpent attacking us from behind. Not immediately, anyway. I needed to establish common ground.

"Starlight told us it was important that we talk with you, but that was the extent of his explanation..."

Xuanwu wheezed out a laugh. "He was likely as high as a kite, searching for his next great journey with *Bear Necessity*." Then he smiled to let us know he was not casting judgment on Starlight's hobbies.

I smiled faintly, nodding. This tortoise even knew the name of Starlight's *bong*? They *had* to be close friends. But I was damned curious what Xuanwu meant by Starlight's *next great journey*.

I idly imagined Bill and Ted's sequel, *Bogus Journey*, before refocusing.

18

I realized that, rather than answering my question, Xuanwu was watching the three of us with curious amusement—primarily Claire. "A white bear of the cold North," he said, smiling at her and dipping his beak respectfully. "Yes. We could be friends, Claire Stone." He enunciated her name very distinctly, as if branding it into his memory.

"Thank you," Claire said, sounding uncertain whether that had required a verbal response or some unknown gesture particular to the culture.

"And you, Cain," Xuanwu said respectfully, turning to face him. "The world's first murderer. What's *that* like?"

Cain narrowed his eyes. "About as much fun as talking to a ninja turtle, apparently," he said in a cool, dry tone.

It was alarmingly silent for two excruciatingly slow heartbeats. And then Xuanwu burst out laughing. "I think we could be friends, too. You do not mince words. Yippee Ki-Yay..." he snorted, chuckling softly.

Cain nodded, hesitantly accepting the praise, and looking mildly surprised he hadn't earned another slash on his shirt for his sharp tongue.

"Callie...Penrose," Xuanwu said slowly, enunciating each syllable strangely. "The White Rose," he added, as if tasting the cadence of the words. He studied me silently for a time, his glittering dark gaze making me uncomfortable. "Do you know what the color white represents to the

Chinese?" he finally asked. I shook my head, not wanting to hazard a guess. "White symbolizes *death*, for the most part."

I pursed my lips, not knowing whether he was trying to offend me or warn me. "Okay."

"And flowers that grow from thorny vines are often attributed to pain and unhappiness, because they all have a tendency to creep into the most unwanted of places, despite our best efforts to tame them, avoid them, or hide from them," he explained, gauging my reaction.

Instinctively, I wanted to try hitting him again, but knew it wouldn't get me anywhere—and that he would likely slice my top clean off before I could do so. I thought about the creature before me—one obviously deeply rooted in a Taoist belief system. And I wondered why, out of all the things he could have said to start a conversation, he had chosen to focus on our names and attributes. First Claire being a white bear, then Cain as his brother's murderer...

And now specific elements of one of my monikers—White Rose—culturally translating to *Death*, *pain*, and *unhappiness*...

And a suspicion abruptly hit me like a swift rock between the eyes. *Exactly* between the eyes, but a few inches higher, in the center of my forehead. Now that I thought about it, he'd said other things that seemed to slither into this epiphany of mine.

"Despair..." I whispered, watching his reaction as I tried to keep my face neutral.

"Perhaps," he replied almost absently, lifting one claw as if weighing something in his hand. If he had meant to imply what I feared, I would have expected some kind of victorious look on his face—excitement, relief—or even fear.

But instead, he was now staring down at his sword, lost in thought.

Was I jumping to conclusions—drawing deeper meanings from his overly cryptic answers that he hadn't meant? Because the word *Despair* was written on my forehead in Enochian script. And Nate Temple was currently hosting a career fair, searching for a candidate for one of his new Horsemen Masks. He had even named each of his new, second string Riders of the Apocalypse—*Hope*, *Despair*, *Justice*, and *Absolution*.

Nate was *Hope*, and as far as I'd heard, the other three were still up for grabs. But that had been over a year ago, so maybe he'd given them all out by now. I was about a million percent sure I didn't want to become a Horseman. I had enough problems, and it sure didn't seem like a good idea to have two groups of Horsemen riding during the Apocalypse. Archangel Michael had been horrified to learn of this second band of Apocalypse Riders, saying that God had never mentioned such a thing.

Which really cranked up the terror meter, in my opinion, telling me that the book of Revelations had been plagiarized or hijacked by other pantheons.

And to learn that my forehead had one of those four names branded across it like I was bought and paid for livestock...

Despair...Even the word made me shiver.

Phix and I had once had a very intense conversation on the definitions and possible interpretations of *Hope* and *Despair*. It had been beyond enlightening, and the more I thought about it, the more similarities I found between her words and Xuanwu's implications.

Phix had told me that Despair wasn't a single-sided definition. That it was a blade to be swung both ways, at whatever target I chose. The user's choice became the definition. Phix's words drifted to the forefront of my mind.

The only way to balance the whips of hope are to know the blades of despair. The world will require that balance, or all will be lost. Hope is nearing his understanding. The world must birth despair.

Even recalling her words, I shook my head stubbornly. I wanted to bring everyone together, not cause pain and suffering. If anything, I would pick Justice—

No. I wouldn't pick *any* of them because I didn't want anything to do with them. Heaven and Hell already had enough reasons to dislike me. Or recruit me. I was smuggling a Holy Spear inside me, for one thing.

I'd also learned firsthand how power could *change* a person. I'd sought nothing but power in my journey through the Doors, and that pursuit had created a monster that I never wanted to see again. A monster desiring of only two things—more power, and vengeance—both to be used to hunt down Samael. I had managed to take a step back from crazy town, but I hadn't forgotten Samael and what he'd done to Cain. His day of reckoning was still coming. Mark my words.

"What does the color black represent?" Claire asked curiously, as if uncomfortable with the growing silence. I felt her studying me nervously from her peripheral vision, waiting for some nonverbal cue that would tell her to attack or to help me escape.

The tortoise chuckled. "Water, of course."

Cain arched an eyebrow suspiciously. "Of course. Because water is black," he said, deadpan.

"Black also represents *destruction*, *evil*, *cruelty*, and *sadness*," Xuanwu admitted, ignoring Cain's sarcasm.

I frowned thoughtfully, snapping out of my inner thoughts. "You don't seem to be any of those things..." Just like Phix had said...the definition not necessarily matching the words—or person, in this case.

He shrugged. "We are all many things at one time or another. We take names, borrow them and their baggage, own them for a short time...but in the end they are simply cherry blossoms on the wind, floating to the next person—and the next, and the next."

"If they are all fleeting and temporary, then why worry about what the colors mean? Or which names define us? If we aren't doomed to fall under their influence, why talk of them?"

He shrugged. "It is something I learned once upon a time," he admitted, sounding as if it were of no consequence. "But even if temporary, names have power—both *over* us and *for* us. Much like a sword cuts both ways. I, too, know what it's like to live a life bonded to a sword," he said, his eyes latching back onto the sword in his lap for a brief moment.

Then he looked directly at me, and there was no easygoing smile this time. I felt my shoulders tense, not understanding where this was going. "I already told you once, I don't have a sword."

He snorted another shotgun blast of gravel near Cain, making him flinch. "We all have swords, child. Your blood is a sword. Your voice is a sword. Your name is a sword. We are all swords. Some just take better care of them than others before passing them on to the next reincarnation."

My mind was spinning, having no idea if this was just a casual conversation, a string of answers hidden in riddles, or if the tortoise was perhaps still mentally sleeping and speaking to us in some sort of fever-dream. Like those moments immediately after a nightmare when you woke up and still felt like you were a petite, white-haired little girl, running through a twisted version of a carnival, your parents nowhere to be found, and a walking, talking, ten-foot-tall octopus with knife tentacles was pursuing you with a maniacal cackle.

A completely hypothetical example.

"Remember that Roland guy? Big prick, am I right?" Cain interrupted, sounding as if he was running out of patience, or perhaps tired of dodging snot rockets. I let out a sigh of relief, thankful for the change in topic.

I nodded my agreement, rolling my shoulders to shake off the imagined feeling of tentacles slithering up behind me.

"I feel like we're running around in circles, chasing our tails," I said, implying both the conversation so far, and my concerns about Kansas City.

"Maybe you *are* chasing your tale," Xuanwu said, grinning sagely.

I folded my arms stubbornly. I couldn't kill the curious part of me, but I also knew when someone was trying to lead me to another topic. He was definitely some sort of Buddhist, although probably an original practitioner rather than one of the many trendy present-day *Burning Man* variations. Maybe he knew the Minotaur, a relatively new fellow Buddhist.

"I don't have time to chase my tail," I muttered. "My city is in chaos, and I need to stop a man who has lost his way. A man who once taught me the difference between right and wrong has forgotten his own lessons."

Xuanwu nodded sadly. "Sometimes, blindly chasing after our forefathers can have disastrous repercussions."

I hesitated. "Four fathers or forefathers?" I asked, clearly enunciating the difference. Because a demon named Johnathan had once called me *the girl with four fathers.*

God—everyone's father.

Titus—my biological father who had given me up to the church as a babe.

Terry Penrose—my adoptive father and personal hero.

Roland Haviar—my old mentor, my father in the teachings of magic and self-defense. The new vampy Michael Corleone of my city.

Xuanwu smiled. "Yes, I see what you mean. Fathers can often disappoint, also."

Even knowing he was baiting me, I still considered his answer in respectful silence for a few moments. Was he talking about Roland—the obvious disappointment in town? Or was this a talk about the Big G? I didn't think so, since Xuanwu obviously wasn't Christian. And Titus was dead, although I had been *beyond* disappointed to learn he had abandoned me, even if he'd had good intentions. Terry had *never* disappointed me. Thinking of him, I really hoped he was safe—but even if he was, none of us would be okay if Roland continued holding Kansas City hostage. Which meant I needed to put a stop to Roland's insanity before checking on my dad. Hopefully, he and Rai were far, far away.

But disastrous repercussions? What was—no. I stopped that train of thought, took a deep breath, and met his eyes, refusing to be led astray. I wasn't going to bite the bait.

"I want to talk about Roland Haviar," I said sternly.

A deep, razor-sharp smile. "And who do you think we have been talking about?"

19

I felt my stomach flutter, replaying our conversation so far. I licked my lips, choosing my words very carefully. "Why would me chasing after Roland have disastrous repercussions?"

He shook his head sadly. "I don't believe you are *blindly* chasing after him, are you? You do not follow meekly in his footsteps. You stand *against* him, correct?"

I nodded my head slowly, poking my brain with a figurative stick. It seemed to do the trick, making me think about his words in slightly different ways. But I soon realized everything he was saying had double and triple entendre—maybe even more.

I finally let out a sigh, realizing I could flounder for hours. I waved a hand back towards the ninjas. A different tactic might help. "You *live* here, now. Thanks to Roland's barrier, we're all stuck here. You send your men out into the streets to either protect innocents—"

"In a sense," he agreed, smirking playfully.

"Heh. Get it?" Cain whispered, nudging Claire. She elbowed him sharply, cutting him off.

I narrowed my eyes at the tortoise before continuing my train of thought. "Or to protect your own interests. You send them to spy, if nothing else. Everyone wants to protect their home. So help *me* help *you*," I pleaded, letting a little exasperation enter my tone.

He nodded his agreement. "I am very concerned about my home." He flicked a claw past our shoulders, indicating the house we had passed through. "I have hidden numerous little treasures inside my humble temple, after all," he whispered mischievously, about as loud as a bumblebee directly in your ear canal.

Cain frowned. "*Dude*. I counted *one* vase and a shrub...I think your stuff is safe."

Claire hit him in the shoulder, shooting him a withering glare.

Xuanwu smiled at the pair. "Even so. They are *mine*, and so they are special to me."

He turned back to find me frowning at his choice of words. *Temple...treasures*.

He shifted slightly on the ground, his shell creaking and cracking with ice as he tried to find a more comfortable position. "Kansas City's plight is not unlike your Biblical War of the Angels—except with mankind. Two men of God—once brothers—having a difference of opinion on how strictly they must follow *His* commandments. Or perhaps whether those commandments should be followed at all..."

"Forefathers," I whispered, reconsidering his earlier comment in a new light.

He waved a hand in a *there you go* gesture. "Precisely. Words, like objects, can serve multiple purposes—have multiple interpretations—depending on how you look at them," he explained.

He was alluding to the difference between *four fathers* and *forefathers*. I nodded. He was talking about riddles, puns, and other word games, which I hated. But he was right.

"Roland's barrier," Xuanwu continued, "also serves more than one purpose. It keeps people *out* as well as *in*."

I beamed proudly, glad that I'd already considered this. I take the wins when I can, folks. Even the tiny ones. "The Shepherds, obviously," I said, perhaps a bit arrogantly. He nodded dismissively, waggling a claw for me to continue—and my confidence ebbed slightly, wondering if he was about to learn me something after all. "The Sanguine Council?"

He leaned forward suddenly. "What an *interesting* theory. Do you know, by chance, who leads the Sanguine Council?"

I frowned. "A council doesn't have a single leader, or it wouldn't be called a *council*..."

Xuanwu smiled. "It would *seem* so. But as we just learned, names can be vitally important—open to any number of misinterpretations. As a wizard, you well know that what one chooses to call a thing, and what that name might imply or infer, is given very careful consideration. It is the very *purpose* of naming—to find the best single word or phrase that achieves a desired result."

I nodded slowly in understanding, but I didn't see any potential wordplay in *council*.

"And vampires are well-known as schemers, perhaps even choosing to call a thing something that it is *not*." His eyes glittered suggestively. "That would be extremely clever, wouldn't it, Callie? Hidden in plain sight, as it were..."

I shivered at the idea. "If they aren't really a *council*...then who is in charge?"

"Another excellent question. It would have to be a very powerful vampire for our conspiracy theory to hold water. A true *Master* of all Master Vampires," he mused, scratching at his beak pensively.

My face paled and my stomach quivered strangely. "Dracula? Are you talking about mothersucking *Vlad Dracul*?" I demanded. "No one has heard from him in forever!"

Cain and Claire both cursed in disbelief.

"Let us suppose our hypothetical Master wanted it that way," he suggested. "I hear Dracula is a collector of all manner of things—both living and non—and we already discussed how important it is to protect our home, our treasures..." I felt like I was about to have a panic attack, but Xuanwu went right on without slowing. "A true Master of his beasts—if he could convince the world that he no longer existed, yet still manage to hold the reins that control all the vampires in the world. One should tread very carefully around a man as clever as that. Or a man daring enough to try following in his footsteps."

Forefathers. He'd said chasing your forefathers could have disastrous repercussions. "You think Roland is, what, after something Dracula owns? One of his treasures?" I hissed.

Xuanwu shrugged, as if we were just having a friendly, hypothetical debate over tea. "Or to kill him and take *all* his treasures. I have no answer to that question. Either would make more sense than believing he is *only* after the Shepherds. He could have ended them *months* ago. The only reason the Shepherds still stand is because he *allows* them to."

I swallowed audibly. Well. I hadn't anticipated him being that powerful, or the Shepherds that outclassed. Claire had made it sound like a stalemate, but Xuanwu sounded utterly sure. Which meant that even if I could have gotten their help, it wouldn't have been enough.

"No vampire has ever been foolish enough to try such a thing. It is said that Dracula can tune in to hear his vampires' thoughts—even across great distances. They are his offspring, after all, bound by cursed blood originating from his own still-flowing veins." He leaned forward. "But those trapped within Roland's barrier are shielded—not just physically but mentally—from outside observation, eliminating the risk of him learning about it." He shrugged. "This barrier would be the only way to pull off such a bold feat. Along with an environmental event that spans continents. Much like the Blood Moon tomorrow evening," he added, as if it was of no import.

"Of course," Claire cursed. "Why *wouldn't* it be during the blood moon."

I felt like jumping to my feet and screaming. What the hell was Roland thinking? If even a sliver of this was true...I locked eyes with Xuanwu, my mind running with possibilities. "You're talking about a ritual...making one place similar to another in order to bridge the two together." Xuanwu nodded very slowly.

And more similarities between the two vampires began clicking together in my mind. Roland shared blood with Dracula. He had made a castle out of his church. He had an army of crimson-eyed vampires specifically *bound* to him.

I licked my lips nervously. "Dracula has a barrier like this around his castle, doesn't he?" I whispered, gesturing up at the sky, even though I hadn't noticed the red haze here.

Xuanwu cocked his head thoughtfully. "I have not visited Dracula's castle, so I could not say for certain. But I have such a barrier *here*," he said, gesturing up at the sky, "to protect my...*one vase and shrub*." He gave Cain a teasing smile, quoting him from earlier. Xuanwu turned back to me. "Only my most trusted men know about it. Hypothetically, I would also imagine only Dracula's most trusted followers would know such a thing. Those on the Sanguine Council, perhaps. One must know one's boss, correct?"

I leaned forward very, very slowly, my hands shaking as I met his eyes. "Someone like the Master of Paris, for example, might know such things, right?"

Xuanwu nodded just as slowly. "Paris is a large, heavily populated city. He must know all manner of things—be entrusted with all manner of secrets."

Motherfucker. Henri Bellerose had snitched on Dracula. No wonder Roland had made him a lieutenant rather than killing him. Roland had needed the inside man to devise his plan. To either rob Dracula or take down the granddaddy of all vampires to steal his throne and take over the Sanguine Council itself. Talk about a long con. And it would both serve his old instincts as a Shepherd—to hurt the Sanguine Council—while absolutely establishing a reputation as the most badass vampire ever.

Cain let out a slow whistle, shaking his head. Claire was clutching her knees to her chest, a stricken look on her face, letting me know she'd had absolutely no idea problems in Kansas City were this bad.

I sat in a daze as well, thinking to myself. *What in the hell did Dracula have that Roland wanted, and what can I possibly do to stop it?*

"You know," Cain began, his voice dripping with sarcasm, "since we're talking hypotheticals, I wonder how this conversation would have gone if you had *led* with that juicy bit of information. *Hypothetically*, we might not have wasted an hour on pointless gossip."

Xuanwu looked over at Cain—not in anger—but with a suddenly haunted look in the depths of those obsidian eyes. His deep voice was shallow and strained, like a dead body being dragged across gravel. "Your hypothetical scenario has been the birthplace of my nightmares for the past —" he glanced at me, eyeing me up and down appraisingly, "twenty-something years."

In the ensuing silence, a feather falling on silk would have sounded as loud as a crystal chandelier shattering to the ground from a twenty-foot fall, and the hair on my arms was either standing vertical or had picked up its own follicle before fleeing from its host, like a snail picking up his shell and deciding to relocate his home.

"Perhaps, man-child," Xuanwu continued, his tone growing sharper and harsher, almost aggressive enough for his words to draw blood as swiftly and quickly as his sword could, "*every single one* of those sleepless nights was filled with me very *carefully* considering the events and ramifications of this meeting. And that I came to the ultimate conclusion that an hour of pointless gossip, as you called it, just might be enough to save all of existence." He was panting loudly, clouds of arctic vapor puffing out of the nostrils on his beak, the scaled skin around his eyes compressed, and the rings piercing his ear holes were vibrating fast enough to look blurred. The claw clutching the hilt of his sword was brimming with growing hoarfrost, crunching as it clenched and unclenched. Clenched and unclenched.

If Xuanwu had whooped our asses when he was feeling calm and collected...

I never *ever* wanted to see him on a battlefield—even if he was on *my* side.

Cain gulped, his face as white as a sheet, and sat perfectly still. A look I'd only seen on him one other time—when we'd first crossed paths with Last Breath, before we learned who he truly was. Other than that time, I'd never seen Cain actually scared.

Xuanwu took a seemingly forced, calming breath, closing his eyes for about ten whole seconds. The features of his face slowly returned to normal before he opened his eyes and looked at Cain. "My apologies, Cain. What I meant to say was that I have given this conversation much thought."

Cain nodded ever so slightly, letting out a breath of his own. "No apology necessary. I was just frustrated with how many gods flirt with open, honest answers." He glanced at me sheepishly. "My sister's time is very valuable. I may be a tad overprotective..." he admitted, squirming on the ground. Claire burst out laughing, Cain's discomfort obviously breaking the dangerous direction the conversation had almost taken. He narrowed his eyes at her. "And my ass was not made for sitting on rocks for so long. It requires plushiness."

Claire choked, laughing even harder, and they began to argue quietly, slapping and poking at each other teasingly.

Xuanwu smiled sadly, his shoulders slumped down and inward, as he watched them banter back and forth. So I was the only one who noticed the now haunted look in his eyes. Like a man sitting in a wobbly wooden chair in an empty, drafty, dilapidated house, watching—for the thousandth time—an old home video of his children playing in the front yard, laughing wildly and shrieking with joy as they chased each other around and around before falling into breathless tickling matches on the soft green grass.

And the lonely man looked on with a lone, happy tear trailing down his dirty, scruffy face, because his children had died in a horrible, preventable accident many, many years ago—and the only way this sad shell of a man knew to banish the screaming emptiness echoing within his broken heart was to watch this video again and again and again.

As a reminder.

As repentance.

As his only salvation from the despair threatening to slip through the numerous cracks in the crumbling walls of his will to live.

Their laughter was the only thing keeping him alive. Giving him purpose.

So he watched. And watched. And watched.

I felt a tear fall down my own cheek, and a faint sob bubbled out from between my lips as Cain and Claire continued teasing each other, entirely unaware. Just like those children in the home video...

Xuanwu started, sensing my attention, and swiftly masked his features.

He pointedly refused to meet my eyes, clearing his throat to interrupt the two children. I wiped at my face quickly, turning to look out at the woods and regain my composure before I alarmed Cain or Claire.

What darkness had Xuanwu seen to make him look upon them in such a way?

Xuanwu spoke, keeping their attention from me for a few more moments. "I needed to understand who you three were. Why you are. Where you've been. Otherwise, I might have been consigning you—and many others—to your deaths. Like handing a child a loaded shotgun because he looked scared—when all that really happened was that he had a nightmare."

I turned to face him, frowning. "It's pretty obvious this isn't a simple nightmare..."

He sighed. "Trying to find the right metaphor is like casting stones at a black kettle," he replied, smirking at the obviously butchered metaphor.

I rolled my eyes, groaning. I appreciated the attempt at levity but my mind was racing with the memory of a petite, white-haired little girl, running through a twisted version of a carnival, her parents nowhere to be found, as a walking, talking, ten-foot-tall octopus with knife tentacles pursued her with a maniacal cackle.

Because I'd just learned it wasn't a nightmare...that the octopus was just as real as the petite, white-haired little girl.

Roland.

Me.

20

I took a deep breath, imagining Terry Penrose stepping into my nightmare to point a firehose—connected to a tank of acid—at the octopus. The resulting screams calmed the little white-haired girl. She may have watched the octopus' demise longer than a child should have. Perhaps she even took notes. But she wouldn't have admitted to either.

Xuanwu placed a claw on my knee, the frigid tips cold enough to instantly make me shudder. "You have time," he said in a reassuring tone. "Some. Roland has everything he needs already, but he can do nothing before tomorrow night. He hides in his fortress for a reason. He will only emerge for the ritual. That is your only chance to act."

I stared down at my boots in silence, considering and discarding ideas to no avail. I looked back up at him, deciding that no matter what, I had to do something. Roland might be pursuing Dracula for personal reasons, but I had been the catalyst to start his descent into madness.

"I need to find a way to break into his church. To get past his wards. Claire says they prevent anyone who doesn't have Roland's express permission."

Xuanwu nodded pensively. "He used strong blood magic to establish his wards. With the Shepherds as his enemies, I would anticipate that his barrier also has secondary protections to block anyone with ties to Heaven. He knows how the Shepherds think—that they have spent hundreds of years fighting the forces of what they see as darkness—and that they have access to powerful magics and artifacts that could perhaps overpower his blood wards." I nodded, knowing Roland well enough to confirm that he likely would have considered such a concern. "And you have ties to Heaven."

I grunted. He wasn't wrong. My blood was a mixed drink of Heavenly liquors.

"Well, I'm not going to add any demonic blood to my body, if that's what you're suggesting," I said.

"I do not believe even demonic blood could enter," he admitted. Which made sense. Roland wanted no one interfering with his heist, and a demon definitely would have been interested in hijacking the chance to rob Dracula —if he really did have such a fine collection of treasures.

Thinking of heavenly blood, a new thought hit me, and I wondered why it hadn't crossed my mind earlier. "Have your ninjas sensed any demons in town?" I asked guardedly, unsure whether mentioning that Samael had been hunting me would make the tortoise uncomfortable—or unwilling to let his ninjas get involved.

Xuanwu shook his head adamantly. "My men say Samael left the city around the same time you disappeared, leading Roland and others to believe him successful in murdering you. Or if not, that he had no further reason to be here with you gone. My men have sensed no demonic presence since. And the barrier around Kansas City is just as effective on demons as it is angels. No one in, no one out," he assured me, decisively.

Although it was a great relief to hear that Samael wouldn't make an already complicated situation worse, I feared what he might be up to outside of Kansas City. He was my responsibility and would die by my hand—when I had the time to get around to it, which meant taking down Roland and his barrier.

I sensed Xuanwu studying me curiously—studying my Seal, specifically. I covered it with my other hand and met his eyes. For the briefest of moments, I thought I saw him studying my forehead thoughtfully, but with no pupils to his obsidian stone eyes, it was hard to tell.

Claire held up a hand like she was in school, looking impatient. Xuanwu smiled in amusement, dipping his beak at her to proceed. "Even if we found a way in, Roland has an army of vampires and werewolves, and two vampire lieutenants standing in our way."

Xuanwu shifted his shoulders slightly, looking resigned to a difficult decision. "My ninjas follow a creed that is deeply rooted in trust and respect. They could follow Hope's murderer," he said softly, staring off at nothing. For a single heartbeat, I saw him murmur as if in prayer, apologizing to some higher power for his decision.

Everyone froze, staring at him. "How about you just *tell* them to help us?" Claire blurted out, missing the most important part of his comment. Cain hadn't missed it, because he was staring at me with a very concerned look on his face, wondering the same thing as me. Xuanwu's words had sent an icy shiver down my spine. He couldn't have meant—

He refocused on us as, snapping out of whatever dark thoughts had crossed his mind. "I do not command them. They follow me out of respect that I bought with *blood*," he said, gripping his sword tightly for a moment, his claws scraping at the frost encasing the hilt. "That same respect could be bought by Hope's murderer."

My stomach quivered unsettlingly, liking his suggestion even worse the second time.

Hope's murderer...

If Xuanwu had meant *hope* as a title or Name—which it sure as hell sounded like—was he really suggesting that I murder *Nate Temple*, the Horseman of Hope? That was a fat *no*.

Xuanwu cleared his throat, his face a grim mask. "Such a person might be strong enough to destroy Roland's barrier from *within*—it's only vulnerable point, as is the case with most rituals. And they would have an army of silent assassins to keep enemies preoccupied."

I shuddered at the confirmation of both the barrier's weak point—something I'd already realized—as well as if he'd truly been asking me to become an assassin. But how *else* would one earn the respect of other assassins other than by becoming one herself? Xuanwu had *bought their respect with blood*. It was the only way. Even still, doing so wouldn't get me inside the church. It would just grant me the muscle to destroy the barriers once I did find a way inside.

Claire and Cain were sharing significant looks with each other, looking deeply troubled.

They needn't have worried. I could never kill Nate. I would just have to find another way.

I decided it was time to change the topic, turning to address Xuanwu with a calm, determined face. Let him take that as he would.

"Earlier, you made it sound like you knew we would eventually meet. That you knew about this conversation for a very long time..." I said, watching him closely. "Why did you come to Missouri, Xuanwu?" A demon I'd killed had once been very interested in Missouri—in the various flavors of power flocking to my state—both in St. Louis and Kansas City. Boston, Massachusetts had also been on his radar, but most of his interest had been devoted to Missouri.

Because of Nate Temple and me.

So why had Xuanwu chosen Kansas City over St. Louis?

He sighed wearily, waving at the air as if to imply *everything*. "Many events transpired to lead you to this moment. Many plans—both foiled and victorious, brought you here. To me. Now. The same can be said for each of my kind—gods—and many others. Children dance to the songs their parents sing, sleep to the lullabies their parents read, fear what their parents tell them to fear, and stand up to whom their parents tell them are evil." His gaze grew distant, staring at something only he could see. "So many children..." he murmured, trailing off.

I frowned, my forearms pebbling with gooseflesh. "What do you mean, *so many children*?" Cain and Claire also looked discomforted by his words, studying each other silently.

He snapped out of his thoughts at my question but didn't meet my eyes as he answered. "You three. Nate Temple. Quinn MacKenna...and many, *many* others. The black sheep of the family always garner the most interest, the most attention, the ones who need to be watched...not just mortals, either," he added scornfully, clenching his sword with both sets of claws. "We gods are also children, you know. We, too, carry the burdens our parents left behind. We, too, feel obligated to honor the preparations our parents set into place."

I scoffed. "I was abandoned on the steps of a church, Xuanwu. I wasn't *prepared* for anything except *pain*," I muttered. I did not whine or cry as I said it. I had simply decided to accept the simple facts of my past rather than wallow in victimhood. The Doors had taught me much. A small part of me still felt betrayed and bitter, but it was a deep, slow burn somewhere in the darkest depths of my soul, and it was hard to hear unless I dwelled on it.

"Perhaps *preserved* rather than *prepared*," Xuanwu suggested. "Saved, even. We all die someday—parents, gods, mortals. And usually at the hands of babes with blades," he said.

"Babes with blades are my kryptonite," Cain grunted, as if hoping to lighten the mood. Claire hit him absentmindedly, seeming more focused on Xuanwu than in supervising Cain.

Xuanwu finally looked up at me. "We are all children, first. Even Samael, Roland, Henri, and Dracula. We are all just playing with the toys our parents gave us, growing up to shuffle our feet to a carefully choreographed dance." I thought that was a rather dire position for a Buddhist to take, but I didn't say anything. "A party has been planned for us, and the invitees are still arriving to play their part. Gods included," he said, touching his own chest. "Consider this a rehearsal dinner. Where do you want to seat the guests? Beside whom? You ask, *why Missouri*. I say, *thank you for the invitation to your debutante ball*. The party is about to start, and I wouldn't miss it for the world. It's better than waiting aimlessly for the end."

I pondered his words, not liking them one bit. I didn't buy into fate. And nothing about current events reminded me of a party. It was a war. Against whom, I didn't yet know. But every pantheon was indeed getting seated in preparation. There was no denying that. I'd heard Nate bring it up several times. The End War. The All War. He was a Catalyst for it, even though neither of us knew what that meant, exactly.

Dark clouds hung on the horizon, and Freaks were flocking to Missouri —preferring to huddle shoulder to shoulder with once enemies rather than remain in solitary hiding where they could be easily picked off or perhaps recruited. Like animals in the wild sensing a storm, the Freaks of the world sensed something coming and were instinctively drawn to certain places around the world. Why Missouri? I didn't have the answer either. I had been hoping Xuanwu would.

"Who is hosting this party? And who intends to crash it?"

Xuanwu was silent for a very long time. "With everyone wearing masks, it is hard to tell, but those who planned the party went to a lot of effort to attract *everyone*...whether by flicking them on the nose, stealing something from them, binding them with an oath, or befriending them. It is important to know who your true allies are—whether each guest you encounter is actually your friend—or looking for the chance to stab you in the back. Loyalty is essential. It is why the vampires bond each other through a powerful bloodline."

I frowned. "That tactic apparently has a few glaring loopholes," I argued, alluding to Roland murdering Haven and turning on Dracula, his supernatural forefather.

Xuanwu nodded absently. "Although, it is better than doing nothing. Perhaps they didn't have powerful enough blood. The right blood can both *create* bonds and *break* bonds..."

I rubbed at my temples, feeling a headache coming on. "This party is just going to have to start without me. I haven't picked out my dress yet. I'll just have to show up fashionably late." I met his eyes stubbornly. "After I kill Roland."

The conviction in my words made my stomach flutter after the fact—only just now realizing that I truly meant it. No matter what he was up to with Dracula, he'd done things here that could not be forgiven. He had made good on his oath to Fabrizio in a way I hadn't considered before now. He had filled the streets of Kansas City with blood—*his* blood—flowing in the veins of every vampire he created who bore the crimson eyes.

And it was time for that blood to nourish an unexpected surprise.

A rose growing from the concrete, whose vines would strangle and choke every vampire with crimson eyes in Kansas City.

Xuanwu nodded in respectful approval, knowing how hard it had been for me to say it out loud. "Then I will save you a seat. You should consider that maybe Roland's actions—even if unbeknownst to him—may be part of the party's entertainment..."

I grunted in reply.

Xuanwu exhaled loudly before climbing to his feet with the aid of his sword as a cane, chips of ice and stone again cascading down his shell and shoulders at the motion. "Perhaps information on Roland was the least vital information you learned today," he said mysteriously.

We climbed to our feet, taking a moment to stretch out our backs before following him down the trail to his home. Cain and Claire brought up the rear, giving us some privacy. Xuanwu tried to speak softly enough for only me to hear as I stepped up beside him. "*Long does it take, for a rose vine to creep, but they choke, and they crawl, they're relentless and never sleep*," he murmured to himself, shaking his head and grinding his beak as he stared off at nothing.

Of course, we all heard it though, because he was flipping ten-feet-tall and loud as hell.

"You have much to consider if you are to find entrance to that which has no entrance. To speak loud enough for deaf ears to hear. To show the blind what you *truly* look like, *White Rose*," he said, winking.

And I suddenly realized that he had seen me for who I was, not the dark-haired demon woman. I hadn't even *thought* about that.

He reached out to flick my hair with an icy claw that was large enough to have gripped my face like a basketball. "Brunette truly does not suit you. White is a much more appropriate color."

I stood there for a moment, stunned. But he was already ambling past us, the ground thumping beneath his feet and sword—but no divots or craters marked his passing—almost as if he stepped precisely so as not to disturb his surroundings.

Maybe Starlight had told him about my affliction. Or Xuanwu had seen through it because he was a god. So...what was Starlight's excuse? Was he a...*god?* The thought of a perpetually high god made me realize, rather abruptly, that I needed to tinkle. I hurried after Xuanwu, motioning for Claire and Cain to follow.

We soon reached the garden and Xuanwu halted, staring out at the apple blossoms in the distance, inhaling deeply through his nostrils. "You are always welcome to my sanctuary if you ever need to clear your mind."

I nodded, smiling. "It is a beautiful home. Especially without the ninjas guarding the grass." That earned a snort of surprised laughter.

The sun was rising, and I could see faint whirls of steam rising up from Xuanwu's carapace. He didn't seem to mind in the slightest, so I didn't think it was any cause for concern. In fact, he looked like it had relaxed him.

"Safe journey, White Rose. We shall meet again soon. I hope." He hesitated before handing me a small object the size of my palm. "Bleed on that and whisper your commands when you think my men are ready to *follow* you, *respect* you, *trust* you. *Silence will fall*," he rumbled in a meaningful tone, enunciating the key words. I closed my fist around the small cold object, nodding grimly.

When I murdered hope.

"Until then, my men will treat you much as any other faction in town." He eyed me up and down pointedly, frowning at my hair, as if to remind me of my demon disguise. "To keep up appearances, for a demon has no allies and many enemies. Any aid given to such an unanimously despised creature would not go unnoticed, dulling a perfectly capable blade that could have been wielded at a later time in a surprise attack."

I dipped my head in understanding. The ninjas would throw a lot of pointy things at us if we stepped out of line. Unless...I earned their respect.

Instead of dwelling on that, I ushered Cain and Claire back towards the house where we saw Yín waiting for us with a big old grin. The ninjas were conspicuously absent, and despite his smiles, Yín didn't speak as he led us back the way we had entered.

When we reached the hallway with the pond and stepping stones, Cain quickly leaned over to peer inside the clay vase, pulling away before Yín could notice. His disappointed frown made me grin. *Such a child*, I thought to myself with a sense of adoration for my brother. As we exited the home, said our silent goodbyes to the guards and Yín, I had already set my mind to the task at hand, figuratively rolling up my sleeves and clenching my jaw as I walked back to our car in silence.

It was time to stir some shit up. But first, I needed a new bra.

21

Claire was snuffling at the air, her window cracked—but even that slight amount of air seemed to disgust her. "This is a stupid risk," she repeated for the third time.

Flip. Snap. Flip. Snap.

I squinted against the light from the morning sun, absently fondling the obsidian turtle figurine Xuanwu had given me. It was ice-cold to the touch and easily fit nestled in the palm of my hand. I pocketed it with a sigh, not wanting to think about his request.

Flip. Snap.

Roland's church stood about fifty yards away. *So close, but so far*, I thought to myself. Claire was right, but I was finished with playing nice. The meeting with Xuanwu, although enlightening, had put a shot clock on the Roland problem—and raised the stakes for failure.

Flip. Snap.

The first thing I'd made abundantly clear to Cain and Claire after we left his house, was that no one was to talk to anyone—at all—about what we'd learned. We couldn't know for certain who was already on Roland's payroll. So the whole Dracula thing was remaining a secret.

Flip. Snap.

Claire growled audibly, gripping the steering wheel hard enough for it to make a rubbery complaint. I wanted to let off some steam, too. It had only been late last night when I killed half a dozen vampires. You would think that would be enough to sate my appetite.

Flip. Snap.

But it wasn't. I wanted to put a stop to Roland. To make Henri Bellerose squeal in agony as I tickled his toes with razor blades for baiting Roland into the Dracula heist. He must have played off Roland's grief at losing me, promising him that Dracula had the metaphoric Holy Grail to save me, or avenge me, or whatever Roland had needed to hear.

Flip. Snap.

Hell, maybe Dracula did have something in his collection that could do such a thing. One tiny misunderstanding—I wasn't dead.

Flip. Snap.

"Cain, I swear to holy hell," Claire snarled suddenly, "I will snap that thing in half and shove it up your ass if you don't stop it right now."

Silence.

Flip. Snap.

She spun, growling as she lunged at him in the backseat.

He dove out of her reach, swatting at her hands. "Fine!" he snapped, shoving the burner flip phone Claire had picked up for each of us into his pocket. "I'm just so *bored*," he said in a toddler's whine. Then, before we knew it, he simply hopped out of the fucking Jeep.

My heartrate tripled as I looked at Roland's church in fear, wondering if anyone had spotted—or scented—Cain. Thankfully, nothing changed, us being too far away for anyone to really pay attention. There were only a handful of Regulars on the street, and most of them were entering or exiting a coffee shop a few doors down. So Cain blended in easily as he slipped into a shaded alley to study the church. I slowly turned to Claire, saw her open her mouth to argue, and then I hurriedly jumped out of the Jeep, also having to swat at her hands to make my escape.

I shuffled over to Cain, ignoring his mischievous grin as I casually eyed the street. I had asked Claire to drive us here in hopes we might be able to get a lay of the land while all the vampires were sleeping.

The view of the church from the alley gave me a better angle on the property around it, so I was able to notice a lot more guards on patrol than I had seen a few minutes ago—a pair of young, shirtless men pulling weeds, a trio of girls smoking beneath a tree, and even a half dozen men and women doing jumping jacks in a row. I also spotted a pair of huge, shaggy, supposedly-napping dogs lying in the cool grass.

To Regulars, the sleeping beasts looked like huge wolfhounds, but to the supernatural community it was a giant middle finger. They didn't care to be seen out in the open because no one dared to talk.

Because they were all werewolves. All incredibly good looking, and all dangerous as hell. There had to be at least two dozen of them spread around the perimeter of the church. I studied them anxiously, trying to see if I recognized anyone. Even from this vantage, I didn't see anyone I recognized, but there was a stone wall around the church, concealing some of the grounds where a dozen or more werewolves could be lying in wait.

Claire finally decided to climb out of the car, muttering under her breath as she joined us. Maybe one of the two lieutenants would be bold enough to risk a little morning sun, step out for a stroll, and I could nab them, dragging them back to my apart—

I muttered a curse under my breath, reminded of my eviction notice. I turned to Claire. "If I kidnap one of them, do we have anywhere to take him?"

She shot me a smoldering glare. "First of all, we're not going to waltz up there and kidnap anyone. We'd be torn to shreds. Second of all...yes. I've got a cave."

"Really?" Cain hooted, leaning forward. "A fucking *cave*?"

"You have a problem with that, Candy?" she asked, baring her teeth.

He shook his head, leaning back and smirking at the nickname. "I actually thought it sounded kind of cool. Like a lair."

"Oh." She thawed slightly. "Well, it's not like I can go sign a lease on a new apartment or go back to my old house with these assholes looking for me," she grumbled, glancing towards the church.

I gritted my teeth, mentally adding one more reason to the *Let Me Count The Ways I Hate Thee* list I was compiling for Roland—my justifications for why he needed to pay for what he'd done. Why he needed to die. Claire was forced to live in a fucking cave? Definitely going on the list—right below *stealing Callie's stuff and hoarding it like a creep*. Other reasons included obvious crimes, but also more heinous, overarching ones.

I couldn't let him become too powerful—or risk him losing his fight to bring a very pissed off Dracula back here to Kansas City.

I had to get rid of his barrier around the city. Because if there was a war coming on the horizon, the Freaks of Kansas City—whether they wanted to or not—needed to be able to enter the fight. If this impending war was as big as everyone seemed to fear, we weren't fighting for a single city or a specific faction within the supernatural community—but all our continued existence. Or at least our freedom from this big bad enemy who obviously intended unpleasant things for us. Otherwise, it wouldn't have been called a war.

Roland had also betrayed his own values—becoming that which he had once hunted. I had to put him down for his own good. The old Roland would have wanted me to. If I thought too hard on that, I began remembering every single good time we'd had together—

I closed my eyes for a three-count, centering myself, my purpose. Once confident that I was back in control, I opened them again.

"Let's hope a skanky demon's stank doesn't travel further than others," Claire teased, pointedly leaning away from me. I nudged her with an elbow, narrowing my eyes. The breeze was blowing the wrong way for that to be a concern. The bitch. She smiled back innocently.

Le Bone's attack had been exceedingly clever. Making me look and smell like a demon during the one time my face might have gotten everyone to lower their figurative guns—fitting right into Bellerose's ploy to entice Roland to rob or kill Dracula. It had made me an outcast—even from my potential allies. Because demons had no friends.

"We really need to catch one of them," I murmured. Because we needed to know what was going on inside the church. Le Bone should have been dead, and he'd had no ability to do magic when I last saw him a year ago. And he obviously held some kind of authority, because last night he'd ordered his vampires to *kill the demon*, and they had died trying to obey that command. Maybe he really was the mysterious second lieutenant.

"Even if we kidnapped one of them, it still won't get us past the ward," Cain said, jerking his chin at the church. I grunted, spotting a very faint red hue surrounding the entire building, almost like fading fog. Roland's ward around the church. Invite only. I felt the power as a gentle hum—even from across the street.

"And nothing matters until tomorrow night," Claire added.

I was assuming Xuanwu's warning about the Blood Moon had meant the party started at moonrise, or full dark. He hadn't elaborated, and I figured it was better for us to show up too early rather than too late. That's when we would make our move on his church.

No. *My* church, not Roland's church. My name was on the deed. Sure, I had granted Roland access to it, letting him use it as his base of operations, but I was technically still the owner unless he'd lawyered up somehow to get me removed.

But Xuanwu had been pretty confident—and I begrudgingly agreed with him—that the ward would also stop anyone tainted with Heavenly blood. And the demon illusion around me would also complicate matters—either with the guards, or the ward itself. I let out a frustrated sigh, cursing how intelligent Roland was—how he thought everything through so completely. Then again, I wouldn't have the talents I had today without his lessons. The student had come to slay the master. Tomorrow.

I watched the Regulars occasionally exiting the coffee shop, shaking my head. They really had no idea what was going on. Still, I sensed a tension around them, some primal instinct that they were in more danger than they should be. None of them listened to this instinct, but they subconsciously felt it. To be honest, I felt it, too. But my shoulders were tense from unseen eyes, sensing silence watching me from a distance. Unless it was my overactive imagination warning me to keep an eye out for ninjas.

"We can check out Abundant Angel and the Shepherds after," I said, shaking off the thought. "I'm not even sure we should bother with them. This really has nothing to do with the Vatican like we originally thought. They're just defending their—"

I caught motion in a sheltered carport near the front of the church grounds and zeroed in. Bellerose himself shambled out from beneath the carport, and my fingers flexed instinctively, wanting to risk it all and take him out with one climactic immolation like Sodom and Gomorrah, except fangier—Suckem and Vamporrah.

But I immediately froze, blinking in disbelief. Henri's once chiseled, and handsome face was now a glistening, scarred ruin, like he'd been doused with Holy Water. Gone was his confident swagger and deep undertone of authority. Although as tall as a scarecrow, his shoulders were slumped and his crimson eyes—which had been a misty gray last time I had seen him—darted about anxiously as he shuffled to the front door of the church, slipping meekly inside beneath a red haze that briefly settled over his shoulders like a gauze curtain. Then he and the red haze were gone as the door closed.

The power I had sensed as it settled over his shoulders—scanning him to verify he had permission to enter—had become a momentary sharper, buzzing sensation compared to the constant gentle hum of before.

I turned to Cain and Claire, my eyes wide. "Did you *see* that?" I whispered.

Cain nodded woodenly. "That...didn't look like a man in a position of power..."

"Look!" Claire hissed, jerking her chin back at the church.

I turned to see two more familiar faces stalk out of the carport. Two beautiful women with dark hair, eyes roving the street alertly. And their eyes glinted crimson in the light of the rising sun. The Paw Patrol—*just yelp for help*.

Paradise and Lost.

Claire growled under her breath. "They used to be so cool," she complained. "They had already been building a pack before you left. But now?" she said angrily, narrowing her eyes. "Let's just say that working for Roland has increased the demand. Wolves have been popping up from all over the city to join, having lived in hiding since the old pack disbanded. Working for Roland must have its perks because they have faced zero challenges to their unique shared-Alpha arrangement."

I grunted. I knew Paradise and Lost—how determined they were. With or without Roland's backing, they would have kept their position as Alphas. Still, Roland's influence would have definitely limited dissenting opinions.

If I looked just right, I could see faint shimmers of red in the eyes of the other patrolling wolves—those who weren't wearing sunglasses, anyway. None of their eyes were as vibrantly crimson as Paradise and Lost or Henri Bellerose, but to someone who knew to look, it was unmistakable. They all shared a blood bond with Roland.

Paradise and Lost walked up to the entrance to the church and opened the doors, strolling inside without issue. Like with Henri, I spotted the faint ripple to the air—as if they had walked through a crimson gossamer curtain. The crimson haze didn't seem to bother them in the slightest as they passed the threshold. Maybe they couldn't even sense it, and it was simply because I was a wizard that I had seen and felt it.

I tried to think back on my time spent training with Roland—anything Roland might have taught me that would give me an idea how he'd made his ward. But nothing came to mind, leading me to believe that one of his lieutenants had been behind it—trying to make a ward that mirrored the one around Dracula's castle. But Henri...that had been a broken man. That hadn't been a man playing a secret game, that had been a hopeless wreck—a shell of a man.

Cain suddenly grunted, drawing his dagger as he leaped in front of me, deflecting a projectile so it slammed into the brick wall rather than my throat. I craned my neck to look past his shoulder, ready for a fight.

A figure stepped forward from the shadows, directly into the sunlight, his fangs glinting in the sun as he spoke in a honeyed, Southern drawl. The sun seemed to reflect off his skin in a faint shimmer that wasn't quite a sparkle—

Nah. It was a fucking sparkle.

"Well, well, well..." he drawled like a friendly Good Samaritan, "looks like we have some spies. And did I hear you say *kidnapping*? We don't take kindly to kidnappers in these parts."

And then he was striding closer, not a flicker of concern in those eyes. Not crimson eyes.

I just stared at the newcomer, dumbfounded. "Alucard?" I gasped.

The Daywalker froze, narrowing his eyes with a frown. "No one is supposed to know that name, here." He looked me up and down, assessing me. "I guess being a demon has its perks. Pity it doesn't come with a severance package for a sudden, violent, horrifically painful and messy death."

And he resumed his measured pace, claws extending from his fingertips.

Cain grinned from ear-to-ear, licking his lips as he drew his dagger. "I've wanted to do this for a very long time."

Alucard halted, eyeing the blade with amusement. "You sure you want to do this? Here?" he asked, smirking darkly.

Cain squared his shoulders. "I don't pick the ballroom. I just fucking dance, disco ball."

Alucard hissed at him like a cat doused with a hose.

22

My momentary feeling of relief at seeing a familiar face had popped like a pricked bubble, even as my mind raced to process what was going on here. I *knew* Alucard Morningstar. He was a Daywalker Master Vampire from St. Louis, and he was friends with Nate Temple. Could this mean...that Nate was trapped here, too? That sent both a flutter of anxiety and hope through me. If I could convince Nate it was really me, I had a very formidable ally to help me storm Roland's church.

Then again...

It might mean Nate was working *with* Roland to avenge my presumed death.

Xuanwu's request whispered in my ears, but I forcefully shrugged it away. Was this what the Black Tortoise had meant? Had he been warning me that Nate Temple was in town and that he had allied himself with Roland?

No. Claire would have known—or at least heard—about an event like that. And it would have been one of the first things out of her mouth upon seeing me. Also, Nate was not one to hide behind closed doors. He was the guy to blast all the doors down with fiery whips and a laugh. There was no way he was in town without anyone knowing.

Cain risked a quick look back at me, startled. "Wait. You know this ass-clown?"

Alucard frowned at the three of us, obviously not recognizing me. He finally dismissed me and turned back to my defender. "Not sure where you've been, Cain, but you really should have brought Callie back with you. Nate Temple isn't going to be pleased to learn you misplaced her. Luckily for you, Roland won't let you live long enough to face Temple's wrath."

I placed a hand on Cain's shoulder, holding him back for a moment. "You're working for Roland?" I asked anxiously.

Alucard frowned at me again. "I don't remember saying you could talk, demon. I would hand you over to Roland as a gift, but he's got more important things to do with his time. Which means you and I will get to know each other very well over the next few weeks. You know, as I'm stripping the flesh from your bones and asking you very nicely to tell me your demon name," he said, his lip curling up in an anticipatory grin.

Claire chose that moment to hit him in a tackle, having been largely ignored up until this point. Alucard saw it at the last moment and rolled clear, kicking her off him and into a dumpster near the Jeep with a loud crashing sound. Cain also lunged, swiping at the Daywalker with his bone dagger. He got close enough to slice Alucard's shirt, but the crazy vampire just laughed as he jumped clear and kicked Cain in the chest hard enough to stagger him. Howls erupted from the direction of the church, catching the sound of our skirmish and sending reinforcements.

"Nowhere to run, now, my sweets," Alucard drawled.

I gritted my teeth as I saw Alucard's hands begin to glow with golden light. I knew how fast and deadly he was, and he obviously saw only a brunette demon woman, not Callie.

Knowing I didn't have time for a long, drawn-out fight—maybe not even a short, brutal fight—with the werewolf guards inbound, I closed my eyes as Alucard squared off against both of my friends. Claire had been sidestepping as if to put herself between me and the approaching werewolves. If I didn't end this quickly, we were about to see Roland very fast, and judging by Alucard's comment—it might be more accurate that we were to be executed before ever getting the chance to waste Master Roland's time.

And it sure seemed Alucard was on Roland's payroll, even without the telltale crimson eyes. Was...*Alucard* the mysterious second lieutenant?

And a devilish thought came to mind. We'd been looking for someone to kidnap...

I closed my eyes and focused on a power I didn't often use—and didn't entirely understand. All I knew was that it had once helped me chase down an extremely fast supernatural being or two, allowing me to see a few seconds into the future in order to overcome their supernatural advantages.

Cain hadn't fared well against it, so I was betting it would work just as well on Alucard.

The Silvers purred at my touch.

I opened my eyes and time abruptly slowed down for everyone but me. Simultaneously, a storm of silver rain suddenly splashed over everything in sight—a torrent of rain that no one but me seemed to notice. As each raindrop struck a physical object, it stuck like silver paint, and soon the entire scene was soaked with the dripping, silver liquid—which was an entirely different experience than the last time I'd used them, catching me momentarily off guard.

But no one else seemed to notice, blinking languidly and moving as if underwater. The silver scene illuminated other things—like a web of thin crimson ribbons extending out from the street behind Alucard in the direction of the church, and I knew it indicated the paths that the incoming wolves would take upon arrival. I even knew it would be about a minute before they arrived—when I had expected they were already on the way. Maybe they had to get permission slips from their mommies, Paradise and Lost, before they were allowed to cross the street. Or they obeyed the leash laws and were trying to wake up their vampire leash-holders.

Or maybe they had a hell of a lot of faith in Alucard handling the problem himself.

I noticed a thicker, braided, crimson and gold rope of power extending directly out from Alucard, and knew it signified his ties to Roland, or perhaps his ties to the ward around the church. That he was indeed working on behalf of the Red Pastor. Whether that was through some bond or a handshake agreement, I couldn't tell. But the thickness and darkness of that rope of power gave me cause for concern. The gold was crackling with light while the crimson was trying to smother the gold, warring against each other for dominance even though they were braided together—and stronger for it.

Regardless of what that might signify, we only had a few minutes to get the hell out of here. I sensed eyes suddenly latch onto us like grappling hooks, so I glanced back, deeper into the alley, only to find familiar silhouettes with rapidly shifting shadows, not at all encumbered by my Silvers and their ability to enhance my perception of time. Xuanwu's ninjas didn't advance or retreat—they simply observed us. I let out an uneasy breath at the thought of attempting to run past them to escape the wolves and Daywalker.

Whether they were here to attack the demon or Daywalker, only the next few moments would reveal. And they weren't slowed down like everyone else. Were they immune to the Silvers? I really needed to have a sit-down with Solomon and find out what he knew about them. All I knew was they were somehow related to my Heavenly blood.

There really was no other direction to take, though, because one look at the Jeep now revealed a veritable net of thin crimson ribbons slowly snaking over it—inbound guards—telling me it would be a race to see who reached it first, and the odds weren't good.

Unless I changed something.

I felt pressure building in my temples, threatening a debilitating migraine if I held the Silvers any longer. That was a new sensation. Then again, Kansas City was very different these days. Maybe Roland's wards were impacting the Silvers. And my power was touching more people than the last time I'd used it—more variables to predict. I needed to move. Fast.

I assessed Cain for an opportunity. He had one foot raised as he prepared to leap towards Alucard, and I saw a ribbon of chrome leading ahead of him, depicting his intended course of action. He was going to wildly miss his target. Alucard faced Cain and was in the process of flinging his hand towards him. I saw a crimson and gold ribbon of smoky light suddenly wink into existence between Alucard and Cain's chest, showing me the Daywalker—unlike Cain—was *not* going to miss his target.

I was apparently working with junior varsity material in Cain.

I walked between the two, my head feeling as if it was about to split open at the strain of holding the Silvers any longer. I bit down, clenching my jaw as I rotated Cain's shoulders just enough to avoid Alucard's strike. Then I hurled a blast of air at Claire's stomach, likening her to a white cue ball in a game of pool so that she would hit the side of the Jeep. The power hit her and she drifted off her feet like I'd struck her with zero gravity. Then I crouched down and prepared to replicate a *Mortal Kombat* finishing move on Alucard.

With a shuddering breath, I released the Silvers and simultaneously exploded upwards from my crouch, leading with my fist. The true colors of the city exploded back to life as my ears popped at the sudden concert of sound in the alley. I heard a surprised, pained grunt, a crash, a shriek, and saw Claire clip the Jeep before cartwheeling over it. I winced but didn't hold back on my uppercut.

My knuckles struck Alucard's chin, cracking like popcorn at the force of the blow, right as his blast of golden light screamed past my face towards Cain—who was abruptly halfway through tripping over his own two feet, a consequence of the adjustment I had made to his body position suddenly warring against the momentum he had put into his intended leaping attack. As a result, Alucard's bar of fiery light scored a molten line of fire into the brick wall behind where his target had stood a millisecond ago—and that bar of light abruptly pivoted to shoot straight up the wall in a scorching sizzle of burnt brick before winking out as my uppercut knocked him clean off his feet.

Cain was already climbing back to his feet in an attempt to grab Alucard before he landed. Cain's eyes danced wildly with confusion over his body apparently stroking out in the middle of a flying leap, but he didn't waste time whining about it. He'd had a good run since his Old Testament days. Experiencing his first stroke after thousands of years would impress even the most critical of doctors.

He managed to grab Alucard from the air on the vampire's descent and had the courtesy to offer up a bent knee to break his fall. I was proud to see that chivalry still existed in this dark new world. It was my prerogative as a sister to make sure my brother wasn't just an uncouth lump of hair, muscle, and testosterone...

That he also had class—a refined Statesman in the art of manliness.

Alucard felt very differently about Cain's gentlemanliness as his back snapped, crackled, and popped, and breath blasted out of his lungs. Cain helpfully delivered a right cross to the Daywalker's already broken jaw in an attempt to set it back into place from my uppercut. Alucard went limp like all men do after their typical three minutes of glory, leaving his dance partner to clean up the mess.

Cain dutifully scooped up the dazed vampire and grinned at me. "Leverage." Then he bolted towards the Jeep—which coughed to life as Claire frantically waved at us from the driver's seat, urging us to hurry, her eyes wide with alarm as she stared over our shoulders.

Cain flung Alucard into the backseat, unceremoniously cracking his nose across the roof of the vehicle before shoving him further inside and jumping in after him.

Remembering what I had seen in the Silvers—as well as what Claire had obviously seen behind me—I was already hurling balls of fire over the hood of the Jeep.

"What the fuck?" Claire screamed, eyes practically bugging out of her face as my fireballs seared paint from the hood of her Jeep. Because she had been so focused on the threat behind *me* that she hadn't seen the two werewolves only a few yards away from *her*.

Instead of lunging for the door, I dropped into a baseball slide and blindly flung my hands straight up, hurling a blast of air where I had just been standing. I gasped as I felt a faint whisper of cut hair, and looked up to find a matte-black katana blade hovering where I had just been standing.

The ninja grunted in surprise at his missed strike, and then again as my blast of air caught him and sent him and his sword flying up and to the right, slamming both into the brick wall. I was already climbing to my feet and diving into the open passenger window as I flung a shield up behind me in the event more ninjas were attempting to filet my spine into a Spicy Callie Roll.

I smelled burning fur and howls of pained outrage from Claire's side of the Jeep as two forces slammed into the shield that I had cast out behind me on my side of the vehicle. I managed to scramble into my seat and stared back through my shield, expecting to see magical swords about to pierce it, but three ninjas had instead used it as a launching pad to hurl themselves *over* the Jeep and right into the gang of smoldering werewolves that were clawing at Claire's door. The ninjas somehow made it look like I had *meant* to catapult them over the vehicle, when in reality my shield had been a solid vertical wall.

Regardless, I was ecstatic to see Rocky, Colton, and Tum-Tum cut into the werewolves like they were pitching a reboot of the classic film to Amazon Studios—and that they were worth every penny of the steep budget.

"GO!" I screamed at Claire, who was staring in disbelief at the ninjas fighting the wolves just outside her window. Paradise and Lost—now in wolf form, but unmistakable to me—circled the ninjas angrily, drool spilling from their massive fangs as their thick, long fur bristled at their new foes—at the poachers who had interrupted their hunt. The ninjas were smoky apparitions, looking like they were enshrouded with black, dry ice. The only thing making them look like more than fog were their matte-black blades lashing out and flicking fresh droplets of blood on our windshield as they moved to their next wolf, ignoring the surprised *yips* and *yelps* from their targets.

I punched Claire's thigh, snapping her out of her instinctive need to protect her territory—the bear inside her struggling to break free and play with the other monsters. Her hands and forearms were currently thigh-thick bear arms gripping the steering wheel hard enough to tear it free if she accidentally sneezed, and she was panting wildly. But my punch had snapped her out of it enough to make her shake her head and stomp her foot down on the gas.

She spun the steering wheel sharply, and the left front quarter panel clipped one of the wolves as our right rear bumper scraped against the car that had been parked in front of us. A cringeworthy *screech* let us know that one of the wolves had either raked a claw at the side of our vehicle or that one of the ninjas had tried slicing our Jeep in half with a sword. Claire corrected the wheel and we sped down the street in the direction of Roland's church and an alarming number of new guards glaring at either us or the fight still raging behind us.

The rear windshield shattered and I felt a slight tug on my bicep as I ducked in surprise, but Claire didn't let up on the gas as she muttered a steady stream of curses without pausing for breath. We raced past the church to see the wolves glaring at us up close as we made our escape. None of them pursued or shifted, but their eyes let me know it wasn't by choice but by command. I glanced back, verifying we didn't have anyone chasing after us in a car, and saw Alucard's eyes beginning to flutter open.

"Ernghh—" Alucard began, but he was interrupted by a meaty *thud* as Cain casually drove a powerful elbow strike down into his temple, knocking him back out.

"Hush little baby," Cain cooed sweetly. Confident that his prisoner was neutralized, Cain finally looked up at me, brandishing a matte-black throwing star from the shards of glass pooled on his lap. More of the glass covered his shoulders, hair, and the sleeping vampire. "Fucking ninjas," he muttered, pointing past me at the dashboard. I turned to see another throwing star firmly embedded in the upholstery just above the radio. "Pretty sure that's what took out the back windshield. I didn't hear a gunshot," Cain said.

I shuddered, deciding to leave it where it was and hope Claire didn't hit a pothole because it might test the limits of the airbag sensor.

We rounded a corner and were fully out of sight of the church a moment later. I let out a breath of relief, thumping my head back against the headrest. "To the bear cave!" I cheered weakly, lifting a pathetic fist in the air.

23

Cain followed us down a slight decline, dragging the still unconscious Alucard behind him by the boots, not bothering to be concerned about the Daywalker's head. In fact, I was pretty sure his smile widened each time Alucard's nose snagged on a large rock or depression in the ground.

He dropped the boots and put his fists on his hips, taking one long look around the cave. Then he cleared his throat, and spoke like a radio announcer, his voice echoing in stereo.

"And now, I bring you never before seen footage of Claire's lady cave—a surprisingly vast space, replete with all manner of mysterious and elusive spots that appear to have never known a man's touch. Despite these secrets, the entrance shows frequent, heavy use—"

"No one will ever find your body, Cain," Claire warned in a cool tone, cutting him off.

He grinned at her playfully. "I practiced it in the car," he admitted, sounding quite pleased with himself.

Claire was silent for a time, but a crooked smile finally broke through and she let out a sigh. "Okay. It was pretty good," she admitted at last, shaking her head. "Let me show you where Starlight keeps his...stuff." She led him off to what appeared to be a make-shift room off to the side, walled off by one of those tri-fold partitions. A fluorescent glow kicked on and I heard them discussing something back and forth in low tones.

Which left me with Alucard. I kept my magic ready in case I needed to subdue him at a moment's notice. I also didn't take my eyes off him, even though my mind was far, far away.

I had tried calling Nate on the drive over here—but he hadn't answered. I had briefly considered calling some of his friends to at least let him know I was alive—perhaps not mentioning that I had kidnapped Alucard—but I had ultimately decided against it, knowing the rabbit hole of questions that decision could throw me into.

It would all be over tomorrow night. One way or another.

Kansas City was my problem. And it wasn't my place to tell anyone what Alucard had or had not been up to on his extended vacation—a distinction I was determined to discover for myself over the next hour or so.

Cain returned, snapping me out of my thoughts. His face looked a little pale as he exited the small room with Claire—who looked ready to shift if Alucard woke too early—a few paces behind him. Cain held up a pair of thin wooden bracelets with no chain between them. They almost looked like reeds from a wicker basket.

I arched a brow, not even bothering to verbalize how woefully inadequate—

Then I saw the word branded into the side of each thin wooden ring —*Vampyr*.

"Right? You ever seen something like this?" he asked curiously.

I shook my head slowly. "We can give it a shot, but be ready to yank them off. I don't want to hurt him. Not until we can talk to him."

Cain nodded in understanding, knowing full well that Alucard was friends with Nate and what kind of repercussions hurting his friend could have. He touched the wooden rings to Alucard's wrist briefly to make sure they wouldn't incinerate him or anything. Nothing happened. He waited for my gesture to proceed before unclasping one and closing it over Alucard's wrist with a faint *click*.

Alucard stirred slightly, but that was it. Maybe they weren't what we thought. Cain repeated the process on the other wrist, and the moment it clicked closed, Alucard jolted upright into a kneeling position like a lightning bolt had struck him on both nipples, arching backwards with his chest out so fast that he even popped a few buttons on his shirt, sending them zipping past me like mad hornets.

He panted, head tilted back and baring his teeth up at the ceiling, unable to move. I noticed the tips of his clawed fingers were each sunk an inch into the dirt floor at his sides. I studied him with concern, but other than obvious discomfort, he didn't show any signs of agony. Just fury at his extremely awkward and uncomfortable restraint. The word *Vampyr* on each bracelet glowed crimson and gold. I silently took a few steps back to make sure Alucard couldn't see the demon lady in his peripheral vision. I knew he could likely still smell me, but it was the least I could do to put him at ease. I wanted to find out what he knew.

To corroborate Xuanwu's hypotheses.

I shot Cain a concerned look and he hesitantly peered down into Alucard's eyes, as if to make sure they hadn't rolled back into his head. Alucard gnashed his teeth at him but that was it. Cain turned back to me, shrugging. "I think he's fine." He turned back to Alucard. "You fell asleep in the car, champ. All tuckered out from your big day. It was *so* adorable—"

"I will rip your throat out with my bare hands, Cain. Take the damned reeds off and let's see how you measure up to a real man."

Claire grunted. "What *is* it with men and measuring?"

I shrugged, not wanting to speak out loud yet. I'd told Claire about Alucard often enough in recent years that this was probably very strange for her—to feel like she knew someone she had never met—until this first in-person meeting when she planned on torturing him for answers. Unless she'd crossed paths with him at some point without me knowing.

The space looked to almost have been an old mining cave or something, judging by the narrow entrance. It was replete with candles, blankets, dressers, and several rooms carved into the rock. Like a bomb shelter. One narrow path led deeper into the mine, but it looked to have been abandoned, unused by Starlight or Claire, judging by the rubble on the floor and no obvious signs of frequent use. I smirked, recalling Cain's flamboyant show a few minutes ago. He loved nothing more than getting under people's skin, but he seemed to take particular delight in tormenting Claire. The rest of the cavern was made of sandy soil and rock, looking like it had been lovingly cleared and swept clean by one of the two bears.

Chairs, a table, a small firepit, and even an industrial shelf full of dry goods and canned food filled up the far end of the cave. I shot Claire a questioning look. She nodded. "I've been here for a while," she muttered self-consciously. "Starlight comes and goes."

Cain stiffened from whatever he had been murmuring to Alucard, blushing.

Neanderthal. I could practically hear the *that's what she said!* But why the blush?

I smiled brightly at Claire, ignoring Cain as he resumed his threats for Alucard to cooperate. "Give me a quick tour? I'm homeless, so this is a step up."

Her lips quivered—either saddened for me and my lost apartment, or grateful that I hadn't judged her creepy lady cave, I wasn't sure—and she nodded eagerly, gripping me by the arm to guide me around the cave, whispering conspiratorially. For a few minutes, we were just two young girls with no real problems, simply excited to show off what meager possessions we had accumulated in our time apart. Two ravens comparing shiny things we had stolen and woven into our nests.

The cave was much larger than I had first thought, and she scooped up a flashlight to take me down the rubble-strewn mining path to show me a surprisingly large hot spring tucked a few hundred feet back. I stared down at it, noticing the mounds of melted wax surrounding the edge of the pool from dozens and dozens of melted candles.

"You have a fucking hot tub?" I demanded, scowling. She nodded sheepishly. "Screw you," I muttered, storming back the way we had come. I didn't get far before I realized she held the flashlight. I folded my arms across my chest, waiting silently for her to stroll her lazy ass—because she did, in fact, take her sweet ass time, grinning like a cuntasaurus when she finally reached me—to guide me back to the cave proper.

She reached out and grabbed my hand tightly. "Maybe you can move in and we can kick Starlight out. He's hardly ever here, anyway," she offered softly.

I found myself smiling at the suggestion. It sounded *fun*. I squeezed her hand back. "Thank you, Claire bear. I didn't mean to call you a cuntasaurus."

"Wait, you called me a *what*?" she choked.

"Oh. I thought I'd said it out loud back there..." I mused, continuing on since I could now see light just ahead. I smiled at her grumbling curses. Love sounded like that sometimes.

We came back to the cave to find Alucard all by himself, still restrained, but Cain missing. Before I could shout out an alarm, I heard him whistling to himself from the room where he'd found the *Vampyr* reeds. Claire grimaced before guiding me over, as if she hadn't wanted to show me that particular area.

I stepped into the room and froze, blinking rapidly. Two tables stretched out side by side against the far rock wall, and upon those tables was Starlight's vast array of...

Well, primarily torture implements, I think, although I couldn't find an immediate use for many of the strange items. The ones I did recognize made me cringe, though. Everything from handheld guillotines to knives, masks to needles, and a rack of stoppered vials labeled with tiny scribbles and scratches in an unknown language. The rock wall was painted with crude symbols that made the hair stand up on my arms, even though I didn't quite know what it said. A bookshelf occupied the opposite wall, and every book in the collection seemed to be over five hundred years old, never having left the confines of the cool, shady cave.

Seeing an open book on a small desk, I grimaced upon seeing the faded, dark brown splotches decorating the aged pages. Blood. More—but different from the wall—sinister symbols filled the pages in red ink, and the paper looked old and thick, as if they were actually hide rather than paper. *A book made of skin*, I thought to myself, shivering.

I briefly imagined this as a classroom, a laboratory of sorts where Starlight learned the alphabet, orchestrated his torture victims' screams to sheet music, swam in the hot tub, and memorized the numbers of chaos as a young cub.

Druidic torture 101. Pop Quiz Thursday, Cubs! Highest grade gets a pot of honey! Make 'em squeal!

One book caught my attention, the title page showing a large tree beneath a single word. *Bioloki*. I frowned at it for a moment, struggling with the pronunciation—like biology?

"Welcome to my penthouse of pain," Cain said, snapping me out of my thoughts. I walked over to him, scanning the table he was perusing. From over his shoulder.

There were many more...undefinable items on this table. I chalked it up to me being a prude on the elements of torture, more than happy to admit that I didn't know what I didn't know—I slept a lot better for it.

Seeing just how many tools Starlight had made my stomach do a little flip-flop. The cute little stoner bear was some kind of executioner or questioner. Or he had been. No wonder the other larger bears gave him a very wide berth.

Cain held two items in his hands, considering them thoughtfully. With a shrug, he took them with him and left the room, motioning for us to join him. Alucard was rightfully pissed off when he noticed our return—generally cursing our existence, threatening our souls, and promising dark things he would do to our flesh once he broke free.

"I will burn your hearts to ash—"

"Easy, Little Brother, or I'm calling Nate," I told him tiredly, using the nickname I knew Alucard used for Nate. He stiffened sharply, his eyes narrowing in suspicion. Or anger.

Sure to stand in full view of Alucard, Cain glanced at his two items, silently debating. He held a strange, triangular-bladed device in one hand, and a cassette player with headphones in the other. He finally grinned at Alucard. "I'll admit, I don't know what either of these do, but I'm mighty curious to find out." Alucard set his jaw defiantly. Cain hefted the cassette player and headphones, his eyes lighting up as he made his decision. "This one is probably terrifying," he said, and then he promptly slid the headphones over Alucard's ears.

I pursed my lips. It was probably a recording of some sickening sound that made you want to stab through your own eardrums. "Cain—" I said, suddenly reconsidering this approach.

Alucard had gone very, very still, blinking in shock. Then...a ghost of a smile tugged at the corners of his mouth. "This...well, this one's not really what you were thinking. In fact, I would really appreciate it if you turned it off. Some things should be done in private," he added, seeming to be biting back outright laughter.

Cain frowned, tearing out the headphone jack to let us all hear the tape.

And sounds of...well, a whole lot of what resembled hyper-enthusiastic Jazzercise students recording a home-workout series rolled out from the tiny speakers.

I'm lying.

It was totally an audio tape of a group sex-a-thon.

Cain's face turned beet red and Claire actually doubled over, cackling wildly.

Alucard finally let his own laugh join Claire's in a chiming duet when several of the 'students' breached some kind of world-record plateau in their 'training'.

Simultaneously. Impressive.

Cain thumbed it off hurriedly before the screams of passion could blow the speakers. He scowled in the direction of Starlight's office. The sickened look on his face told me he was considering some of the other things he may have unknowingly touched. It might have been a table of pain implements, but it apparently also held a selection of *pleasure* devices as well. Maybe even the pain implements resulted in certain...pleasurable pains.

Starlight was *nasty*. Claire's laughter had been replaced by a similarly disgusted look to realize she had been living in a cave with a stoner hermit who had a sex dungeon ten feet away from where she went to sleep every night.

"Claire, do you have any hand sanitizer?" Cain asked very softly.

"Um, I think we have some gasoline."

"Even better," Cain said, seeming to perk up.

I sighed, hiding my own smile from my friend, Alucard. Hearing him laugh had brought back a flood of old memories. "You *have* to tell Nate about this," I told him absently, knowing Nate would get a real hoot out of it.

Alucard grew very, very quiet at my familiar words, and I instantly remembered we weren't old friends. Not anymore. His laughter had momentarily taken me to a world that should have been. The world that had been.

But right now, he saw only a demon. I let out a regretful sigh.

24

Thirty minutes of infuriating conversation had led absolutely nowhere. In fact, Alucard now seemed even *more* determined to distrust me—*because* I was trying so hard.

In essence, it didn't matter what stories I told him that only Callie would know. In his mind, a demon had kidnapped Callie, tortured all these memories out of her, and then kidnapped him—for reasons unknown. That was what really seemed to annoy him. What we wanted with him, and why we thought he would care about Callie Penrose—a woman he hardly knew.

Ouch.

I couldn't necessarily blame him. Still, I was almost ready to give torture another go—after a more thorough review of the implements available, of course. I was running out of ideas, energy, and patience. Since my return home, I hadn't once stopped to catch my breath. I'd tasted the ultimate betrayal, almost had a friend die, been attacked numerous times, and had even met a turtle god who made me run the equivalent of a mental 5k while reciting prime numbers and hopping on one foot.

To say my patience was low and my temper high was the understatement of the year.

I must have remained silent for too long. Alucard—still locked down by the *Vampyr* bracelets in that extremely uncomfortable kneeling position, his face aimed at the ceiling and his back arched—managed to hiss at me. "Stop wasting both our time with this ridiculous farce and just kill me already. Callie Penrose is dead, and if you were as familiar with Nate Temple as you pretend, you would already be running back to Hell with your tail tucked between your legs." He paused for a moment. "But he would find you even there, wouldn't he, *demon*?" he added, laughing huskily.

I rolled my eyes with a snort. Not because the threat was empty—it was anything but that. Simply put, I knew Nate would never harm me—

Then a thought slithered into my brain and my breath caught. Unless... Nate couldn't recognize me either. If he thought a demon had kidnapped and tortured his friend...yeah.

Nate might just kill said demon for retribution—only realizing too late who I really was.

Cain stepped in before I could respond, snarling down at Alucard from only inches away. "If it was up to me, I would just kill you. Callie Penrose is quite literally the only one I have ever met who saw beyond my past to uncover the man beneath—the man I didn't even know *existed* anymore. She pulled that man out of me, accepted me, dusted off my coat and straightened my shoulders to stand up tall, and asked if I would stand *beside* her. She..." his voice cracked harshly, "she calls me *brother*..." he finally whispered. "Do you have any idea what that *means*? To *ME*?" he roared, gripping Alucard's shirt with both fists. "And you think I would just waltz back into town with a demon rather than Callie? I'd rather die." He turned to me, eyes gleaming wildly. "Strike me down, demon. If this vampire is right, why do you stand there and let me disrespect you?" He stretched his neck suggestively, panting.

A minute stretched and I just stood there. Alucard watched suspiciously.

Cain finally turned back to him. "I guess she must be Hell's most pathetic demon. Or...I'm *right*. Do you think any of us wants to be here? Callie went through hell for the last year, and when she comes back expecting to hug and kiss old friends that she thought she might never see again, she finds *this* disaster," he gestured wildly with one hand, implying Kansas City in general, and not Claire who had been standing directly behind him.

Claire arched a cool eyebrow at him, folding her arms. Luckily, Alucard couldn't see far enough to notice. He was too busy staring into Cain's eyes, looking either slightly ashamed or considering. I couldn't quite tell from this angle. Regardless, Cain was getting through to him.

Cain continued, leaning closer and closer as he spoke. "Her old mentor is now a tyrant, her best friend is forced to hide in a fucking cave, and to top it all off, a Daywalker she apparently respected—for some reason I can't even begin to fathom—is groveling before a psychopath vampire king like a little *bitch!*" He spat on Alucard, forcefully releasing his fists as he panted, balling them at his sides instead.

I stepped forward suddenly, holding him back. "Enough, Cain. It's okay, just—"

Cain glared over my shoulder. "Fucking *coward*! Callie is twice the man you'll ever be. She's risking everything to fix what *you* helped *make*. Do you know she can leave the city whenever she wants? She doesn't even have to be in this shithole, dealing with clowns—

I shoved a finger over his lips, cutting him off and shaking my head sternly as I shifted to block his view of Alucard. I really hadn't wanted that bit of information out there. Not at all. Especially not if Alucard was on Team Roland.

Alucard had gone eerily silent. Even with Cain's slip, I realized there really was only one way to handle the Daywalker.

Confident that Cain wasn't going to reach over me and stab him, I turned to face Alucard and then stepped into his line of sight. I wasn't sure if he would even hear my words correctly or if he would hear me spout some demonic taunt, but I could get Claire to translate for me if that ended up being the case.

"Swear on your friendship with Nate Temple that you won't attack us if I release you. You're free to go, but I just don't feel up for a fight right now. I refuse to fight Nate's friend—not out of fear, but out of respect for the man you once were. Out of respect for the friendship you have shown Nate in the past. If that still means anything to you."

Alucard's eyes were full of suspicion and doubt as they flicked my way. "Nate *is* my best friend. *Always*," he promised me. I didn't react in any way whatsoever. "I swear not to attack you—any of you—if you release me. Although I make no promises for when we meet again," he added. "I swear this on my friendship with Nate Temple. On my own power, even."

Without fanfare, I reached down and unclasped the *Vampyr* reeds from his wrists, taking a few quick steps back to get out of immediate reach.

Alucard let out a groan of relief, flopping down onto his side for a moment, his feet probably asleep with pins and needles and his muscles likely spasming at the sudden release of tension. He scrambled unsteadily back up to his feet, watching the three of us as if expecting us to attack him.

"Nate would be disappointed to see you now, but your sister would be proud of what you have become," I told him sadly. "Mark my words. If you remain on your path, Neveah will see you sooner than you wish." I turned my back on him, ignoring the stunned look on his face. "Go. Before I change my mind, Alucard. And for your sake, I would get as far away from Roland as possible. He dies tomorrow night—as do his associates. Helping me might absolve any crimes you did in his employ."

I walked over to one of the chairs and sat down tiredly, shoving my hand in my pocket and pulling out the silver butterfly charm Nate had given me. In the hectic schedule after my return, I had almost forgotten about it. I smiled at it sadly, thinking of kisses.

I wondered if keycard access to Roland's church came with the added bonus of some kind of magical oath that prevented them from disobeying the Red Pastor. It would make sense and would explain their subservience.

He studied me suspiciously. "Can you really leave Kansas City?" he asked, attempting to mask the eagerness practically dancing in his eyes. He also tried to hide the pain my previous comment had caused him. Or...maybe he'd heard something else entirely since my words were sometimes dubbed over by demonic Google Translate. Regardless of that risk, I decided to continue speaking directly to him rather than subbing Cain or Claire in to speak for me.

I let out a bitter laugh at his question. "It's complicated. If it works, I might just run off to Fae with Nate and let this world burn," I growled, biting back the sudden threat of tears. I wouldn't, really. Not until Roland was dead, anyway.

Claire looked over at me sharply, surprised by my words. The pain in her eyes stemmed from a deep well of empathy for the mental surrender that had birthed my comment—not the comment itself. That I was so hurt by current events that I was ready to throw the towel in. I waved off her concern, staring down at the silver butterfly charm to center myself. Would Nate know me or would he see a demon as well? If that happened...

I wasn't entirely sure that I hadn't meant what I'd said about giving up. Of running off to Fae with Nate. A lifetime spent running, fighting, and solving my problems with immediate violence. Washing the blood off in a crisp pond with Nate every night. Then sitting around the campfire after to warm up. A lifetime of moments.

Of mornings.

Of evenings.

With Nate...

Yeah. That'll do, pig.

Alucard made a strange noise and I looked over abruptly, fearing he had broken his promise. He was staring at the charm in my hands. His lips moved silently like he was muttering a spell. If I hadn't known he was incapable of such a thing, I might have incinerated him on the spot by pure reflex. "Where did you get that?" he rasped.

I glanced down at the charm. "Nate gave it to me."

"When?" he demanded.

I narrowed my eyes, not appreciating his tone. "At Chateau Falco. Before he went to Fight Night against Mordred."

He studied me, not speaking, seeming to be arguing with himself internally. Had Nate mentioned this charm to Alucard? "Where did he get it?" Alucard asked me.

I frowned. "A friend in Fae. Barbie, I think he said her name was. A silver sprite who loves sexy time." I realized how that had sounded and clarified. "In *general*, she loves sexy time. Gets a rush from it," I said, trying to clarify the source of her power.

Alucard flashed me a genuine smirk. "Yeah. She does."

I narrowed my eyes at his lecherous grin. "You better not be saying Nate fucked a fairy or I'll kill him. Slowly. And I'll practice my technique on *you*," I snarled, clenching my fists.

Alucard's brief humor evaporated. Then I realized he was staring at my hands, not scared off by my *tone*. I glanced down to see claws sprouting up from between my fingers. I regained control of my thoughts, banishing the apparent jealousy that had taken over, and they disappeared.

Another thought surprised me. He'd...heard my actual words, not a demonic threat dubbed over my words.

Alucard was slowly shaking his head, looking like he'd been struck between his eyes. He cocked his head, appraising me up and down with a confused frown. "Is...it really you, Callie?" he asked, bewildered. "What the *hell* is going on here?"

I nodded, having no idea which part of our strange conversation had convinced him. My scalp suddenly flared with heat, and I let out a gasp of surprise. I spun to face Claire, pointing at my hair where I had felt the sensation. She nodded excitedly, but she followed it up with a wary look towards Alucard—who had begun laughing hysterically under his breath. "This is so incredibly fucked up," he muttered between gasps of laughter.

Cain and Claire were staring at Alucard uncertainly, likely assuming his laughter signaled a rapid downward spiral into insanity.

"Are you telling me," I began, feeling suddenly angry, "that all I had to do was flash some claws at you to convince you who I really was?" I snapped, realizing I was actually really, really pissed off, now. I felt relieved but I was also shaking with fury. I could have whipped out my claws in the fight if I'd known that was all he'd needed to see to be convinced.

He took a few gasping breaths, trying to silence his laughter. "No," he wheezed. "I'm not laughing at *that*," he tried to explain, fighting another bout of giggles. "Nate...never fucked a fairy!" he abruptly belted out, his laughter returning twofold as the words echoed through the cavern. "But you can bet your ass I'm going to tease him about it the next time I see him!"

Cain had walked over and was staring at the laughing Alucard, nodding satisfactorily. "I knew I nailed my speech. Especially that live-action part," he said matter-of-factly. "That pendant and fairy sex thing was a little helpful, I'm sure." He patted me on the shoulder consolingly, not even remotely joking.

I placed a hand on his shoulder, watching the giggling glampire. "You're right. It must have been your speech," I lied.

"Fairy fucker!" Alucard cackled, plopping down onto his back and laughing at the ceiling, blinking through his tears.

Cain gave me a somber look. "This is entirely unhelpful. Not to mention unprofessional."

I nodded absently. We'd convinced—and possibly broken the psyche of—Alucard. And we were still no closer to a way into Roland's church. What a colossal waste of time.

25

As the Master Vampire tried to master his laughter, I made the decision that I wasn't going to tell him about Dracula. Just because he finally saw through the spell making me look like a demon did not mean he was on my side. He'd worked for Roland well before I came back to town, knowing full well how wrong Roland's actions were. Running and hiding in a cave like Claire had been forced to do was more honorable than working with Roland.

As Roland's second lieutenant, Alucard was complicit in the Red Pastor's crimes. Period. Judgement on those crimes would come later...

After he had outlived his usefulness. Now, he was a tool for me to use. Nothing more.

Cain had moved some folding chairs into a lopsided circle, somehow leaving Alucard all alone before the three of us—Cain and Claire seated on my left and right. Alucard smirked faintly, catching the subtle hint, but he sat down without comment. His eyes drank me in like I was some kind of optical illusion. Probably because I still didn't look like myself, even though he had learned otherwise. A conundrum. "I don't understand this demon thing," he finally said, waving a hand at me. "I can see...a Callie-*esque* person, but you still look different, like a flickering hologram. That white streak in your hair wasn't there earlier."

I nodded, trying to focus my rage—putting his crimes on a shelf for later.

"Thank Le Bone for that. He hit me with some whopper of a magical spell last night and this was the result—"

"Le Bone is dead," Alucard interrupted, frowning in confusion. "He was executed by decapitation almost a year ago. I was there. Roland called it axe-communication," he chuckled hollowly. Cain echoed him, but his laugh sounded amused. "I even helped burn his corpse after. A welcoming gift to Kansas City," he added dryly.

I blinked a few times, my mouth clicking shut. Dead. I sensed Cain and Claire shift uncomfortably on either side of me, not liking that news one bit. I pursed my lips, thinking furiously. I turned to Cain, arching an eyebrow. He shook his head, silently telling me he was confident he had seen Le Bone.

In a way, hearing Le Bone had appeared to curse me—from beyond the grave, apparently—actually made me feel a whole lot better. Because it was *suspicious*.

Someone who could cast a spell to make *me* look like a demon must have been able to cast an illusion over *themselves*. Yet they had chosen to look like Le Bone—a dead man. An easily verifiable fact if someone did a little digging. That was either a huge mistake...

Or a hidden message of some kind.

I was dismissing the possibility that Le Bone was a zombie out of sheer ick factor. Then again, maybe Claire had been correct. *Necromancy*...I shuddered. That was way out of my wheelhouse. Barring further proof to the fact, I chose to keep that one out of my analysis.

This assailant could have chosen to appear as any random stranger that I had never seen before, making me waste a bunch of time fruitlessly searching for him. It was almost like whoever had cursed me had *wanted* me to spin my wheels—but only for a little while. Buying time.

That was...baffling, but it showed me this assailant was either the world's greatest idiot, or brilliant. Did that actually make him a potential ally? I ran through potential suspects, but kept discarding them, always ending up on the same theory.

Anyone openly standing *against* Roland—Fabrizio's Vatican crew—was immediately out of the suspect pool, because if any of them had seen Callie Penrose suddenly reappear, they would have bent over backwards trying to convince me to talk some sense into Roland.

The only other suspects who might have wanted me to stay away from Roland would have been other vampires who fully *supported* Roland and his goals—but any vampire caught concealing the fact that Callie Penrose was, in fact, alive and well, would have been spit-roasted above holy fire faster than you could say three *Hail Marys*. so loyal vampires were most likely out, too.

It had to be a third party—of which Kansas City had plenty, all in hiding.

Or...an enemy hiding in the shadows—someone who *openly* supported Roland, but did *not* support him in *actuality*. A vampire stupid enough—or clever enough—to disguise himself as a man most knew was dead. He had faith enough in me to believe I could work from the shadows while hunted as a demon by *everyone*, to get my answers without immediately derailing Roland. But...why? To steal Roland's prize?

And this person knew I was alive only minutes after I returned to Kansas City, which made my every orifice pucker. Had a member of the Sanguine Council made it into Kansas City before the barrier went up? Working behind the scenes to derail Roland's conquest?

Or maybe...it was Henri Bellerose—despite how weak he had *appeared*. Had that been camouflage? Henri wanting Roland to spearhead the whole Dracula heist and then steal it from him after the dust settled—if Roland survived.

That was typical for vampires. Schemes. Games. But why show his hand to me in a way I could easily see through? Henri would have been better off disguising himself as a stranger.

Dracula...

The thought crept in so stealthily that I almost jumped in fright. Was that even possible? Could Dracula have done this to me? Somehow picking up on Roland's secret plan and using some ancient vampiric power to shut the shit down from the shadows? Had I been...

Dracula'd?

I realized Alucard was still staring at me, waiting for my reaction. I forced my face to remain calm even though my heart was practically bursting through my chest. Alucard would know something had frightened me—able to sense heartbeats since he was a vampire—but I kept that last suspect to myself. The barrier prevented Dracula from coming here. It had to. Or Roland would never have dared to consider it—to go through all this work.

I took a calming breath. "Fine. Some unknown person who *looked* like Le Bone cast this illusion over me."

He nodded thoughtfully, scratching at his jaw. "I'll admit, we all thought

Haven's necklace was malfunctioning when it started *dinging* last night, but after we saw the aftermath in the alley...what you did to them..." He trailed off, studying me as if he'd never met me before—like his respect for me had instantly skyrocketed. "Anyway, it caused quite the panic. Paradise and Lost sent a few vampires off to investigate, tracking your movements through a few alleys with the necklace to verify that the impossible was true. That a demon had managed to break through the barrier that we knew for a fact *blocked* demons. The barrier that blocked everyone, even Roland, its maker."

I stared at him for about three seconds, not wanting to reveal any ignorance, but I was feeling plenty ignorant. "What necklace?"

"It goes off if a demon is within a few hundred feet of it. An artifact Roland took from Haven after he killed him. It hadn't made a sound since Samael left town, apparently. The last time we used it was when we scoured the city right after the barrier went up—to make sure no demons were trapped inside with us."

Cain was muttering something to himself under his breath but I didn't bother trying to decipher it. If the vampires had a necklace that could track a demon, and it worked on me...

Then why hadn't my boots reacted when Claire had put them on, pointing at me? Maybe they only worked when I wore them. Regardless, between my boots, the necklace, and what I'd heard so far, it was becoming blatantly clear that no other demons were in town. Roland wanted them out for his big plan, so whoever Le Bone had really been, at least he wasn't a demon. At least he hadn't been Samael in disguise.

Given the circumstances, it was a relatively small relief, but a relief, nonetheless. It also enabled my conspiracy theory. That someone within Roland's flock was a schemer—who just so happened to have access to an artifact that could keep tabs on me if I came too close, too early. In which case they could instantly call up an army to keep me at bay until my assailant was finished with his machinations.

"Anyway," Alucard continued. "Paradise and Lost were still freaked out about the alley slaughter this morning. They even asked *me* to help with guard duty, and I haven't been asked to do anything useful in *months*." He arched an eyebrow at me. "You really did a number on them. It looked personal. *Very* personal..."

I nodded, not denying it. I even felt marginally pleased that I had caused a panic among their ranks. Those...*things* I had executed last night had been true monsters—and that appellation had nothing to do with them being vampires.

"Roland's vampires deserved worse than I gave them," I said calmly, not attempting to hide my double meaning—that Alucard was *also* one of Roland's vampires. He got the message, leaning back ever so slightly. "They didn't know the meaning of the word *consent*," I added, deciding it was wise to dial back the threat. No use putting him on defense so soon.

He cocked his head, frowning for a moment. Then it seemed to suddenly dawn on him, and his eyes smoldered as he stared off into the middle distance. After about ten seconds, he turned back to me. "Yeah. Okay. You did me a favor, then. I suspected such...*tendencies* about a few of them, but I never had any proof. Otherwise I would have found a way to take care of it myself."

He bowed his head to me, and there was no question that his unspoken *thank you* was authentic. I nodded back, acknowledging his gesture in the same manner it was delivered.

26

I let out a frustrated breath, thinking on the demon angle. "And you're *certain* that a demon can't break through Roland's barrier?" I pressed, needing to be certain.

He nodded grimly. "Roland and Henri summoned a demon just before the barrier went up. Then Roland *sacrificed* the demon—along with many others—to *power* the fucking barrier. Trust me. No one is getting through that thing until Roland decides to take it down. It's why Paradise and Lost were so freaked out about the necklace *dinging* yesterday."

Henri again...

I kept my face composed, wondering again if Henri could be the one behind my demon affliction, playing everyone like puppets despite the apparent broken man demeanor I had seen outside the church. Maybe that had been a disguise in itself. Like the *Usual Suspects* movie with Kevin Spacey as Keyser Söze. Because I knew for a fact that Henri had been an extremely powerful vampire, and that even Roland had tread carefully around him before all of this. I turned to Alucard, thinking.

"Is there *any* chance that Roland is being played?" I asked, taking a risk. "That someone else is actually behind all this madness?"

Alucard shook his head sadly, looking as if he empathized with my pain. "Not a chance. I've been here from the beginning, Callie. As much as I hate to say it, this is all Roland."

I kept my gaze steady, reading him for any sign of defeat. I hadn't seen any crimson glow to his eyes like Roland's other oathbound followers, but with the Silvers there had definitely been some tie between the two—even if it had seemed conflicted, Roland's crimson cord battling with Alucard's cord of golden light.

Was Alucard his own man or was he a pawn? Either way, he was a criminal working for Roland. Worse, he might not even know about that sinister crimson cord latching onto him, thinking himself independent when he was in fact a puppet of Roland. I kept all these thoughts from my face as I studied Alucard "What about Henri? Every time I hear Roland has done something terrible, Henri is never far away..." I suggested.

Alucard...

Let out a harsh, incredulous laugh, his momentary empathy evaporating in an instant. Cain and Claire shot me considering looks, as if silently asking if they could kill Alucard yet, but they didn't speak out loud.

Alucard slowly regained his composure, dabbing at his eyes with his sleeves. "I'm sorry to laugh. I get it. Really, I do. It's just...you haven't been here. Haven't seen what Roland has truly become," he explained, regaining that momentary sympathy. "I suspected Henri at first, too, refusing to accept the fact that Roland had changed so utterly. But that all changed in one fateful day," he said, losing the amused smile. "The day Roland earned his nickname, the Red Pastor."

I leaned forward, wondering how this could be any worse than what I'd already heard about Haven. "Enlighten me, vampire," I said, coldly, not appreciating his outburst.

He nodded in resignation, propping his elbows on his knees.

"Henri is an old, and very powerful, vampire—but he couldn't use magic like Roland. However, old vampires run across all manner of interesting tidbits as the years go by, which apparently really seemed to interest Roland." That tracked with Xuanwu's theory—that someone had told him about Dracula. "Those conversations were before my time, but I do know that Henri gave Roland the books on how to make his barriers—since Henri was unable to do anything with them himself, not having magic at his disposal."

"What books?" I asked almost feverishly, thinking that Solomon might have some solution in the Temple that could counteract the books.

Alucard shrugged unhelpfully, deflating my excitement. "Magic books.

All I can tell you about the barriers is that blood powered them, and I only know *that* because I saw some of the sacrifices in person." He sensed the frustrated look on my face and lifted his hands helplessly. "Look, I don't know anything about magic. I don't even know enough to *make up* a story. I've spent time around Nate, and all I can tell you about his magic is that when he lifts up his hands, a lot of people die. How?" He wiggled his fingers dramatically. "*Magic*. Other than that, I have no fucking clue. I can't tell you what I don't know. But I *can* tell you that even the Shepherds were stunned by the barriers—probably because it cut off their reserve troops and they never could figure out how to take them down."

I sighed in frustration, waving him on to continue. He sounded genuinely annoyed—as if he had been mad at himself for not having an answer long before I ever asked the question.

"After the barriers went up without a hitch, Roland began to grow reclusive—not spending much time with Henri or myself. We had kind of expected the opposite after such a big win. Or at least some inkling of why he'd wanted the damned things in the first place. Because as soon as they were up, he no longer seemed concerned about the Shepherds constantly bothering us in the streets. He told us to keep them busy, and to keep the infestation of spies from snooping on the church," he said, eyes flicking to Claire meaningfully, "but it was an offhanded command, like he was just trying to get us to leave him alone."

He absently scuffed his boot on the floor, either collecting his thoughts or gathering his resolve, I wasn't sure.

"That's when I began to grow nervous that my time was coming to an end—truly realizing for the first time that I had no way to escape. I wasn't in the circle of trust anymore. Hadn't *ever* been in the circle of trust, as a matter of fact. I began to fear that maybe Henri had done something to Roland. That Henri had even killed him or subjugated him somehow..."

I nodded. "That exact thought had crossed my mind," I admitted.

Alucard looked up at me, his eyes haunted. "Apparently, a rumor just like that began to spread through the vampires, and Roland happened to hear about it. He called a meeting that very night, and told us to all wait outside in front of the church. There were about a hundred of us, give or take, all wondering which one of us was going to pay for spreading rumors. Or if we were going to find out that the rumors were, in fact, true."

He kept his eyes low as he continued. "The doors kicked open and a bloody sack of a broken man was hurled down the steps. We all thought it was Roland's dinner," Alucard said in a hollow tone, still staring at the ground. "But when that bloody man lifted his head to turn back and look at the entrance of the church, we realized it was *Henri Bellerose*. Roland calmly walked down the steps, his once-white dress shirt literally dripping with blood, and he grabbed Henri by the hair, ignoring his screams, his apologies, his pleas. I will never forget that image. I see it every time I look at Henri," Alucard whispered. "That was the first time I heard one of the new vampires call him the Red Pastor...and he said it like he had gazed upon God. It was just a terrified, awed whisper that night, but it soon became a title to be feared by all."

We sat absolutely still, stunned silent.

Alucard met my eyes briefly. "Then Roland ripped out Henri's fangs with his bare hands."

My eyes almost bugged out of my head at Alucard's blunt delivery, and I thought I heard Claire gag. Good god.

"Does that mean he's no longer a vampire?" Claire asked incredulously.

Alucard shook his head. "No. He's still a vampire, and that's the point. He's an old, powerful, Master Vampire...who now needs help eating his food."

"Holy shit," Cain breathed, folding his arms. "Roland neutered him."

Alucard nodded with a mirthless smile. "Roland bound Henri's power into those teeth, inscribing them with symbols right there on the steps of the church for all to see. He even explained it for us non-wizardly types—maybe for Henri, too. It was a blood oath that forced Henri to always serve Roland—that Henri would starve to death and wither away to nothing without Roland's support. He called him *Renfield*."

Cain was shaking his head numbly, having met Henri and knowing full well how powerful he had been. Renfield...like that character in the original Dracula lore.

"Henri is literally a servant now—a brittle husk of the man he'd once been. He lives with an ever-present fear, now, like he's always one loud sound away from running for his life. But he *can't* run and he knows it. He can't do *anything* that might bring direct or even indirect harm to Roland. He can't even take his own *life*. It's disgusting. Worse than death, and all because of a *rumor* that challenged Roland's authority." Alucard shivered, rubbing at his arms forcefully. "And Roland did *that* to the man who gave him the barriers..."

He turned to look at our horrified faces, nodding somberly. "I see it in your eyes. Sense it in your heartbeats. The distrust, the suspicion of me..." he shook his head and finally shrugged. "You wonder why I haven't fought Roland or tried to run away and hide in a cave...maybe now you understand," he said softly.

I sat frozen in my seat, unable to speak. I hadn't even known such a thing was possible. A Renfield. One thing was for certain. Henri had just been dragged kicking and screaming from my dwindling suspect pool.

27

Something he had said in his story caught my attention. Something I had almost missed because I was so focused on Henri's plight. "You were his fixer, weren't you? You were the one who bought off the politicians and media. That was your role for Roland."

Cain and Claire both made soft, startled sounds.

Alucard nodded, not looking proud. "It's a talent of mine. It's how I took over New Orleans, back in the day. Before I grew bored of the politics and packed up for St. Louis."

Cain grunted again. "Just like that, huh?" he said dryly.

Alucard shrugged. "I used money and influence to make the humans in charge look the other way. Or, I made them an offer they couldn't refuse. For those unwilling to take hush money or succumb to blackmail, I offered to *turn* them. You'd be surprised how many suddenly preferred to take the money," he said thoughtfully. "Anyway, I took over the city not through violence, but through business and handshakes. Politics. Roland said he wanted minimal human casualties—but I'm pretty sure he just didn't want outside interference."

As disgusted as I was about Alucard's part in all of this, I had to give him credit. His tactics had a far lower mortality rate than open war. And as much as I hated to admit it, I had no evidence that Alucard had done anything unforgivable. No murder sprees or anything. Just...white collar crimes. Which only added to my frustration.

No matter what suspicions I held, there had been no faking Alucard's fear of Roland. That didn't vindicate him or anything, because everyone was afraid of Roland—even his most devoted followers. Like Henri Bellerose.

I suppressed a shudder. If Roland could make a Renfield out of a vampire as strong as Henri, who was to say Roland hadn't already completed the pair, making *both* of his lieutenants his Renfields? His blood slaves. Or that he *intended* to when his schedule cleared up. The look in Alucard's non-crimson eyes told me the latter was currently on his mind.

Alucard hadn't let slip any hint that he knew of Roland's ultimate goal, but I knew the Daywalker was exceedingly clever, a Master Vampire in his own right before he ever became a Daywalker. His ability to overthrow the city through politicking was proof of that.

But what did that mean for me, now? I wasn't about to offer up answers. Not yet. I simply couldn't risk it. I needed to see Alucard prove which line of the sand he was on with action, not words. To burn the bridge behind him, so to speak.

"You know why I'm here, Alucard. Why I kidnapped you..." I said, taking a big risk. "I need a way into the church. I need to see Roland face to face. Now more than ever..."

Alucard was shaking his head before I even finished speaking. "He's not the man you remember, Callie. Trust me. I don't even know what he is anymore. I almost ran screaming when he passed me in the hall the other day, so unfamiliar with seeing him that I feared he was there to kill me. He was muttering under his breath about a castle and the blood moon tomorrow night. He didn't even seem to notice I was there."

The three of us grew very still, but Alucard hadn't noticed and kept on talking.

"I think he's starting to lose it," he finally said, glancing up at me warily as if fearing my response. "I don't think seeing you miraculously alive will do anything but give him that final push over the edge," he said very softly.

I nodded, trying to keep my face relaxed and my voice devoid of any particular interest as I asked, "What is happening tomorrow night during this Blood Moon?"

Alucard frowned absently, not seeming overly concerned. "A sermon. Just like he does every Friday. I call it his black mass," he muttered. "But not where anyone can overhear."

I stared at him blankly. Roland did this every Friday? If he was attempting a ritual tomorrow night, maybe he'd begun practicing the steps a long time ago. To perfect the spell without anyone noticing. I nodded to myself, getting more confident with each passing second.

I looked up to find Alucard studying me silently. "I hate to break it to you, but if you really do know a way to get out of Kansas City, take it. If you happen to have an extra pass, I wouldn't turn it down. Give me an oath to swear and my life is yours. I only came here in the first place because Roland called me, sounding distressed. I figured I could hang out with him for a few days, get him back on his feet. He didn't tell me about your disappearance or any of this other crazy shit he had planned, and by the time I learned about it, it was too late."

He was silent for a few moments, then he finally let out a breath. "I know how this all looks. I could be working for Roland right now, feeding you just enough information to buy your trust so I could escape with you. I would suspect the same if I was in your shoes. But it's not like I have much choice. Disobey Roland and I die. I'm just lucky not to have wound up like Henri," he muttered. "Yet." Then he barked out a humorless laugh. "Who would have thought I would have ever been thankful for imprisonment?" He noticed us watching him and waved a hand. "Do yourself a favor and get out of town while you still can. You don't need an invite to my pity party. Just..." he cut off abruptly, averting his eyes in shame, "tell Nate that I'm sorry. That I would rather die fighting by his side than live forever like *this*," he whispered, vehemently.

The barely bottled up fury in his voice when speaking about Nate served to instantly snuff out my own building frustration. To see him respond so emotionally...

It wasn't the reaction of a powerful vampire losing a powerful *ally*. It was a man talking about losing his friend. I found my anger cooling to learn that at least Alucard still maintained that sliver of honor.

Nate was an arrogant bastard, but he had a roguish charm and a streak of loyalty a mile wide. Despite his many mistakes and flaws, he really was good at picking up strays and putting them back on their own two feet. In building *families*—not just an army of *allies*.

And making them stronger as individuals through tough love. A different playbook from Roland.

I took a calming breath, closing my eyes for a moment. "Do you have any word on Nate?" I asked in a soft tone. The last time I had seen Nate had been inside the Doors, and he'd been living on a mountain, looking like he really needed to get back to civilization before he turned savage. He had looked haggard, worn out, exhausted, and a hint of madness had danced in those green eyes.

Then again, that madness could have been because I declined to accept the Horseman's Mask he had offered me. Thinking of Nate, I felt my stomach flutter as Xuanwu's request whispered in my ear again. That his men could follow hope's murderer.

Alucard smiled distantly, staring off at nothing. "Tory tells me that Nate fought Mordred again in Fae, but that's it. Hearing what's happened here... we agreed it was best not to give me any information that might be...taken from me. I do know Nate's apparently been living in Fae ever since that fight. Almost a year, now. That's all I know for certain."

I frowned in alarm. He'd been *living* in Fae? For a *year*? With the time flowing strangely between our realms, did that mean he'd actually spent *years* in Fae or a few *months*? Hearing this, I also wondered again if my seeing him on my trip through the Doors had also been real—like my meeting with Starlight or my parents outside the church the night they abandoned me.

I put my concerns for Nate on a shelf and digested everything I'd learned so far.

There was one way I might be able to get a definitive answer about the demon disguise infecting me, and it was looking more and more like I needed to entertain it, despite the risks to my soul. I knew no one was going to like that plan, so I wisely kept my mouth shut.

All in all, it was gearing up to be a really shitty day.

I settled my gaze on Alucard. "We're not going anywhere," I told him firmly, drumming my fingers across my knees. "We need answers, and you need to put proof to your words. Let's marry those two goals. You and Cain will find out anything you can on Roland's Black Mass tomorrow—even if you think it's trivial. Can you explain away your abduction? Maybe say that the demon left you alone and you broke free," I mused, tapping my lips. Then I grinned delightedly. "She was too preoccupied speaking with *another* demon to notice your escape."

Alucard flashed his fangs wickedly, a spark of anticipation igniting deep in his eyes at the newfound sense of purpose. "Give them something to fear that's more important than my abduction—another demon. That's genius," he said, nodding his approval.

I shrugged. "It's a talent of mine," I said, repeating his earlier humble brag. "You sure you're up for it?" I asked, glancing at his wrists.

He nodded, eyeing the *Vampyr* bracelets warily. "Nothing a little sunshine won't fix." He turned to me after a brief pause. "Does this mean you trust me?"

I smiled darkly at him. "Of course. That's why I'm sending the world's first murderer with you. To keep that trust alive...or not."

Cain grinned delightedly. "Cool," he said, thumbing his dagger fondly.

Alucard sighed, nodding his head in resignation. It was better than any other option open to him and he knew it.

"Good. I've got a few things of my own to look into. We will meet back here tonight."

Cain extended a hand, offering to help Alucard to his feet. The two studied each other in silence for a moment or two before Alucard finally traded grips with him, dusting off his hands immediately after. Cain smirked at the potential slight, but Alucard may have just been doing it out of habit. Noticing the twinkle in his eyes, I doubted it.

"Follow me, disco ball," Cain said, "we need to find some wheels." He paused to frown at me suspiciously, as if only just now realizing we would be left unsupervised. "And what things are you going to look into?"

I shrugged innocently. "Claire and I will head to Solomon's Temple to hopefully find some answers from a wise man. They are in short supply here..." They each narrowed their eyes at me. "I need to ask some uncomfortable questions. And I need to check on Phix."

Cain's gaze grew harder. "And murder hope..."

Alucard flinched, catching the reference to Nate Temple. "Hold on a damned minute—"

"Let's keep talk of zoo animals out of this," I told Cain meaningfully, interrupting Alucard. Cain nodded in understanding—no blabbing about what Xuanwu had told us about Dracula—but Alucard looked to have about three dozen new questions. Cain was going to have a rough day. "Keep Alucard honest, learn what you can, and meet back here tonight."

"You will stay out of trouble?" Cain pressed. Then he grunted. "Never mind." He rounded on Claire, pointing a commanding finger. "You, woman. Keep her out of trouble or I'll spank your hairy ass."

"You say the sweetest things," Claire grinned. "I'll be sure to tell Kenai about you."

Cain grinned. "You do that. But keep her safe." His smile shifted to something cold and final—no longer amused but a deadly warning.

Claire nodded, unperturbed. "I only just got her back. I won't let her out of my sight."

With one last wary look, the two men finally turned to leave the cave.

Once confident we were alone, Claire turned to me. "What stupid idea is percolating in that head of yours? Which domino are we really knocking down first?"

I smiled, letting out a breath. "I love you, Claire."

She shrugged self-importantly. "Hairy chests don't solve problems, they *create* problems. Women, on the other hand, create solutions to *end* problems," she said matter-of-factly. "But I will be there to keep your head on your shoulders. Figuratively and literally."

"I need to make a long-distance phone call." I wasn't about to share details until it was too late for her to stop me.

She studied me suspiciously, just like Cain had. "Call them collect so they have to pay for it. Otherwise, I'm not sure we can afford to borrow more trouble."

"Relax. We're just going to go feed some pigeons," I said, smiling darkly.

"I think everyone has made it perfectly clear that you aren't getting into Abundant Angel," Claire said. "The Shepherds are a waste of time, anyway. Roland doesn't care about *them*," she said, heavily implying who Roland *did* care about. Dracula.

"We're just going to feed them. Throw out some bread crumbs," I said innocently, not correcting her misconception.

She let out a long sigh and nodded. "Well, it's only wizards, I guess. You've thrown down with them often enough."

"Sure have," I said cheerfully, trying not to look guilty.

28

We had driven to an old abandoned warehouse I had once been held captive in. Good times. Back then, my captors had intended well and had prepared the space for my imprisonment accordingly. I was banking on that preparation now, knowing I would need every bit of it—plus some—to survive. The juice was worth the squeeze, though. I hoped.

Claire looked ready to shift at the slightest sound of a rat or gust of wind against the exterior walls of the metal building. She knew when I was being shady, even when I was trying to hide it. And she'd been to this place before too—when she'd invaded it to try and save *me*.

"I don't think Shepherds hang out here," she muttered sarcastically.

I smirked, finishing up the circle before wiping loose hair out of my eyes with my forearm. "Who said anything about Shepherds?" I asked sweetly, climbing back to my feet to inspect my work. It was flawless, in my opinion. Then again, I didn't really have a guidebook on how to do this, and had never spent much time practicing rituals of any sort. I had never been interested in this witchy type of magic—rituals, spells, and complex incantations. I was more of a fast and hard kind of wizard.

I was hoping that I'd stored up a fair amount of good will with my intended target, and that it would be enough to let me skate by any steps I may have overlooked.

Although banking on Divine Intervention seemed a bad bet, I was willing to take the odds.

I took a deep breath, clicked my heels together for good measure, prayed that I remembered enough of Roland's teachings—ironically—to not be smited on the spot and...

I spoke Archangel Michael's name out loud in a bold, authoritative, confident voice, pulling deep on what I remembered both Roland and Father David had tried to hammer into my memory over the last decade.

"Archangel Michael! Archistrategos! Supreme Commander of the Heavenly Hosts! I call upon your aid!"

Claire gasped in horror, having no idea what I'd intended. The walls rocked as if a mortar had struck the ground outside, or as if a giant fist had pummeled the wall itself—like an apartment neighbor banging on the wall at three in the morning, telling me to pipe the hell down.

Like a good neighbor, I decided to turn the volume knob up instead.

And I spoke Michael's name a second time. "Archangel Michael! The sword in God's right hand! The Angel of Death!" I bellowed.

The very walls of the warehouse began to rattle and quake, metal squealing and protesting even as some of the bolts cracked and snapped, raining dust down from the rafters. Claire squeaked behind me, practically panting, but not daring to speak out loud and potentially ruin my plan—not that it would have mattered one way or another.

My stomach fluttered nervously as I prepared to say it a third time. "Archangel Mic—"

A sharp crack of lightning struck the ground about an inch from my foot, ruining my circle, numbing my feet, and singeing my eyebrows. The temperature in the warehouse dropped by about thirty degrees the millisecond before I was tackled by a manifestation of an Angel's sheer will, sending me grunting and gasping to fly across the room, bowling Claire over behind me like a struck pin. Even as she fell, I heard the familiar sound of fabric exploding as she shifted into her better than ten-foot-tall polar bear form. She roared a challenge at the threat, her new form ready, willing, and able to take a helluva lot more damage than most could dish out.

I tried to get up only to realize a hand the size of my torso held me down, throbbing with an arctic chill that threatened to freeze the very marrow in my bones. Icy vapor clouded around me, veiling my attacker, but a face suddenly emerged from the fog—a face as cold, merciless, and brutal as any I had ever seen. A warrior's face. A veteran's face. The face of a man who had lost brothers in a war that my puny mortal mind could not even pretend to *begin* to comprehend.

And...it wasn't Michael.

"You ignorant, vapid, witless *child*!" Eae snapped, his teeth actually clacking together as if he was itching to bite my nose off. His breath was like dry ice, making my tongue instantly dry out and turn numb. "What devilry is this?" he demanded.

"Eae..." I managed in a breathless whisper. "Imagine seeing a guy like you in a place like this. Remember the last time we—"

He lifted me a few inches from the ground and then slammed me back down, banging my head against the solid concrete hard enough to make my vision wink out for a moment. Claire snarled furiously, claws scraping at the concrete in warning, but any direct attack on her part would only result in my instant death. Eae had me dead to rights so didn't even bother looking up at her.

I struggled to focus on him, realizing that he looked a lot angrier—and more powerful—than the last time I had seen him. Than *any* time I had seen him.

"How *dare* you speak about the last time we met," he snarled viciously. "I don't know how you broke through the barrier—or what you hoped to accomplish here—but I vow to send you right back to Hell at my earliest convenience." His arm quivered, and his massive claws began to tighten on my chest as he shook me, eyes dancing with rage, making my head flop back and forth like a bobblehead doll.

I stared at his great massive wings—like clouds of stone, glass, and metal fragments suspended in shifting gel. Except the tips of his feathers looked sharp enough to shave a layer off of a hair follicle. Claire's warning growl changed in pitch, almost a coughing bark, and I realized she was aiming it away from Eae.

Eae's grip lessened marginally, and I flicked my eyes to see three men staring at us.

And one of them was familiar.

Arthur—the homeless man I had introduced to Father David for a job at Abundant Angel Catholic Church. He looked harder, his hair swept back into a warrior's ponytail, and a long scar split his cheek, deep enough to now be a permanent indent in his flesh. His eyes glittered with calm, cool authority. Determination. I couldn't look into those eyes without feeling both pain and fear. That ultimately, his predicament was all my fault. Both for current events and for me placing him in the hands of the church—to be scooped up by Fabrizio as a future Shepherd thanks to Roland's ex-communication.

And no one but me even knew who he truly was. At least it had been a secret the last time I had seen him. Even from this distance, I knew the two hooded figures flanking him were wizards, and although young, they looked battle-hardened. Shepherds in training. Just like I had once been under Roland's tutelage. And look how well that had turned out for me—pinned beneath an avenging angel of the Lord and stuff. Their careers were on the fast-track.

Their rise to the ranks of full Shepherd was predicated on a current Shepherd falling in battle, and I couldn't help but grimace inwardly at the irony there. One man rising as another fell—just like the angels in that ancient battle with Lucifer.

"I thought I smelled SHIT," I murmured, smiling faintly to ease the tension. "Shepherds in training," I explained.

Arthur's lips set into a grim line, finding no humor in my quip. "If you would be so kind," he began, turning to address Eae with a respectful dip of his chin, "kill the demon or incapacitate her. We could keep her in the cells below the church until we figure out how she slipped past the Red Pastor's barrier. Or how she intended to siphon up more of her ilk from Hell and smuggle them through this cursed barrier. Then you can send her back home."

Too late, I realized what was going on, even though it seemed truly impossible. My stupid demon disguise was strong enough to even trick an *angel*? Give me a break! What the hell powered this thing?

Another thought made me wince. I'd asked Eae if he remembered the last time we met. Me, looking like a fallen angel, and casually asking an angel about the last time we'd met.

And *Eae* literally translated to *demon thwarter*...

No wonder Eae had looked about ready to kill me.

"And the bear?" Eae asked coolly.

"The First Shepherd likely has many questions for her. He will be sorely disappointed to hear that a friend of the White Rose now consorts with demons." He said this matter-of-factly, but his voice was tinged with empathy and disappointment.

What name had they heard me shouting if not Michael's?

I wondered, very briefly, who would have appeared if I would have said Michael's name a third time—whether it would have summoned Michael or someone much, much worse. And if Michael had answered the call, only to find a demon behind it…a fearful shudder rocked me from neck to tailbone at the mere thought of that. Thankfully, Eae seemed convinced that it wouldn't have worked, regardless. Thank god. I had dismissed the demon disguise concern, assuming that surely an angel would be able to see through it.

On the bright side, maybe I had just won a ticket to Abundant Angel—a chance to convince Fabrizio who I really was—

"This one was obviously attempting to summon a fellow demon," Eae said, interrupting my train of thought as he flexed one of his wings high, the fanned feathers seeming to twinkle maliciously at the tips. "I would rather keep this city demon-free, as it has been for the past year. I think it's best to cut out this first sign of cancer before it spreads."

Arthur dipped his eyes respectfully. "As you wish, Eae. Take down the bear," he commanded the two wizards beside him, already dismissing me entirely. My eyes widened in stunned disbelief. No trial or conversation? Just swift judgment? This wasn't like Eae at all.

Eae locked eyes with me, his smile stretching wider. "And beheading is less paperwork," he admitted, in the cold, merciless, soulless tone of a true devil—an accountant.

"No—"

His wing was already descending, and I knew it was sharp enough that I might not even feel my head separate from my body, because everything had spiraled downward so fast that I didn't even have time to try *considering* throwing my power against it.

Two pinpoints of crackling blue flame within a thick white fog appeared out of nowhere and pounded into Eae's wing, deflecting it enough to slam the tip down beside my ear rather than my neck. It sunk a few inches into the concrete with a sound that made my ears pop.

Eae spun wildly, knocked from atop me, and roaring with outrage. I gasped, coughing weakly as I struggled to my feet, stunned to find Last Breath—now in his huge bipedal white lion form—squaring off against Eae not five feet away from me.

I now had a new appreciation for his name, since he'd arrived just as I was certain I had taken my last breath. But how the hell had he found me, here in this random warehouse? And...why hadn't he arrived to back me up *sooner?*

Claire had knocked down her two would-be captors—one was groaning on the ground beside a SHIT-shaped dent in the aluminum siding, and another was cursing from within a tower of toppled pallets.

Arthur held a sword steadily before him, his eyes flickering from me, to Claire, and finally to Eae and the albino lion dude, gauging which one he should focus on. He didn't look scared but determined. It was hard to see Last Breath as anything other than a demon. What else was strong enough to stand up to an angel?

"Don't kill them!" I shouted at both of my allies. "They know not what they do!"

Eae bellowed in outrage, hurling Last Breath off his chest and into a support beam, denting it with a shower of falling dust, before rounding on me with a glare. He glanced sharply back at Last Breath, a hesitant frown slowly crossing his features.

Arthur shouted out, his eyes focused entirely on Claire. "That thing was hunting the White Rose the last time I saw her. Might even be her killer. Do *not* let him escape." The two SHITs were climbing to their feet, now, murderous frowns on their faces. Arthur spared a pitiless look at them. "Not you two fools!" he snapped, hurting their little feelings. "Get back to the church. This could be a diversion." They nodded, looking both unhappy they were not permitted to fight yet also alarmed at the potential danger for the church if this was indeed a diversion—perhaps even the herald of a demonic *invasion*. They sprinted for the exit, not bothering to look back.

Which was surprising. Arthur—a non-wizard—facing down a shifter polar bear all by himself, and not looking even the slightest bit concerned?

Arthur followed their departure with his eyes as if making sure they weren't ambushed by yet more of my secret demonic allies. In the distraction, I darted towards Claire and squeezed her furry arm—thankfully she had seen me coming in her peripheral vision or she might have instinctively decapitated me by sheer reflex. "We're leaving!" I shouted at her. "We can't beat them without killing them." Claire's ears tucked back against her head, but she kept her eyes locked on Arthur as I lifted the Seal of Solomon towards my lips.

Because it was the only way I could think of getting us to safety. I wasn't about to battle it out with two of my old friends. They were just doing their jobs, battling what they thought was a demon. They certainly wouldn't entertain a friendly debate on the virtues and vices of Callie Penrose—let alone give me the time to convince them who I really was.

Eae spun, aiming his angelic laser focused glare our way. His eyes darted to the silver ring on my knuckle and his lips parted wordlessly. I hesitated, feeling a flash of heat on my scalp as the Seal touched my lips. Last Breath suddenly gripped Eae by one of the wings and hurled him directly past us at Arthur—who was now sprinting towards us in an attempt to stop whatever he thought I was doing. The Angel slammed into Arthur, sending them both tumbling.

And the strangest thing happened as Last Breath grabbed onto Claire's outstretched paw.

Namely, my two friends simply disappeared, violently ripped from my grip.

Before I could react, the scene before me froze like I had snapped a polaroid picture with my eyes. Then, like a newspaper catching alight, that polaroid picture bloomed with silver flames at the edges, racing inwards in an ever-shrinking ring of silver fire. It was surreal.

My eyes were riveted on the center of that photo.

At the incredulous look on both Eae and Arthur's frozen faces. The silver flame met in the center and everything disintegrated to ashes, leaving me briefly hovering in a gray void of nothingness.

Then, like a pane of glass hit by a rock, the void simply shattered into billions of shards, and I thought to myself, *what a lovely means of teleporting. So soothing and relaxing.*

Darkness swallowed me up and then shat me right back out.

I closed my eyes in order to truly relish the unique experience.

To me, it corroborated my theory that even different planes of existence were operated by disgruntled, bitter, government employees who were counting down the hours until they could collect their pension and quit the jobs that they so loathed. Their one respite being those small opportunities that allowed them to cause as much anguish as possible to those poor, unfortunate souls forced to step in front of their greasy service windows.

Those customer service representatives handling me now were having the time of their lives.

29

My existence was darkness—no source of light or sound—as I imagined hold music while waiting for the complaint department of inter-realm travel.

Your experience is not very important to us. Please remain in limbo for the next available operator. Wait time approximately five eternities.

Then, in reverse this time, a needlepoint of flame bloomed to life before me and expanded outward in a raging wash of fire, eating away at the darkness to reveal a cavernous room of tan and red-flecked marble pillars. Tables laden with beakers, test tubes, books, and dozens of alchemical ingredients surrounded me as the fire finally reached the edges of my vision and hissed out like a puff of steam. I stood motionless, waiting for the other shoe to drop and something entirely abnormal to happen again. Maybe with ice this time.

But thankfully, nothing changed. I assessed the room warily, wondering where I was. Where my friends had gone. Had Eae done something to interrupt our travel, metaphysically kicking my ankle as I ran away?

"Who knows what an angel can do," I murmured out loud, my voice echoing in the large marble chamber. The carved pillars were at least three times as wide as my waist, and I followed them up, and up, and up to finally spot the ceiling very high above, making me feel like I was in a canyon. I spun in a slow circle, searching for any other signs of life.

Just to be sure, I walked a quick circuit around the room, ignoring the doors that most likely led off to other rooms, verifying Claire or Last Breath weren't hidden behind a couch or something, unconscious and choking to death on their own tongues. No luck.

Despite there being no sunlight, two mature trees leaned against the outer wall, seeming to grow out of the marble tile floor, the branches spreading wide with budding pink and white flowers decorating the leaves. I almost jumped out of my boots when the branches shifted slightly as if at a breeze. Except there was no breeze in this enclosed space. I nervously looked away from the trees.

A few couches and chairs littered the room, along with wardrobes, dressers, and numerous worktables cluttered to overflowing with even more varied collections of bizarre and strange items. Articles of clothing, shoes, and papers littered the floor, were draped over furniture, or lay in piles here and there, as if someone had left in a hurry, packing whatever they could grab in ten seconds or less.

It felt at once both cozy and clinical, like it was both a work space and living quarters.

With nothing else to do, I walked up to one of the tables that looked more recently used than the others. A handwritten journal lay open, and the pages were scrawled with what looked like a dozen different calculus equations. Except the variables looked like runes—demonic, angelic, druidic, Norse, Greek, zodiac, kanji, and even a few crude Hieroglyphs. I grunted at the complexity of the gibberish, shaking my head. "Looks like some unholy union of cutting-edge mathematics and various alphabets conceived a child—the language of creation," I muttered absently, thinking out loud. My voice was immediately swallowed up by the vast space, making me feel like I stood at the bottom of a well.

I frowned, wondering where that thought had come from, why I'd called it *the language of creation*. Maybe it was because the equations consisted of symbols taken from the alphabets of a large variety of known languages. And letters, numbers, and symbols were the building blocks—the beginnings—needed to create language.

After a few moments, I was startled to realize I was leaning closer to the page, muttering under my breath and shaking my head—and I didn't recall having moved. That was alarming, but my subconscious mind seemed to have chugged a bottle of Mountain Dew, cracked its knuckles, and then stepped up to the control station.

"Not the language of creation," I said out loud, thinking over my earlier definition. Something about it just seemed wrong—or incomplete. "Alphabet...*al*...*pha*...bet," I murmured, breaking down the syllables in order to pinpoint exactly what was bothering me. And that's when it hit me.

Alpha. Alpha meant *the beginning*.

Conversely, Omega meant *the end*.

Alpha and Omega—*the beginning* and *the end*.

I realized I was nodding satisfactorily, leaning away from the paper with a sensation of accomplishment. I shuddered at the alien duality—my subconscious and conscious mind working as a team without my express choice. But...they were right. *I* was right.

This wasn't the language of creation—a collection of individual *alpha*-bets...

This was a singular collection taken from those earlier, beginning alphabets to form something entirely new. I shuddered in realization.

This was...an *omega*-bet—*the language of the end*.

For some reason, that thought resonated within me like a perfectly-tuned guitar chord. Realizing that, I felt decidedly uneasy. Like the equations had purred to life at my revised definition, even though the revision hadn't truly felt like my mind had birthed it. More like...

I'd *read* it from the equations, understanding it on some abstract, subconscious level.

Why in the world was someone building the omegabet—*the language of the end?*

I let out a nervous breath, deciding not to let myself study the equations too closely anymore. To give them only a cursory glance from here on out.

The equations were all jumbled together, implying that the previous half of the journal likely led up to the current theories on the open page before me, and I was expected to simply accept how the author had gotten to this point in their savant-level ramblings. Although I was no expert—despite what my subconscious thought—I sensed the equations were incomplete.

I flipped the thick leather page backwards to see hastily scrawled diagrams, thumbnail sketches of a sword, a pyramid, a lightning bolt, an hourglass, a broken halo, a hammer, two mountain peaks, and a feather. Feverishly flipping more pages, I found moon cycles, star charts, pages of

Fae spells, a very rough map, a hurried drawing of a mountain and a rainbow —with a winged unicorn zipping towards it as if to impale the arch—and a few pages full of ornate family trees, using only initials to mark the branches.

I suddenly felt very self-conscious.

This was probably something I shouldn't be looking at without permission, let alone unsupervised *and* without permission. It wasn't mine, and this all looked very personal. Like a diary of a mad man. Yet...much of it looked hauntingly familiar, although I couldn't quite place why. Perhaps my imagination was still running wild after my unexpected inter-realm Uber driver had suddenly kicked me off his intergalactic Vespa to land here.

I shook my head and took a step back, briefly taking in the rest of the long work table. On the far edge sat a collection of leather strips arranged to form the outline of a shattered sword—laid out in order so that the pieces needed only to be shifted closer to complete the blade. The pieces were made of old black leather, darker than coal, and seemed to be weighing down yet *more* scraps of paper filled with yet *more* diagrams, calculations and hastily scribbled notes. Just beside that rested a pile of old jewelry, consisting of enough precious stones to make a jeweler drool, and a bluish-green serpentine dragon figurine about the size of my palm held down a pile of long white feathers.

Three marble pedestals, about chest height stood near a plush, high-backed velvet chair with tall arms. The outermost pedestals each held a rectangular glass box that was about six inches tall and open on the top. The box on the left was full of opal white marbles, and the box on the right was full of smoky black marbles.

The center pedestal had a velvet cloth draped over the flat top. Two of the white marbles rested atop the cushioned fabric and there was an ivory handwritten notecard as well. I took a step closer to read it.

Mem

Or

E's

I turned away, wondering if it was more of the omegabet or something.

My attention was pulled away by a nearby stack of small animal skeletons and beakers of dried blood resting above unlit burners. Rituals, written in blood, filled pages and pages of scattered papers surrounding the skeletons, like some cheeky practitioner had forgotten to tidy up after their dark sacrifice to Satan.

I shivered, averting my eyes. Whoever lived here didn't appear to be a *help-an-old-lady-cross-the-street* type of person, and I was suddenly reminded of the demon Johnathan's workroom I had discovered what seemed like a lifetime ago. It had been crammed full of notes about Missouri and the influx of beings coming here. Was this another such place? Had I found some other member of his demonic terrorist sleeper cell?

I finally shook my head, turning away. I needed to find out where I was before snooping any further. What if the owner was here and walked in on me? If Eae had redirected me here, I was betting the owner wouldn't be entirely pleased to meet me, because Eae hadn't been pleased to see me back in that warehouse. He had seen only an enemy. A demon. A fallen brother.

Or...maybe this had nothing to do with Eae. It could be a reaction from trying to travel back to Solomon's Temple in spite of Roland's barrier. My breath caught, wondering if I was actually inside Roland's church. Or maybe Abundant Angel. There were levels below the Shepherd's church that I had never visited...

All in all, having my method of travel hijacked was not a promising prospect.

It sure didn't feel like Solomon's Temple. The stone was different than any I had seen in my brief visit yesterday.

"*Dessspaaiiiiiirrrrr*," a voice hissed in a rasp like dried leaves tumbling over brittle twigs.

I jumped instinctively, spinning in the air like a startled kitten.

30

I crouched, ready for an attack as my eyes darted back and forth from shadow to shadow, trying to pinpoint the source of the hissing voice.

Despair, it had said. And in the creepiest way possible.

"Hello?" I called out nervously. I jerked my head left and right—even upwards, to check if the voice belonged to someone overlooking the laboratory from a balcony or something. Empty. I licked my lips nervously. "I didn't mean to—"

"State your name, wanderer," the male voice hissed, seemingly coming from first the tree and then on the opposite side of the room entirely—as if it had just Shadow Walked mid-sentence. Except I had felt no magic.

"State *your* name, creep," I snapped back, glancing back and forth for any signs of movement. But I saw nothing. "And stop hisspering at me." Silence ensued. Then...

A deep, rumbling chuckle rolled out from behind a dresser, but by the time I turned to look, the laughter was on the opposite side of the room again, near one of the trees.

"*My* name..." it mused. "I haven't heard my own name in," another chuckle, "many moons. But we are not here to speak of *my* name, wanderer. There are rules, you see..."

I narrowed my eyes. "Rules to what?"

"To conversation, to answers, to enlightenment." Each statement came from a different point of the room as he hopped about, making my skin crawl. "To reach those lofty heights, I must have your name, wanderer. I've been waiting so, so long to hear you say it, after all."

I rolled my shoulders, feeling like a finger had brushed the back of my neck at his words. I thought about his request very carefully. I had broken into his home. It was the least I could do. "Callie," I breathed respectfully. "Callie Penrose. Look, I'm *really* sorr—"

"Your *full* name," he hissed in a slow, gentle drawl, seeming suddenly much closer. How was he moving about so quickly without me sensing anything?

I frowned, momentarily confused by his question. Then it hit me. Solomon was part of my name. I *had* used the Seal of Solomon to get here—wherever *here* was—so it was likely safe information to share. And if he had really wanted to kill me, I was pretty sure I would already be bleeding out. I hadn't even caught a glimpse of him yet. "Um. Callie Solomon Penrose," I said, not sure which order to list my names in. Any other time, I might have given serious thought to how this stranger knew I hadn't shared the whole truth, but I was talking to a teleporting, invisible, hissing creature—and somehow, I knew it was a creature, not a person—in a dark magic laboratory where they studied the *language of the end*.

Certain questions simply didn't manifest at this level of insanity.

"Your *first* name. Your *given* name," he urged, almost hungrily, as if licking his lips.

I shuddered anxiously, wondering who exactly I was talking to. He was obviously powerful yet remained hidden rather than attacking. Almost...like he was frightened of me. But the way he had phrased his question this time...almost like—

I flinched at a sound behind me, spinning to find a wooden crib on the floor not ten paces away, rocking back and forth with a steady *creaking* sound.

I caught a flash of a blue tail with fins sprouting from the sides—almost like those on a Koi fish—disappearing around the corner of a table beyond the crib, fleeing on silent feet after his freaky fast delivery.

I stared at the crib, my pulse suddenly thumping loudly in my ears. The crib itself wasn't familiar—made hastily from loose vines and branches—but it was a very meaningful, very secret, symbol that held special significance to me. The old crib that I'd once found in Terry

Penrose's garage as a young teenager. Inside that crib, I'd found a hidden carved message...

And paired with this creature's question...

I realized I was panting, eyes darting from the crib to where I had seen the tail vanish.

My *Xuanwu After Dark* conversation suddenly began to take on yet *another* epiphany, like washing a filthy window to let the light through. His comments hit my mind now like fastballs striking a catcher's mitt—*slap, slap, slap*.

We all have our crosses to bear, our swords to carry...

Your blood is a sword. Your voice is a sword. Your name is a sword. We are all swords. Some just take better care of them than others before passing them on...

We take names, borrow them and their baggage, own them for a short time...but in the end they are simply cherry blossoms on the wind, floating to the next person—and the next, and the next...

But most impacting of all Xuanwu's comments was when I thought we had been discussing the Sanguine Council and their clever trick of hiding a name.

...Well-known schemers, perhaps even choosing to call a thing something that it is not. That would be extremely clever, wouldn't it, Callie? Hidden in plain sight, as it were...

But...how had Xuanwu known my secret, and why hadn't he simply spoken clearly?

And *this* creature also seemed to know my secret, knowing that placing a crib before me would be significant—the answer to his question. This stranger wasn't asking because *he* didn't know. He was asking whether or not *I* knew. He'd said *he'd been waiting so long to hear me say it...*

Which meant he probably knew other things...

I took a deep breath. Like prying my fingers from a boulder that I had carried for decades, my lips began to move, releasing the burden—the question—I had carried for so, so long.

"Ex..." I began, cutting off to lick my lips. "Excalibur..." I finally whispered, voicing the crude message I'd found carved into the base of my crib that day long ago.

Ex. Callie. Bur.

A name hidden in plain sight. I'd always thought it an explanation for where my name had been derived.

The weight of my secret vanished, and I briefly felt as if I would float up into the air—nothing magical or anything like that. Just the relief of unburdening a secret. The soothing serenity of knowing I no longer had to lie or omit—

Then the magical part happened, shattering my soothing serenity like a bull in a china shop. An unseen, metaphysical claw abruptly clenched my soul in a godly fist—taking my breath away as it squeezed—and then tore away the name I had spoken. I gasped, my knees buckling at the strangely horrifying sensation—at the hollow it left within me.

But...I realized it wasn't necessarily *pain*. It was more like a ravenous hunger that had left a hole in my stomach—a vacuum. Then, like nature does, it began abhorring the bejeezus out of the vacuum, slowly redistributing the contents of my soul to more efficiently capitalize on the new vacant real estate. This happened in a gurgling, bubbling, liquid sensation, like filling up a king's chalice—a grail.

The pieces of black leather at the far end of the table abruptly snapped together with a metallic *clang*—which was startling on the principle that it had moved by itself so suddenly, but also because leather didn't *clang*—making me jump with a startled squeak.

The leather sword shape—now one solid piece—disappeared in a puff of smoke.

Or...*mist*.

"What the hell just happened?" I asked no one in particular.

A hissing, gleeful laugh was the only response, coming from several points around the room—here one second, over there the next—making me dizzier than I already felt from the soul mugging I'd just survived.

31

I suddenly had an image of Ariel in *The Little Mermaid* having her voice taken from her, and only realizing too late that the bargain with octo-twat Ursula had been inadvisable.

Part of me wanted the name back. Right. Now. Although, I didn't actually feel like anything had really been *taken* from me. I hadn't actually lost anything. I'd never used the name, so nothing had changed. Xuanwu's riddled words echoed in my mind again, pounded at me, like an aggressive mantra trying to calm me down in a stern dad voice.

Your blood is a sword. Your voice is a sword. Your name is a sword. We are all swords. Some just take better care of them than others before passing them on...

We take names, borrow them and their baggage, own them for a short time...But in the end they are simply cherry blossoms on the wind, floating to the next person—and the next, and the next...

I had just carried it for a time, not truly owning it. But how had he known about it?

Xuanwu had very purposefully guided our conversation, telling me he had already considered every possible outcome of our talk. As upset as I was with him for speaking in riddles, he *had* given me true answers—especially about Dracula. He'd helped me.

Maybe.

Because I was sure he had his own motivations as well. He had mentioned a party—a war—coming to the world, and that everyone would need to pick a side. I didn't know him well enough to stake my life on which side he would pick.

I let my conversation with Xuanwu replay at half-speed in the background of my mind.

Like...a plodding tortoise as opposed to a hare.

I wasn't a fan of being used, and with Nate off battling Mordred—King Arthur's son—I was beginning to realize this Excalibur situation—whatever it was—may have driven a wedge between *us*. That Nate would think *I* had hidden this knowledge from *him*.

Because in my wildest fantasies, I had never considered that I might be the *actual fucking sword*. I had simply thought I'd been named *after* it.

Yet another reason to go visit Nate—maybe a slightly lower priority than the murder bit.

"Oh, Callie..." the voice chuckled, snapping me out of my reverie. I had almost forgotten he was still lurking about somewhere. "I am delighted to *finally* make your acquaintance."

And I gasped to see a surprisingly long, serpentine dragon suddenly crawling head-first down the tree nearest me, his body hugging the surface like a Komodo dragon on the beach. His long, muscular legs were bent more than ninety degrees at the elbow, making me think he could have stood upright on his back two legs if he so chose. He reached the tile and made his way towards me, his body easily transitioning between the vertical descent and horizontal walk as if he was a snake. His scales glistened from green to blue and back again, seemingly of their own accord since there was no direct light to cause a change like that.

Down his back was a ridged fin that moved like a rippling flag as he sashayed my way. Despite his long, narrow body, his head was a short, wide, bearded affair, reminding me of a Pug's squashed, flat face. Two smooth pointed bone horns arced back from his temples, protecting the back of his neck, and two long whiskers—similar to a catfish—draped down either side of his jaws to hang below his chin like an exaggerated flesh mustache. He was about eight feet long from snout to rump, not counting the long tail, and as he drew nearer and I got a closer look at his thick, muscular legs, I was even more confident that he could stand upright.

He paused a respectful distance from me and snorted out a puff of steam, rearing his head up on his snake-like neck until it was level with mine. Then he calmly lifted one leg and slammed his clawed foot down upon the crib, shattering it to pieces. "It served its purpose."

I narrowed my eyes at him. "Who the hell are you?" I demanded.

Like a cobra slowly rearing up to strike—and with apparently as much expended effort—his front legs and torso rose off the ground, bending at the belly where his thick back legs flexed to support the shift in weight. I stared incredulously. He wasn't a shifter dragon—he was an actual dragon. He was a smaller version of those Chinese dragon puppets you see in festivals and parades with about five guys underneath using wooden poles to make the puppet appear to writhe and bob as they moved—like a snake with legs. He didn't have wings and I was curious what other differences he might have from the shifter dragons I knew. He'd snorted steam, so I was betting he had some kind of spitting magic. Fire?

He studied me, now standing fully upright, flicking his tongue out to taste the air.

"I, the hell, am a messenger," he replied in his basso hissing whisper, sounding amused.

I frowned. "Look," I said. "I already asked you to stop hisspering. I feel like I shouldn't have to ask again, you know? Just talk normal. It will be easier for me to understand you."

He let out a great, big, booming laugh, his flesh-stache bouncing and whipping wildly about. "How refreshing," he finally said—without the creepy hissing factor—after his laughter had died down. "One who speaks her mind."

"Yeah," I admitted, realizing I was feeling a sort of kindred spirit vibe from the dragon. Although I knew he was dangerous, something about his aura just seemed in harmony with mine. But I'd been wrong before. "I didn't ask for your occupation. I asked who you *are*."

He nodded. "My name is Qinglong, the Azure Dragon. You may know my brother, Xuanwu," he rumbled, sounding amused.

My mouth fell open and I stared at him dumbly. "You...you're the dragon of the East," I whispered, recalling the carving on Xuanwu's door. "You represent the Spring season and wood, right?" I asked.

He nodded, pointedly glancing at the trees in the room. "Quite."

Of course. Wood. Budding trees. I shook my head, not entirely sure which of my dozen questions to focus on first. I closed my eyes, took a deep breath, and relaxed, still feeling punchy from the soul mugging. I finally opened them again, feeling less anxious, and smiled at him. "It's a pleasure."

He smiled in response. Or maybe he had curled his lips at me to reveal his fangs. I wasn't entirely sure.

My eyes drifted to where the leather sword-shape had been, and I found myself frowning again. "You wouldn't be here if you didn't have answers. And you knew about the crib," I said, jerking my chin at the pile of now broken sticks. He nodded calmly. "I thought they carved *Excalibur* into my crib to let me know what had inspired the name they chose for me, but *whatever* just happened tells me I was a bit naïve."

He had followed my gaze, glancing over at where the leather had been on the table.

"Why was Excalibur hidden within me and then taken away?" I pressed. Because it was obvious that something had just been taken from me. Not an actual sword, but...a *piece* of one, like Xuanwu had hinted.

I am more than just a name. I am all. And I am nothing. Just a piece of this world, riding out my part to play in life like any other, Xuanwu's voice murmured in my mind.

Qinglong nodded, approving of the way I'd chosen to ask the question.

"Excalibur was too powerful to leave out where anyone could scoop it up. It was decided that the sword needed to be dismantled, and the pieces safely hidden until it was the right time to reunite them again. Knowing how powerful your blood mix was—Nephilim *and* dark wizard *and* Solomon—your parents knew you would be strong enough to keep the Name safe. The sheath, as you saw, was not strong enough for any extended period."

I sat back, shaking my head. This was just ridiculous.

Qinglong continued. "When you came here and spoke the Name, you transferred it back into the sheath—its vessel. Since it immediately disappeared, I'm guessing it thought it was time to reunite with the other pieces. Otherwise it would have remained here."

I found that I wasn't particularly concerned where it had gone. I'd done my part. The hatchling had left the nest, for better or for worse.

Not my sword, not my problem. That's what I say.

"Part of me was just sucked out of my body. I'm pretty sure that kind of thing has consequences."

He shook his head, his flesh-stache whipping about wildly. "There are no lasting effects, just a...mild readjustment period. A few days, at most."

I narrowed my eyes, even though I could sense he was right. I already felt my soul knitting itself back together, and there was no longer a noticeable hollow pit within me.

"I...was a drug mule used to smuggle a piece of Excalibur?" I asked, gritting my teeth.

Qinglong thought about it for a few moments. "There are a few additional details that we need to discuss..."

32

He held out his claws, gesturing at the room around us. "I have waited here a long time to meet you, Callie. This space has waited a long time for you to discover her secrets. Your mother's secrets."

My pulse quickened and I licked my lips. "My...mother?"

"Yes. She requested my assistance...in the event she couldn't be here," he said empathetically. "When she passed, I came to fulfill my promise and wait for you. To help you, in a small way."

I suddenly felt very numb. "With Excalibur's Name."

He nodded. "Yes. Among other things." His gaze settled on the journal I had been perusing, and I felt my face flush. "I'll admit, I had my doubts about her and your father's plan. About you. About all of it. But...when I saw you decipher the omegabet..." he trailed off, shaking his head slowly. "That was both terrifying and inspiring."

I blushed. "It just kind of happened," I admitted. "I can't read it or anything."

He gave me a very intense look, locking eyes with me. "Most wouldn't have spared it a second glance, but you discovered the name in minutes. That kind of skill is not typical. Even back in the age of the greatest wizards the world has ever known."

I scoffed. "I'm definitely not one of the greatest wizards. Not even close."

He regarded me thoughtfully. "Not yet. But even they had to start somewhere. You might surprise yourself. I know you are already surprising me."

His eyes flickered to my forehead for the briefest of moments. Of course. It had been the first thing he'd said to me. Instead of letting the moment slip, I pounced, pointing at the hidden symbol marking my forehead, and leaned closer. "Mind telling me about this?"

He shook his head. "Your parents didn't know. They searched and searched, but never found any answers."

I sighed angrily. Archangel Michael hadn't known either, so the answer was plausible.

"But you do?"

He shook his head. "I can read it, but it means nothing to me."

I let out a breath. "I need to sit down. That Excalibur thing left my legs wobbly, and it would be embarrassing if one of the world's greatest wizards fell off her own two feet."

He chuckled, motioning me towards a long couch. I sat, letting out a breath of relief, and Qinglong merely squatted on his hind legs on the floor, still much taller than me. I scanned the room, shaking my head. My eyes settled on the dark ritual altar and I grimaced.

Qinglong noticed my attention, grunting thoughtfully before turning back to face me—his eyes latching onto the Seal of Solomon on my finger. "Dealing with devils is dangerous..."

I nodded knowingly. Being of the Solomon bloodline, dealing with devils was kind of our shtick. I knew I had a few devils in my life—Cain, Dorian, Roland, just to name a few. Not even considering the literal devils I had killed or held bound inside my Seal. Or Samael pursuing me. I shuddered, dismissing the thought.

Qinglong's head absently shifted slightly from side to side, just like a cobra, but I could tell it wasn't any kind of warning gesture. "Your mother spelled the Seal of Solomon so that it would take you here the first time you tried to visit the Temple with it. We are in her laboratory—and living quarters—within Solomon's Temple. It is now all yours, of course." He spread his hands about the room, indicating the books, artifacts, and varied collections with a sweep of his claws. "This represents the summation of her life's work, locked safely inside Solomon's Temple like a vault within a vault."

I took in the red-flecked marble pillars and floors—very different from the white surfaces I had seen in the rest of the place. No wonder I hadn't immediately recognized it.

My eyes drifted to the journal, and my breath caught. The journal I'd been reading...it had been my mother's work. I'd been reading her notes and equations on the omegabet...

I leaned back in the couch, shaking my head slowly, trying to take it all in. "Why did she see fit to keep you here for so long? Surely she could have just left me a key and a note."

He shook his head adamantly. "I am its protector. Relying on a ward for more than twenty years is asking for trouble." I nodded, knowing he was right. "She warded this laboratory to maintain her privacy—a place where she could complete her work without fear. You see, she discovered that she was being watched—her very thoughts read by others. She needed a way to pass on her research to you without handing it over to her enemies as well... so she hired me to keep them out. To bar them from spying on her work." He glanced at me, gauging my reaction. "You will need that protection now, Callie. This is her legacy to her daughter."

I nodded, thinking back on the journal and the bizarre notes. "Solomon had intended to take me here, I think."

Qinglong's lips thinned, and he spoke almost defensively. "I was under very strict obligations—*no one is permitted to enter before Callie*," he said. "No one. Solomon shouldn't have tried entering. Not that he remembers anymore," he muttered.

My stomach fluttered nervously. "What happened, Qinglong?"

"Solomon tried entering your mother's laboratory before you. I defended the door. It's why your mother bonded me in the first place. I am a Door God. I guard the entrances to sacred places and Temples. Letting in positive energy and barring negative energy."

My mouth suddenly felt dry. I didn't want to appear ungrateful, but I was pretty sure my mother wouldn't have wanted Solomon injured. Then again... if this room was in Solomon's Temple, the only people that *could* have tried entering—other than me—was Richard and Solomon. So maybe she *had* meant to keep them out.

"You're a...bouncer?" I asked, hoping I could ease the tension, because he was obviously frustrated, and I didn't particularly like the idea of a frustrated dragon this close to me.

He turned to me, narrowing his eyes. "A bouncer *god*," he said, enunciating the last word.

I smiled. "I don't want to come off as disrespectful, but I have a question." He nodded. I licked my lips. "Did my mother distrust Solomon or Richard?"

He furrowed his brow—or the equivalent of such a gesture on a dragon—and shook his head resolutely. "She trusted them absolutely. Everyone in the Temple is blood bound—a family. But she said that *no one* could enter without your express permission—and only *after* you and I met. I did as obligated," he repeated.

"What...did you do to Solomon?" I asked carefully, already having a pretty good idea.

"I put a growth in him. It will kill him, eventually."

My eyes widened at his matter-of-factness. Was he talking about the black veins? "Um. What kind of timeline are we talking? And can you...*ungrow* it?"

He didn't immediately answer, and the silence stretched between us until I began to fidget. "He has three or four days. I can...*ungrow* it," he said, smirking at the phrase. "Or at least shed some light on how you can heal him yourself. But not *yet*." He took a breath, settling lower on his haunches. "It is time for you to learn some things, and you will not relish the experience. For that, I am truly sorry. I only do as obligated."

And that last sentence sounded like a felling axe chopping down an ancient tree.

Thanks, mom.

I studied Qinglong sidelong, trying to find similarities to him and his brother, Xuanwu. I wondered if he was also a ninja or something different. He had talked about wizards with familiarity and had mentioned guarding doors. Maybe that put him in a different field than his brother.

"I'm not going to pause for questions," he said sternly. "I am going to share what your mother and father needed you to know. Although you likely have many questions, many of those will have to wait until a later time. Understood?"

I nodded, idly glancing at the black and white marbles atop the pedestals. At the note.

Qinglong snorted. "And you say you are nothing special," he muttered.

I turned to him, frowning. "Pardon?" I asked, confused.

He pointed at the marbles. "Those are memories your parents preserved for you to view—*at a later time*," he said, emphatically. "Exactly what I was just referring to, the questions that would have to wait."

I shook my head wonderingly. "Memories?" I asked softly, re-reading the note in my mind. *Mem. Or. E's*. Of course.

He nodded. "Your mother distilled her most significant memories into those marbles. You will experience events of her life from her point of view—as if you were seeing through her eyes. She wanted to be certain that no matter what happened to her, she would still be able to pass on certain things she thought you needed to know."

My eyes widened incredulously. I hadn't known such a thing was possible. Even thinking about how to replicate such a feat made my brain hurt.

"The white marbles include narration—where she went back over her memory to provide footnotes or other information pertinent to the memory she may not have known at the time. The black marbles are without commentary. Raw memory."

I grunted, shaking my head. "How do they work?"

"Simply place the marble on your tongue and make sure you are seated. Your mind will go into a trance of sorts, like a daydream, and you don't want to later come out of the memory only to realize your body fell down and got a concussion on the side table. Limit yourself to no more than a few experiences per week. They are...addictive. Many a wizard has grown to depend on them, their bodies wasting away in the process. Dwelling too long on the past can be toxic to your health—even more so when magic enters the equation."

I nodded slowly, reconsidering how beautiful they were with a slight shiver.

He dusted his claws significantly. "Now, let us talk about Calvin and Makayla Temple, your parents' best friends..."

33

I froze, staring at him blankly. Hold on a second. Best friends?

First Excalibur and now this? Calvin and Makayla Temple. Nate's parents. The parents who had hidden so much from their son, lied to him, and generally made his life a living hell. And now I learned that they had been sniffing around my family tree, pissing on the trunk.

I knew we leased space to them for the Armory, but best friends? I wondered if Qinglong knew—or cared—that Nate's parents were dead.

Spoiler alert: they're deadsies.

"Okay..." I said, hesitantly.

"Your parents fought side by side with the Temples, searching out clues, weaknesses, and information on an enemy who was not yet known back then. They searched out powerful artifacts and weapons, storing them in the Armory." I nodded to let him know I was aware of that, at least. "One of those items was Excalibur. They knew it—along with many other items—would be crucial to winning this upcoming war. But despite their best efforts, and many victories, they ultimately came to the conclusion that they were a generation too soon. That the war would start much later, and too late for them to be of proper help—because they had already drawn too much attention to themselves. Their enemies knew them intimately, and it was only a matter of time before the enemy took them out of the equation."

I nodded woodenly, thinking of all the secrets Nate's parents had kept from him. How even now, he was learning new facts about this upcoming war his parents had warned him about. Hearing that my parents had been their friends, and that my mother had wanted this laboratory to keep her research safe, made me realize that maybe Nate's parents hadn't been *able* to tell him the truth. They knew they were being watched, so couldn't openly tell him anything...therefore, they cleverly hid breadcrumbs in his path—like I was beginning to learn my parents had done for me.

And Xuanwu's cryptic comments suddenly made more sense. He'd been talking about this upcoming war but hadn't wanted to say it where he could be overheard. Or he hadn't known if he could trust me yet.

"The families—for you and the Temples are not the only such children involved," he added with a sideways glance, his look letting me know that those details were none of my business, "decided that rather than giving up, they could help empower the next generation. But in a fit of irony, the only way they could do that—and keep you children safe from the enemy—was to put as much distance between them and their children as possible. And they had to make it like they took all their secrets to the grave. If anyone had suspected they had passed on those secrets, or powers, they had accumulated to their children...none of you would have survived. Unlike some of the others, your parents didn't have money or allies to keep them safe. And they thought raising you here in Solomon's Temple would make you separate from the world, unmotivated to help. So..." he trailed off, gesturing with his claw.

"They left me on the steps...to protect me," I whispered. "Hiding my identity from everyone. And then hid the Seal of Solomon in Kansas City..." I said, momentarily reliving that night I'd visited in the Doors.

He nodded, a proud look on his face. "They spelled the Seal—and your crib—so that you would one day find them, in one way or another. You would have felt drawn to them."

I shook my head slowly, staring off at nothing.

"It was the only chance they had to guarantee you lived long enough to potentially become a threat—to let you, year by year, gather up the pieces they so carefully hid along your paths. Along the paths they hoped you would take. Maybe a nudge in the right direction every now and then," he added with a flicker of a smile.

"Live to fight another day," I said softly, shaking my head.

To learn that Nate and I—and other children—had been part of some sinister plot, part of some design...it made me want to chew rocks and spit bullets.

I took slow, measured breaths, trying to study the big picture compared to what was happening in Kansas City right now. Maybe these things were what Xuanwu had been referring to. About children. *Babes with blades*, he had said.

The Temples had orchestrated this like a murder mystery dinner, setting up numerous gods and legends to cross Nate's path in St. Louis and now he had a veritable army. And they had helped my parents—

I slowly turned to Qinglong. "It was their idea to hide Excalibur's name inside me, wasn't it? Calvin and Makayla." I wasn't sure if I was furious or... grateful. I just felt cold.

Qinglong nodded mercilessly. "Excalibur granted you an added measure of protection, concealing your true aura. Your bloodline. And it was undetectable," he added with a gentle smile. "The Temples also suggested putting you in the care of Abundant Angel Catholic Church. They had heard good things of the pastor there, that he was a good man."

I grew lightheaded for a moment, staring at him in open disbelief.

Qinglong nodded. "And in return, they extended the lease for their Armory, hoping that one day their children would meet. And have the tools necessary to succeed where they had failed."

"And who is this mysterious enemy?"

"The *Masters*," he said soberly. "Whatever information your parents discovered about them is in your mother's journals and memories. But essentially, they are a conglomerate of gods, monsters, and other supernatural beings or entities who intend to establish a new world order—with Regulars and Freaks as their servants. To go back to the old days when they were feared, revered, and worshipped, rather than mocked, parodied, stereotyped, and romanticized as they are in current times. Their stories perverted into Disney movies rather than the grim parables they actually were."

I shook my head. "They want to come out of the woodwork—reveal themselves to the world," I breathed. "Putting the *monster* back in monsters." It would be chaos—mass attacks, magic used openly, basically flaunting the shit out of the gifts we had that others did not.

"That is likely step two. Right now, they are consolidating their power—getting rid of the competition so they can become the last one standing in their respective fields."

I stared at him, blinking slowly as I tried to process it all. "You mean making sure there is only one God of Thunder rather than ten across different pantheons, for example. So the last one standing will receive all the worship and fear for themselves...all the power for themselves," I breathed, horrified. Because many creatures needed worship, stories told about them, sacrifices, prayers—or any other number of ways people showed their affections to gods—in order to remain powerful. But...if they were the last one left, they would receive all that power for themselves.

He nodded slowly. "You begin to comprehend the repercussions.

I stared off at nothing, thinking about it like a string of dominos. Consolidate power then cause chaos and mass panic as they reveal themselves to the world, and then sit back and reap the waves of power resulting from the populaces' terror or worship. Something like this, if done right, would essentially make them new gods. Because they would have killed all the old gods.

"The old gods are dead, long live the new gods," Qinglong murmured.

"They're taking a page out of the old books. Kids rising up to defeat their parents and take the thrones. All the pantheons did it. The Greeks, the Norse..." I waved a hand.

"Precisely. And...your parents did the same with you. Fighting fire with fire."

I nodded numbly. And my parents thought I was equipped to handle something like this? "It seems like I'll need to make some new friends," I said slowly. "A *lot* of new friends."

"Just remember that the Masters don't care for collateral damage. It is all or nothing to them. They want to wipe the slate clean, so do not expect honor or fair fights. They want to burn it all down and rise from the ashes. Which means they've got eyes and ears everywhere, surveilling anyone they might want to utilize or take down as a threat. Or any of their associates in hopes of getting information on their targets."

"That's why my parents made this laboratory. To stay undetected."

He nodded. "Even here, think thrice before you mention the Masters to anyone. You never know who might be in their pocket—whether that person even knows it or not. Outside this room, I wouldn't even think too hard on them, let alone speak of them—and only to those you trust completely. Mere words won't be enough. You need *family*. You need blood oaths, and with *your* blood," he said, jerking his chin at me, "they'll have no *choice* but to be loyal to you. Your blood mix isn't just powerful enough to create bonds," he said, leaning forward meaningfully, "it is also strong enough to shatter them."

And I suddenly remembered breaking unbreakable chains when Johnathan the demon had tied me to a cross. I shook my head in wonder. Holy crap...

"Outside this laboratory," Qinglong continued, "I recommend acting as if you have no idea there is anything to be concerned about. Because if the Masters even think you're onto them, you're already dead."

I frowned thoughtfully. "I guess that's why I've never heard of them. Like one of those elite secret societies. Global domination won't work if everyone knows who is pulling the strings." He smiled at my example. "Is there any obvious way to indicate them? Like a glow or something?"

He shook his head, rolling his eyes.

"Fine. So in a way, this is an arms race. Or a draft pick. For all of us, both Masters and whatever we are," I said, frowning to myself. I would need to come up with a cool name. "Because if we can't find the Masters, maybe we can start stealing their prospects, start siphoning off their power in any way we can find. Before they get too powerful to handle."

He thought about that and finally shrugged. "I have not read your mother's journals. That seems like one approach—to kick sand in their faces—and it comes with obvious risk, of course." He gave me a considering look, underlining that risk.

"What exactly are Nate and I supposed to do about them?"

"I cannot speak for Nate Temple, but I'm sure his parents—like yours—found a way to give him what they thought he would need." I grunted. Not in a way that made Nate happy. "I imagine that the two of you will face many temptations in the years to come, and your parents' hope was that you would consider each other a moral compass, as it were."

There was simply too much to worry about, and I felt like I was going to crack. I had been on the edge with just the Kansas City drama, and now all of this? "The Masters..." I said, shaking my head.

"Original pantheons won't matter for long—they will make alliances, go to war, or make handshake deals to take out their foes. Then, of course, they will turn on one another. It's a battle royale, a free-for-all. Good men will make deals with devils, anything to survive one more round."

I nodded, running down that idea. "Maybe that is why so many people are acting strangely. A priest becoming a tyrant. A fierce Shepherd becoming a frightened sheep. It's why everyone seems to have become what they are not. Acting against their natures."

I thought about something else I'd heard from Xuanwu. *Black Sheep*. I was the Black Sheep of my family. As was Roland. Eae. Samael. Alucard. And so many others. Hell, Nate's friends in St. Louis were all Black Sheep and they seemed to be doing pretty well together.

A fleeting suspicion crossed my mind—whether our parents had set us up to fall in love with each other. Judging by all of their other scheming, it wasn't beyond the realm of possibility to tack on *arranged marriage* and made my stomach squirm unhappily ever after. My feelings for Nate were my own, not some fabricated equation.

Right?

Another sobering thought slithered into my ears like an oiled snake, making my shoulders twitch. "*Master* Calvin Temple helped you come up with a way to protect me from...the *Masters*," I said, emphasizing his title and the name of our enemy being the same.

Qinglong nodded. "Calvin believed that one of the first Temple ancestors here in the States was one of the first Masters. The one who set their entire plan in motion. He felt a personal responsibility for it, hence his devotion to the fight."

Good god. Nate would love to hear that.

"How do I know you're not one of them?" I asked guardedly.

He smiled, nodding. "I am blood bound to this room by both your father and mother. But your blood is even stronger than theirs. Much stronger..." he mused, curling his flesh-stache with his claws. "Perhaps we could renew that oath. A gesture of faith."

Wanting to see how such a thing could work—for future use—and wanting to know beyond a shadow of a doubt that I could trust Qinglong, I extended my arm.

Qinglong accepted it carefully and made the smallest of punctures in my wrist with one of his claws. Then he lowered his head and lapped up the small pool of blood. I grimaced at the ritual and pulled my hand away when he was finished. I stared at him as he licked the blood from his lips.

"That's it?" I asked, finally realizing he wasn't going to say anything about it.

He nodded, smiling. "I am now bonded to you," he said. "Not as any kind of servant or anything, but if you focus, you'll sense a...harmony between us."

I closed my eyes, doing as he said. And...he was right. Nothing extreme, but a faint hum, like a silken string between his chest and my own. And despite its size, it was as strong as cable wire. I opened my eyes, shaking my head in disbelief.

"See?" he said, smiling. "You can feel me, now. If ever you see me and do not feel it, you will know I found a way to break your oath. Highly unlikely, with your blood."

I nodded slowly, still trying to wrap my head around it. "Being a Master has a lot of perks. Why wouldn't you join them?"

He smiled, shaking his head. "My existence *consists* of sharing powers with my fellows. If I'm to die standing by it, reincarnation will be kind to me for my steadfastness."

He had been locked up here for a while, so I didn't bother asking him about Dracula, presuming he wouldn't know much more than I already did.

"Lock up behind you on your way out," he said in a faint, hissper. And I turned to see he had disappeared.

"Hey, fix Solomon!" I shouted. But no one answered. Damn it.

34

I heard a noise behind me and spun, ready to hurl magic and grab Qinglong by the flesh-stache until he agreed to heal Solomon of the black veins.

So I was more than surprised to see Claire and Last Breath standing in an open doorway I hadn't even noticed, staring at me with concern. I saw an old bloody handprint on the interior frame of the door—likely my mother's ward to protect her laboratory from the Masters.

"Don't come in!" I snapped, holding up my hands urgently. "It's warded!"

My friends gave each other a long, silent look, but they didn't approach. They tapped their ears and made a shrugging gesture. I frowned. They couldn't hear me? Wow. That was a relief. Good to know I hadn't had this whole secret conversation about an evil secret society hell-bent on overthrowing humanity with the fucking door to the hall open.

No wonder Qinglong had disappeared so abruptly. He'd probably sensed them.

I held up a finger, telling them to give me a minute.

I didn't wait for an answer as I made my way over to the table and scooped up the dragon figurine I had noticed earlier. The one that looked just like Qinglong. His brother had given me a black tortoise figurine, so I was betting this was also some kind of totem—one that Qinglong had given to my mother.

Maybe it would help me find him later. I shoved it into my coat pocket, glad that it was small. I took one last look around the room, my eyes lingering on the space where the sheath had been. Excalibur's new vessel.

I shook my head, walking towards them. I kept my wounded wrist out of their immediate sight and waited for them to turn around before smearing a bit on the frame, right beside my mother's print. I lifted my hand, holding it up to her print, smiling sadly. She'd...done her best. I was still pissed at her for it, but I thought I understood it. She was the mom who took a bullet to save her daughter.

It's just that no one else had ever known there had been a shooter.

"Thanks, mom," I whispered, pressing my forehead against her print.

Then I walked through the opening and closed the door behind me.

"Glad to see you're alive. We haven't been looking for you or anything," Claire said coldly, folding her arms.

I let out a breath, nodding. "How long have you been standing there?" I asked.

Claire was wearing a fluffy robe, and I remembered she had shifted in our fight back at the warehouse—what felt like a million years ago for me.

Last Breath was in full-on lion mode, sans armor, scowling at the door warily.

"Just got here," she murmured absently, her eyes also pinned to the door. "Who..." she began, trailing off as she cocked her head suddenly, sniffing much more intently as if she'd caught a dangerous scent. Qinglong. Was he still here? I couldn't feel him through our strange blood bond, so I was doubting it.

Last Breath had already flung a big meaty paw across Claire's chest, even though the door was closed. "Are you...feeling okay, Callie?" he asked nervously, staring at my arms.

I frowned. "I think so."

"What were you doing in there, and why couldn't we hear you?" Claire asked, settling her eyes back on me.

I stared back at her for a minute, not entirely sure how to answer. What could I tell her? "A guy with a mustache," I finally whispered. "Well, a flesh-stache, technically. And the room is warded from eavesdropping."

"You were doing a guy with a flesh-stache," she said flatly, the beginning of a grin tugging at the corners of her lips, "in a room warded from eavesdropping." She nudged Last Breath with an elbow. He found it about as humorous as I did.

"No. Never mind." I indicated the room behind me. "This was my mother's laboratory."

Claire's face wilted at the dark change in topic. "Oh. It's...nice," she said lamely.

Last Breath was shaking his head in open disbelief. "And you're sure you feel fine? Nothing strange in your arms or chest?" he asked again.

I frowned at him, then glanced down at my arms, inspecting them. I lifted the neck of my shirt but saw nothing wrong. "I'm fine. Why?" Was he talking about the demon disguise?

Last Breath let out a relieved sigh but didn't look entirely relaxed. "It's just..." He waved a hand at the doorway. "Solomon tried to enter this room and was knocked unconscious. He doesn't remember any of it, and he woke up with black veins. I found him right here, still in the doorway."

I let out a breath. "Yeah. He...well, he wasn't supposed to go in there. My mom booby-trapped it." I didn't want to admit that there had been a freaking dragon living here without their consent. I knew I would have to soon, but I just needed a minute to myself. Qinglong had said he would shed some light on how to help Solomon, but at least I knew we had three or four days.

I could find Qinglong before that. We'd bonded. Or I would go pummel Xuanwu into telling me where his mustached brother would likely go after a twenty-odd-year prison sentence. Maybe Qinglong had just needed to go potty. Because I hadn't seen a restroom.

"I think I know how to help Solomon, but it's going to have to wait a few days," I said, ignoring the flat stare from Last Breath. "Trust me on this. I'll tell you all about it soon, but right now I just want to get away from here." I pointed at the door adamantly. "Just to be safe, no one enters this room without me. My mother's ward is still active, and I need to figure out how to take it down before anyone else ends up like Solomon."

Last Breath nodded thoughtfully, staring at the wooden door. "Your mother was a very clever wizard." I could sense the million questions on his mind, but I didn't say anything.

I realized, in that moment, that she hadn't told Last Breath or Solomon about any of this specifically *because* they would have tried to talk her out of it. Or they would have poked their noses into the Masters and gotten themselves killed in a failed attempt at vengeance.

They carried guilt, thinking they had failed her. Guilt they never should have had to carry.

But I knew that somewhere out there, beyond the veil of life, she was smiling.

Because she'd saved their lives from unseen bullets, too.

35

The chirping chorus of singing birds rolled over me, increasingly louder, as we neared the balcony—the only part of Solomon's Temple I felt familiar with. At some point, Last Breath had shifted back to his human form—turning back into Richard, in my mind—and had snatched up one of the ever-present robes seemingly hanging everywhere. So I looked like I was escorting the two of them to the spa for a romantic massage or something.

Richard and Claire had tried speaking with me on the way through the halls—about seven hundred miles of them, it had felt like—but I had walked in a numb haze for most of it. I remembered ultimately telling them a fabricated version of the truth—that my mother had spelled the Seal of Solomon to redirect me to her laboratory upon first use and that I'd learned some things from my mother's effects. I said nothing about the Masters, though. I wouldn't until I thought more on the blood bond ritual Qinglong had shown me.

Both for their safety and my own.

There was pretty much only one person I wanted to see right now. Because Xuanwu had given me a job, and speaking with his brother, Qinglong, had served to verify some truths for me. I needed to murder hope.

Upon hearing what I'd gone through—even the redacted version—the two of them had grown very quiet. After a time, Claire had started telling me what they'd been up to—since I'd forgotten to ask. Whoops. I learned that they had checked on the still unconscious Phix and caught Solomon up on events in Kansas City before searching for me. When Richard hadn't been looking, I'd mouthed the word *Dracula* to Claire, silently asking if she'd shared that information with them. She had shaken her head *no*, and I'd let out a soft sigh of relief.

We finally reached the balcony and I took a deep breath of fresh air, imagining my parents doing the same in their day. Maybe Calvin and Makayla Temple, too. All staring out at the beauty below as they strategized how best to deal with the Masters and protect their kids.

Other than repeating the word "Wild," again and again, Claire seemed to have gotten over her shock of seeing Solomon's Temple—after an apparently extensive inspection—and she now acted more familiar with it all than I could even pretend. I couldn't even really remember what I had seen on the walk back to the balcony, I'd been so lost in my own thoughts.

I would have to figure out a way to get anyone else into my mother's laboratory without poisoning them, of course, but that could wait. I didn't want to unlock the room only to leave again for Kansas City. My Seal and blood mix had been the key to get inside the room unscathed, so maybe I could use one of those to break the ward my mother had put in place.

For the fifth time, Richard appraised me up and down, checking that I was unharmed—other than the small cuts on my palms. "I'm glad you're okay, Callie. I got to that warehouse as fast as I could. The moment I sensed you were in danger, I came."

I had begun to nod at the first statement but hesitated at his last comment. He hadn't said that before, or I hadn't heard him. "You...*sensed* that I was in danger?" I asked, arching an eyebrow.

Richard nodded. "Much stronger than the others before it."

I blinked several times. He had sensed me in danger other times. Probably when I'd been fighting Alucard and Claire, but that sensation must have been significantly stronger when Eae was about to behead me. And Richard could just, what, appear at my side to protect me?

Richard nodded at me from within his high-necked robe, letting me know I'd spoken out loud. I opened my mouth to ask a question, thought of a better one, and then an even better one. Ultimately, I decided to just keep them to myself for later. I was on a timetable. I needed to focus on Kansas City. Solomon's Temple could wait, and I had a job to do for a tortoise.

"I'm pretty sure Eae recognized me right before the world caught fire and burned away," I said, flicking my hair where I had felt the flush of warmth when Eae had last looked at me.

Richard was frowning at me in confusion, but Claire smiled broadly, elbowing him. "I told you she wasn't listening when I told her." She abruptly wrapped me up in a hug, patting my hair soothingly and squeezing tightly, and I knew it had nothing to do with my hair.

It was the first time I had let her touch me since leaving my mother's laboratory—she was hugging me for every painful word that had left my mouth on our walk, letting me know she was there in any capacity I needed. I hugged her back, feeling my shoulders relax at the physical contact of a caring, empathetic heart. I hadn't known how tight my shoulders were.

"I love you, Callie," she whispered. "I'll always be here for you, even if your cat's a dick." Richard grumbled unhappily.

I laughed, squeezing her back tightly.

I remembered her trying to hug me a few times on our walk back to the balcony, or to hold my hand, but I had rebuked any physical contact, feeling too raw.

I definitely hadn't heard her tell me I looked like myself for the first time since last night. For Claire, it had been the first time in over a year that she had actually *seen* her best friend.

"I never saw any demonic form," Richard said, squinting at me as if I was an optical illusion that he could overpower through sheer will. "But I do need to speak with you about something. Privately."

Claire bristled, but I placed a hand on her shoulder, still staring into Richard's eyes. "It's okay, Claire. Wait here for a minute," I said, motioning Richard to walk with me.

Claire folded her arms, glaring at Richard. "She's just going to tell me later!"

I smirked, shaking my head. We walked in silence for a minute or so, putting enough distance between us for Claire not to overhear...whatever it was Richard wanted to say.

"Lot of weird stuff going on, Callie..." he said after a few more steps.

I frowned. "You mean the guy with the flesh-stache?"

He pursed his lips, shaking his head. "I still want to hear about that, but I was talking about your apparent demon disguise," he said, gesturing at me with a wave of his hand, "And your friend from the alley."

I came to a dead halt. "*Excuse* me?" I asked in a frosty tone. "You mean the vampires trying to molest Phix or the guy that sucker-punched me?" I demanded.

He turned to face me, shaking his head uncertainly. "You knew that man, Callie. He approached and you *spoke* with him..."

I stared at him incredulously. "What the *hell* are you talking about? He *attacked* me!"

Richard was shaking his head firmly. "No. He did not. I saw the whole thing. This is the first chance I've had to talk with you since then," he explained. "And I've never seen this demon disguise Claire keeps talking about..." he reminded me, eyeing me up and down.

Part of me was furious that he would insinuate such an allegation, calling me a liar. But...another part of me felt an intangible terror at the implication. Richard, judging by his face right now, was entirely sure of himself. One of us had to be wrong...

And that event had been a blank spot to me. Just that flash of light and then a familiar looking man walking away. Le Bone. Which meant...

I took a calming breath, ignoring the tingling sensation in my fingers at the thought of something happening to me that I couldn't remember. "What did you see, Richard?" I asked.

I think he could tell by my tone that he'd managed to freak me out. "A man approached you. You held up your hand for us to give you some privacy, so I thought it was a friend of yours. You spoke briefly for a few moments, and then I think you shook hands. Then you did something with your magic. Your Silvers..."

My heart skipped a beat, and I suddenly felt like I was going to vomit. I...had done this to *myself*? Why? And why couldn't I remember any of it? Why hadn't Cain remembered?

"All I remember is a flash of light and falling down," I told Richard, taking a deep breath to calm down. "Cain remembers the same thing. It's why he was getting his ass kicked when the vampires came out of nowhere. He was already on the ground, just like me. In fact, being on the ground is the only reason that electric net hit Phix instead of me..." I said, realizing that for the first time.

Richard frowned at the contradicting story. "You and Cain both fell when you used your Silvers, and the man left a heartbeat before the vampires descended. It was so sudden that I didn't see it coming. My guard was down because you were speaking with this man without any apparent concern. Then Phix was injured and I had to return here, or I would have asked you about all of it sooner. I didn't even realize it was a big deal until Claire mentioned your demon disguise."

I shivered, wondering what could have possibly happened. I had absolutely no recollection of any of this. Could he be wrong? Had he seen some kind of illusion?

"Richard...is there any chance that maybe *you* saw something that didn't happen? An illusion?" I asked carefully. "You are the only one to have seen this scenario."

He shook his head firmly. "Not a chance. I know illusion. Which is what makes this so confusing. I don't sense anything around you right now. And I should if it's an illusion cast upon you. Maybe it's because you did it to yourself? Much like how you said Cain also senses no demon disguise on you."

I sighed. I had no idea. "What did this man look like?"

He shrugged thoughtfully. "A guy."

I blinked at him, waiting for more. "You sure it was a guy? Some of them have orbs of delight on their chests," I explained dryly, indicating my own chest, "but those guys are called broads, dames, women..." I waved a hand as if the list went on forever.

His face reddened. "It was a man. I couldn't see his face. He was powerful, but I couldn't decipher what kind of power. And since you knew him, were speaking amicably with him, I didn't press. He was obviously a friend of yours."

I shook my head. "I...don't know what you're talking about. I don't remember any of that..." This only made Richard look more concerned. Why would I do such a thing to myself? And who could have possibly *convinced* me to do such a thing?

I looked at Richard sharply. "Samael?"

Richard snarled. "I would know Samael's stench anywhere. It definitely wasn't him. I did not recognize the scent. I do not think I even picked up on a scent, actually..." he said, as if only just thinking about that. "Some kind of metal, maybe..."

I was simply relieved to hear the conviction in Richard's voice when he'd denied it being Samael. All this just served to confirm that someone was indeed playing a game, and it did likely have to be someone I knew, since he'd approached me openly and I hadn't been alarmed.

Or...the person had done something to disarm me and Richard hadn't sensed it. Richard had said the man was powerful and had only a *metallic-maybe* scent. Maybe a Sanguine Council member *had* snuck into town before Roland's barrier went up. Vampires could lull their victims if they were strong enough. I had a certain tolerance for vampire enthrallments, having trained with the Shepherds, so the vampire would have had to be *very* powerful. High-ranking vampires only.

Of course, that admission brought *vampire numero uno* to mind.

Dracula.

Oh, god. I hadn't spoken with Dracula, had I? Dracula was probably the most notorious for enthrallment. Probably the bestest the world had ever seen.

Maybe I really *had* been Dracula'd!

I shook off that thought. Whoever had done it didn't really matter right now. I couldn't do anything about it at the moment. I turned to Richard, smiling weakly. "It's okay. Thanks for telling me this. I'll figure it out," I reassured him as I guided him back towards Claire.

36

As we walked, I tried inspecting myself magically, wondering if I could sense my own magic affecting me. But I found nothing. I was too good to catch myself, apparently.

I studied Richard discreetly as we walked. He was frowning to himself, not liking the situation one bit. He was of Asian descent...or had chosen to appear so. But I knew he could shift into all manner of appearances. Why had he chosen this one? Had he always chosen so?

Qinglong had warned me about trust—but he had also confirmed I could trust Solomon and Richard. That we were family and shared a sacred bond. And Richard had leapt into a fight to save me in the warehouse. He had literally saved my life.

I shuddered, the reality of that only just now hitting me. Eae had almost *killed* me. Beheaded me. I had never seen that cold look on his face before. Well, cold, sure, but not as cold as that.

I wasn't sure how much time I'd lost speaking with Qinglong, but I needed to get moving, and I had an idea or two about immediate steps I wanted to take, even after hearing Richard's story about my friend from the alley.

"How does your ability work?" I asked, as we reached Claire again. "Sensing me in danger. Can you spy on me?" Claire looked ready to grab me by the ear until I shared my private talk with Richard, but I gave her a stern look.

Richard scoffed. "No. I can't hear you or anything. It's more like...a feeling in the pit of my stomach. I knew you were in trouble, and where you were—because of your ring—but not what the trouble *was*. It felt dire, so I rushed to you as fast as I could. I almost wasn't fast enough to stop the angel," he admitted guiltily. "It's been some time since anyone wore the Seal of Solomon, and I had almost forgotten what it felt like to share that bond."

I glanced at him. "My mother..." I said.

He nodded somberly. "Yes," he said, keeping his eyes downcast as he continued. "We were quite the pair before she took off the Seal and hid it from us..."

Seeing him now—a strong, but seemingly young, Asian man—in a fluffy white robe casually talking about keeping me safe from monsters almost made me burst out laughing. But...he had done the same thing for my mother. Before she had met my father and run away with Calvin and Makayla Temple.

Claire snorted abruptly, drawing my attention away from Richard. "Jack-pot," she said, grinning from ear-to-ear.

I followed her gaze to see—

My mouth fell open.

Claire laughed at me. "This place is fucking *wild*, right? I've seen more man-meat here in the last hour than I've seen in the past few *months* in Kansas City."

Richard was waving his hands wildly, trying to silently warn Claire's victim.

Sensing this, Claire began jogging backwards, grinning at us. "You two catch up. I'm going to go talk to the naked dude," she said. Then she spun and skipped towards the lounge chairs thirty yards away.

Where Solomon was sprawled out on a deck chair, ankles crossed and his hands folded behind his head, unaware of our arrival up until that point.

He was as naked as a baby.

But the sound of Claire approaching must have finally alerted him, because he turned to look, swiftly peeling off a pair of sunglasses to blink at Claire with rapidly widening eyes.

He instantly dove for a towel lying beside his chair.

"No need to cover up on my account, sailor. I just wanted to say—" she cut off with a strangled squawk, "my god! What the hell is *that?*" she demanded, skidding to a halt and blatantly pointing at him.

I raced over, my face flushing at her choice of words. No matter what Solomon's bait and tackle looked like, there was a certain level of tact required when describing it in a group setting. Namely, *not to describe it in a group setting.*

I left Richard in my dust and skidded on my heels to find Solomon wrapping the towel around his waist and standing to face us. I opened my mouth to verbally spank Claire for her rudeness, but I let out a gasp of my own upon seeing Solomon.

The black veins looked much more prominent than last time I'd seen them. They fanned across his chest and upper arms in stark contrast to the clean white towel. But what had really thrown me was that freaking *thorns* were growing out from the skin of his shoulders where a knot of black veins connected in a particularly large dark mass. A trickle of blood oozed out from the wound, making me wince.

I shook my head in both disgust and guilt. "Those..." I began, lifting my hand to point, "those aren't black veins. They're roots!" I hissed incredulously, wincing further as I noticed a few additional thick and wickedly curved barbs piercing his flesh—as if they were clawing to get out of his body.

Roots...like from a tree. And trees were made of *wood.* Qinglong—represented by wood and Spring—had admitted to putting a growth in Solomon, but I hadn't taken it literally. Solomon was known as one of the wisest men in the world, according to stories. So did that make him...

The tree of knowledge.

I would, of course, never say that out loud. I shouldn't have even thought it.

And guilt threatened to consume me because I knew the guy who could cure him, but instead of offering up that information, I was thinking of jokes.

Solomon hung his head and nodded. "The sunlight seems to keep them at bay," he said tiredly, waving a hand up at the sky. Something about that tickled my memory, giving me an idea. But I didn't immediately voice it. It probably wouldn't do to tell them that the dragon hiding in Solomon's

Temple had done this to him. *Oh, and he's a friend. Wicked flesh-stache*. Yeah... First impressions mattered. I would hold off on this one. Because according to Qinglong, Solomon had time—no matter how bad he looked right now.

And I simply had no time to help him.

"I didn't mean for you to see me like this," Solomon admitted. He didn't sound embarrassed for himself, but more like he hadn't wanted to share the burden with me. That he hadn't wanted sympathy or a doting eye. Just a man suffering his injuries in privacy, not wanting anyone to offer their help.

Richard stepped up beside me. "I didn't realize you were out here, Solomon, or I would have led them away," he said apologetically. "Let me walk you back to your rooms. I need to go check on Phix anyway, so we're heading in the same direction." He shot me a very flat look, demanding that I drop the topic right now, even though it was a blatant lie about Phix. He and Claire had already checked on the sphinx.

I nodded, still deeply unsettled by Solomon's condition. "We'll wait here," I told him.

I'd wanted to pick Solomon's brain on a few things but seeing him like this...I realized how callous it would be for me to ask his help while not admitting the solution to his predicament was within my grasp. Kind of. I couldn't tell them about Qinglong without starting a long, long, *long* conversation—and possible fight. I didn't have time for a long conversation. Or a fight.

I watched them leave, smiling faintly at how careful Richard was to appear like he wasn't ready to catch Solomon the moment he might fall. But to someone like me, who had spent years in martial arts—paying attention to foot placement, posture, and balance—it was obvious that Richard was Solomon's personal nurse. And he was so good at hiding it that Solomon probably wasn't even aware of it. Or he had accepted it with the finality of a man who knew there was no hope of a cure, accepting the despair and resigning himself to simply watching the ticking hand of the clock of life, relishing each spastic *click* of the second hand.

I shooed Claire over to the balcony, forcibly turning her shoulders to look out at the garden. "Leave the men in peace," I told her, attempting to hide my own frustration.

I couldn't justify taking the time to help Solomon right now.

Because after speaking with Qinglong, I had grown very confident that Roland's plan to mess with Dracula might just be a plot of the Masters.

Whether he knew it or not.

And that was a big, dark concern, consuming my every thought since leaving my mother's laboratory. Just how bad was Roland these days?

37

Claire leaned out over the railing, sweeping her blue eyes over the gardens, a dazed smile plastered over her cheeks as she slowly shook her head in awe. "Solomon's Temple," she murmured. Then she nudged me playfully with her shoulder. "Sweet digs, sister. Much better than my lady cave sex dungeon."

I nodded absently, but the questions racing through my mind were too murky and numerous to let myself truly enjoy the moment. I grunted at a thought. The White Rose didn't have time to stop and smell the roses. Go figure.

"I haven't really had the chance to explore it yet," I said, leaning down on my forearms and breathing in the rich, earthy smells from the gardens. "As soon as I arrived, I heard about Kansas City." I studied the sweep of luscious greenery, but I just couldn't get into any happy thoughts. "You know, it would have been incredibly helpful if Alucard had mentioned that the Shepherds had an angel on the bench, let alone one I personally knew," I grumbled.

Claire murmured her agreement. "Shocked the hell out of me. What also shocked the hell out of me was when my usually intelligent friend decided to try summoning a fucking archangel," she added in a very dry tone, "while she was stuck in a spell that made her look, sound, and smell like a demon. That one really shocked me."

I grunted. "This is exactly why I didn't tell you. Michael and I are cool. We go way back."

Claire shot me an astonished look. "Way back, eh?" she said doubtfully.

I nodded. "He took me to his place once. Helped me out of a pickle."

Claire stared at me. "I think you're grossly exaggerating your friendship."

"You're just jealous that I'm friends with angels."

She rolled her eyes. "Yeah. One of those angel pals of yours just tried to kill me. I don't think I'm in the market for meeting any more of your friends." She picked at the railing with a fingernail, looking lost in thought, or debating something heavy on her mind. Finally, she made up her mind. "I must be a terrible friend to not know about your psycho angel pals. Too absorbed in my own little world, not bothering to tell you about all my adventures—"

I swatted her in the arm, cutting her off. "Yeah, yeah. I get it," I muttered. "While you were off playing *find the honeypot* with Kenai in Alaska, I met some new people."

"Find the honeypot..." She chuckled huskily. "That's not a half-bad idea. By any chance, did you *finally* play any games with Nate while I was gone?" Her eyes abruptly twinkled with mischievous excitement. "Maybe something *super* weird with your magic—"

I cut her off with a forceful shove this time, my face aflame. "No. None of that. Unfortunately." I added the last bit because it was true. I was also hoping it would appease the horn-ball enough for her to let go of the topic. "Like I was saying, I ran into Michael about a year ago. He wanted to talk to me about the whole Nameless thing, imprisoning a fallen angel inside my ring."

Claire shivered, fingering the bracelet on her wrist—a band of creamy leather about the size of a watch with no face, and scribbled with unfamiliar dark runes. Seeing those, I hurriedly averted my gaze, not wanting to think about the omegabet I'd somehow translated in my mother's laboratory. The bracelet made Claire bulletproof—courtesy of Darling and Dear—although it hadn't offered much help against Angel Eae.

I sighed, brushing off the thought. Claire had been there the night I trapped Nameless.

"You didn't mention anything about Michael when you were telling me about the Doors," she said, frowning.

I shrugged. "I didn't tell you about the croissant I ate that morning either, Claire," I muttered, rolling my eyes. "It's not like you handed over your diary of the last year either. It wasn't important at the time. Now, it is. When we figure all this crap out, we can rent some cheesy movies, get drunk, and overshare to our hearts' desire with a sleepover. Right now, we don't have time," I snapped, more harshly than I had intended.

She was quiet for a few seconds, letting me get my breathing under control. "Easy, Callie. I wasn't picking a fight. Just...I've *missed* you," she admitted, her voice cracking slightly. Then she leaned over the balcony and I saw a tear fall onto the railing below her.

That single drop startled the hell out of me. I hadn't said anything *that* mean.

She refused to meet my eyes as she spoke. "I give off this brave face, flaunt my body, make suggestive jokes, but inside..." she trailed off, blinking another tear onto the balcony. "Inside, I'm fucking *screaming*, Callie!" she finished in a hoarse whisper.

My own eyes misted up and my breath caught at the level of pain in her voice. Even still, it didn't make any sense, catching me entirely by surprise. I turned to her suddenly. "Did Kenai—"

"No! Nothing like that. It's not boy trouble," she muttered, waving a hand. "It's...well, it's *everything*, Callie. I'm a goddamned polar bear!" she blurted out, as if she'd been bottling up that simple statement for far too long. "My life has shifted into this incredibly frightening nightmare. And it just keeps getting scarier! I used to be a veterinarian, Callie. And today we fought a fucking *angel*! One who would have killed you if Last Breath hadn't jumped in at the last second to save your ass. *Think* about that!" she sobbed angrily. "I've been searching for you for a *year*, Callie. I *finally* find you...and you were almost *beheaded* in front of me not twelve hours later! I would have lost my ever-loving *mind*..." She shuddered, panting desperately and no longer caring that she was openly crying.

I stood entirely still, numb to the bone. I...*hadn't* thought about that. Definitely not in that way. It would have utterly shattered Claire. No matter how tough she was. Hell, she'd been on the verge of going feral the moment I set my eyes on her in my apartment. One gentle nudge away from losing her humanity entirely. My death would have been a drop-kick.

"Sure, there are parts of this that I love," Claire continued, wiping at her nose with her robe as she regained some of her composure, "and parts that terrify me. But mostly...it's all just so *much*. At first, I bottled it in as a coping mechanism to keep my own sanity. Letting the aggression and instincts of the bear take over is actually a huge relief. I've pretty much been relying on it to survive. But that human part of me—Goldilocks, I call her—is slowly starting to come out of her hiding place, and I'm not sure where she fits anymore. *If* she fits anymore," she whispered.

I couldn't take it anymore, blinking through a blurry film of my own tears, each word from Claire feeling like the stab of a knife to my heart. I wrapped my arms around her and pulled her close, petting her hair. "I had no idea, Claire. You put on such a brave face that I didn't even think to press you on it. I thought you had embraced your new...changes, like the bear had helped you open up or something." I thought a little levity might help. "You know, *I am woman, hear me roar*."

Claire didn't laugh. Not at all. "How would you know? You haven't really been here, Callie," she said, with a touch of exasperation in her voice that made me wince. "You run off to St. Louis, or Italy, or some magical realm. Or you tell me to get out of town for a while because Kansas City isn't safe. You're either here and want me gone, or gone when I am here," she whispered, twisting the knives buried in my heart. "So I head back to the bears in Alaska, because I don't know what to do when I'm all by myself, Callie, and I can't afford to let anyone *know* that!"

"I'm *so* sorry, Claire..." I whispered, squeezing her tightly.

She finally warmed up to me, her body no longer rigid and unyielding. We stood that way for a solid minute until I was sure it was okay to talk again.

"Silly old bear," I whispered, ignoring the tears spilling down my cheeks as I nuzzled her hair. "You don't have to pick one or the other. You're a BAB either way."

She pulled back, frowning up at me with her tear-filled, red-rimmed eyes. "A what?"

I smiled. "You're either a Bad Ass Bitch or a Bad Ass Bear. BAB." She smirked slightly but gave me only the most pathetic of shrugs in response. "I went through a similar thing last year...an internal crisis. That's what I called it anyway," I told her, trying a different tactic.

"All the White Rose stuff?" she asked. I nodded. "When I first heard people talking about the White Rose, it took me a while to realize the boogeyman everyone was talking about was my best friend." She studied me thoughtfully. "Heard you killed a lot of monsters. More than a lot..."

I nodded. "I did," I admitted. "I was having trouble finding my place in the world. I didn't want to belong to any of my old groups. I was also pissed off that a few of my old groups had turned their backs on me. On Roland. I went dark, Claire. Really dark. I lost my way."

Claire squeezed my biceps reassuringly. "That's okay. It happens. Usually only once a month, though," she said, smiling. "I'm glad to hear I'm not the only schizophrenic girl on the streets of Kansas City. What does that say about me?" she mused rhetorically.

I laughed faintly, wiping at my nose. "I really could have used you as a sounding board, so I guess I kind of know what you mean about the bear thing. I'm sorry I haven't been here for you."

She smiled. "Our friendship would be pretty boring if we didn't bicker about something every now and again. Just imagine if we were always sane... how boring that would be."

I smiled, nodding. "Yeah. Who wants stability in their relationships?"

I thought about everything Qinglong had told me, that I needed to find out who I could trust. That I needed to find a way to form special bonds with them—strengthened by something stronger than words—a blood bond like the one I'd shared with him.

And I realized that if I couldn't trust Claire, I was pretty much done with life. I had tested her time and time again, even pushing her away to such an extent that she thought I had snapped a fuse and turned demonic the night I trapped Nameless.

But she had seen through my ruse. She was my cornerstone. My rock.

Even still, there was the chance that one of these Masters could have chosen her for that *exact* reason, turning her against her knowledge—using cats' paws like Qinglong had warned.

"Let's go sit down. I'll tell you what I've been thinking lately. I could use a fresh pair of eyeballs," I said, guiding her over towards a wicker couch not far away. Hearing her open up about her troubles, what she'd felt—but never shared—as a result of being turned to a shifter bear against her will...well, that had been as genuine and honest as friendship could get.

Turning your back on everyone or bottling up your pain only led down dark roads. I'd experienced something similar a year ago. The White Rose had been a heartless killer who had pretty much turned her back on everyone, trying to do the right thing but not having defined her purpose.

So while it was wise to be perceptive, alert, skeptical, and reasonably paranoid...I needed to have at least one person I could count on when things turned to hell. Brothers—like Cain—were great, but there just wasn't any substitute for girlfriends.

Sisters before Misters was a rule for a reason.

"Can you do me a small favor?" I asked, my heart suddenly beating erratically.

She nodded, not looking back at me as we walked. "Sure."

I took a deep breath, set my shoulders, and stepped up beside her. "I need you to drink some of my blood."

She froze, blinked a few times, and then slowly turned to look at me with a thoughtful expression. She opened her mouth, but then closed it. Finally, she shrugged her shoulders. "Okay. But we already shared blood as kids, remember? I didn't *drink* it, though," she said pensively, resuming her walk. "Think that makes a difference?"

I flinched, feeling as if I'd just been struck between the eyes.

She...was *right*. We'd done one of those childhood blood pacts where we sliced our palms and shook hands to prove our undying friendship.

"Fuck me..." I breathed, catching up with her. Was *that* why Claire was always so reliable? Had we *already made* one of the blood bonds Qinglong had shown me? Even though she hadn't *tasted* my blood, we'd *exchanged* blood. Wasn't that even *more* meaningful?

I closed my eyes, focusing inwards like I had done with Qinglong. Almost immediately, I sensed a low, steady *thrum* between us, and I saw that a cord of light as thick as braided rope connected us—much stronger than what I'd seen with Qinglong. But he'd been a god and I hadn't *exchanged* blood with him like I had done with Claire so many years ago.

"Just to be clear, that wasn't you asking me for a second favor, right?" she asked, having stopped with me when I closed my eyes. "I'm all for taking one for the team, but—"

I opened my eyes, laughing as I realized she was referring to my *fuck me* comment. "No! That wasn't a request, jerk." I gripped her shoulders, shaking her excitedly. "I can trust you!"

She narrowed her slowly darkening eyes, looking about ready to punch me right in the mouth. "Of course you can, idiot." She cocked her head quizzically. "What's going through that head of yours?" she asked, frowning uncertainly. "Did you doubt me?"

I laughed, shaking my head fiercely. "No! Well, *yes*, but not because of anything you did. It's..." I struggled with where to start. "It's Hocus Pocus stuff," I explained, waving my fingers dramatically. "But I can tell you all about it, now!"

Because my previous explanation to her and Richard had been topical, avoiding so much of what I'd learned from Qinglong that might put them—or me—at risk. Now, I could actually get into the Masters thing. Well, we weren't protected by my mother's laboratory, so I would still need to be careful, but I now knew for a fact that Claire was on my team.

Sensing Claire staring at me warily, I wrapped her up in a hug, squeezing tightly before shoving her onto the wicker couch. "Let's chat. You have no idea how much better I feel to get this off my chest..."

And I began to tell her what I had learned, what I suspected, what I planned, and what I needed her to do.

The look on her face as I unveiled my plan was priceless. It was fuel for my heart, slowly repairing the damage it had taken to learn of my parents' decisions, and more importantly, of how badly I'd screwed up as a friend to Claire. Pretty soon we were both crying and snotting all over each other.

Sisters before Misters. A very powerful magic.

Take heed, gentlemen. Never interrupt one of these rituals, unless you want to volunteer yourself for the sacrificial altar...

We will oblige you.

38

We talked for half an hour or so, maybe longer. And as I listened to stories of her time in Alaska—very detailed stories as opposed to what she'd told me before—I felt my soul stitching itself back together, stronger than ever. To know beyond a shadow of a doubt that I could trust her—that she couldn't be turned by the Masters...

I had needed that more than I had cared to admit. A rock to clutch onto in a raging river.

Because I was definitely about to jump back into the white-water rapids of current events in Kansas City. Hell, I was about to stir shit up from the Missouri to the Mississippi river, from Kansas City to St. Louis, and it was absolutely going to cause some flooding. My crazy plan actually excited me. I felt like I'd spent so much time sitting down and being beaten in the face with knowledge—from Xuanwu to Qinglong—that I considered the risk of physical danger much like a tube of *Icy Hot* on sore muscles.

It was time to remind everyone who I was. In a way they would never expect.

Catching Claire up on my own journeys—how I briefly became Kansas City's Jackie the Ripper with my White Rose letter jacket, more depth on my experiences through the Doors, the dragon living in my mother's laboratory, and other things—had been a great feeling, too.

Because something many people didn't understand was that there were two levels to a story. Much like the part of the iceberg visible above the ocean's surface was one level of a story—the factual side. But the gargantuan size of the iceberg below the surface was the real meat of a story—the emotional side.

Put another way, the bricks of a story—the facts—were held together by messy, goopy mortar—the emotions. Without that sloppy gunk, you just had a tower of loose rocks.

And since Richard and Solomon had stepped away, we had nothing better to do. Well, I had one thing I needed to do, but I needed Richard's help to do it.

I'd approached this whole mess in Kansas City too timidly. I'd been running around everywhere demanding answers—like a rookie level policeman trying to put a report together so that he could fill out the paperwork and set it on his boss' desk and clock out for the day.

Like trying to learn martial arts by only watching fights from the audience or on a TV.

There was a time and place for that type of learning, but it was usually only *after* you'd stepped into the ring a time or two and bloodied your nose. A way to add some perspective to your wounds.

To truly *learn* the thing, you needed to *do* the thing.

There was no substitute for a good punch to the jaw to really deliver an understanding of the nature of fighting to one's basal ganglia. So far, I'd been screaming and hollering at the TV, complaining when my fighter lost, yelling at the referees, cursing out the opponent.

But it had really been the time to *act*. To get punched in the jaw. To spit out some blood, tongue my loose tooth, and grin through a bloody maw at my enemy as I climbed back to my feet with my fists up.

Because I had a piece of work ahead of me, and no amount of planning was going to get the job done.

My fight with Eae and Arthur had firmly put me in the Shepherds' bad graces. I really didn't see a point in seeking out the First Shepherd anyway, even if I could, but it wasn't going to make my job any easier, either. My real problem was with Roland and his Dracula obsession. Whether he intended an alliance of some kind or to harm Dracula in some way—robbery or murder—didn't really matter. Both resulted in dire consequences for my city.

I saw Richard walk through a different set of tall doors to reenter the balcony alone, Solomon nowhere in sight. I closed my eyes for a moment, focusing. Then I opened them again to smile as he approached, shoving the object Claire had given me into the back of my jeans. I didn't ask where she'd gotten it, but she had to have stolen it since she'd arrived here naked. I guess that also meant she'd stolen it from me, in a way.

"Is he okay?" I asked as he slowed a few paces away from us, probably wondering why we looked all splotchy and sticky. Rituals were messy and he was wise enough not to comment on or question the dark arts of sister-craft.

"Sleeping," he answered tiredly. "He's getting worse. I'm not sure how much time he has left, to be honest."

I'd assumed as much, judging by the thorns poking out from his flesh. Claire was giving me a stern look. "He will be fine for a few more days. I'm sure of it."

Richard narrowed his eyes at me. "Care to elaborate?" he asked, his voice strained.

"My mother left a journal that talked about the ward she used. I'll need to study it, but I know for a fact he has at least three or four days. I'll take care of him well before then or arrange for him to be taken care of if I'm unable to make it back in time," I promised. "Don't worry. I won't let anything happen to him, Richard. But I need you to drop it. Now."

He clicked his mouth shut stubbornly, but finally gave me a stiff nod. "Okay."

"I need your help. And I need you to not ask me any questions about it."

He looked up sharply, considering the serious look on my face. "What would you have me do?" he asked, not necessarily answering me. I waited patiently, arching a brow at him. He finally sighed, rolling his eyes. "Okay. No questions other than *that*," he finally muttered.

"Who's a good boy? Dandy lion is a good boy! Yes he is!" Claire cooed in her old veterinarian voice—the one she had used for sick pets before and after their check-ups.

Richard curled a lip at her. "What I would do for a Klondike bar right now."

Claire laughed, clapping her hands. "Nice."

He grunted with a satisfied look on his face before turning back to me. "So?"

"I need to visit the Armory. Right now. I need to do a little therapy shopping."

His smile evaporated, replaced by a sickly grimace. "That's...dangerous," he finally said.

I nodded, climbing to my feet. "I'm counting on it. But when a lady needs to shop, she doesn't need to do it tomorrow," I said, already walking towards him with purposeful strides.

He raked a hand through his hair, muttering something under his breath. "Follow me, I guess," he finally mumbled dryly. "But you're not allowed to go alone."

Claire piped up immediately. "Oh, I'm coming, too. I don't care—"

I held up a hand, cutting them both off. I took a moment to consider my plan. Finally, I turned to Claire. "I need you to stay here in case Phix wakes up. She might know something useful." She opened her mouth to protest—that Richard should be the one to stay behind since he had been caring for Phix anyway and knew the Temple better than anyone—but I used my womanly laser eyes to let her know it hadn't been a request. That I needed her—specifically—here, and that I wasn't able to explain why in front of the drooling man-creature behind me.

She let out her breath in a huff, nodding begrudgingly. "Fine, but I'm waiting by the door," she muttered.

I smiled gratefully, turning back to Richard. "Lead on...Dandy lion."

His glare darkened and he nodded stiffly, sensing that something significant had just transpired, and that he hadn't been a part of it—even though he had seemingly won the sidekick lottery to join me on my shopping trip.

The two of us followed the lion like lionesses.

"About you somehow casting this demon disguise upon yourself but not remembering it," Richard said, conversationally. "That's probably significant."

I nodded absently, studying the halls he led us through. "Probably."

He glanced over his shoulder at my blasé response. "You had to have a very good reason to make yourself forget what you did, and why you did it."

I nodded, still studying the walls. It really was a beautiful place. "Probably."

His shoulders bristled at my clipped tone and another seemingly unconcerned answer.

"And I don't understand how your mother spelled the Seal to redirect you to her rooms. It should have been impossible to do such a thing. No spell can tie itself to this place. Well, Nate Temple's Armory is tied here, but he is leasing a secluded part of the Temple from us. We just placed an access door for him inside Chateau Falco—which is about the second safest place on the planet, I would imagine."

I nodded distractedly, studying a room full of statues—a ridiculous number of them. "And look at where we're going," I mused, as if speaking to myself, still not meeting his eyes.

I could practically feel Claire grinning behind me, and from the look on Richard's face in my peripheral vision, he could see her amused grin, too.

He grunted angrily, his bare feet slapping the marble floor tiles a little louder than before. I smiled to myself, holding out a hand behind my back in the universal *stop* gesture to discourage Claire from antagonizing him more than I already was.

We passed a library of sorts, shelves climbing at least three stories, and I saw that the far end of the room featured a pair of wide glass doors stretching all the way to the ceiling to let in light—or fresh air when opened. Tubs, baskets, and barrels packed loosely with scrolls filled one corner of the room, but we were already striding past it before I could discern anything else.

"What do you know about Dracula?" I asked casually. He glanced back at me, frowning. I knew Claire had kept Dracula's name out of her story when catching them up to speed, so I wasn't concerned about him reading too deeply into it. I pointed at the library we had just passed and shrugged. "Figured this place must have metric tons of documents, studies, relics, and other snippets of information. Solomon was known as a wise man." I indicated the obviously elaborate halls, the exquisite marble, the priceless paintings hanging from the walls. "Wisdom pays well."

He nodded slowly, turning to walk backwards. "Solomon likes to collect information. What did you want to know?"

I shrugged. "Just a thought that crossed my mind, what with all this vampire drama on my plate. Other than sucking blood from helpless humans, what other trouble did he get into?"

Richard thought about it, still looking suspicious that I had an ulterior motive, but he finally nodded, turning around to resume a normal walk, answering me over his shoulder.

"Vlad Dracul..." he began, collecting his thoughts in a lecturing tone, "made a deal with a devil for power—and was cursed with vampirism for his meddling. Other than the obvious, he was also a collector. Built a secluded castle where he could hide his treasures from prying eyes. Not a lot of neighbors," he added dryly. "They just kept disappearing."

I smiled faintly. Right. "So...much like Solomon, then," I said casually.

Richard's shoulders stiffened, but he didn't look back at me as he took a deep, calming breath. "I hadn't thought of it in quite that way before, but yes," he admitted. "They're practically identical. Except for the devil bit, of course." I ignored his deadpan tone.

"What might Dracula have collected over the years that could interest someone today?"

He slowed, turning to look at me again. "I'm not sure what's really going on here, but if you have a specific question, or care to fill me in on the details, I can probably be a lot more helpful."

"You probably could," I agreed, gazing past him, "If I was asking a specific question or cared to fill you in on the details."

He stopped abruptly, his lips curling upwards in a snarl.

I paused, arching an eyebrow at him. "Did you have...*a question*?" I asked, emphasizing the last word to remind him what he had agreed to a few minutes ago on the balcony.

He gritted his teeth, face growing darker, but he shook his head stiffly and turned on his heel, resuming his walk. It was a full minute, and a few turns from the main hallway before he answered my question. "Everything in his collection would be desirable. It's why he collected it in the first place. It depends on what you are interested in," he said, voice tight with anger. "But it doesn't really matter what anyone wants. His castle is a puzzle. Those who enter die or are never heard from again. I'm not sure I've ever actually met anyone who survived it. Some have entered the guest areas by invitation, but Dracula's Castle dwarfs even this place. It's like saying you survived Solomon's Temple when you really just sipped tea on the balcony," he said, pointing a thumb over his shoulder back the way we had come.

I pursed my lips thoughtfully. Interesting. What was Roland up to?

"We're here," he said, halting before a tall oaken door covered in a woodland motif of trees, wild beasts, fairies, a cave standing atop a hill, and a calm, secluded pond.

"You better pick me up something cool," Claire muttered.

39

I frowned at the door, wondering if the carving itself held any special significance or if it was just an elaborate piece of art. It had taken a long time to create, down to the finest details on the fairies' wings and their twinkling eyes. I sensed no specific magic, though, so turned to Richard, patiently waiting for him to open it.

"I remember the way back," Claire said helpfully into the thick silence.

I held up a hand. "This is an invasion, according to the lease agreement, right? We need permission to enter their space. Don't we?"

Richard nodded stiffly. "Like I said. Dangerous."

I turned to Claire. "Mind sticking around here for a while? We shouldn't be long, but you can keep the door open for us. In the off chance any of Nate's friends are in the Armory and see me as a demon, I'd rather make a run for it than fight them."

She nodded slowly, not having considered that, even though I'd shared my plan with her on the balcony. To be honest, the thought had only hit me as we walked through the Temple, as I had been testing Richard's patience.

"It's still part of Solomon's Temple, though," Claire said. "Maybe you won't look like a demon over there." None of us knew why my disguise wasn't apparent here. Richard hadn't seen it at all, of course, and he had other reasons to be concerned. Like my frosty attitude towards him and my mysterious guy friend from the alley.

I shrugged. "*Maybe* isn't going to keep a werewolf from ripping my face off."

Claire's fists balled up at her sides, her anger and protectiveness jumping to life at the casual mention of very likely danger just three feet away. She slowly turned her threatening glare to Richard. "You better keep her safe, pussycat. Or we're going to have a problem."

He rolled his eyes. "What is *up* with you two?" he finally asked. "Have you both forgotten that I pledged my life to her?" he demanded, pointing at me.

I studied him thoughtfully, keeping my face blank. "You can do illusions, Richard. And not considering your version of events for a moment, I thought someone cast an illusion on me to make me look like a demon. Then you return, and suddenly that illusion is gone. And you have a wildly different story that no one else can corroborate." I shrugged, having spoken in a tone that didn't accuse him of being a liar, but simply stated contradicting facts.

Regardless of my caution, Richard looked as if I'd just punched him in the jaw for saying *good morning* to me. Then, understanding and concern dawned as he realized I was right. Or at least that I wasn't wrong. I'd checked him earlier for a bond to me—upon seeing him return from tending to Solomon—but it had been a flimsy line of power compared to what I shared with Claire. And I didn't want a bond born from prior obligation, carried over to me out of an antiquated sense of duty. I wanted his bond for myself. So, taking a page from Qinglong, I wanted to extend our lease, so to speak. To know—not assume—that we were on the same page.

Too much was at risk.

"If you doubt me," Richard rasped in a barely restrained growl, "tell me to my face, but you better also be ready to tell me what you need me to do to *rectify* that doubt."

"Are you sure about that?" I asked, locking eyes with him. "You want to have my trust?"

He nodded resolutely. "Yes, Callie. I. Do," he growled defiantly.

"Then suck my blood," I told him without hesitation, cutting the pad of my finger on the dagger Claire had given to me on the balcony. Silver-ish red blood beaded up on the small wound. I was startled to see that the silver color was visible. It wasn't always the case, and I hadn't discovered what made it come into play or not.

Richard stood there with his mouth hanging open, momentarily thrown for a loop.

Without missing a beat, Claire suddenly grabbed my wrist, stuck my finger in her mouth, and lapped up the blood. Her eyes instantly sprang wide and she jumped backwards, her shoulders momentarily rigid. She flexed her fingers absently and managed to relax her shoulders before meeting my eyes with a stunned look. I watched her, just as surprised. What the hell had *that* been all about?

Her voice shook slightly. "I...think the silver struck me on a *genetic* level," she breathed. "It hurt for a second, but it's gone now, thank god. I didn't even consider that aspect."

I shivered. She was right. Shifters weren't fans of silver, which meant my blood was *actually* silver, rather than just *looking* like silver. I'd already told her about the bond of light between us, so she hadn't needed to do this. Then again, she knew how badly I wanted to trust Richard—especially after what he'd told me in private—so she had volunteered herself without hesitation. Also, it offered the alpha-male a challenge he could recognize after having to suffer through our female mental gymnastics for the past few hours.

Or, in man-speak...a gauntlet thrown. Time to man-up. *Do you even lift, bro?*

I closed my eyes for a moment, focusing on the cord of light I had seen on the balcony with Claire. And I almost gasped with joy to see it was now crackling with silver sparks like a sparkler! Apparently, my blood was a little bit more potent these days compared to when we had been in our wonder years.

Another thought hit me as I opened my eyes, slightly dampening my momentary joy. That the cord of power between us looked awfully similar to what I had seen extending to Roland's vampires and wolves. I suppressed that thought with a shudder, turning to Richard.

Claire was staring at him with a smug look. "Too pussy to try it?" she teased.

He narrowed his eyes at her, drawing up his resolve until it felt like a physical presence wrapped around his shoulders. He didn't break eye contact with me as he approached, gently lifted my finger to his lips, and licked up a drop of my silver blood. He grimaced distastefully, swallowing several times. "Not as good as the red kind, but it will do in a pinch."

It was interesting to see that silver didn't have an effect on him like it had with Claire—like it would with any shifter.

"Was something significant supposed to happen?" he asked coldly.

I closed my eyes, checking the bond between us...

And a warm smile split my cheeks. A thick, pulsing, white and blue cord of light connected us—much stronger than earlier. I opened my eyes and let out a breath.

"Thank you," I told him. "I learned some frightening things in my mother's laboratory...and I needed to be sure of your loyalty. I'm sure now," I said, smiling.

Richard nodded, some of his temper cooling at the mention of my mother. "Oh. I didn't realize..." he trailed off, frowning at a new thought. "Did she say I was untrustworthy" he asked, sounding wounded.

I held up my hands in a calming gesture as I shook my head adamantly. "No. The opposite, in fact," I reassured him. "It's just...there are some bad things coming our way soon, and I was informed that I really needed to verify where everyone stands before the bullets start flying. That simple promises and words wouldn't be enough. That they could be easily broken." I was silent for a few seconds, letting him digest that.

He finally nodded. "That makes sense. And you thought blood was some kind of lie detector?" he asked, not in a mocking tone but a thoughtful one.

I nodded. "My blood apparently is."

"As much as I hate to admit it, you were right to check," he finally said. Then he grinned. "Does this mean you can now tell me about the...fleshstached man you met?"

Despite his humor, I gave it serious thought. "You have to promise not to be upset..." He nodded eagerly. "My mom brought a dragon home. He lives in her lab. But he's nice, and he knows how to help Solomon."

Richard's face paled with concern and...well a whole slew of emotions, flickering from one to another like he was having a seizure.

I held up a hand. "He won't talk to anyone but me, and no one can enter without me. But what he did to Solomon was under my mother's orders. *Anyone* trying to enter her lab without me gets hit with the thorns," I said, fudging the truth a little bit.

He sputtered wordlessly, struggling to verbalize a coherent string of letters or sounds.

"I think he's about to cough up a hairball," Claire said, taking a step back.

"The sooner we get this over with, the sooner I can look into healing Solomon," I reminded Richard, eyeing the door.

He finally took a deep breath, shaking his head. "You are just as infuriating as your mother was."

I curtsied politely.

He glanced up at the door as if gathering his courage. "Why are we really going in there? Because I don't believe it's about shopping. Why do you need to see Nate Temple?"

I took a measured breath. "I need to murder Hope..."

Claire made an unpleasant sound behind me, but I paid her no attention, my mind already made up. I had given this a lot of thought—not even counting the cryptic advice and hints I had been given, like murdering hope to gain an army of ninjas.

Another perk of having an Armory next door might be that I actually *could* rent some of those items. Powerful, dangerous items. Artifacts and weapons deemed too powerful to leave out in circulation. They shouldn't be left on shelves to collect dust. Maybe there was something in the Armory that was strong enough to break down Roland's barrier—or at least the front door of his church.

"Okay. You sure about this?" Richard asked after a few moments. "If you trust me, of course." He flashed me a teasing smirk, taking the sting out of the question.

I nodded, squaring my shoulders. "Let's do it. Claire, keep this door open in case we need to run back through."

Claire nodded, and Richard opened the door. Dust fell as it opened, and the loud creaking sound seemed to echo for miles—both inside Solomon's Temple *and* the Armory. Soft, ambient light shone from the hallway ahead of us, the walls more of a sandstone than the white marble on this side of the door. Then again, my mother's lab had different stone as well. I'd briefly visited the Armory before, but I hadn't known I was the landlord back then.

No monsters or friends of Nate jumped out at us, and I let out a breath I hadn't known I'd been holding. I stepped through the door at the same time as Richard, keeping my eyes alert. I opened my mouth to tell Richard where we needed to start our search...

And Pandora rounded the corner, coming to an abrupt halt to blink at us a few times.

"Oh, dear. Look at what the cat dragged in," she said, eyeing the two of us.

She lifted a hand and the door slammed shut behind us.

"Shit," I muttered, ignoring the sounds of Claire pounding her fists on the other side of the door. I stared at Pandora—one of the most dangerous people I had ever heard about.

Her box was famous for all the wrong reasons...

Her eyes twinkled in anticipation, practically glittering with malevolence.

40

Pandora wore a sheer, practically transparent, toga that left one shoulder bare, toed the line between covering her breasts and emphasizing her side boobs, and finally ended just above her knees like a summer dress. Her skin was the color of warm caramel, and her hair glistened as if in sunlight, despite us being in a dim hallway. Her eyes glittered with wisdom—both the kind you wanted to learn and the kind you fled screaming from.

She smiled warmly at Richard. "Landlord," she said, curtsying deeply, barely dodging a wardrobe malfunction.

He smiled back politely, keeping his eyes averted from her body in a chivalric attempt at decency, hiding his uneasiness behind class. "My lady," he said with a formal bow.

I suddenly realized that I was way overdressed for this pajama party compared to her Pandora's Secret negligee and Dick Heffner's robe.

She turned to me, eyeing me up and down appraisingly. "Landlady," she said politely at the base of another curtsy. "Glad to finally have you back where you belong. I hate it when things just wander off. I swear, sometimes I feel like I'm herding cats." She absently caressed a leather belt hanging over her forearm as she spoke.

I let out a breath of relief. "I thought you were going to kill us," I admitted, having feared she would see me as a demon like everyone in Kansas City.

"On principle, it isn't advisable to kill one's landlady, Callie."

I gave her a genuine smile, my gaze absently settling on the leather strap laying across her forearm. My smile slowly faltered, ultimately turning into an outright frown. I pointed at it, my hand shaking. "Where did you get that?" I whispered, suddenly recognizing it. It was the sheath from my mother's lab. The piece that had disappeared when I had spoken my name.

Excalibur.

She smiled. "It returned a short while ago—a safety precaution either your parents or Nate's parents must have put in place. I'll keep it safe until you're ready to deliver it in person," she said. "And you'll need to give it to him willingly, like I did."

I nodded woodenly, realizing I wasn't quite sure how to take any of her three statements. "Who...do you want me to give it to?" I finally asked, picking one.

She grinned from ear-to-ear. "That's the spirit, sister!" she cheered, licking her lips.

I replayed the words in my mind and immediately felt my cheeks heating up. "That wasn't what I meant!" I hissed, realizing it sounded downright scandalous in the wrong context.

"Oh. I must have missed that memo," she said. "When it was my turn to give it to him, I gave it to him in a hot tub." And this time, her smile was in no way innocent, cute, or playful. It was downright feral and dripping with heat.

My face blushed furiously, entirely crimson. I was sure of it.

She smiled at me. "Oh, I get it now! You think I'm talking about Nate!" she hooted. Then she held up a hand, shaking her head. "Don't worry, I would never bang a Master," she said, chuckling.

I shuddered at the look in her eyes, wondering how literal she was being with the last part. She wouldn't bang Master Temple or...one of the bad Masters Qinglong warned me about?

I steadily regained control of my breathing. "Why do I need to deliver it?" I asked. "Can't you do it for me? The sheath obviously chose you for a reason. I've apparently been carrying it around for a long time, circling the block without an address."

Pandora was already shaking her head. "You need to officially bequeath

Excalibur to the King, relinquishing your claim to it." She lifted the leather and sniffed it loudly. "It still smells like your soul," she explained, carefully placing it back on her forearm. "And something else I can't quite place," she added, pensively tapping her lips. "In any case, it's tainted with whatever lady musk you have going on. It needs to be cleansed. Freely given to the King."

I shook my head, dismissing the lady musk comment as I stared into her eyes. "Did you help Nate's parents do this to me?"

Pandora studied me thoughtfully. "I always do as I'm told."

I scowled at her, tapping my foot impatiently.

Pandora dipped her chin in acknowledgment, carefully considering her words. "Know that Calvin and Makayla Temple did their best—what they thought was best. Always. No matter the cost. They always took the path less traveled, and that has made all the difference..."

My patience was wearing thin. "Yes or no, Pandora."

She smiled. "Yes, I helped Calvin and Makayla...after they helped me. Gave me new purpose. Gave me shelter. Protected me from the world of embers and sparks. I had hoped those would fade away one day, but I was wrong. So, so wrong..." she said, sounding frightened for the first time since I'd entered the Armory.

Her words sent chills down my spine, even though I didn't know what they meant—embers and sparks.

Pandora continued on, and I realized she was smiling at me. "I'm not sure Nate ever caught what I meant when I told him Excalibur was around here somewhere. It's almost like he forgot I ever said it...Solomon's Temple, Nate Temple's Armory," she explained, winking at me. "Kind of obvious they would be connected, right? It's amazing no one saw that coming."

Richard cleared his throat lightly, reminding me why we were really here. He was right. I had promised myself to put all of this on the backburner. I had enough going on already.

Pandora smirked at him over my shoulder, understanding the not so subtle hint, but not taking offense by it. She smiled sweetly at me. "Anyway, I'll keep this here until you're ready to deliver it yourself. After you finish murdering Hope."

Richard made a strange coughing sound behind me. My spine locked rigid as I stared at Pandora, ready to bolt like a frightened rabbit. Taking a gamble, I met her eyes. "I don't put much stock in fortune cookies." Her lips curled up in a very amused smile, but she didn't speak. Since she didn't kill me on the spot, I pressed on. "I need to see Nate," I said, hoping she could bring him here for me rather than me risk searching for him myself.

She studied me thoughtfully, her eyes growing distant as if seeing something that wasn't there. Then they locked back onto me like a bird of prey. "Why do you seek Nate Temple?"

Considering that momentary distant look, I realized she wasn't asking a simple question. Pandora was playing a game. "I fear for my friend."

Pandora studied me, waiting for me to continue. When I didn't, she leaned closer, sniffing at me. "Fear..." she mused. "What a delicious sentiment. But remember, Callie, if we leave our toys on the shelf too long, sometimes they get picked up by others. Or wither away under a blanket of dust and broken dreams of what never was."

My heart was racing, but I kept my face collected as best I could. "I would never leave Nate on a shelf. Not willingly."

"What do you call leaving your toy alone on a shelf for a year?" she asked softly.

I lowered my eyes, not sure if she was talking about Nate or...something else entirely.

"I learned the secret of life. The meaning of it all," I finally said. "It cost me a year."

Pandora sucked in a sharp intake of breath, suddenly leaning closer, the fabric of her toga catching on the tips of her breasts as if aroused by my comment. She licked her lips, breathing huskily. "That's a slippery piece of knowledge isn't it? How long did you grasp it?" she whispered.

I tried not to lean away from her sudden animalistic energy. "An eternity. A heartbeat." I shrugged helplessly. The fact that she even knew it had been fleeting at all was eerie.

Pandora slowly calmed, closing her eyes for a moment as her breathing returned to normal. "What did it look like?" she finally asked, almost too softly to hear.

I smiled sadly, remembering my time on the roof with Solomon and Last Breath. "A broken man and a vapid little girl, holding hands before the end of the world," I whispered back, just as faintly.

Pandora clucked her tongue. "Ah. That's a good one."

"What did it look like to you?" I asked, curious.

"A box," she said, her voice strangely flat.

The hair on the back of my neck stood straight up and Richard shifted uncomfortably from foot to foot. A box. Pandora's box. She noticed the look on my face and nodded languidly. "I told you...yours was a good one."

I forced my shoulders to relax and met her eyes. "I thought I came here for advice, but now I grow concerned for Nate, which is—"

"You came here for love."

After a moment, I nodded, surprising even myself. "I guess you're right."

"Remember, eventually we all end up killing that which we love most."

"Not this girl," I said firmly.

She cocked her head at me, looking disappointed. "So, you are no longer here to murder Hope? That's unfortunate."

I blinked, my smile faltering slightly. "I've already told you I've learned to not put too much faith into words. Gods cast riddles like men throw dice—to gamble, to cheat, and to play games with human lives. I'm no gambler."

Richard murmured approvingly behind me, but Pandora studied me curiously, somewhat taken aback by my comment.

Then she blinked rapidly as if only just seeing me for the first time. "You read the omegabet..." she breathed, sounding stunned. "Oh, dear."

I winced, not really sure how to respond. "Just a little..."

She studied me pensively. "And they thought I was dangerous," she finally murmured, eyeing my forehead—the invisible-not-invisible brand. Before I could even open my mouth, she continued. "Wordplay is not inherently wicked, and it is not only used to gamble, cheat, or play games. Sometimes it is the safest—and only—way to share secret knowledge, requiring the student to earn the right to the lesson. To the Seeing." She seemed to place special emphasis on that last word but continued talking before I could think on it. "Much as a sword can murder or absolve, grant or take power, justify or decapitate. Words are weapons, child. Much sharper than any blade or magic." She pondered me critically. "Sometimes words mean exactly what they say. Even if you do not yet have the capacity to realize it."

Sensing her passion, I let a few moments pass before speaking.

"I mean Nate no harm whatsoever. In fact, I would rather the world burn than raise my hand against him."

Pandora smiled sadly. "Oh, child. You will raise your hand against him. Never promise what you cannot do. I already warned you that mankind always ends up killing what they love most in life." She gave me a sad, hopeful smile. "You will find Nate at home, but he is lonely."

"Why is Chateau Falco empty?" I asked nervously.

"Chateau Falco will never be empty, my sweet. Nate is home, with friends, but all alone. He's stuck in a dream, searching for a nightmare, crying as he laughs."

My skin threatened to vibrate right off my bones. "What are you talking about, Pandora? I really need to make sure he's okay," I demanded, feeling panicked.

Pandora cocked her head quizzically. "I just told you he is not okay. He struggles to find the end of the story. Only you can give that to him."

I shook my head willfully, finished with her word games. "I need to see him."

Pandora finally nodded, and then walked up to a nondescript door I hadn't noticed a few feet away from us. She opened it, studying the contents thoughtfully. Then she closed the door, knocked on it a few times, and then reopened it. Snow flurries flew inwards, blanketing her in fresh flakes. She shivered, brushing them away as she turned to us. "There you go. I'll leave it open for when you're ready to leave." She arched an eyebrow at me, smirking. "If you decide you want to leave," she giggled, rolling her hips suggestively.

Then she began walking backwards down the hall, watching me. "Remember, blades cut both ways, sweetie. Sometimes what you hear isn't what you hear. What you think isn't what you think. Killing is often just a balance. Wordplay, right?"

Then she began singing to herself as she turned away, skipping down the hall.

"Bah, bah, black sheep have you any wool? Yes, sir, yes sir, three bags full. One for the Master..." She trailed off, glancing over her shoulder just enough to let me see the smirk on the profile of her face. Then she was on her way again, continuing her song. "One for the dame, one for the little boy who lives down the lane..."

She let out one last giggle before skipping around the corner, out of sight.

I stared at the empty hallway, thinking on her song, narrowing my eyes against the flurries of snow drifting into the hallway and settling upon our feet.

The word dame had two definitions. The most popular was an old crone, but another was the female equivalent of a knight...

Richard cleared his throat, drawing my attention from the empty hall. "I don't think I will ever understand women. Let alone intelligent, powerful women," he mused, speaking almost as if to himself even though he'd drawn my attention first.

I smirked, shaking my head. "Misogynist."

His face purpled. "That's not what I—"

I laughed as I grabbed his arm and tugged him into a world of snow and ice. "Get furry and angry. It's the only thing you menfolk are good at," I teased.

In response, he dropped his robe and transformed into his massive white lion form, standing head and shoulders above me. I wondered where he stored his armor, since he wasn't wearing it this time either. I knew the armor was magic because when I'd knocked off his helmet upon first meeting him, the piece had fallen to the ground and disappeared in a swirl of vapor.

He snarled savagely as he was pelted with three snowballs—right in the snout—as fast as rapid-fire gunshots. I jumped behind him and accidentally stomped on his tail, making him yowl loud enough to cause an avalanche.

That's when I saw the army of tiny snowmen turn to face us like they shared one hive mind, and whoever had made them had used the charcoal pieces to give them all frowny faces.

"Come on, Hobbes!" I shouted, shoving him ahead of me. "Get furry and angry! It's the attack of the deranged mutant killer monster snow goons, and they look pissed!"

Even missing the Calvin and Hobbes reference, Last Breath obliged.

I loved my homicidal psycho temple cat.

41

I realized—seeing Nate battling dozens of deranged killer monster snow goons—that no matter what anyone said, I would never be able to kill this man. Not that I could not, but that I would not. The world could burn if that was the requirement to save it. And it had nothing to do with romance. Simply put, I loved this man. On every level I could contemplate. As a friend, as an ally, as a peer, and hopefully, one day, as a lover. Beneath his snarky arrogance, he was a gentle and kind soul, always willing to go the extra mile to care for—

He impaled an airborne snowman with a gnarled staff as tall as he was, spinning to swing it like a baseball bat to decapitate a trio of snowmen behind him. He was laughing as wind and snow whipped up his hair, and his cheeks were covered in stubble and flecks of blue blood from the snowmen he'd just murdered. Wild at heart.

A gentle and kind soul, I reminded myself.

He wore faded jeans with no shirt or shoes, but the cold didn't seem to touch him. Grimm—his homicidal unicorn—galloped around the perimeter of the camp, spearing snowmen left and right, laughing like a lunatic as he hurled startlingly disrespectful curses and taunts back at the dead and dying left in his wake.

Last Breath shot me a very stark look before sighing in resignation and leaping into the fray. I did the same, flinging balls of fire back and forth, scorching lines of snow goons into white and blue Slurpee juice until the camp looked like a convenience store invaded by a gang of teens at the height of summer. Something about the fight was just so undignified that I found I was grinning like an idiot, too. I almost felt like dancing as I slaughtered the harmless little guys.

Until one flung his nose at me and it detonated about a millisecond after I flung up my shield—orange grit exploding like shrapnel across the surface. After that, I took them a bit more seriously. They consisted of three spheres—one each for the head, the body, and the base—and they scooted across the snow like they were fans of Johnny 5 from Short Circuit.

Many of them had missing noses, which explained the carrot-colored craters here and there in the snow. An alarming number of stick arms and lumps of coal littered the slush as well, indicating many more snow goons had been here before we arrived.

Nate had glanced up sharply at my first fireball—eyes briefly widening to see me and a giant white lion opting in to help him clean up the mess—before he went right on back to killing snow goons, no longer laughing as openly as he had a few moments ago. Soon enough, only a few snow goons remained, and I even saw some trying to drag themselves away from the carnage—their bodies consisting of only two sections, the head and chest—leaking blue blooded smears behind them like amputated soldiers in a war movie.

Grimm took the time to calmly trot towards each of them, and then stomped his hooves through their heads without even bothering to look down. With a final snort, the unicorn turned to stare at us, lowering his horn in silent warning. I let out a breath, shaking my head at the ridiculousness of the fight, and waved at Grimm.

He continued staring at me, only moving his head to keep Last Breath in his line of sight as well. Now that the brief fight had ended, and I was no longer tossing fireballs, I realized how cold it was here. We stood on what seemed to be a small plateau beneath the peak of a very tall mountain, higher than even a blanket of clouds that hovered about fifty feet below the edge of our plateau. I had no idea where we were in Fae, exactly, but I could sense a vibrancy to the air that confirmed we definitely weren't in Missouri anymore.

Nate yanked his staff out from the ground, shaking blue slush from the end before he turned to stare at us as well. His face was blank, assessing us warily.

"You said you were friends, right?" Last Breath asked from the side of his mouth.

For the first time, I realized music was actually playing from a Bluetooth speaker perched atop a boulder. Katy Perry of all choices, and Grimm seemed to be unaware he was subtly bobbing his head to the beat. No wonder I'd felt like dancing during the brief fight.

I had never pictured Nate—or Grimm—as a Katy Perry fan.

"Hey, Nate," I said, breaking the awkward silence.

He dipped his head in acknowledgment. "Hey."

My smile faltered slightly, and I wondered if I might just look like a demon to earn such a hollow greeting. Because it always helped to think of things like that after the fact. Keeps your reflexes sharp.

The shirtless, barefoot man before me—still showing zero discomfort at the frigid chill—was more Wylde than Nate, more Fae than human, more savage than civilized, but I refused to think of him as anything other than Nate. Even so, I needed to tread very carefully here. To not appear threatening in any way whatsoever. Last Breath already seemed to have come to this understanding and had dipped his head politely at both Grimm and Nate before lowering his eyes—like one would do when confronting a wild or hyper-dominant animal.

I'd seen Nate in dark moments before, but never one this severe. He was one heartbeat away from destroying the world, and I wasn't sure he would feel any remorse in the action if he chose to cross that line. Why had his friends left him alone here like this? Couldn't they see what the Land of the Fae was doing to him?

Calm. I needed to keep him calm—

Grimm snorted, scraping one hoof at the snow in front of him in a not so discreet warning as he glared at Last Breath. "Who's the pussy—"

Nate flung up a hand, instantly cutting Grimm short, and the two turned to look behind them. My mouth fell open as a small, blonde-haired little girl hopped out from an igloo I hadn't noticed tucked against the wall of the mountain—the door tall enough for her to simply walk through. She wore a cute little blue dress with white polka dots, long white stockings, and shining yellow flats that definitely weren't suitable for the top of a mountain.

Then again, she had no coat either, and this was Fae, so I kept my mouth shut. She silently turned off the music and swept her gaze over the field of snow goons—now just blue slush, hunks of coal, orange grit, and amputated stick arms—with piercing blue eyes.

The little girl threw her hands up. "Great. Now we're going to have Bumblenuts circling the mountain in an hour—" Her eyes locked onto me and she blinked. Then they latched onto Last Breath and they rapidly switched to ecstatic glee. "Kitty!" she shrieked before sprinting towards my lion. Last Breath's eyes widened, and I grinned.

As if her arrival had been a white flag, the tension in the air lessened and Nate motioned for me to join him at a firepit circled by stumps, boulders, and a heavy log. I sighed in relief, making my way over to him.

The blonde little girl looked so cute and bubbly with her polka-dotted dress and deep blue eyes that I found myself grinning absently at her. She looked vaguely familiar for some reason that I couldn't quite pinpoint, as if she reminded me of someone.

Last Breath handled her exuberant affection well, allowing her to pet and tug on his mane. He even suffered her relentless chattering with an amused look on his face. "My werewolf friend, Gunnar, is bigger than you. Have you ever considered putting ribbons in your mane? Because I'm probably definitely going to put ribbons in your mane." I smiled to myself as she peppered him with more questions in a constant stream, barely pausing to take a breath.

I joined Nate beside the firepit, and blinked upon realizing the flames were bright blue, almost the same color as the snow goon blood. The coals looked like glowing chips of arctic ice. I even felt gusts of cold air occasionally flaring out between the usual waves of heat—like the fire couldn't quite decide whether it wanted to be an air conditioning unit or a heater when it grew up.

We sat silently, staring into the blue flames. Not trusting myself to say the right thing in his current mental state, I decided to wait him out. He finally let out a breath, poking the fire with his staff. The tip didn't seem to be flammable for some reason. In fact, it didn't really look like wood, now that I was closer to it—more like metal or stone.

"Lightning bolt," he said, noticing my glance—even though his eyes hadn't been focused on me. He'd caught me eyeing his staff from his peripheral vision.

You know what I mean.

"We set lightning traps since we're up so high," he explained. "And...we don't like lightning very much," he added in a vaguely suspicious tone. "Anyway, the bolts freeze when they hit our traps. I kept this one as a reminder to keep one eye on the sky." Then he grunted and let out a harsh, cold laugh as if he'd made a joke.

I nodded slowly, not completely following, but not wanting to appear judgmental. "It looks kind of...pretty," I admitted, studying it more closely. I swore I could see swirls of color within the grains of...whatever element it was.

He nodded. "This one hit a...rainbow I made," he said stiffly, as if he'd changed what he'd been about to say. Then he hurriedly set the staff down beside him. "You chose a hell of a time to visit. But that should be the last attack of the day," he assured me.

So casual about it, I thought to myself. Be careful.

He reminded me of a live electrical wire, yet he looked completely calm at the same time. I wondered again who had thought it a good idea to leave him alone up here like this. Even I could see it was changing him, and I'd only been here ten minutes or so.

The little girl skipped up to the fire, tugging Last Breath by the paw. She stared at me thoughtfully, cocking her little head as she pointedly gazed upon my forehead. I squirmed beneath her assessment, feeling like a subject in a science experiment. Then she eyed me critically from head-to-toe, seeming to stare through me—or possibly inside me. Her dimples were as deep as bullet holes, and her cute blue eyes made me feel like a white rabbit targeted by twin hunting rifles. "I'm Alice. Nate took me on an adventure. We had a fairy tale story with backwards dragons and knights," she said by way of introduction, not even giving us a minute to introduce ourselves. "Have you decided what you are here to do?" she asked sweetly.

I blinked once. Twice. Her outward demeanor and age had initially led me to assume she was nothing more than what she seemed—a beautiful little girl. But hearing her name and staring into those deep blue eyes now, I heard a small warning bell ringing inside my ears. Alice...she was Alvara's daughter. The mother and daughter Nate had promised to take to Fae—in direct violation of their still-standing banishment. On some instinctual level, I knew she was incredibly powerful, young enough to be led by her emotions, and her emotions were suddenly suspicious of me.

I nodded my head, trying not to show fear, wondering where her mother was. "Yes."

She nodded somberly, eyes calculating. I remained perfectly still. Nate folded his arms behind his head to lean back against a stump and grinned—a little of the man I knew shining through.

"Why are you wearing Demonskin? You're supposed to be royalty. It's confusing. Unless this is a masquerade ball." She turned to Nate. "This isn't a masquerade ball, is it?"

I stiffened for several different reasons, trying to shrug off Nate's sudden interest—like a wolf locking eyes with you in the middle of the woods when you were miles from habitation. He finally turned back to Alice and shook his head. "Not that I'm aware of."

"How do I take off my...Demonskin?" I asked her, not realizing my curse had a name. I'd assumed it wasn't visible at the moment. Nate had definitely recognized me, or he would have attacked on sight. Maybe the Demonskin was the source of the initial tension I'd felt from him. She had also mentioned a *masquerade ball*, just like Xuanwu had.

Alice frowned. "It's not *my* Demonskin. How would I know how to take it off? It's tied to your soul, and *that's* about as tangled up as I've seen in a long time. Worse than his was." She shot Nate a long-suffering look, but he was grinning, not saying a word to aid me. She turned back to me. "You must have big family problems to go to such great lengths."

Her words bit deep. "I'll try to take care of that," I said, wanting to punt the child off the cliff. Of course I had big family problems, but that didn't explain why I'd used this Demonskin on myself. Whoever had convinced me to do this was going to pay. Which was one of the reasons I was here.

Her personality was very...loud. Not necessarily in volume, but in energy. It would have been a lot more entertaining if she'd been targeting someone else, the tiny, Napoleonic bully.

"Your forehead is dusty. Royalty should keep their crowns clean," she said, eyeing my forehead again.

Nate coughed into his elbow, his shoulders shaking. "I'm not sure how to clean it, Alice," I said with a sigh, her comment making me think of what Pandora had said about toys collecting dust on the shelf. And a crown was another word for a head.

"You don't clean it. You must dominate it. Like he did. His shines like the sun, now."

He blinked at her. "I have a tattoo on my head, too?"

I sure couldn't see anything on his forehead.

Alice nodded absently. "Different, but the same language as hers. But you have so many other problems going on," she huffed, gesturing in his general vicinity without actually looking at him, "that I wouldn't worry too much about it."

He frowned darkly at that—but not until she looked away from him.

"It seems being royalty is harder than I thought," I said.

Alice sniffed. "We haven't even gotten to the royalty bits. Those are just the lady bits."

Nate coughed violently into his fist.

Alice casually picked up a snow goon's head and set it in the kettle over the fire to boil. I almost gagged at that imagery but managed to keep my composure. "I'll make some tea for you. Can't have a decent reunion without some tea. Right, Nate?"

"Right, my lady," he said seriously.

Was this actually Alice from the Lewis Carroll stories? I watched as she very carefully set four stone cups down beside the fire. She glanced at Nate and pointed to one. He nodded. Then she turned to me, pointing to a different cup. I nodded, wondering why this felt ritualistic.

The smile that split her cheeks upon my nod made me wonder what I had just agreed to.

She then glanced at the other two cups, shook her head, and stood to her feet. "Kitty and I will be in the igloo. Grimm will leave to scout the camp borders and search for threats."

He snorted. "And slaughter them mercilessly." Then he took off to the skies, obeying the little girl without question. He almost seemed eager to be away.

When I turned back to Alice, she was already tugging Last Breath away by the paw, leaving Nate and I alone with the four cups. Two had tea in them, even though I hadn't seen her pour anything. "Be careful with her, Nate," Alice teased over her shoulder. "*She's* seen the omegabet. *You* haven't seen the omegabet."

Nate watched her, scratching at his jaw and looking perplexed. "Sometimes, she says things that I can't even *begin* to comprehend," he explained in a low whisper, dismissing her comment. "She's been teaching me Fae magic. There is a lot to learn. And a very steep learning curve."

Alice scoffed, hearing his whisper even from across the clearing. She glanced back at him from over her shoulder. "You are only taking twice as long as I feared. Which is quite good, considering my mother gave up all hope with you." She turned to me, scrunching her nose. "Speaking of hope, I would appreciate you saving the murder until after tea."

Then she slipped into the igloo with Last Breath, leaving me all alone with my victim.

Well.

Shit.

42

Nate tensed, leaning away from me in a swift jerk. He studied me warily, eyes narrowed ever so slightly. I held up my hands, shaking my head in a calming gesture. "Wordplay," I assured him in a gentle tone.

Nate's unease slowly changed to deep thought. And like a wild animal looking at an open cage, he continued to study me, suspicion flickering in the depths of those eyes. I smiled warmly at him.

I hadn't seen Alice grab tea leaves from anywhere, but our cups were emitting a minty scented steam. I handed Nate his cup of tea, taking one for myself and leaving the two strangely empty cups beside the fire. Instead of speaking, I studied the two empty cups thoughtfully as I sipped the warm tea. Flavor exploded across my tongue, much more intense than any mint tea I'd had before. I licked my lips, smiling down at the cup.

Nate sipped at his own cup, but I could feel his eyes on me, still waiting.

Alice's comment had gone off about as well as a bucket of gasoline hurled at a fire. I needed to establish trust, like Qinglong had told me. But it wouldn't be through a blood bond. I'd already decided how I would bond this man to me. I'd made the decision shortly after speaking with Xuanwu—several of his statements taking time to reveal their true meaning. But each step I'd taken since had only confirmed my decision.

"Alice asked if you knew what you were here to do..." Nate said softly, rather than asking about the obvious statement she'd parted with—about murdering hope.

I nodded confidently. "About some things, I'm conflicted. About one thing, I'm convinced," I admitted, pointedly refusing to look at him.

"What are you conflicted about?" he asked softly.

I smiled inwardly at his choice of question—not that it was any easier to answer, but it spoke volumes about the man before me. I let out a breath, thinking of my talk with Qinglong. "I have something I need to talk to you about, but I can't do so right now." He frowned, opening his mouth to argue but I held up a finger. "It's not that I don't want to tell you, it's that it would require time I don't have." I took a measured breath, closing my eyes for a moment, knowing that, in order to be honest, I had to say this next part. "And it would take an objective, non-emotional mindset that you don't currently seem to have. It would detract both of us from our current... battles," I said, settling on a word. "You with Mordred, and me with Kansas City."

He studied me thoughtfully, definitely not pleased, but he apparently trusted and respected me enough to finally nod. "I...think you may be right," he finally said, his voice slightly raspy. "To be honest, this is about as clear-headed as I've felt in quite a while. Which means I'm clear-headed enough to realize how much further I still have to go."

I smiled reassuringly. "Thank you."

He glanced at me curiously. "Why even bring it up if you didn't want to talk about it?"

I stared into the fire, giving his question deep thought. "We have both suffered too many lies from those we care about. I have this information I need to share with you, but neither of us can afford to discuss it yet. In my opinion, choosing not to let you know I have this information feels exactly the same as an outright lie. I figured the only way to be honest was to let you know I have it, but that I'm not ready to talk about it yet. Otherwise, if you found out later and thought I had hidden it from you..." I shuddered at the thought.

He tensed. "I wouldn't hurt you, Callie. Jesus—"

I gripped his hand suddenly, cutting him off. His skin was hot to the touch, and he froze like a startled deer. How long had it been since someone had touched him? For him to react like that meant it had been too long.

"I know you would never hurt me, Nate. It's just that...I couldn't bear knowing you thought I had lied to you. So, an unpleasant middle-ground is better than nothing."

He studied me in silence, his face expressionless. I turned back to the fire, releasing his hand and feeling very small under his gaze.

"Thank you, Callie," he finally said. We sat in silence for a time, the fire crackling between us. "And what are you convinced about?" he finally asked. I felt him shift his gaze away in my peripheral vision.

I didn't look up, staring instead at the smoldering blue fire, at the glowing coals that looked like neon blue lights one might see illuminating a pool in the evening. I continued watching the dancing flames until I had regained my composure. I turned to Nate, my voice clear and confident. "I want to see it."

He tensed, shooting me a surprised look. It slowly began to morph into a frown, and he opened his mouth.

"I want to see it," I repeated in a firm tone.

He studied me silently. "Why?" he finally asked.

Unbidden, a smile slowly stretched over my face. "I need to make sure it matches my boots."

His eyes widened and he grew very still. I waited, nodding my head as I pointed at the satchel lying beside the log at his feet—the Darling and Dear satchel I had given him. Ever so slowly, and in complete silence, he reached inside his satchel without looking, and withdrew a white stone mask that glittered like sunlight striking fresh snow. He stared down at it for a second, a smile creeping over his face as if the two had just shared an inside joke. Then he shook his head, his smile fading as he extended it towards me.

My heart began to skip as my fingers drew closer. The moment my fingertips touched the surface, I gasped as the Horseman Mask stuck to my skin like a magnet and my every sensory receptor exploded, overloaded with input for the space of a single, eternal second.

Then it was gone, my skin tingling sharply in its abrupt absence, seeming to hum on a molecular level as it resonated with the Mask now cupped in both of my hands—which I didn't recall doing—like I was holding a purring cat. The interior of the Mask was a sort of crystal, looking sharp and jagged with veins of silver streaking throughout. I ran a finger over the interior, not liking the concept of putting sharp jagged stone against my face.

I gasped as my finger brushed through what felt like velvet, seeming to want to latch onto my fingertip and hug it tightly. And my forehead pulsed a single time, like a cool breeze over damp flesh. I shivered.

Nate chuckled. "Creepy, right?"

I nodded, unable to peel my eyes away from it. I didn't even need to ask, knowing exactly which Horseman Mask it was. "Despair," I said in a breathless whisper.

It hummed stronger, warming my hand as it responded to my voice. I turned it over in my lap to inspect the front and instantly felt myself smiling. What appeared to be a beautiful woman's face stared back at me—even though what looked like a ragged bandage covered her eyes. And from beneath the bandage, three rivulets of silver streaked down the surface from each eye. Six tear drops for the Sixth Horseman.

On a not so distant level, I was very pleased to see this, because deep down I had been fearing I would lose my eyes at one point and actually be wearing a bandage around my head in the flesh. My vanity purred, pleased.

Although the Mask was so detailed that it almost looked like actual flesh, it was most definitely the same crystallized white and silver stone, glittering whenever the light hit it just right. I noticed a faint indentation on the forehead—a horizontal crescent moon, points up. I frowned thoughtfully at that, fairly confident that it didn't match the word *Despair* branded into my forehead. But for the moment, it didn't matter.

I set it on my knees, finally looking up at Nate. I was silent, studying the growing frown on his face with absolutely no reaction on mine. I let the silence stretch, not reacting as he began to twitch and fidget subtly.

"What are the rules on workplace romance?" I finally asked.

He blinked. Then he leapt to his feet, breathing huskily. "I know the boss. I'm sure he won't mind..." he said carefully.

"Good," I purred, allowing a wicked grin to finally touch my cheeks. "Because that would have been a deal breaker." Because I had realized that my love for Nate had actually been a predominant factor in instinctively wanting to decline—not the dangers the job entailed, even though I had lied to myself about it with that line.

I hadn't wanted to choose the Mask of Despair *over* Nate.

This was the way I wanted to bond *with* Nate.

I lifted the Mask in my hands, gauging its weight. Although it looked dense, it felt no heavier than a thin tank top.

"You can change its shape," he said, pulling out the coin hanging from a chain around his neck. The moment he touched it, a dark charcoal Mask with a single golden streak down the center appeared in his hands. That gold streak looked more like a fracture, or a bolt of electricity than a naturally occurring element of the Mask—like mine with the silver streaks. The stone was so dark that it was hard to make out what the face looked like. A moment later it was a coin again. "Just imagine what you want it to look like," he said.

I thought about the silver butterfly charm he had given me the day we first kissed, the one currently in my pocket, and I smiled. With a faint curl of vapor, a new silver butterfly charm sat in my palm.

"You're going to have to teach me how to use it," I said, grinning down at the butterfly.

He grimaced slightly. "There's kind of a learning curve. I can share my experiences and help you as best as I can, but I think each Mask is entirely unique. They seem to adapt to the user's abilities or inclinations. At least that's what mine has seemed to do." He thought about it. "Each seems to have its own personality. It might be best for you to figure it out on your own, rather than me limiting you by telling you what to do. You aren't an extension of me, of Hope—"

"I'm Hope's counterpoint. Despair and Hope, two sides of the same coin. We are each other's murderer," I said, smiling faintly, alluding to Alice's comment, finally.

Nate nodded his agreement. "I had...hoped that was what Alice meant, but only because I've spent a lot of time around her recently and know how she thinks."

I had much I wanted to discuss with Nate. About the Masters, our parents, and what we'd each been up to this past year. But that conversation would have to wait for another day.

Or maybe that conversation was for a *couple* days. And nights. With a lot of alcohol, room service, and privacy for miles in every direction. I glanced up at Nate, trying to conceal my rapidly blushing cheeks. "You know...and I'm just spit-balling here, but it might be a good idea to take this training seriously. Go somewhere secluded. Very secluded, mind you. Just to be safe. And we will need food and drinks. Shelter. And no one knowing where we are. You know, so we don't get distracted. Because training is important. Very important—"

Nate burst out laughing, part of the man I knew shining through this more primal version. "Deal. We will...dedicate ourselves to this *training*."

I smiled much wider than any training warranted. "It would be a good time for us to talk about things, too. Rather than these brief meetings, we could get into bigger topics. Like the one I brought up earlier..." I said, my smile fading.

Nate nodded, looking surprisingly serious and...eager. "I think I would really like that, all scandalous insinuations aside. I think sitting down with you and just talking would be fascinating, believe it or not." And I could tell he was being sincere.

"Of course it would," I said, sniffing pompously.

"Out of curiosity, who told you to murder hope?"

"A lot of people," I admitted. "Including Pandora. Others didn't necessarily say it outright, but now that I think about it...they might have been saying the same thing in a different way, and I just never caught it."

Nate grunted, grinning in amusement. "Welcome to my life. Someday, maybe you'll have a crazy mountain of your own."

I smiled, taking in the mountain as I carefully pocketed the butterfly charm. "Maybe a beach," I said, rubbing my arms. "In a very general way, how do I use the Mask? Some kind of ritual or spell?"

He grinned, shaking his head. "Just slap it on and hold on for dear life. It might not fully wake up the first time. I used mine a few times before it really opened up."

"You say that like it's alive..."

He grimaced. "It is, in a way. I brought it to life with some of the Nine Souls from Hell." I blanched, and he waved off my concern. "Don't worry. They aren't tainted by demons or anything. I technically fed the Souls to the Masks, so if anything, the Masks *ate* them."

Horrified, I pointed my boots at my Mask, but I felt no tingle signifying demonic presence. I let out a sigh of relief. He was right. He nodded satisfactorily.

I held up the Mask, meeting his eyes. "Things are going to get wild soon. We will need these more than you know."

He read between the lines, nodding slowly, curiously...excitedly. "Come back whenever you're finished in Kansas City. We need to do some talking. And *training*." His eyes glittered mischievously.

I nodded. "Pandora told me I had to come back anyway. I need to deliver something to someone for her."

He studied me thoughtfully but didn't ask for me to elaborate. "I...would like that, Callie." He hesitated for a moment, debating something on his mind. "I would offer to come help—if you needed it—but I might cause more damage than help, in my current state. I need to finish clearing my head."

I smiled back at him. "You already helped, Nate." I held up the Mask meaningfully. "I've got it from here."

Last Breath was peering out from the igloo—with Alice doing the same a few feet below him. I waved at the pair, letting them know we were finished and ready to leave.

They hurried over, and I couldn't tell who was more anxious. Last Breath—to escape the tiny terrorist—or Alice. Nate grinned, pointing out the silver ribbons tied into Last Breath's mane. I chuckled, shaking my head.

"I'll be back. Soon," I told Nate, just as Alice and Last Breath reached us. Alice grinned at the charm in my hand, nodding her approval. Then she tapped her forehead, pointed at mine, and gave me a thumbs up.

I sighed, smiling in spite of myself. I'd felt a cold chill on my forehead, so something had changed with my brand to earn her open approval.

"Give them hell," Nate said, smiling. Grimm landed near the igloo, drawing our attention. He was chewing on something that seemed to still be alive, struggling weakly in his jaws.

Nate suddenly tensed, glancing at Grimm and then rapidly back to me. "Wait. You don't have a horse! It's kind of a requirement."

I cocked my head, glancing at Grimm thoughtfully. An idea came to me, but I didn't voice it. "I'll figure something out," I told Nate, shrugging. I motioned Last Breath to follow me back to the still open portal leading back to the Armory.

I didn't say *giddy-up* to Last Breath. But I really wanted to.

43

We stepped through the portal, back into the Armory, expecting to find Pandora waiting for us. To my surprise, the hallway was empty. I closed the closet door behind us, halting the gusts of snowflakes that had formed a blanket of powder across the hall, leaving a trail of our boot prints. I called out her name, waited a few moments, and then followed Last Breath to the door leading back to Solomon's Temple. A large, roaring bear was carved into this side of the wooden door, and I very wisely—without saying that I feared Claire was waiting on the other side, ready to attack on sight—let Last Breath open the door first.

She had been waiting.

She hit him in a bear tackle, pummeling him into a glass cabinet where their combined bulk shattered the contents, and the furniture itself, in a shower of glass, wooden splinters, and whatever else had been on display inside it. I watched a tall, ancient vase slowly topple and crash to the ground, marveling as vapor slowly escaped the cracked clay with an audible chorus of relieved sighs from whatever had been stored inside. Something sentient, obviously. Last Breath sneezed repeatedly as he inhaled some of the vapor.

Claire, not noticing the vapors or caring about the damages to Solomon's antiques, continued punching Last Breath in the face and chest, her bulky, oven mitt-sized paws doing a real number on the furry lion.

"Claire!" I finally shouted, cupping my hands around my mouth. She froze, whipping her head around to face me, blinking a few times. "We have work to do. Leave the poor guy alone."

Rather than wait, I began striding down the hallway, paying no attention to my surroundings, thinking furiously about next steps and the silver butterfly in my pocket. Claire caught up to me, maintaining her bear form since the hall was wide enough to mostly accommodate her mass. As long as she took wide turns, Solomon's antiques were safe. Last Breath gave her a real ass-chewing as they followed behind me—but not about her decking him. He was pissed about the broken cabinet and vase. I tuned him out, double-timing it to the balcony. I didn't think I needed to head there to travel back to Kansas City, but the walk was doing me some good, giving me a sense of purpose.

I'd already told Claire my plan back when we'd spoken on the balcony, and nothing had changed. I spoke over my shoulder, not slowing. "Things are going to get dicey in Kansas City, so keep your ears open," I told Last Breath, "or whatever it is you did when you sensed me in danger earlier. Fair warning, I'll be in various forms of danger pretty much the entire time, so use your best judgment, I guess."

"You're not going to ask me to join you?" he asked, sounding surprised.

"I figured it's best you stay here to watch over Solomon and Phix. If she wakes up and finds no one else here, she might—"

"Claw the furniture?" Claire growled in a surprisingly comprehensible growl. I glanced back at her, impressed. She shook her shoulders, bumping into a dresser in the process. Last Breath lashed out to catch the vase wobbling on top, shooting a glare at Claire—who was pretending not to notice.

"Something like that," I said in reply. I glanced back at Last Breath again, not slowing my walk. "It's probably best to use you as a last resort. Fabrizio and Roland both know about you hunting me before I disappeared. It would be hard to explain you at a demon's side."

He nodded stiffly, not disagreeing, but not necessarily pleased about it either. It was very hard to take him seriously with Alice's silver ribbons in his hair, but I decided not to mention them in case he didn't know. He really looked like a dandy lion now.

"Keep Solomon alive until I get back. I have a friend who may be able to help ease his discomfort, but I need his help in Kansas City. He loves sunshine, so might be able to at least buy Solomon some more time until I figure out the permanent solution."

I'd gotten the idea to use Alucard from Xuanwu cursing out the thorns trapping his feet back when I'd first met him, that *without sunlight they just festered and multiplied.* Also, his brother Qinglong had told me he would *shed some light* on how to help Solomon. Maybe they had already given me the antidote.

Whatever Roland was after, he would have it soon. I missed a step, suddenly considering the fact that we had just gone to Fae, and that time flowed differently there. Not wearing a watch, I began to run. What if Alucard and Cain had been caught? What if they thought we had been caught? Had we missed our meeting at the cave? How long had we been gone?

Shit. Shit. Shit.

"What's wrong, Callie?" Last Breath growled, glancing left and right for any sign of threat.

"I don't know how long we've been gone!" I snapped.

"Then stop running and kiss your ring!"

I skidded to a halt, grabbed a fistful of Claire's fur, and kissed my ring.

This time, there was a flash of momentary bright light, like we had stepped outside after watching movies for a few hours in a dark basement, and then we were stumbling across a sandy floor in a dim, cool cavern.

I glanced left and right, panting. That had been much better than my last experience with kissing the ring. Then I frowned. "How did we end up here?" I asked, thankful to find Claire standing beside me. We were in the cave she had taken us to, but I had no idea how we had arrived here over any other place in Kansas City. Was it because I'd been thinking about the cave and meeting Alucard and Cain here?

Claire pointed to an old alarm clock on one of the small dressers, showing that it was about seven o'clock. Judging by the warm light outside the cave, I was betting early evening, not morning.

The real question was what *day* it was. Had we been gone a week or a—

"Finally!" Cain snapped, stumbling out of one of the side rooms wearing only his jeans and clutching a dagger in his fist as if he'd expected us to be intruders. He was tugging a shirt on, seeming to have a hard time while juggling his dagger.

I let out a sigh of relief. "You're okay!"

He cocked his head quizzically. "Of course I'm okay. Are you okay?" he asked, frowning in concern at the obvious mania tainting my voice. Also, Claire was pacing back and forth across the room, still in bear form—as if she expected trouble. I was pretty sure she was just concerned about the tasks ahead of her.

I waved a hand at him. "We're fine. We just got caught up in some drama and feared we had lost track of time. When is the Blood Moon?"

"Tomorrow night. But unless you found a way to get inside the church, I don't see why it really matters."

I glanced around the cavern, frowning. "Where is Alucard?"

Cain snorted, finally sheathing his dagger into the waist of his jeans. "He's charging, I think."

"What is that supposed to mean?

"He said he was low on power so needed some sun," Cain replied, pointing a finger towards the cave entrance.

Claire made a chuffing sound and I walked over to her to place my hand on her back before she could leave. Her fur quivered at my touch. "Thank you," I whispered, encouraging her for the job ahead.

Her ears wilted and she nuzzled me with her massive head for a moment. Then she ambled out of the cave to retrieve the environmentally friendly vampire.

"I figured I could use a recharge, too, so found myself a bed," Cain continued, watching our interaction thoughtfully. His features grew suddenly serious, and he leaned closer as if to tell me an important secret he'd learned while spying on Roland—even though we were the only ones left in the cave. "Did you know Starlight has a grow room here?" he whispered.

I blinked at Cain, finally shaking my head in disappointment. "He grows marijuana here?"

Cain had a troubled look on his face. "Not just marijuana. He has some really strange looking plants in there. One of them even looks like it's made of scales. Weirdest fucking thing I've ever seen," he muttered, shaking his head.

That...was actually a lot more concerning than Cain apparently knew. Because I'd once seen a tree like that, and it hadn't just been a tree. I waved a hand at him. "Leave Starlight to his hobbies. He's probably only growing ingredients for his potions."

"His drugs, you mean," Cain muttered, as Claire appeared at the entrance with Alucard. The Daywalker continued walking towards us, but Claire made a low grumbling sound and turned away, shuffling back outside —likely to keep an eye out since she had already heard my plan, and wasn't necessarily pleased about her role. She understood it but didn't like it.

I motioned for the men to join me, sitting down on the floor for us to have a team meeting. I caught Alucard and Cain up on the important parts they had missed, and then I asked what they'd learned—which was nothing useful, apparently. At least the vampires had bought Alucard's fabricated story of escaping the now *two* demons in town. Paradise and Lost had hurried him inside the church to strategize on how to take the demons out. Cain had watched from an adjacent building, tracking patrols and guard movements. I considered all of this in silence, thinking.

I finally waved a hand. "That's fine. I've got a new plan."

Cain frowned dubiously. "I liked our first plan—find a way inside the church. What it lacked in complexity, it made up for with impossibility." Alucard smirked momentarily, but quickly wiped a hand over his face when he caught me glaring at him.

"My new plan is better. It's loud, messy, and bound to piss off a lot of people."

"I love it when she talks dirty," Cain said, nudging Alucard.

Alucard was watching me, pointedly ignoring Cain. "That's great and all, but you still need to get into the church..."

I waved a hand dismissively. "No. I've been looking for a key, but what I really need is a Molotov Cocktail," I said. "If I can't break in, I need to force them out." Alucard leaned back, blinking a few times before nodding, motioning for me to continue. "I need to stir up a lot of trouble, and piss off as many people as possible, in a relatively short amount of time. Any ideas?"

Cain frowned. "Dorian is hosting a party tonight," he suggested.

Alucard nodded instantly. "Bellerose might attend. I heard him mention it just an hour ago. And he hardly ever leaves the church."

I clapped my hands eagerly. "Perfect!" If enough supernatural factions from around town went to this party, it would be the perfect place to make a scene—and I needed a big scene for my plan to work. "How do we get an invite?"

Cain shrugged. "I'm always welcome at Dorian's parties."

"Even with your recent actions? Being the last person to see Callie alive?"

Cain scoffed. "You kidding? If anything, it will get me the VIP treatment. Everyone will want to hear what I have to say."

I smiled wickedly and casually mentioned what I had in mind. The looks on their faces changed from abject horror to stunned disbelief and finally to grim resignation.

"Are you sure about this, Callie?" Alucard asked. "Because it sounds like a Nate Temple plan, and those are usually dicey at best."

I smiled, shaking my head. "This one is all me, but I did just talk with Nate." Seeing Alucard abruptly tense, I held out a hand. "I didn't mention you at all. Figured it was best since I refuse to lie to him. The way I see it, Roland won't be a problem much longer, one way or another. Whatever you need to tell him after is up to you."

His shoulders sagged in relief. "Thank you. Is...he doing alright?"

I nodded. "He's gone through a rough patch, but I think he's on the mend. He's clearing his head in Fae."

Alucard looked mildly jealous—probably because Fae was a place where one could unleash their inner id—letting go of all civilized thought. A great place to be a monster. I wasn't about to let him know how close Nate had looked to madness. Alucard had enough to worry about here. "What do you want me to do?" he asked. "I feel like there is a lot going on that is not being said..." Cain leaned back on his hands, lifted his eyes to the ceiling, and began to whistle innocently. Alucard pointed a thumb at him, looking at me. "See? He's been doing that every time I ask him a question."

In answer, I lifted my wrist towards Alucard. "I need you to suck it."

44

Cain's whistle faltered as he burst out laughing, falling over onto his side as he hooted. Alucard looked surprisingly annoyed. "You know I don't really need to drink blood anymore, right?" he said, but his eyes had locked onto my wrist, some small part of him giving lie to his words. Or that even if he no longer *needed* to, he still *enjoyed* doing so.

"I just need you to suck it and not ask any questions. No one needs to know," I added, wondering if he was embarrassed about it.

Cain was rolling back and forth now, laughing harder.

Alucard shot him a dark look before curiously studying my face. Finally, he shrugged and took hold of my forearm. His fingers were warm and tense. He shot me one last look, as if to verify I was sure. I nodded and he lashed out with his fangs, so sharp and swift I didn't actually feel any pain until he sucked, and that was instantly washed away by a wave of endorphins as his vampire venom counteracted the pain—a natural gift that helped lull his victims.

He pulled back sharply, lapping at the wound one time before shuffling backwards a foot on his rear. His last lick had served to begin healing the bite, the skin already knitting back together. He had closed his eyes and his fingers were flexing at his sides as he visibly shuddered. "I've never tasted anything like it..." he whispered under his breath, eyes still closed as he licked his lips.

I closed my eyes, focusing inwardly. Almost immediately, I sensed a hum of power and saw a bright golden cord connecting us. I also realized that there was no crimson and gold cord, but that had only been seen in my Silvers. Since he was now bonded to me, I leaned forward. "Once you learned what Roland had truly become—not when you first came here in good faith—did you ever work for him willingly?"

Alucard opened his eyes, cocking his head. "Of course not. He's gone fucking mental."

I wondered if I had asked the right question, flipping through a dozen before realizing they could all be answered in ways that could have multiple meanings—or only lead to further questions, which I didn't have time for. "Do you, Alucard Morningstar, swear to serve me and my interests over *anyone* here in Kansas City right now? Do you swear to serve me over any vampire whatsoever?" I asked, wanting to make sure I didn't give him a conflict with Nate. "This is a temporary agreement. One week, let's say. I'm not trying to steal your soul, but I need you to swear it." I studied him, letting him see the sincerity in my eyes.

He slowly nodded his agreement, and then cleared his throat before repeating the oath verbatim, adding only the time-duration to the end.

I sensed the bond between us hum louder for a moment, a reassuring sensation, and I let out a breath of relief. "Thank you, Alucard. I'll explain later, but right now we don't have time."

Cain had stopped laughing and was staring at my arm. He climbed to his feet and approached me. "I'm a bandwagon kind of guy," he said, indicating my other wrist. "But I refuse to swap saliva with disco ball."

I smiled at him. I already trusted him with my life, but it was a distant worry snuffed out to have him volunteer. When I had checked my bond with Alucard, I'd already gotten a peripheral glance at my bond with Cain—apparently established due to our choice to adopt each other as siblings—and it had reminded me of a gnarled, unbreakable tree root. Instead of biting my wrist, he pricked my finger and wiped up the drop of silvery crimson blood with his calloused fingertip and stuck it in his mouth.

He stared down at his hands for a few moments, his frown growing deeper. "I don't get a high off it?" he complained. I shrugged, not having an answer. I closed my eyes and smiled to see that our tree root bond was now thicker, gnarlier, and pulsing strongly.

Alucard was staring at his fingers, looking awed by whatever my blood had done to him. I probably should have done a little more research on my idea before suggesting it. The last time he had sucked blood from another supernatural—a Beast Master—he had evolved into a Daywalker. I hoped I hadn't also changed him into something new, but I had needed to know I could count on him—that he hadn't been swayed by these Masters. Or Roland—

With sudden fear, I realized I may have just broken his access to Roland's church. I calmed myself enough to bring up the Silvers—just to get a quick glimpse—and let out a breath to see the cord between him and the church still there, but more golden than crimson now.

"Was that all you needed me to do?" he asked, snapping me out of my daze. I released the Silvers, hoping what I'd seen didn't mean that Alucard was still somehow bonded to Roland. Then it would become a question of power. Was my blood stronger than Roland's blood?

That was the underlying point behind this whole thing—the student fighting her mentor.

The Horseman fighting a Master Vampire...hopefully not an *actual* Master...

I shook my head at Alucard's question, shelving my inner fear. I would find out soon enough. "You're my inside man, so no party for you. Resume whatever you were doing before we crossed paths. And you understand what you're to do tomorrow?" I asked.

Alucard pursed his lips, nodding. "I got it." He didn't sound eager or hopeful.

"Trust me," I said, reassuring him. He sighed, nodding. "Let's get moving," I said, climbing to my feet and striding out of the cave and into the approaching evening air. Alucard and Cain hurriedly darted out in front of me as if it was a competition to see who the best protector was. I rolled my eyes as I mentally made a list of anything I might need. Fading sunlight warmed my cheeks, making me smile. "Cain, I'll need you to—"

A meteor struck the earth a few yards away, causing dust and debris to roll out in a cloudy ring that sent me into a coughing fit. I sensed frigid air, like someone had opened a freezer in front of me, but I couldn't see through the cloud as I waved my hands to clear it, ready for a fight.

"Ah!" Cain yelped. "The fucking angel found me! Run for your lives!"

And Eae materialized from the center of the cloud. He unfurled his wings, using them to bat both Alucard and Cain in different directions—

each over a dozen feet away—and he didn't even look at them as he did it. He just stared at me. I heard Claire roar in the distance, but it sounded very far away.

I held up a hand for my friends to stand down as I stared Eae in the eyes, wondering what he was doing here if he wasn't going to attack the girl with the Demonskin in front of him. Maybe...

"Callie?" he asked in a hoarse whisper.

I nodded slowly, careful not to make any threatening moves. "Yes, pigeon. Yes." That was something I'd heard Nate call him once. Or had it been *feathers*?

Eae shuddered, and suddenly scooped me up in a tight squeeze, wrapping his wings around me in a cocoon of...*Heavenwy gwow*, as that impressive clergyman in *The Princess Bride* would have said.

"How did you know?" I squeaked, my ribs creaking at the force of his hug.

I heard Cain and Alucard muttering darkly about sucker-punching, cheap-shot angels having no honor for a fair fight, and other things that just shouldn't be said to an Angel of the Lord. Blasphemers.

"You opened a portal to Solomon's Temple," Eae laughed, ignoring their taunts. "To see a portal *at all* was astounding, given the barrier around Kansas City, but to see Solomon's Temple...I *knew* it had to be you. Even someone who had stolen your Seal wouldn't have been able to use it to travel there."

Eae finally relented, holding me at arm's-length and tucking his wings behind his back. They were different from my own wings—which I hadn't dared attempt using the last few days in case they appeared as a horrifying set of scaly, demon wings or something. Ick.

"A demented little..." Eae frowned, shaking his head as he obviously reconsidered what he had been about to say. "A demented little *bear* told me where I might find a pretty rose." He glanced at Cain and Alucard with a judgmental sneer, silencing their *still* ongoing taunts. "He was quite...disturbing.

I frowned, wondering what games Starlight was playing.

"If you can see me, do you think you can convince Fabrizio and the others who I am?" I asked, wondering if having them as allies might help with the chaos. "You're an angel. They have to believe you."

He shook his head. "After Nameless Fell, they no longer hold the same respect for angels. I choose to help them for my own reasons, but I am not permitted to enter the church."

I grunted in disapproval. Even angels weren't trustworthy these days?

"They all heard you shout, 'kill them!' back in the warehouse," Eae explained. "I can't deny or refute that. I heard it, too."

I gritted my teeth. "I shouted *don't kill them.*"

He waved a pale hand dismissively. "Even Arthur believes you're a demon. I am here on my own, child. If I give them further reason to doubt an angel..." he shuddered at the thought. "It might just sever their faith in God entirely. If men of the cloth can't trust an angel, all hope is lost."

I considered this update, realizing it might just provide a different opportunity.

Eae studied me thoughtfully, eyes riveted on my forehead. "I can still see it, but it's faint through the illusion. It's...changed," he mused pensively. Then he sighed, a frustrated sound. "Even still, every sense at my disposal screams you are a demon," he said, shaking his head in disbelief. "How did this come to be?"

I considered lying but, given the circumstances, I decided that was wholly cruel and unfair. He was risking losing his only allies by coming here. So I told him about the mystery man somehow convincing me to order from the alley's *you pick two* menu—casting Demonskin on myself and then a memory-wiping spell. Because I was a glutton for punishment, I voiced the same question I'd asked everyone. "Any chance it could have been Samael?" Because if anyone would know a demon's abilities to break the rules, it was Eae, the Demon Thwarter.

He shook his head after a moment. "Not a chance. I would know if Samael was in town. And this cursed barrier blocks demons as well as angels. I railed against it repeatedly, even damaging my wings for a time. I was unable to pass through it." Jesus. That was hardcore. "I will think on this riddle."

I nodded angrily, taking a calming breath. A thought hit me, now that Eae wasn't trying to kill me. "Do you know Michael?" I asked.

He jolted, eyes flicking up to the skies. He let out a nervous breath. "Know is a very...familiar word. Why do you ask?"

"I met him...last year, I guess." I very carefully considered my words, fairly confident that if Eae wasn't close friends with the Archangel, the Archangel probably wouldn't want me blabbing his secrets. "He showed me some...things. I was summoning him when you stopped me in the warehouse. Do you think he would be able to help? To make it through the barrier with his...Archangeliness?"

Eae paled, taking a step closer and gripping my shoulders meaningfully. "If so, he would have immolated you on sight. He wouldn't have given you the time to prove who you really are. I'm telling you, Callie. This Demonskin, as you called it, isn't some simple Glamour. It fooled even me. Powerful enough to fool an Angel..." He shook his head, appraising me warily. "How you managed to do such a thing to yourself...it's rather alarming. I've never seen such a powerful disguise."

I let out a breath, shaking my head clear of the shattered hope that Eae might have been able to help me. "Well, whoever convinced me to do this didn't realize they inadvertently handed me a shortcut." I told him my plan and watched him just stare back at me like a lifeless statue.

I think it was a look of encouragement. Yeah. Definitely.

45

Eae hadn't been encouraging me. "Did Nate Temple give you this plan? It sounds like one of his idiotic, dangerous and...usually successful plans," he finally admitted with a sigh.

I pointedly ignored Alucard nodding his agreement. "No. This was my idea." Part of me smiled at the fact that I would now—or very soon—share a bond with Nate Temple. Not just one of manipulative parents, love, or magic, but...a bond of family through our Horseman relationship. It was another braid tying us closer together. Something that would only strengthen our relationship. Maybe when we started our...training, I would see what added benefits a blood bond might have...

Feeling my cheeks heat up to have such thoughts before an angel, I chose not to burn Eae's virginal ears. Michael had gotten very twitchy when asking me about Nate's new Horsemen, claiming God had never mentioned them. Thinking on that now, I decided it was probably very wise not to confront Michael...as one of the new Four Horsemen.

I leaned close, murmuring under my breath so softly that even Alucard's vampire hearing wouldn't have caught it. "Roland is after something Dracula has in his possession, and he's making his grab tomorrow night. I don't have time to find out exactly what it is or what it does, but if I can simply stop Roland or trip him up in the middle of his spell, it won't matter. I don't have time for half measures. You know my purpose, Eae. I just want to end this suffering."

Eae obviously sensed I was keeping some information back from my associates but gave no indication my whisper had been anything important. Instead, he stared very pointedly at my forehead, at the Enochian script branded there—even though only a few could see it on the best of days. "To end the pain and suffering? Or...to *bring* it?" he asked, softly enough that no one else could have overheard.

I pointedly kept my hands from touching the Mask of Despair in my pocket. "Both," I promised him, unblinking. Then, since I had no other choice... "I have become Despair. I am number six."

Eae stared at me, his face a mixture of horror and concern.

I let him stew on that as I reviewed my plan, wondering if anything had changed. Having Eae here might actually be a godsend. I turned to him, gripping his wrist urgently. "Eae, I'm going to need you to bend some rules..." I told him part of my plan, and how he could help.

He smiled faintly at my first request, nodding easily, but my second request...

He glanced back at where Claire had entered the woods to keep watch from further away. He grimaced, looking uncertain as he turned back to me. "They aren't the men you remember, Callie. Are you sure you want to take that risk?"

I smiled bitterly. "Actually, it's more like the Shepherds have taken off their sheep clothing to reveal the very wolves I always knew lurked underneath," I muttered. "But my plan—although dangerous—is solid." I tapped my head with two fingers. "Psychology wins every time."

He gave me a withering frown. "*Faith* wins every time, Callie," he corrected.

I grunted, not unkindly, but letting him know I wasn't buying what he was selling. "How has that gone for you—or anyone—in my absence?" He wilted slightly, having no rebuke. "Enemies are gathering outside Kansas City's gates. Some are already within. I have come to kill their dreams, immolate their desires, and crush their tiny kingdoms. Kansas City isn't theirs. They hoped to reshape my city, to bring their war to my streets, to take what doesn't belong to them, to abandon what promises they once held dear..." I said in a frosty but calm tone. "They didn't know that true *Despair* lives here, and she sits on a throne of broken dreams—built from all the lofty aspirations of those who tried and failed before them. I will show them fear in a handful of dust. This is how their reign ends," I promised in a low growl. "Not with a bang, but with a *whimper*," I snarled, realizing I was panting and gripping the Horseman Mask—the silver butterfly charm—in my pocket.

Eae had taken a subconscious step back from me, staring at me like he'd never seen me before. I released the charm and waved a hand to let him know he didn't need to find me a straightjacket. I took a calming breath, regaining my composure. "Everyone I thought I knew has shown their true colors in my absence—becoming the worst possible forms of themselves the moment they were left unsupervised. And predators are circling the city—or are already inside—working to capitalize on that. I will destroy them. All. No faith, power, or alliance will prevent me from creeping through their defenses and choking them to death with my bare hands. They will be an example to all those who think to try the same in the future."

This was no longer just about Roland or my hurt feelings. It was so much more, now. Because the Masters would do far worse in the long run. I needed to make such a spectacle of this event that everyone stepped well clear of Kansas City for a good long time. Not just because Roland had turned tyrant and intended to make a bridge between my city and Dracula's Castle. No. This fight was also to let the Masters know—whoever and wherever they were—that my home was too big of a threat to face. That I was too big of a threat.

I heard a bellowing roar in the distance, and then a ball of flame struck a tree not fifty yards away from us. "Claire," I breathed, my fists suddenly flexing in anger.

Eae had spun towards the sound as well. "Shepherds," he growled. "Was this part of your plan?" he asked, sounding hopeful. I shook my head. "Then they must have followed me."

Cain cursed. "Time to skate, Callie. Now." He shoved Alucard towards a car that I hadn't paid any attention to, jumping into the driver's seat and turning the key.

A Geo Metro. Badass. Because we'd left Claire's Jeep at the warehouse. Damn it.

We weren't fast enough, because a lone Shepherd burst clear from the tree line, slowing to stare at Eae, who had already turned his back on the Shepherd and spread his wings out wide in order to momentarily conceal me and the car. Thankfully, Claire was still roaring in the distance, so I knew she hadn't been taken down, but this ambitious little sheep had been smart, sneaking past our sentry.

Eae gritted his teeth, glaring at me. "Hit me and run. It's your only chance. Our only chance. They won't bother asking questions of a demon, they will just kill. And if they think I'm assisting you, all hope is lost. I'll be there tonight, and I'll make sure Claire is safe in captivity. Go!"

My eyes danced wildly. I wanted to kill the Shepherds for daring to attack us, even though Claire being abducted had been part of my plan—it just wasn't supposed to happen right *now*. Claire's past friendship with Callie gave her a good chance at surviving, but if they thought Eae was here consorting with a demon...

He was right. I had no other choice.

So...

I struck an Angel of the Lord. Hard. I took out all my frustration on him, sending him flying into the car, rocking the tiny car up on two wheels for a few seconds before it came crashing back down. The airbags went off, pounding Cain and Alucard—my driver and navigator—in the faces. Damn it.

Hopefully I hadn't just destroyed our escape pod. Or my pilots.

Eae crumpled to the ground, groaning, and as his eyes locked onto mine, they looked shocked. Not a feigned reaction for the Shepherd's benefit, but genuine surprise at how hard I had hit him. I ignored it, seeing Cain and Alucard sluggishly working to deflate the airbags as they coughed at the cloud of dust from the safety devices.

I slowly turned to face the Shepherd and decided our only chance at escape was for me to use an ancient, secret magic that was simply too powerful to use very often—the consequences too detrimental to mankind.

But desperate times...

So, I took a calming breath, relaxing my features as I summoned a power given to me at birth—a power I had perfected over years of meticulous study and practice until I had finally mastered the craft.

I hit him with my R.B.F.

Resting Bitch Face.

My celestial power washed over him on a molecular level, and he froze as if turned to stone, his magic useless against such an unstoppable, alien force.

In addition to the paralyzing effect of my Resting Bitch Face, he had also just witnessed me bat aside an angel without effort. I snarled at him and then hopped into the car, slapping Cain on the shoulder. "Drive!" I hissed.

Cain grumbled something vaguely affirmative and gave it some gas. I flew halfway into the front seat, not realizing he'd put it in reverse. I heard a crunch and a pained groan from outside the broken window before Cain slammed on the brakes so abruptly that it sent me toppling back into my seat. I glanced out the window to see that Cain had run over Eae's wing.

"Jesus!" Alucard cursed. "Take the *wheel*!" he snapped pointing at Cain's hands. They were gripping the windshield wiper and turn signal arm like he thought it was a dirt bike.

Cain, for his part, stared at the steering wheel, looking more baffled at why the car had gone *backwards*.

Alucard shifted the car into drive with another curse and Cain shifted his hands to the steering wheel before giving it gas again...

Without turning the wheel.

Of course, this caused us to run over Eae's wing *again*, eliciting another sharp groan and crunching sound.

Cain jerked the wheel hard, swerving us onto a side dirt road rather than choosing to drive past the Shepherd scout. I just hoped this road didn't lead to a dead end.

I also hoped the Shepherds would be too busy checking on Eae and keeping the furious polar bear restrained to pursue us.

"You okay, boys?" I asked, glancing behind us to make sure we were safe.

"I'm ready to party," Cain murmured dazedly, running over a stump and making me hit my head on the ceiling of the tiny car.

"Wooo," Alucard cheered pathetically, right as Cain swerved the car to avoid some obstacle his raptor-like focus had caught in the dirt road, the motion causing Alucard's head to strike the window hard enough to make me wince. Given Cain's groggy state, I gave it even odds that we had been in danger of actually hitting anything. Alucard groaned, clutching his head with his left hand and gripping the *oh shit bar* above the door in the other.

I sighed. "It's all going according to plan," I muttered, glancing at the clock on the dash. "Do we have time to run an errand before we go to the party?"

Cain nodded, putting about 110% of his attention into gripping the steering wheel with both hands.

"Good. Let's drop Alucard off near the church. Then I'll tell you where to go."

"Can we get some Tylenol first?" they asked in stereo.

I sighed. "Sure."

46

We pulled into the circular drive outside Dorian Gray's mansion and I waited for the limo driver to get out and open my door. I gave him a pointed sniff, refusing to meet his eyes—to let him know I wasn't pleased at how long it had taken him to do his job. I accepted his hand, begrudgingly, and climbed out of the vehicle, sweeping an elitist look over the mansion and the steps leading up to it, as well as the exotic cars idling in a line or parked off to the side, all with drivers seated behind the wheels, subserviently waiting for their masters to summon them.

Perhaps even their *Masters*...

Cain had called Dorian and simply asked if anything interesting was happening tonight. Dorian had arranged for a limo and driver without even asking if Cain needed a ride. He'd only asked where Cain wanted to be picked up—seeming eager to see his friend, but not wanting to ask anything directly over the phone.

Cain had been right. Everyone knew he'd been one of the last to see Callie Penrose alive, and he had indeed been given the VIP treatment for this party.

Cain hadn't mentioned anything about his plus one, so everyone was in for one...hell of a surprise. As I waited for Cain to get out of his side of the car and join me, I eyed the servants with a barely restrained sneer. The heavily muscled, scruffy men wore cowboy hats, belts with huge flashy buckles, and crocodile skin cowboy boots.

Just inside the door, tan-skinned—both sprayed and natural—curvaceous women wore elaborate, feathered headdresses, tasseled leather riding chaps that covered only the sides of their long legs, and moccasins.

Welcome to the Wild West.

I waited impatiently as Cain walked up beside me. He wore dark slacks, a loosely buttoned white dress shirt and boat shoes—like he'd just stepped off his yacht. Except for the white leather collar around his neck that we'd picked up at Wal-Mart, he looked like a man in charge of himself and those around him. His face was blank as he handed me the end of the attached, matching leash we'd also bought, and I flashed him a dazzling smile, patting him on the head. "Good boy," I cooed.

Then I made my way up the steps, tugging the leash gently for him to follow.

I strode up the stairs, not making eye contact or even acknowledging the offered drinks. I clucked my tongue for Cain to follow me into the living area where sounds of merriment and vice danced through the air like vultures circling a fresh battlefield.

Dozens of people—some dressed in similarly themed outfits as the servants at the door—filled the room, clutching stemmed glasses and cigarettes, chatting amicably or dancing wildly to club music that poured out from a side hallway. Conversation in the room dimmed noticeably upon my entrance and I scanned the crowd distastefully, not making eye contact with any of them.

I almost flinched in surprise to find Starlight across the room. He wore the largest and most outlandish feathered headdress—like those reserved only for a chief or shaman—I had ever seen, with red and black-tipped feathers as long as my forearm. The headpiece trailed all the way to the ground, resting on either side of him so that it resembled a feathered, hooded robe.

He hadn't noticed my arrival, thankfully. He was seated on a brightly colored Persian rug with long tasseled knots on either end, about two feet wide by three feet long, and he was shaking the corner like one would a set of reins on a horse, muttering under his breath.

Several partygoers were gathered around him, standing on their feet and seeming to cheer him on. Then, with a sudden booming applause, he shot up into the air, nearly tumbling off the...

Damned flying carpet!

I'd seen that before, which meant the mysterious Mike Arthur was around here somewhere. I couldn't see him through the crowd, and instead found myself staring up at Starlight hovering over the crowd. He clutched a three-foot long pipe in his hands and began puffing contentedly, blowing perfect smoke rings out over the crowd as they continued to clap and cheer. I shook my head, suddenly remembering my purpose.

I managed to peel my eyes from the bear to find one person facing me squarely, staring openly at me rather than from the corner of his eyes like most people were doing.

Dorian Gray.

He wore a tight-fitting silver suit with a crisp white dress shirt and a silver ascot, and his perfectly-messy shaggy hair brushed his shoulders. I kept my suddenly screaming hormones in check and gave him an amused nod. Then I glanced pointedly at a seating area with a leather couch and chairs, currently occupied.

Dorian dipped his chin and swiftly cleared the guests out of the way with brief touches of his finger, smoldering winks, and empty promises of later scandalous sin. The men and women left with hungry, anticipatory grins on their faces, encouraged by whatever dark desires Dorian had just suggested.

I walked over to the couch, tugging Cain's leash, and sat down, patting the seat for Cain to join me. My white jeans and white blouse seemed to glow against the dark leather of the couch, and I crossed my legs as I set the leash on my lap and held up an empty hand in an expectant manner.

Dorian stepped aside to intercept one of his servants and plucked two glasses of a deep red wine from her tray. He handed one to me, cast a brief, thoughtful look at Cain's battered face and leather collar, and then decided to keep the other for himself before sitting down across from me.

Cain, who already looked like a tortured raccoon from the airbags, kept his eyes downcast, but didn't attempt to hide what looked like an impotent fury and deep inner shame.

"Pleased to meet you, Miss..." Dorian trailed off questioningly.

"You may call me Meridiana," I said, drawing up the name from an old text on demons I'd read years ago—a succubus who had allegedly helped a certain Pope Sylvester achieve a high rank in the Catholic Church over a thousand years ago. It seemed fitting and was abstract enough to slip past all but the most devoted demonologists—if any heard me claim it as my name.

Dorian stiffened in recognition. Damn it. Dorian could loosely be described as an incubus. I forced a slow smile onto my face. "Ah, you've heard of me. How...delightful."

"It's an honor," he said, dipping his chin politely, ever the good host. "And what brings you to my house of sin?" he asked, eyeing Cain warily.

I sniffed disdainfully. "There was, quite literally, nothing else interesting to do in this town with that child vampire locking all the exits. Nothing left to entertain me after I killed the White Rose. My new dog mentioned your penchant for depravity. I figured I may as well have a drink before I die of boredom." I sipped at my wine, grimacing in disapproval.

Dorian's lips set into a thin line, but he kept all other emotion from his face. "You...killed the White Rose?" he asked neutrally. He made a good show of it, but I saw his fist clench at his side, and his eyes darted to Cain and his leash again.

I shrugged. "Someone had to pluck that flower. My brother and sister failed, so I decided to give it a go. Honestly, I don't see what all the fuss was about."

The revelers within earshot had grown uncomfortably silent. Dorian sipped at his drink, his hand shaking ever so slightly. "Thank you for honoring me with your presence. Perhaps you will find entertainment within these walls. All manner of...*enjoyment* is available." As if on cue, a male and female servant drifted up beside me, sitting on the arms of the couch. The two began kissing each other, their hands questing unashamedly across hot, flushed flesh, and within seconds, moans and gasps bubbled up from their throats as their passion grew more frantic and desperate.

I calmly and coldly elbowed the man in the ribs hard enough to make him yelp and tumble from the couch, falling on top of the woman in a tangled, painful, completely unerotic sprawl. I took another sip of my wine as if nothing significant had happened.

"They were too willing," I murmured, by way of explanation. "Takes all the fun out of it." I gave Cain's leash a quick tug, jerking his head. "Right, my sweet?"

"Yes, Mistress," he rasped, keeping his eyes down.

"Good boy," I purred, patting his thigh. I turned back to Dorian. "The White Rose wasn't a total disappointment, as you can see. I got a dog after all." I let out a lilting laugh as if a thought had just come to me. "I've practically gone domestic!"

Dorian licked his lips. "I feel I should warn you that the White Rose had allies who might not take kindly to your news," he said very carefully. "Or your acquisitions," he added, obviously implying my treatment of Cain. I was mildly impressed to hear the undertone of a threat—that he didn't take kindly to my treatment of Cain. I knew Dorian was a lot more dangerous than he let on, but to stand up to a demon—one who so casually admitted to killing the infamous White Rose and who currently held Cain on a leash?

That was ballsy. And loyal. I sensed no flash of heat on my scalp, and saw no recognition in his eyes, though, so he still didn't see who I really was. I couldn't risk him seeing Callie.

I snorted unconcernedly, deciding I needed to crank up the demon factor. "Well. Whatever shall I do?" I said, feigning fear. I let a vicious smile creep back over my face and belted out an amused laugh before guzzling down my wine. After a few moments of nearly complete silence—the only sound was me tapping my fingernail against the stem of my glass—I turned back to Dorian, a curious look on my face. "That vampire preacher isn't still upset about his precious flower, is he? Is that who you were implying?"

Dorian nodded, pursing his lips. "He's *quite* upset, as a matter of fact."

I tapped my lips thoughtfully. "Hmmm. Perhaps he would open the doors to Kansas City if I gifted him her head. Something to remember her by. Like a cut flower."

I laughed sadistically, loudly, slapping my knee.

A stark contrast to the stunned silence around me.

47

I saw Dorian's jaw clench almost imperceptibly. "I...am not sure how wise that would be. Can you not leave Kansas City on your own?" he asked, frowning.

I narrowed my eyes in irritation. "Not without opening a doorway to Hell, and I would rather not invite old associates of mine to my new home. It's such a nuisance getting wrapped up in their schemes. I've never been a fan of politics. I'm more of a field agent, you see." I paused, thinking. "I've also never been a fan of sharing my things. I worked very hard to get here, and not all demons work in concert. We all have our own motivations and goals. Kansas City would be torn apart between our interests."

"I see."

I let out an impatient sigh. "How about this. Anyone who has...questions," I enunciated sarcastically, indicating I really meant grievances, "over this plucked flower, is more than welcome to meet me at church tomorrow night. I hear the moon will be a sight to behold—the perfect backdrop for an informal wake outside that ramshackle church the vampire so bravely hides in." I began clapping my hands delightedly. "Oh, yes. That is a splendid idea."

On cue—even though no one else knew it was orchestrated—Cain let out a low growl.

I yanked the chain hard enough to send him crashing to the floor at my feet. I swiftly lifted my foot and kicked him in the ribs, my heel sinking a few inches into his flesh. "Quiet, dog. She is no longer your bitch to mourn. You are mine, unless you need further reminders..." I said, leaning down. I dipped my finger into his wound and plopped it into my mouth with what I hoped sounded like a sexual purr.

Cain blanched, shaking his head. "No, mistress. Apologies, mistress."

"Good." I saw the incredulous look on Dorian's face—as if he had never seen Cain before.

A man standing a few feet away suddenly shrieked, staring down in horror at Cain's bloody puncture wound. He lifted those terrified eyes to mine and let out another shriek.

Then he was running. Directly toward the easiest path to escape—the huge glass window that took up almost the entire wall to display the front gardens. He leapt at it with a desperation that proved his full commitment to risk bodily harm rather than spend one more moment in my presence. He struck the window with his face, breaking his nose, and bounced backwards to land on a side table inside the living room, shattering it before crashing down to the ground with a whimper. He squealed like a stuck pig as he rolled back and forth, clutching his gushing nose and getting blood all over Dorian's rug.

"Wow," I said bluntly. "He hit that really hard. How did it not break?"

Dorian shrugged. "It probably hurt a lot worse than it looked. Although not bulletproof, that glass is old and thick."

Starlight piped up, exhaling a thick cloud of smoke from his magic flying carpet. "Wait for it," he said, almost feverishly as he stared at the window.

Everyone stood transfixed, watching the young man roll back and forth, still clutching his face and screaming in agony. One of his arms was also bent crooked, but no one offered to help him. A few seconds later, I opened my mouth to speak and—

The glass shattered, crashing to the floor in a deafening sound, covering—and likely slicing into—the injured young man.

"There it is," Starlight said, nodding satisfactorily.

Dorian sighed, snapping his fingers impatiently. Two cowboys scooped up the bleeding, broken man and carted him out of the room.

I shook my head in disbelief and finally turned back to Dorian, trying to remember what we'd been talking about. He looked nonplussed, as if this sort of thing happened often. He glanced at Cain, reminding me.

I nodded, allowing myself a prideful smile. "Cain was there when I beheaded the bitch. Got uppity with me. But I needed someone to carry my things, so I showed him mercy. My Father was always trying to teach me about mercy, but I never truly understood it until I found this specimen." I kicked him in the side again and he fell over with a cracked rib, his side still bleeding. He hurriedly assumed a kneeling position on all fours. I sniffed disdainfully and then propped my feet onto his bleeding back.

I turned back to Dorian. "Anyway, spread the word, Mr. Gray. I'm sure there are more than a few who would like to ask me questions." I leaned forward, licking my lips—which still had Cain's blood on them—as I whispered secretly, "And I am so bored right now that I honestly don't know whether or not I am peeing." I leaned back with a shrug, glancing down at my jeans and letting out a sigh of relief. "Let the peasants come with their... grievances. I could use a few more henchmen," I said, allowing my eyes to settle upon Cain. "I already took her dog, but I hear she had a cat as well..." I said, my eyes lighting up.

Dorian nodded slowly. "The Sphinx...I haven't seen her lately, but she has been prowling the streets for answers about the White Rose."

"Pity," I said. "Well, if the cat is too scared to come tomorrow, perhaps there will be others with...pointed questions. I welcome anyone and everyone."

"Why did you do it?"

I glanced back, smiling. "Because I could." Then I scanned the room. "I hear the pastor has found something I may be interested in. I love trinkets. Perhaps I'll take it off his hands at church tomorrow."

Dorian paled, but didn't offer any hints at what Roland might be after. "And if he doesn't want to part with his possessions?"

I waved a hand. "Anyone who disagrees can meet me outside the church tomorrow night." My eyes swept the room, refusing to make eye contact with Starlight, who was studying me with a pensive frown, still hovering above the crowd. I clucked my tongue in what I hoped portrayed boredom. "Come along now, Cain." I climbed to my feet and flung my glass carelessly up at the second-floor balcony without looking. It flew towards a very particular painting on the upper level. I noticed Dorian's shoulders stiffen almost imperceptibly. My gaze might have rested on his for longer than a heartbeat before I was leading Cain out of the room and back towards the entrance. Still, I felt no flash of heat on my scalp. He hadn't recognized me.

Dorian would either understand the subtle message—that only Callie would have known how important that painting actually was to Dorian—or would fear that Meridiana knew. Either way, he would be doubly sure to get as many people as possible to the church.

I felt Dorian following us from the room at the same time I spotted Paradise and Lost saunter down the stairs, staring straight at me. They were in human form—two exotic, dark-haired beauties with crimson irises.

Henri Bellerose lurched behind them like an old puppet with broken strings, his eyes hollow and empty. His face was a melted scar and he walked with a slight limp. He looked at me absently and then took a nervous step closer to the wolves, seeking their protection.

Jesus. He wasn't even a *shell* of his former self. And he definitely wasn't a criminal mastermind duping Roland into his ploy to take over the Sanguine Council. It looked like Alucard had been *generous* with his explanation of Henri's current mental state. He truly was Roland's Renfield.

"Well, hello there..." Paradise said, the two wolves spreading out slightly to divide my attention. Henri chose his guard and drew closer to Lost, quivering behind her. Cain curled his lip up at them, but it didn't look heartfelt. More like he was simply going through the motions of protecting his new boss.

I smiled at the wolves. "Oh, goodie. Party favors."

Dorian stepped in abruptly, holding up his hands. "Not inside! I welcomed you here as guests. No fighting inside my home or there will be repercussions even you three couldn't fathom," he said, suddenly rippling with shadows that limned his body like a cloak whipping in the wind.

Paradise and Lost curled their lips up, practically quivering with violence.

"Obedient little bitches, aren't you?" I said, smirking at their suddenly tense shoulders. "Now, we can take care of this here or you can return to your boss and give him my message. Then again, your headless corpses might serve as a flashier invitation to my party."

The werewolves glared, shoulders flexing. Henri's scarred, melted-candle face, paled.

"Last warning," Dorian said in a threatening tone.

They finally backed down. "We will see you soon, demon. Get your affairs in order."

"Until tomorrow night, mortal worms," I said in a lilting tone. "And be good little bitches for your boss," I said, jerking my chin towards Henri. "He looks like he could use some tender loving care until Roland has time for you again."

They stiffened at the jab, but quickly regained their composure. "I fear you've got it backwards, demon. Henri is currently experiencing the displeasure of our Master, Roland Haviar. Isn't that right, Henri?" they asked, too sweetly.

The broken, melted vampire nodded stiffly, looking utterly ashamed that the rest of the party was watching in stunned disbelief, witnessing his impotence.

The werewolves began laughing darkly. Then they left. Henri followed, practically clutching at their jackets.

I kept my face neutral, but I really wanted to curse. I'd hoped Bellerose was really behind it all, either influencing Roland to some extent, or the one who had tricked me into spelling myself. Really, any backbone at all would have made me feel better.

I carefully spun in a circle, pointing my boots towards Dorian just to be sure a real demon wasn't lurking amidst the party guests, but I sensed nothing. I slowly spun in all directions, pretending to study my audience. No tingling sensation at all.

We left the mansion and were about to hop into our limo when a comet struck a nearby Rolls Royce, shattering glass, bending metal, and injuring the driver still inside.

I stared at the angel, smiling giddily.

"Meridiana," Eae snarled. "You dare show your face after what you did in Paris?"

I scoffed. "That was three hundred years ago, Eae, my dear. I don't even remember who I ate for breakfast this morning."

"I swore to you that I would make you pay for that. I'm here to collect, with interest."

Dorian jumped in hurriedly. "Hold! No fighting here!"

I let out an annoyed breath. "Fine. I won't fight him...as long as the Shepherds give me back my teddy bear." I pointed at Cain. "My dog misses his old friend," I explained, meeting Eae's eyes with a savage grin—trying to duplicate the look I'd seen on Nate's face in Fae. "Or I will burn their church to the ground next."

Eae growled, his wings abruptly flaring out.

I grinned. "No one likes premature ewingulation."

Eae snarled. "I will make sure the bear is there tomorrow night...if you promise to face me in battle."

I thought about it, smirking. I finally nodded. "But let the mortals have a go at me, first. You and I can fight once they are all rotting in the streets. Like old times, eh? Like Paris..." I cooed.

He snarled furiously. "Deal! We fight last. I look forward to it." Then he took off for the skies, and I heard Dorian let out a relieved breath.

I turned to him, still smiling. "Brothers," I said. "Can't live with 'em, can't live without 'em, am I right?"

He nodded back with a faint smile, but his eyes let me know he was eager to get me the hell off of his property.

We finally hopped into our limo—still idling and waiting a few cars down from the door like we had requested—and left Dorian's mansion in our rear windshield. Before the doors had even closed, Cain had snatched up a clean towel intended for the small bar we had ignored in the backseat of the limo, and shoved it over his wounded ribs, shooting me a silent, furious glare. I leaned my head on his shoulder, holding it in place for him. The gesture seemed to calm him significantly. I must have put on a very good act to get him this worked up.

"That window..." Cain murmured, shaking his head. "Poor bastard."

I grunted, laughter unexpectedly bubbling up from deep in my belly. It helped ease the tension between us, which had probably been his intent.

We had the driver make about four wrong turns, taking side streets and back alleys, before pulling up to a fancy hotel downtown that we had arbitrarily picked earlier. We didn't wait for him to open our doors this time—simply climbing out and striding into the lobby like we owned the place.

Cain's leash got very significant looks from the wealthy guests, as well as my white head-to-toe outfit, but we paid them no mind, striding through the lobby and making our way onto the elevator to the parking garage on the lower level. He had kept the towel balled up in a fist, covering the bloody wound as best he could as we walked past those in the lobby. In the elevator, he peeled it off and checked the wound with a grunt. His healing ability had kicked in enough to close the wound, so he tossed the bloody scarf into the corner of the elevator. He strode out of the confined space the moment we heard *ding*.

We climbed into the battered Geo Metro in silence. Part one of my plan was done.

Now it was time for Cain to do his.

"Tell Alucard to be ready and to keep his head on his shoulders."

He shot me a wary look, silently telling me to watch my ass. I nodded and held up a fist.

Now...

I faced what seemed the hardest challenge imaginable, on multiple levels. And I had to do it alone. It was the only path—to take not the path *less* travelled, but the path *never* travelled.

The path that was no path.

The path that was all paths.

Tomorrow, I would have to be a demon. An Angel of Death.

Tonight, I had to become *nothing*.

48

I stood at the base of the steps leading up to Xuanwu's home. The same guards from last time studied me in silence. I didn't move. Didn't look up.

"Sanctuary," I breathed, soft enough to almost be unspoken.

I was claiming sanctuary from my biggest enemy. Myself.

They studied me for what might have seemed an uncomfortable length of time to most people. Not me. I'd been forced to sit in silence in pitch darkness in the middle of the woods—the kind of woods with active predators—for an entire night in my education as a SHIT. Roland had taken a very old school mentality when it came to teaching his only ever student.

So I stood on the porch, head bowed, and waited, willing to accept refusal if that was what they chose. Yín approached on silent feet, holding out his forearm. I gently rested my hand over his and followed him into the house. I let my eyes trail over the door when he paused before it. I didn't actively assess it, second guess myself, or look over at Yín. I acknowledged its natural state—taking a moment longer to scan Qinglong's depiction in more detail.

After an indeterminable length of time, the doors opened of their own accord and Yín led me inside. He paused at the threshold and I took off my boots. I slipped into a pair of wooden-soled clog sandals but kept myself firmly rooted when he took a step to lead me away. I felt him glance at me, but I kept my eyes downcast. I touched my clothes with two fingers and shook my head slightly.

Then I rested my hand back on his forearm and allowed him to take me in a new direction. We walked through several of the traditional, rice-papered sliding doors—I had finally remembered their name, *shōji*—until I found myself in a room full of armored mannequins. A tall, wooden, tri-fold privacy divider stood in the corner of the room—illuminated from behind with a candle—intended to use in changing clothes.

I slowly walked behind it and undressed—even my undergarments—carefully folding my clothes as if it was the most important thing I had ever done. I set my jacket on top, hesitating only a moment as I considered the dangerous items within the pockets. Then I slipped into a spare silk robe with long, wide openings at the sleeves. I folded one side of the robe over my bare body, tying a thin silk ribbon to another that was set just inside the interior corner of the robe, binding it closed. Then I folded the second half of the robe over the first, tying those silk ribbons together as well. I pulled on a pair of silk pants, and lifted a wide, silk sash, studying it thoughtfully.

I let out a light breath and stepped out from behind the partition to stand beside Yín. I handed him the sash and then turned around, lifting my arms. He didn't even murmur as he began wrapping it around me in a practiced gesture, finally folding the end in on itself.

I dipped my head in thanks and let him lead me to the first pedestal. He then lowered his arm before stepping back to let me move about freely. I took a measured breath, keeping my eyes downcast as I tried to get a feel for the set of armor before me on the pedestal—through smell, hearing, and touch—before I finally lifted my eyes to actually see it for the briefest of moments. It was exquisite red-lacquered battle armor.

I moved on to the next pedestal, performing the same process. Then again. And again, turning down more battle armor sets of various colors, styles, designs, and time periods, until I stood before the last pedestal. I breathed in deeply. A crisp, simple, almost cold warmth. I listened to the faint breeze slipping through a gap in the *shōji* ahead of us, and the almost playful kiss as that breeze touched the outfit before me. I tasted the air and imagined strawberries and sunshine.

I smiled faintly, my memory trying to bring up a pleasant past, but I forced it back down.

I looked up to see a white set of ninja garb. I nodded one time, allowing myself a genuine smile of approval, silently announcing it as my favorite. Instead of reaching for it, I turned away, spotting a canvas robe and pants on a hook in a forgotten corner. I approached and slipped them on over the silk under-robe and pants I already wore, wrapping a cloth belt around it all, tying it close to my body so I could move freely.

The sharp silence was akin to the sound of a blade slipping between two ribs. That I had chosen this rough canvas over the others—especially after smiling in approval at the last set.

I stepped up to the *shōji* and waited. After a few moments, Yín approached to slide it open and step through before me, the familiar garden behind him bathed in moonlight at this late hour. The moon hung full, large and bright enough to appear close enough to touch with my fingertips.

Despite the time of night, two rows of dark, living shadows sat facing each other with bared, black blades resting across their laps. I could sense a cold, detached readiness radiating outwards from them—a calm betrothal with death. A romantic passion with the taste of a foe's last dying breath.

I didn't stare or openly look, I observed the scene with all my senses—relying upon my eyes least of all. Three monks sat in silence before a statue of Buddha, and beyond the statue was the same field of swaying grass and apple blossom trees. The flowers looked engorged with moonlight and tranquility, pregnant with serenity, screaming silently, loving violently...

In perfect, effortless harmony.

I felt curious eyes settling upon me. I didn't check which of the ninjas it was. That wasn't why I was here. I was here for myself, to clear my head—not to talk or make friends or convince anyone of anything. I noticed a rack of weapons: staffs, blades, dragon-whips, throwing stars and knives, spears, chained swords, cudgels, nunchakus, butterfly swords, triple-chained staffs, and other weapons I had never seen before.

I picked up an old, worn staff—twigs bound by wire were wrapped around one end—that was leaning against the rack of priceless, deadly weapons. It was definitely the plainest weapon available. I gripped the staff, dedicating myself to its purpose, washing all other thought from my mind. Tomorrow would be hectic, chaotic, loud, violent...

But tonight...

I began wordlessly sweeping the deck with the old broom.

Yín momentarily lost his countenance and sucked in a startled breath. I didn't smile or acknowledge him as I continued to sweep, focusing my entire self on the perfection of such a simple, complicated task. I thought of the countless feet that would cross—and had crossed—this space since its construction.

I breathed in through my nose and out through a slight opening between my lips. I was here to find my center—but I would *buy* that precious commodity. I would *earn* my keep.

I soon began to sweat, furrowing my brow as I swept from one end of the deck to the other, carefully sweeping the dust and dirt into a neat pile. I swept back my sweaty hair, and took a few deep breaths, waiting for my heartrate to slow. I detached each hand from the broom, flexed my fingers a few times, and then regripped the weapon, ready for my next bout.

I went back to the beginning of my gauntlet for a second run, sweeping anything I had missed into the first pile I had made. My arms shook slightly, as if I had spent an hour swinging a sword. I was breathing raggedly, my vision momentarily throbbing as it threatened to tunnel closed. I fought it, regaining control of my breathing and steadying my pulse. Once composed, I used a dustpan to scoop up the mess and deposited it into a nearby trashcan. I carefully replaced the broom where I had found it, lovingly returning it to its place with the same care I would have used to tuck a friend's child into bed.

I quieted my mind, thanking the broom for taking care of its family and keeping their home free of dust and negative energy—an unsung guardian for these warriors and monks.

I didn't pretend to be a part of the family around me. I wasn't doing this to earn their respect. I was searching for inner peace, and Xuanwu had offered me sanctuary. My actions were an attempt to learn from them, to steal their secrets for myself. Even if for only a night.

I was a thief.

I turned back to the weapons, eyeing them thoughtfully. I did know something of my own that I could gift them for their accommodation in my quest for inner peace. I stepped up to a cabinet sheltered beneath an awning and, after pulling open a few drawers, found what I needed. I laid the items out on a wooden table, clearing anything in my way to form a clean workspace. I then brushed the table free of any dust and debris, mopping up a few wet oil stains and picking out a burr wedged into the surface of the workbench. Satisfied, I set a stool before my workstation and walked back to the weapons rack. I grabbed the butterfly swords—feeling a special affinity towards them after my time with Nate—and brought them back to the table. I had noticed a few nicks in the edge.

I set both swords—forearm length twin blades as wide as my hand—down on the table. I was careful to keep the tassels clear as I pulled out a whetstone. The blade only needed a bit of work. I flipped the stone over, checked the grit on each side to make sure my instinct had been correct, and then added a small amount of oil to the surface. I pressed the blade to the stone at the proper angle with both hands and slid the blade horizontally towards me. Like Roland had made me do for hours at a time. I lost myself in the repetitions. Occasionally adding a few more drops of oil.

My fingers shook as I polished the first butterfly sword with an oiled cloth, dried off my fingers with a second cloth, and then combed my clean fingers through the tassels to untangle a few threads.

Then I set it aside and scooped up the second blade, repeating the process. I felt eyes boring into my back and I paused, keeping my shoulders relaxed. The eyes drew closer and I soon felt a powerful presence directly behind me, as well as frigid tendrils of air raking across my shoulders through my sweat-damp robes. I could have turned and touched my observer, but I remained motionless, staring down at the blade, waiting.

After a few moments, the observer departed, taking the cold with him.

I resumed my work, losing myself in the motions as I squinted down at the blade in the moonlight. This one had taken longer than the first, and I sat there gripping the table, my breath coming in shallow pants, the middle of my body a gaping hollow. Now that I had stopped moving, my shoulders shook in the cool breeze, my robes thoroughly soaked.

Despite moving well past my limits of hunger, and thoroughly exhausting myself, my mind felt sharp and clear, devoid of fears, concerns, and emotions. My therapy was having a beneficial effect, preparing me, re-forging me into a sharper blade.

I felt eyes on me again—not the same as before—and knew they belonged to more than one person. They watched intently, and not just my act of sharpening their blades, but the set of my shoulders, the way my hips settled into the stool, the tilt of my head, the way my damp hair hung loose, the shaking in my hands, the hunger in my belly, the mind guiding my actions.

They didn't just *watch* me. The minds behind those eyes took in all that extra, often-overlooked data about me, and came to a crystal-clear conclusion. A definition for me. I wasn't sure how I knew such a thing—all from glances felt upon my back—but I was certain of it.

I finally stood from the stool, stretched out my back, carefully picked up the sharpened, polished, and oiled blades, and returned them to their place on the weapons rack. The eyes followed my every move, my every thought.

I took two steps back from the rack, lowered my eyes as I bowed faintly, and then I slowly turned to find my next chore.

The world suddenly tilted; I lost my balance as my vision rapidly dwindled down to a tunnel, threatening to drown me entirely in a fog of darkness.

49

Soft, sure, feather-light hands caught me so gently and swiftly that it felt like nothing had actually touched me. I simply stopped falling, but so gradually and smoothly that I couldn't pinpoint the exact moment I had stopped. It was the strangest sensation.

My vision slowly expanded, widening out from the momentary narrow tunnel. Dehydration. I was dehydrated.

I hadn't eaten or consumed any significant amount of liquid since my return to Kansas City from the Doors. I began to open my mouth to apologize but a silk finger pressed my lips closed the moment before my lips parted, anticipating my thoughts before even I had.

I did not nod or make eye contact with my savior. He pulled his finger away. The man—apparently very strong—suddenly swept me off my feet so effortlessly and smoothly that it felt like a choreographed dance. Then he was carrying me back to the house and through two rooms before slowing in a dimly lit room that featured a wooden square of flooring seeming to float in the center of a pond. A low table with a single pillow occupied the wooden floor, and a small waterfall bubbled over tiers of rocks before falling into the pond. Dozens of large orange and white koi fish circled the pond, swimming lazily.

A bowl of rice, a pair of chopsticks, a small cup, and a clay jug of tea sat on the table. My savior set me back down, supporting my shoulders with both hands in his feather-light, strong-as-iron, grip. I carefully knelt down on the pillow, moving slowly so as not to lose my balance or let the blood rush to my head. It took me a moment to realize my savior no longer touched me, and that I couldn't recall when he had broken physical contact.

But I knew he was still in the room, those eyes as piercing as I had felt outside. The same man who had approached me from behind to observe me sharpening the blades.

I scooped up the chopsticks and spun them up into my hair to hold it back rather than use them to eat the rice. I thought I heard a muffled sound, but it was soon replaced by the gentle whisper of the rice paper door sliding closed, leaving me in the room to sip my tea in peace, and to watch the koi fish.

I drank the tea until it was finished, appreciating this new clarity of mind. I had passed the state of hunger that hurt—I didn't know exactly when—and now felt a hollowness within my core. At the same time, I felt fuller in other ways, in other places.

My mind attempted to consider my savior—his identity, his purpose, his decision—but I succinctly slashed those errant thoughts to ribbons.

I noticed, for the first time, a small bell with a silk ribbon tied to the end sitting on the floor beside my pillow. I picked it up and gave it a faint jingle, the sound startlingly loud after the silence I had cloaked myself in so far this evening.

The *shōji* ahead of me slid open to reveal a young woman kneeling on the other side of the threshold, her eyes downcast as she held out a hand to encourage me to join her. I left the dishes on the table and very carefully climbed to my feet.

I entered the room to find it much warmer than any I had been in so far. Soft, gentle hands trailed down my neck and over my shoulders, as one would touch a skittish horse in order to bond with it. I wasn't successful in hiding my instinctive flinch, but the hands never slowed or reacted other than to trail down my ribs and around my waist. My skin tingled where she touched me, like she was drawing lines of electric current down my body—faint blooms of energy seemed to pop beneath my skin in a pleasant, relaxing way.

She untied my belt, slowly unwrapping me, never breaking the contact of her fingers to my body—if one hand untied or unwound, the other continued to drift and dance up and down my lower back or shoulders. She folded the sash into a neat square and set it down beside me before moving on to my sweaty canvas robe. She was surprisingly fast, but thankfully motioned for me to take off both pairs of pants myself. She took them from me, never meeting my eyes, but smiling to herself as if listening to her favorite song in her mind.

I wore only my sweat-slicked silk robes, now.

She slowly turned me to face her, untied my second sash and folded it into a neat square faster than I could have curled it up into a tight ball. She set her surprisingly warm hands on my shoulders, squeezed gently, and then trailed the pads down my biceps, dancing and tapping as they drifted down my forearms, my palms, and my fingers, which she gently gripped and used to guide me down into a kneeling position, mirroring the motion herself until we knelt before each other, as my robe billowed around me.

I stared wonderingly at her pale flushed lips, her delicate chin, and the porcelain hollow of her throat, counting the slow throbs of her pulse from the veins visible beneath her thin skin. My breathing was deep and slow, but my heart was racing, and my skin was tingling slightly.

Still smiling to her inner song—seeming to stare deep *within* my body, not at the exterior of my body—she reached for my hip with one hand, her other resting on my upper thigh, and tugged the ribbon loose. She casually fluffed out that half of the robe, letting it fall loosely at my hip and shoulder. Before I had time to even consider being self-conscious about my nudity, she had already untied the second string and flicked the corner of the robe free so that the entire garment fell into a silken pile around me.

Warm air danced over my sweaty chest, and it took me a moment to realize that I had my eyes closed, I was panting, and my body shook with faint tremors. My body felt awakened, my skin tingling with energy as every once-normal sensation was suddenly amplified.

I heard a squishing sound and then the scent of fresh roses filled the room as water splashed into a puddle behind me.

Before I could flinch at the sound, a hot sponge pressed firmly but gently into the back of my neck—hot, soapy, oily water trailed down my spine and lower back, dripping onto my heels and the bottoms of my feet since I was kneeling. The sponge moved, splashed, was squeezed again, and placed on my shoulder to the same effect.

I lost myself in the sensation of hot, scented oil sliding down my body, washing away sweat, dirt, and even the last residues of stress, replaced by a deep, powerful calm within my soul. A distant part of me wondered whether my bather was activating my chakras or if the sheer act of sensual physical contact was causing me to feel this way. To feel as if I was about to explode in one shuddering breath, not unlike a toe-curling, eye-rolling orgasm.

But one of the *soul*. A soulgasm.

Soon I was steaming, dripping wet, and my lips were parted as I relished my newfound euphoria. And then she repeated the process over the front of my shoulders. My back arched and I whimpered like a plucked string on a guitar, feeling as if every note—every squeeze of the sponge—was bringing me closer and closer to some long-lost part of myself.

As far as I knew, I blanked out for a good ten minutes, because I found it near impossible to open my eyes, only stirring because I no longer felt the sponge washing my thighs in soothing, circular motions. Water dripped from my breasts onto my inner thigh, and my body was so worked up I thought I might have to go take a long trip to Fae and pay Grimm whatever he asked to watch Alice for a few hours while I checked out the inside of Nate's igloo.

It wasn't that I necessarily felt sexually aroused but more that my body was so alive right now—so hyper-aware of every sensation—that I wanted to have that last drink and see what happened. I decided she was secretly a tantric goddess, and that was all there was to it.

She had washed away more than dirt and sweat and stress from my body. She had polished off years of tarnish from my soul.

A thick, fluffy robe was placed around my shoulders, trapping in the heat, and a moment later, I heard the partition slide open behind me.

I glanced over my shoulder to see the exotic woman kneeling on the other side, smiling brightly at me as it slid closed. I spotted a cup of jasmine tea before me and a black stone sitting beside it. The word *Hope* was etched into the surface, and I found a grin threatening to split my cheeks entirely in two.

I scooped up the flat stone in one hand—it was as hot as one could get without causing discomfort—and the tea in the other, downing it in one quick pull. A pallet heaped with furs and blankets beside a small fire murmured seductively to me, and I had no willpower to deny its temptations. I slid under the blankets, twitching and biting my lips at the sensory explosions of fur caressing my skin. I tucked the blankets up to my chin, smiling to myself as I clutched my fortune stone to my chest, shivering as the stone seemed to melt deeper and deeper into my chest before sleep embraced me in strong, loving arms that smelled of licorice and mint.

50

I woke to find two sets of garments beside my bed—both wrapped up with a silk ribbon, like gifts—as well as a bowl of fresh fruit and tea. I studied the two sets of garments thoughtfully as I broke my fast.

One set was the clothes I had arrived in—the white jeans and blouse I had worn to Dorian's party—now cleaned and neatly folded up with my Darling and Dear jacket. They had even made sure to fold the jacket so that the figurines and my silver butterfly charms were protected. Still, I unwrapped it enough to verify their safety and authenticity.

This was still Kansas City, after all.

The other set of clothing was the white set of ninja-looking garb Yín had shown me in the armory room yesterday. The same set I had approved of but not worn, choosing the canvas robes instead.

Out of respect—and coolness factor—I chose the ninja set, of course.

I put on the new clothing, taking care to be methodical and conscious of every motion, clasp, or tie, using the process as a form of meditation.

But I didn't immediately leave Xuanwu's home. I still maintained my silence, and the detached calm I'd achieved the previous night had still been with me when I woke. My head was clear and determined, and I felt at peace with my plan of attack for tonight. Even still, I wanted to drink up every drop of this tranquility that I could while I had the chance.

So I silently served tea to several of the shadowy ninjas, paying more attention to their clothing and overall appearance than I had last night. I wore almost identical clothes to them now, only mine were white. I didn't make eye contact with them, but I let myself be more aware of them. They, in turn, seemed more open to having me do so. Which is strange to say, because they hadn't done anything yesterday to make me feel unwelcome or anything, but I felt a mild kinship with them today.

I never saw my tantric bather again, although I wished I could have thanked her in some small way, even if I didn't quite know what that would be. Even a smile of gratitude would have sufficed.

I saw a monk making kanji drawings with a large, fat brush as long as his leg—more like a mop than a paintbrush. The end result was an incredibly complex piece of beautiful calligraphy that he silently rolled up and gave me as a gift, making my eyes water—especially when he placed a finger over my lips as I opened my mouth to verbally thank him.

Later, I saw him using the broom I had borrowed yesterday.

I spent a considerable amount of time sitting before the gong all by myself, staring out at the field of apple blossoms as I meditated upon recent events—simply observing the facts from a slightly different perspective. Hindsight. Occasionally, I felt specters in my mind, shadowy forms politely shifting on the outskirts of my focus, observing and passing on without comment or intrusion—the ninjas or monks watching me from an astral state, I presumed, assessing me, reading me.

Xuanwu came to sit beside me at one point, radiating cold air as we watched the apple blossoms in companionable silence. He eventually placed a claw on my shoulder, kissed me on the side of the head, and left.

I thought about that for a very long time, ignoring the startled looks from absolutely everyone who had seen Xuanwu's gesture of affection.

I finally decided it was time for me to get back to work, and that's when I realized that I hadn't spoken a single word for more than twelve hours.

And mankind did rejoice! Hallelujah!

Yín, as if reading my mind, had been waiting for me. We exited the house and I walked down the front steps, tugging a few straps on my new clothing to get familiar with the apparent weapons straps and buckles hidden all over. They were similar to tactical clothing in that way, just for blades rather than guns and ammo. I clutched the bundle of my old clothes in the other hand as I turned back to Yín, dipping my chin.

"Thank you for your hospitality," I told him. "I needed it." The act of speaking felt both physically and socially strange.

He bowed respectfully. "You are always welcome, White Rose. Thorns and all," he added, winking playfully. His smile slowly faded, and he leaned closer as if to ask a private question. "Why did you visit us in person rather than using the figurine Xuanwu gave you?"

I smiled. "I didn't come here to recruit. I came here to unshoulder my own mental baggage. To cleanse my mind. To prepare. I haven't decided—"

I cut off, suddenly hyper-aware of a shadow in my peripheral vision that hadn't been there a moment ago. It was no more than two paces away, standing beside the trunk of a tree. I slowly turned to find one of the ninjas staring at me. Even as I watched, the flickering shadows faded away, leaving just the man in black, and I somehow knew he was the one who had saved me from falling last night.

I was sure I hadn't seen him today while serving the ninjas tea.

"You do not dictate where a petal falls or where death blooms. That is for me to decide, White Rose," he said calmly, his voice a low hum.

I lowered my chin respectfully, despite his tone. He was a handsome man, even with the three faint scars down his unshaven cheeks, and I could tell he was very strong despite his unassuming, lean body type. He had handled me like a kitten last night and, seeing him now, I was somewhat surprised. He was a few inches taller than me, and the top of his hair was pulled back into a short tail that just touched the back of his neck, leaving the hair on the sides of his head to brush his jaws like scythes. His dark eyes threatened to draw me in until I averted them with a shallow exhale.

"We go where we are needed," he said, "and tonight, we are needed outside a church—no matter what some may or may not *decide*," he said in a low tone, repeating the word I had used a moment ago.

"Thank you..." I trailed off, not knowing his name.

He smirked in amusement. "I am called Ryuu, and I would whisper the name of Old Death into your enemies' ears. As would my brothers."

Yín was noticeably submissive, keeping his eyes lowered and not making any sound that could be taken as an interruption. He respected and feared this Ryuu.

"What would you have my Shinobi do, White Rose?" Ryuu asked.

I thought about that, very hard, realizing there was no way for me to turn him down without looking disrespectful. "I need a vampire captured and brought to me in secret." His dark eyes flickered at the edges, a twitch of amusement at me telling a ninja—a Shinobi, apparently—to be discreet. I would have to read up on their culture after all of this was said and done. My training in the martial arts had only given me a mildly more extensive understanding than the average American.

"What particulars do you require?" he asked. I arched a brow in confusion. He used hand gestures to accompany his explanation. "Tall, short, male, female, fat, skinny, strong, weak or..." he smiled darkly, "or would you have me open Roland Haviar's throat?"

I shook my head firmly, decisively, my eyes flashing territorially. "He is mine," I snarled.

Ryuu dipped his chin, an echo of a smile pulling at the corners of his lips.

"I need someone loyal to Roland, someone devoted to his own wickedness," I told Ryuu. "You have watched these streets. I'm sure you could find one you know to be cruel."

He nodded without hesitation. "I will gift wrap him up and deliver him to you shortly."

I frowned suspiciously. "Do you have a phone so I can tell you where I will—"

"I have no need. I know where you are. Always."

He stepped backwards without a noise, and then simply faded from view as if I'd only imagined him. I shivered slightly at that—and I thought I heard a faint, responding chuckle at my reaction, but that could have been a leaf tumbling across the grass.

I turned back to Yín, shaking my head. "I will return when this is finished. I think I have much to learn," I admitted.

He dipped his head. "We are always learning, always searching for new understandings. You are more than welcome to return."

I hesitated, searching his face. "Why did Ryuu offer his assistance?" I asked. "Does he lead the...Shinobi?" I asked, choosing Ryuu's preferred word rather than ninja, although I wasn't certain of the difference—or if there even was one.

Yín hesitated longer in his response than I had in the question. "That is something you must come to learn on your own, I think. I cannot answer for others, but...I believe fortune has favored you in him. Outside of training his men, I have only heard him speak three times in my years here." His eyes were intense as he ticked up a single finger. "Each time was directly to Xuanwu. And he spoke as an *equal*."

Yín bowed once more and backed away three paces before turning away and leaving me to stand in the garden with the two guards—who had been so studiously quiet that I had entirely forgotten about them.

"You guys should get a radio or something," I said.

They bowed their chins in understanding but didn't meet my eyes. They seemed...afraid. Of me or Ryuu? Or maybe they just really hated music and were trying to be polite.

I climbed into my battered Geo Metro and drove away, staring at every shadow I drove past, wondering if Ryuu was already stalking me.

Speaking to Xuanwu as an equal...

Later. A better understanding of the mysteries of the Shinobi would not help me tonight.

51

I'd gotten some much needed sleep last night, a good meal this morning, and meditating at Xuanwu's house had polished my mind, clearing it of useless factors that only threatened to slow me down. I had needed a clear head for what would happen when I confronted Roland. I had no new insights or changes of heart, but I had needed to verify where my heart stood on the matter. After everything I had learned over the last few days, I'd made my decision. The majority of my focused meditations had been me recalling my visit through the Doors, imagining a world where I had already succeeded in my mission during the blood moon, envisioning my plan in perfect detail, in perfect execution, and the ramifications that would follow my victory.

I had secretly held the Mask of Despair—the silver butterfly charm—in my lap or hand the entire morning, getting to know it on a subconscious level, allowing it to touch my flesh as I meditated. Spending a brief amount of time in Xuanwu's home had really brought on a hunger for slowing down to speed up.

Finally having my own set of wheels and some time to kill, I'd spent the rest of the day running errands, checking around town, and generally getting an understanding of the city's new groove—the pulse. To all outward appearances, my hometown functioned as it always had. I'd driven by numerous police cruisers and had been surprised to see what I took as two distinctly different camps within the men in blue. The older, grizzled police officers had grim, harder looks on their faces, while the younger officers displayed greasy, pleased smiles. The old dogs knew something strange was going on and didn't like it. The young wolves had less concern for duty and obligation to Kansas City's citizens and liked their newfound freedom.

Whenever I drove through a neighborhood that Claire had indicated as a supernatural hotbed of one faction or another, I had found windows shuttered, people not lingering outdoors, and an increased police presence—of the younger, greasier variety.

In fact, there was increased police presence everywhere—except Roland's church. Or, more specifically, the police had cordoned off a two or three block radius around Roland's church, even barricading the streets and forcing people away. I wondered if that was Alucard's work or the usual preparation for Roland's Friday night Black Mass. It served my purposes—less potential for collateral damage—so I didn't really care that much.

I'd—very, very carefully—checked out Abundant Angel Catholic Church, but hadn't gotten very close when I noticed a surprising number of SHITs patrolling the area as far as a block out from the property itself. Claire was in there somewhere, hopefully safe in the cells far down below, but I couldn't do anything about that right now. I just hoped I could count on Eae to do his part. He'd had a good performance last night—which had surprised me. Not that he'd honored his word, but that he had acted in the gray area—on the word of a woman who had already been involved with one angel falling. Despite his support, the thought had to have crossed his mind—that maybe the world was better off without Callie Penrose.

Then again, the current state of Kansas City was the result of a city mourning the White Rose—whether they were aware of it or not. The devil you knew, I guessed.

The carefully concocted story Claire was supposed to tell her jailers combined with Eae's supposed duel with this new demon in town should be enough to get the Shepherds there tonight. I had a backup plan if it wasn't enough to lead the sheep here, but if the first steps of my plan fell apart, the rest would quickly become a crapshoot with a high body count.

The wake of Callie Penrose would be a night for the history books, one way or another.

Roland and Fabrizio would be drawn out to catch a glimpse of the White

Rose's killer—for differing reasons—and I would have everyone's attention for a brief amount of time. Long enough, I hoped.

I'd run my last errand of the day to prepare for my showdown outside Roland's church, and returned to the Geo Metro to find a small origami swan tucked neatly beneath the door handle. A single drop of blood painted the pretty lips of the pretty little swan. I heard the scuffle of boots approach from the depths of the adjacent alley, and a young, greasy-looking man was shoved down onto his knees. He had a gag stuffed into his mouth, and a long metal wire constricted his throat, the end trailing off into the depths of the shaded alley like a leash. I sensed a familiar presence in that darkness, but the wide, terrified eyes of the kneeling vampire before me would have announced who the delivery guy had been better than a nametag.

Or a bloodthirsty origami swan.

The vampire also had a red ribbon tied around his chest, knotted into an elaborate bow—wrapped up like a birthday gift. I smiled, shaking my head slightly as I shot a look into the darkness. Old Death's good friend stared back, unseen, and I knew he was smiling. Ryuu.

I sensed more than just Ryuu in the depths of the shadows, and more eyes watching me from the roof of the buildings towering over the alley, but I didn't try to find them. Shadows had been given life in Kansas City, and it was safest to let them simply be. Curiosity killed the cat, and they were working for me, so I granted them their wish to remain unseen.

I studied the red-eyed vampire before me and finally tugged his gag free, letting him pant for a moment before I leaned down close, right in his face.

"Did you know the White Rose?" I asked.

He nodded quickly. "I've seen her before. At Haven's compound. She came with Master Roland. Before he was a vampire," he elaborated nervously.

"And do you know who I am?" I asked, smiling. "What do I look like?"

"A demon!" He gasped. "Meridiana. A very...pretty demon!" he whined, smiling crookedly as if hoping flattery would save him.

I pulled out a vial from the folds of my jacket, tilting it back and forth to show the vampire what shifted inside. My blood. "What do you see?" I asked, popping the top off.

His eyes danced from me to the vial, but he sniffed at the vial obediently. "Blood and liquid silver?" he stammered, looking uncertain.

I nodded pensively, recapping the vial. Then I closed my eyes and called upon my Silvers, letting a silver liquid form into a ball above my palm, growing larger with each passing second. I had used my Silvers in the Doors to repair the Spear of Longinus, to merge with a broken katana. I imagined that exact sword in perfect detail, now, letting the orb of silver liquid grow and grow, ignoring the horrified whimpers before me.

I flung my hand against the brick wall, exerting my will into the act and keeping the broken katana firmly in my mind as I did. A metallic clang and the sound of crumbling brick echoed sharply in the narrow space and I finally opened my eyes. An exact replica of the katana Fabrizio had allowed me to take into the Doors was embedded firmly into the brick and mortar.

The vampire panted desperately, murmuring incoherently as if praying for salvation. "What did you see?" I demanded.

He opened his mouth wordlessly, eyes dancing from me to the sword like a rat. "A sword called from the depths of Hell..." he rasped hopelessly.

"That's it? A sword appearing from Hell?" I asked, locking my eyes onto his.

He nodded jerkily.

"And who stands before you now," I asked leaning close so he could see my face.

"Meridiana!" he gasped, repeating his earlier answer. He was too afraid to lie.

I nodded, turning away to hide my smile of relief. My plan would work.

"Please. Please just let me go. I didn't do anything—"

The wire jerked tight and a form flowed up directly behind him. Dark fingers flickering with midnight black vapor snatched him by the hair and jerked his head back to stare up at Ryuu's face leaning over him from behind. "You have done quite a lot, vampire. I've seen what you and your friends do to *pass the time*."

I calmly strode over to the sword, unsheathing it from the stone with a surprisingly gentle whisper. I turned my back on the vampire, keeping my breath measured and calm. "Women?" I asked the Shinobi behind me.

"Yes."

I swiftly stepped backwards with one foot, crouching into a forward-facing lunge, and felt a faint, satisfying resistance.

The vampire behind me coughed wetly, a ragged, shocked breath struggling to fill his pierced lung.

My katana made no sound as I withdrew it from his body, still not looking at him. I took a slow breath and spun, decapitating the vampire in one swift motion. Blood fountained from his headless torso before it fell to the ground, the head rolling grotesquely as it came to a stop, face-down in an oily puddle. I studied my blade, giving it a harsh flick of my wrist. Blood flew from the edge and I lifted it to my face, inspecting it.

An exact replica to the one Fabrizio had given me.

And the vampire had given me my answer.

Ryuu practically purred with satisfaction, staring at my face with an approving smirk. "It looks like I'm just as good as I thought," I said out loud, referring to my Demonskin. Only after Ryuu's chuckle did I realize it had sounded like I was bragging about my killing the vampire. I didn't correct myself. Both were true.

"Xuanwu asked me to pass on a message," Ryuu said.

I turned to look at him.

"*Abandon all hope, ye who enter here* is a fitting phrase above a locked door. And the door to Roland's church deserves such a warning."

I considered that in silence for a few moments. "Thank you." I turned away, staring out at the streets, deep in thought.

I'd needed to make sure they wouldn't all suddenly recognize me the moment I used my Silvers in the physical sense—that my Silver sword wouldn't suddenly give me away.

Because I needed this sword. This *exact* katana.

Absently, I wondered why Ryuu hadn't seen me as a demon—if it was an extension of Xuanwu's perception, or simply because he was a ninja warrior badass killing machine. "I'm going to use this Demonskin against them. Be ready."

He glanced over his shoulder at a very strange, almost unnoticeable sound. He slowly turned back to me, a determined frown on his face. "They have the First Murderer. Cain, son of Eve," he said flatly. My breath caught instinctively, but I managed to nod calmly, hoping Alucard could do his part. "He was restrained, scraped up, but otherwise unharmed."

"Who brought him in?" I whispered in a frosty tone.

"The werewolves, Paradise and Lost."

I nodded very slightly. "If any harm comes to him..."

Ryuu nodded determinedly. "They will die first."

I shook my head. "Not just *first*...they die *slowly*. No stealthy kills. You will incite fear with their slaughter."

He nodded calmly. "The death of a thousand cuts."

I wasn't sure what that was—or if it was literally possible to cut someone one thousand times without killing them. "Use silver."

"You tend your garden and I will tend mine," he said, not unkindly but with authority, reminding me he was not a servant but an ally.

"Only red-eyes die tonight, Ryuu. Everyone else is just ignorant or scared. Red-eyes have earned the chance...to hear Old Death's name whispered in their ears."

I crouched down before the growing pool of vampire blood, dipping two fingers into it. I lifted the bloody paint to my chest, pausing to shoot Ryuu a questioning look.

He grinned like a wolf.

So I began to paint my white ninja garb with vampire blood, drawing a large Cross Pattée from neck to navel, nipple to nipple. Finished, I wiped my fingers off on the vampire's shirt.

Ryuu nodded his approval. "I will spread the word. Red-eyes only. And on your signal."

I dipped my chin. "See you there."

"No, White Rose," he said in a breathy whisper, directly behind me. "You won't."

Then he was gone. Something about his tone let me know it hadn't been a personal threat or warning. Just a simple statement of fact. He and his Shinobi would not be seen as they brought death to the streets of Kansas City.

Silence would fall. And blood would flow.

I wondered where Alucard fit into Cain's abduction, and where he would ultimately stand when it was time to lay our cards on the table. He'd tasted my blood, but...

Roland's bond had still been there when I checked with my Silvers.

One way or another, we would find out which blood bond was stronger.

Which warrior was better. Whether the student could defeat the master.

I climbed into my car, staring up at the sky and waiting for the sun to begin its descent. I'd tried calling Alucard, but he hadn't answered—either having betrayed me or unable to speak openly as deep within enemy territory as he was.

I knew Cain was tough—that he could withstand more torture than most men...

But anything done to him would be returned threefold on the wielder, courtesy of me.

I would even let Dorian record it to share with his network of viewers.

A fitting season premiere to the *Return of the White Rose*.

52

When I arrived outside the church, an alarming number of people had shown up for the event. Perfect. With everyone present, I no longer had to be as careful about using magic. They were already here and ready to spill blood. Anything they saw would either make them see who I really was, or they would chalk it up to me being a demon with all sorts of powers—especially since I'd been strong enough to kill the White Rose.

I'd used my magic to cause a mild distraction at one of the police barricades, and then a sloppy concealment spell to sneak my Geo Metro past the cordon. Luckily, it was a tiny car—small enough to easily conceal with my spell and to drive onto the sidewalk to sneak around the barricade. I'd parked on a street pointing directly at Roland's church, and waited in silence, holding the Mask of Despair in my hands, bonding with it.

I felt it was important to do. Rather than just *slapping it on*, as Nate had informed me. No. We needed to have a different relationship. Not just to be used when needed and then tucked out of sight. Pandora had cautioned against leaving our toys on shelves.

I waited until the Blood Moon hung heavy in the sky—large and sinister—casting a reddish-orange glow over the City of Fountains. Then I turned the Mask of Despair into my silver butterfly charm and shoved it in a pocket

—a different one than the silver butterfly charm Nate had given me. It would be embarrassing to mix them up.

Since entrances were pivotal, I turned the key, shifted into drive, and floored the accelerator towards the crowd standing in my way. Seeing and hearing a car at all was startling, so everyone got out of the way in a hurry.

Then I was speeding directly onto the church property, not slowing down as the grinning vampires grew larger in my windshield. Their grins immediately slipped, realizing too late that I had no intention of stopping. I barreled right into them, mowing a large chunk of them down before I opened the door and jumped out, using a shield of air to slow my roll.

Heh.

The car slammed into the door like a crushed can and instantly vaporized into red mist.

But I did count about a dozen vampires felled by the little hunk of metal.

I kept my magic up—in order to keep the other fifty or more vampires and just as many wolves back as I assessed my hard work with a disappointed frown.

Muttering darkly under my breath, I studied the church for a moment. This close, I noticed a fine mist surrounding the church. It throbbed with power and menace, making me want to turn away. It was powerful, and even though I could usually see a ward and have some inkling how it worked, how it was made, and what it did...

This one was an enigma. It seemed to want absolutely *no one* near it—except for those bonded to Roland. The Mask of Despair quivered in my pocket, but I ignored it. Too soon.

We had a show to play out, first.

I silently walked back to the street, feeling absolutely everyone staring at me. I stared right back. Shepherds stood on one side of me and vampires and wolves on the other—those guarding the front of the church trickling into their ranks two-by-two, but still leaving a contingent back as reserves.

Dorian and his Hellfire Club stood between the two—the ones I had almost run over on my way towards the church. I even saw Xuanwu standing before two bald monks in white robes. He drew a lot of attention—many having no idea who he was or why he was here. I mean, he was a giant, frozen stone turtle standing head and shoulders above everyone else, and he was too calm. His eyes settled on me for no longer than they settled on anyone else, like he was watching a sporting event. He held his sword in a stone claw like a cane.

No one tried speaking with him.

Eae was there, perched on the roof of a bus stop for all to see, and he looked anticipatory. His wings were in full display and he wore armor. He glanced back at the Shepherds and I noticed the snarling, roaring polar bear held down by chains and a few SHITs. I also saw Fabrizio at the front of his group, glaring at me with cold eyes. I smiled back. It costs nothing to be polite. Eae turned back to me with a dark, promising smile of his own, so that it looked like the two prize-fighters were taunting each other. The crowd ate it up, and I could soon hear hushed conversations as Dorian wandered through the crowd like a shark, taking bets and bringing the cheer back to church.

I didn't spot any Regulars, thankfully, and since we were in a mostly commercial area—and the police had cordoned off the area—I figured it was about as Regular-free as it was going to get.

I had known that with this many parties present, all strapped for a fight, everyone would be too cautious to be the first to turn on each other. Because that would leave their backs open to an attack from a *different* party. I had needed this tension and chaos. A stalemate.

Everyone waiting to see me fight whoever wanted to volunteer before I squared off with Eae. Which is why I'd gone to Dorian's party last night—to ruffle some feathers. To pick a fight.

With everyone who had a grudge with the White Rose's murderer.

I felt the Mask quivering in my pocket again, hungry to team up, but I kept it there.

My white ninja outfit drew quite a bit of attention. Or maybe it was the red Cross Pattée I'd painted down the center of my chest with the vampire's blood. Ryuu had merely smiled when I asked him, so I was confident I wouldn't offend Yín or Xuanwu. I'd also made my leather jacket white so as not to clash or be recognized. Functional and chic.

Without further ado, I pulled out the silver katana from a strap on my belt—a temporary fix since I didn't have a sheath designed for it—and slammed it into the pavement at my feet. Then I held up the vial of my silver magic, lifting it up for all to see.

"Blood and sword. Petals and thorns of the great White Rose." I spat on the ground. "Any questions?" I asked. No one spoke. They just stared back at me for about a minute.

Fabrizio finally stepped forward, Claire growled louder behind him, railing against her chains and her captors. "Not so much a question as a commandment, demon—"

"Meridiana," I interrupted, not even looking at him as I inspected my nails in the glow of the blood moon. "A Succubus, if you're interested..." and this time I did look up at him, with such a smoldering and suggestive look that he actually blushed. My laugh rang out like a bell in the quiet street, echoing for a few seconds.

His face darkened. "Hard pass, Meridiana." He muttered, straightening his shoulders. "You say you killed the White Rose—one who had the support of the Vatican at her back." I very studiously managed to keep my face clear of anger at that blatant lie, when all I really wanted to do was break my foot off in his ass. The backing of the Vatican! News to me! They'd turned on both Roland and me at the drop of a hat—even after we saved them from both a traitor and the resulting public embarrassment.

In fact, it could be argued that our decision to help them *then* had sort of precipitated *this* fight. Roland wouldn't have been a vampire if we had refused to help them, but Roland had chosen to sacrifice his mortality in exchange for preventing a war between the Sanguine Council and the Vatican Shepherds. "For that," Fabrizio continued, snapping me out of my dark thoughts, "I will personally send you back to Hell. If I fall, Eae will have his chance to do God's work."

Eae bristled at that, but he didn't challenge it. He had to be very careful how he acted today. If he helped me too obviously, the Shepherds might lose faith in an angel—an unacceptable choice with disastrous consequences, according to Eae.

Claire roared again and I bit back my instinctive smile. *Soon, Claire bear. Soon...*

Without Eae and Claire's help, the Shepherds might not have shown up at all, despite Fabrizio's apparent bravado. Claire's part of my plan had been to warn them about tonight—which they would have dismissed as a lie—as well as telling them she'd almost had me dead to rights when the Shepherds and Eae had interrupted us outside of the cave, which they also might have disbelieved—maybe even doubting Eae's worth or loyalty.

Which was why I'd told Eae he needed to go to Dorian's party and pick a fight with me. My terms for our duel lent credence to Claire's claims—the ones they had initially dismissed—and made Eae look willing to die for the cause.

Then him being here now, dressed up in armor...well, yeah. It was convincing.

Eae had a few other small tasks he was supposed to have done, but all I could do was hope for the best.

Alucard suddenly swaggered out from the crowd of vampires to lock eyes with me. "On behalf of Roland Haviar, Master of Kansas City, I'd like to rip your cute little nose off, hell-twat." He glanced at Fabrizio with an amused sneer. "But I've never been one to turn down sloppy seconds." He glanced back to me. "For the record, I wouldn't mind if you killed this one," he said, pointing a thumb at Fabrizio.

I sighed tiredly. "I do have an appointment with the vampire priest I must get to," I said, licking my lips as I pointed at the doors to the church, "and then a wrestle with my brother," I added, blowing a kiss at Eae, "so let's move this farce right along, shall we?"

"You don't want to attract Roland's attention, demon," Alucard said with a sneer.

"Is your new puppy so important to you?" Paradise asked, strutting forward from behind her pack to steal Alucard's sunshine.

Lost stepped up beside her, smirking. "We haven't house-broken him, yet."

Alucard hissed at the two of them. "Back off. She is *mine*. I practically giftwrapped Cain in a bow and let you two bring him in, let you two accept all the credit." Their faces paled in slight shame, but they recovered well. "You *owe* me. Roland will see *my* value for once rather than relying on that lickspittle, Bellerose. We all saw how useless he turned out to be."

Paradise and Lost growled at Alucard. "You're not supposed to even be here. You're supposed to be watching Cain," they snapped, trying to regain some of their authority.

Alucard scoffed. "You want to bring up *more* of your failures in front of your pack?" He laughed. "Fine. You two couldn't get him to say a *word*! Cain must be the pig with the brick house, too tough for the big bad wolves!" he laughed loudly in their faces. "You had to beg for my help *again* to get any answers out of him. And I made him *sing*." Paradise and Lost were furious with shame this time, which was an interesting sight to see. Alucard waved a hand dismissively. "Anyway. He stands no chance of escaping his chains without help. Trust me. Let him rot. He's just another murderer."

I hid the smile from my face. Alucard had brought Cain in—an interesting development—and one that served to earn him some credit with the wolves. Allowing him to even interrogate Cain. Clever. And he'd used our code word, *murderer*, letting me know Cain was in position. I really hoped my blood bond to Alucard was stronger than his bond with Roland.

But this was a show, and a show required entertainment. I would learn pretty quickly if Alucard was just telling me what I wanted to hear. I caught a faint flicker of a shifting curtain in the window of Roland's church, and my heart jumped. Roland? Was he watching?

I hoped so. The whole point of this party was to piss him off enough to draw him out.

I slowly turned to Alucard, my face a cool, blank mask. "You beat my dog?" I asked him.

My tone made everyone flinch. Alucard smiled back at me, nodding. "Repeatedly."

I nodded slightly. "Any last words?" Everyone got way the hell back from us.

Alucard cracked his neck left and then right. "I'm going to hit you where the sun don't shine, hell-twat."

And he leapt at my face.

Ding! Ding! Ding! Round one.

53

I shifted to the side, backhanding him across the face with an echoing *crack* on his way past. The Hellfire crowd cheered raucously, shouting out bets for Dorian to take, but he was too busy watching us with his mouth hanging open. I flinched as about a hundred golf umbrellas snapped to life before the vampires. They held them out in a shield wall and I instantly understood why—they were protecting themselves from sunlight. Alucard.

I quickly dove to my right, rolling to my feet as a blast of brilliant sunshine slammed into the space where I had just been standing. It left a small crater in the pavement, glittering with sparkles. I narrowed my eyes at Alucard, squaring my shoulders and wanting to stay within ten paces of him—close enough to dart forward when I saw an opening.

His next blast came directly at me—a bar of solid light aimed at my chest. I spun away, wincing at the unbelievably raw heat emanating from it, and let it hammer into—and entirely through—the umbrella shields behind me. Puffs of dust and agonized screams erupted for those unfortunate souls who were kissed by sunlight. The umbrellas had been to protect against daylight touching them...

Not a raging hard-on whipping out directly from the sun's nether regions.

And I was fairly confident that I'd caught a hesitation in Alucard's eyes a heartbeat before he unzipped his solar fly. A telegraphed warning?

He cursed, wincing at the damage he'd caused before rounding on me.

Whether this fight was an act on Alucard's part, or entirely authentic, I had to make it look convincing. Impressive. Enough to draw out Roland. But I also wanted to be moderately careful about revealing my skills. There was every possibility that me fighting Alucard wouldn't be enough to draw out Roland and that it would take me fighting Fabrizio and possibly Eae as well. I wanted to conserve my strength somewhat.

Because I needed to make sure I had something left in the tank when he came out. Or I would have to find a way inside the church—and I was hoping my Horseman Mask had some damned clever ideas on that front.

I had to fight better than I usually did, with half of my usual weapons. And Alucard couldn't risk looking weak. The fight had to be intense enough that no one had time to think about anything else.

So...

I scooped up the Silver katana, yanking it out of the pavement, and rushed Alucard. He grunted, flinging his hands at me with another blast, his eyes staring directly at my shoulders. I took a risk and fell into a baseball slide, hoping his look had indicated his aim.

Another bar of fire screamed over my head, but I had already been holding my arm up to shield me from the heat. Another line of poor bastards with worthless umbrellas went down with puffs of dust or screams —those unlucky enough to receive a kill-shot.

I used the momentum from my slide to jump right back to my feet and punch Alucard in the chest. He grunted loudly, taking his own swing at my face. I ducked and gave him a body-shot.

"Told you," he wheezed in a whisper, "I would hit you where the sun don't shine," he coughed, taking a feeble swing at my head, keeping us close. "The vampires," he muttered, regaining his breath. Then he grabbed me and hurled me right back towards the umbrella academy vampires.

I grunted as I hit and rolled, not bothering to hide my smile. I hadn't caught his hint earlier, but it looked like he was really on my side. I came to my feet, stumbling slightly as I veered towards an untouched group of vampires.

Alucard pointed with his eyes, and I evaded as another bar of light—this one actually a triple bar of light that pounded through the umbrellas like rice paper. I kept running and Alucard kept blasting, taking out more and more as Paradise and Lost began to howl—either calling up reinforcements or attempting to tell Alucard to *stop*, I wasn't entirely sure.

They had a point, though. Too much more of this and people would get suspicious.

I skidded to a halt and hurled a blast of air at Alucard, knocking him on his ass. I glanced up at the church discreetly to see someone was still watching from the window, although I couldn't make out a face. Good enough.

I sprinted at Alucard, holding the katana over my head as I swung it down at him. Sparks flared as I missed, striking the concrete. Luckily, this wasn't a typical sword but my Silvers magic or the blade would have snapped. Alucard tripped over his own feet and I caught him with a back kick right in the jaw, knocking him out cold.

I slid the sword into my makeshift sheath before walking up to the Daywalker and nudging him with my boot. He didn't stir.

I bent down to grab him by a leg—just like Cain had done—and dragged him towards the church as the crowd grew still. I stared up at the window, smiling as I dropped Alucard's foot. I placed my hands on my hips and shouted.

"ROOOOOOOOOLAND! COME OUT TO PLAY!"

I waited a few moments, but the doors remained closed.

Then I kicked Alucard once for good measure—making it look like a lot harder of a blow than it was—and turned around to face the Shepherds, keeping the church in my peripheral vision but turning my back entirely on the vampires and wolves. What was left of them, anyway.

"Okay. I think I'm all warmed up, now. Who's nex—"

A bar of crimson light about twenty feet wide suddenly erupted out from the very top of the church, shooting straight up into the sky. It struck an unseen crimson dome high above with an earth-shaking gong like a struck bell.

Damn it. I was out of time. There went my plan to draw Roland out.

54

Other than the initial gasps, the street had gone very quiet, everyone staring up at the crimson beam of light with horror. It hadn't been a blast of power, but more like...

A homing beacon. It rippled with power, seeming to twirl and rotate like a drill.

I averted my gaze to check on the crowd. They all looked on the verge of fleeing for their lives. Well, Dorian's crew did. Some of the vampires looked awed by the crimson beam while others, including the werewolves, looked ready to make me pay for taking down Alucard and hurting so many of them in the process.

The Shepherds looked nervously upon the crimson beam, but they soon shifted their attention to me. I spotted Xuanwu and his two monks staring directly at me, three boulders in the sea of panicked faces of the Hellfire Club behind them. And an idea suddenly hit me.

I reached into my pocket to cut my thumb on his figurine. "Emphasize my words," I breathed, squeezing the turtle in my fist. I saw his clawed fist clench on the hilt of his sword.

I let go of the tortoise figurine and turned to flash a big grin at the vampires and werewolves. My voice rang out like a bullhorn, crisp and clear over the rising sounds of panic. "Hell hath no fury like a demon bored!" I shouted, raising my arms slowly.

And then I immediately opened up my vision to the Silvers and...

I gasped, my smile evaporating. Xuanwu was suddenly zipping straight past me—close enough for me to touch—on his way to the vampires. Despite everyone else suddenly moving as if swimming in honey, Xuanwu was fucking Flash Tortoise. And he was laughing and screaming like a Norse berserker on cocaine-infused mead, his beak spread wide and his tongue lolling out the side of his mouth like a dog on a car ride. In fact, Xuanwu looked exactly as happy as that dog would.

He was a tornado of death. I saw his icy blue katana flick and slash across vampires and wolves without any resistance whatsoever. He targeted specific locations within the vampire and werewolf camps—each victim ten feet or more apart from one another.

To inflict maximum chaos when they suddenly heard screams from all over their camps, rather than all from one front like a typical attack would do. Even with my Silvers vision, he was a blur of tattered robes, icy blue blade, and outstretched claw.

I snapped out of it, returning my vision to normal and forcing the smile back onto my face. I glanced over to see Xuanwu standing beside his monks as if I'd imagined the whole thing. I saw his cloak ripple ever so slightly, followed by the faint *click* of his sword returning to its sheath.

Emphasize, I'd told him. Good god.

I stared down the vampire and werewolf camps just as a dozen of the red-eyed monsters suddenly dropped, clutching their stomachs to hold in their intestines. Then came the howls and screams—from both the afflicted and the untouched. Paradise and Lost spun from me to their army, barking orders, demanding what the hell had just happened.

I stood there, smiling, with my arms outstretched, and within moments all attention snapped back to me. I let out a forced laugh, figuring even if it sounded a bit strange, they would just think demons had strange laughs.

There wasn't a comedy club in Hell, after all. Or...maybe the *best* ones were down there.

Everyone got really freaking nervous to see that the crazy lady in white somehow killed a dozen heavily protected wolves and vampires with a mere thought.

They hadn't seen anything yet. This next part was to take back my toys.

I began to slowly twirl, laughing up at the sky. "Hello, Darkness, my old friend..." I sang.

And clouds of smoke puffed into existence in half a dozen places within the Fabrizio and Roland camps. Men and women began to scream as they fell, and I saw a dozen wizard shields spring into existence near the Shepherds. Werewolves suddenly grouped into small units of four or five—backs to each other as they glared out at the smoke, snarling and biting at the air, their hackles raised aggressively.

Chains snapped and a beastly roar announced that somewhere on the other side of the world, a lady butterfly had flapped her wings...

And a pissed off polar bear rolled over an army of Shepherds in Kansas City.

She barreled through them like a gust of wind through a field of wheat—just with a lot more blood spurts and sounds of snapping bone. Shots rang out as several of the SHITs with more practical foresight unloaded on her with small caliber pistols—and even a shotgun!

I glanced up sharply to find Eae now standing atop the bus stop, his face pale. If Eae hadn't done his other job, I was going to rip his wings off.

Claire, instead of running faster, stopped cold. She slowly turned around, ignoring the bullets hammering into her body, and I let out a sigh of relief. Eae had gotten her bracelet back like I'd asked. I glanced up at him and caught the vaguest of nods before he refocused on the Shepherds with a sickly look on his face.

I felt that. I'd asked him, essentially, to do this to his people. Claire calmly walked up and grabbed the SHIT with the shotgun by the chest and hurled him into a fountain across the street from the church, flushing the little turd.

No one shot any more bullets at her as she calmly loped towards me and settled down on her haunches at my side. She was matted with blood, but I saw the band wrapped around her paw and let out a sigh of relief. Bears could take a licking and keep on ticking, so there had been the chance that she'd take the bullets without having her bracelet from Darling and Dear—the one that made her bulletproof.

I was just thankful she'd been fast enough to get away before anyone decided to try magic or an electric net—which I was keeping a close eye out for.

She pressed up against me with her shoulder, settling down on all fours and tucking her ears back as she let out a great bellowing roar, saliva stretching from her massive fangs.

Then she glanced back casually, looking past my shoulder, and her tongue rolled out of her mouth like a panting dog.

I turned to see Cain walking up to me, as healthy as I'd ever seen, but decorated here and there with blood. From the blood dripping from his dagger, I knew it wasn't his.

"You two just standing around as usual?" he asked. I grinned, squeezing his arm before I turned back to the two camps of very pissed off monsters.

It was time to show everyone what they'd gotten themselves into.

Paradise and Lost gasped incredulously to see Cain at my side, their eyes instantly darting to where they'd last seen Alucard.

But his unconscious body was suspiciously missing, gosh darn it.

I stepped forward, Cain and Claire flanking me with blade and claw. "Know the shadows of Hell! They are mine to command!" I crowed. Paradise and Lost looked horrified, and spun to their surviving wolves, shouting commands. I was surprised the two women hadn't wolfed out by now. What did that mean?

The church doors finally began to open, and a tide of vampires rolled out.

Unfortunately, everyone chose that moment to run towards the center and duke it out rather than letting the unseen shadows continue to kill them. Upon seeing this great flush of vampires—and maybe encouraged by my successes so far, many of the Hellfire wenches began hurling glass jars upon the wolves and vampires, deciding they'd had enough of the current state of affairs in Kansas City.

Which was great. Really. Me, inspiring all these angry witches to team up and fight Roland's army. Any other time it would have brought a tear of pride to my eyes.

Except tonight, that just meant the Shepherds didn't have to try as hard to go after the vampires and wolves. It meant a few of them had time to focus on me.

I saw Fabrizio storming my way, a dark gleam in his eyes, as well as Arthur who looked as if I'd just run over his dog. Oh, and the church doors closed, too. That part had been cool. I hadn't stood a chance at getting there before they'd closed anyway—not through the three armies slamming into each other less than twenty feet away from me.

Simply put, it was pure, unadulterated chaos.

More clouds of smoke erupted everywhere, and ninjas appeared in their wake, slaughtering anyone with red eyes and only harming others if they accidentally pointed something sharp in my general direction. I saw many ninjas go down, but not as many as their foes. They even died in silence, for the most part. The surviving ninjas didn't confront Fabrizio or Arthur, though. Those two just kept chugging my way.

The little holy engines that could.

I turned to Claire and Cain, pointing out Paradise and Lost. They looked like they were trying to regroup their wolves and either flank someone, flee, or escape to the church. "Catch, don't kill. Not yet. Roland might sense their deaths, and who knows what that would do to the ritual," I urged, pointing up at the beam of light.

Cain turned to Claire excitedly. "I've wanted to ride you for a while now, Claire—" He danced back from the sudden swipe of her massive paw, obviously having anticipated her reaction. "Fine. Maybe next time," he said, chuckling good-naturedly. She made a chuffing sound that translated to, *they will never find your body*, and he seemed to find that even funnier.

Then they took off at a dead run, pursuing Paradise and Lost.

Rather than square off against the two Shepherds—because I didn't want to kill my friends—I saw an opening in the battle and took it. I needed to get closer to the church. If Roland wasn't coming out, then I had to find a way in. Fabrizio shouted something at my back, but I ignored him as I slipped through a trio of red-eyed vampires, opening their bellies with my katana as I politely said, "Excuse me."

Because we're courteous in the Midwest.

As disappointed and frustrated as I was with the Shepherds, they didn't deserve to die.

And a direct fight with them would only end in death, because they saw a demon, so would try their hardest to separate my head from my shoulders.

Right about now would have been a good time to get rid of the Demon-skin I had placed over myself in the alley—at least according to Richard. If only I knew how. Thinking of Richard, why hadn't he shown up? Had I not been in enough danger yet?

I heard Fabrizio and Arthur hurling magic and blades at the knot of fighting behind me, so I poured on the speed to increase my lead. I flung out my hand at a pack of five wolves and silver spears as tall as I was erupted from the ground, impaling them at head-level. I was careful to steer clear of their claws and jaws as I slipped past, reminding myself that they were bad.

Unfortunately, a small part of me was more honest. *They were gullible…*

Not having any time for facts in the reality I currently orbited, I forced down the thought.

I blasted fire and air, hurled silver spears, used my katana to carve out an opening or slice tendons, each step bringing me closer to the church. Closer to the real fight. I just hoped that crimson beam of rotating light didn't mean Roland had already completed his ritual.

55

I finally broke through the insanity and into a relatively open space. Apart from all the dead bodies, anyway. I kept jogging, just to make sure I didn't attract attention from those on the outskirts of the fighting.

I turned back to assess the field of battle, wincing as jars of witch's brew shattered and splashed here and there, usually resulting in such perversely horrifying reactions that I knew I would never be able to forget them.

One memorable one was a werewolf doused with purple goop suddenly realizing he had tentacles for legs. I watched him scramble all over the place for a good ten seconds, my brain momentarily shutting down. I snapped out of it when Fabrizio appeared out of the mob to stab him in the throat. I don't know if it was me or the werewolf who looked most relieved.

But Fabrizio was staring at me as he did it.

Arthur was nowhere in sight, thankfully, but I still didn't want to fight Fabrizio. Because I didn't want to kill him. And I needed my energy for Roland. I reached into my pocket to grab my Horseman Mask of Despair, but I was surprised to feel the Crucifix necklace I'd found inside the Doors also in the same pocket. The one that had belonged to Anthony, an old friend of Fabrizio. *A brother*, he had said.

I pulled them both out, allowing the Crucifix to hang in my hand between us, swinging back and forth like I was hoping to hypnotize the First Shepherd.

Which...it kind of did. Fabrizio slowed, frowning. I lobbed it to him in a way that indicated zero threat, and then I slapped on my Horseman Mask, my heart racing with concern over what it might feel like. What might happen next.

I hadn't expected the sensation of a thousand sticky fingers latching onto my face to hold it close to my skin so that it wouldn't fall.

I also hadn't expected it to come with default Silvers vision.

Everything abruptly slowed, and I gasped as the whole battle stood before me like a painted portrait. Fabrizio stood at the forefront of the masterpiece like a man reaching out for help, his face blank with shock as the crucifix necklace slowly closed the distance to his hand—only inches away now.

I saw Alucard blasting the courtyard with sunshine, a ring of vampires flying outwards in slow motion, crumbling to ash even as they flew.

I saw Xuanwu and his ninjas killing red-eyes without ever being seen—for the most part. Some of the ninjas went down, but not very many. Xuanwu never even came close to being sensed. And Ryuu stood at his side, grinning savagely as his katana erupted out of a red-eyed vampire's back.

I couldn't wait to tell Ryuu that I had, in fact, seen him. Smug bastard.

I saw Cain and Claire apart from the general mob, squaring off against Paradise and Lost—now finally in wolf form—looking as if they didn't know or care that any other battle existed behind them.

Dorian Gray and Arthur were nowhere in sight—probably obscured by the hundred other bodies filling the street.

And dozens upon dozens of colorful ribbons whipped back and forth from foe to foe, indicating where attacks would land. I could see it all. And with a little focus, I realized I could speed it back up to the normal flow of time. But I didn't do that.

I glanced back to see Fabrizio clutching the crucifix necklace and staring at me with awe. I felt a flash of heat on my scalp and I gasped in surprise. He recognized me!

Except he obviously hadn't noticed Eae sweeping down upon him from behind, like an eagle catching a fish in the water. Eae snatched him up. In slow motion, it looked way worse than it probably was—as if the force had snapped Fabrizio's neck or at least given him severe whiplash, like in one of those crash test dummy videos. The angel swept his massive wings down to lift the First Shepherd directly over me before looping back to safety.

It was incredibly beautiful to see in slow motion.

And it totally killed the reunion we'd almost had.

With a sigh, I turned back to face the church, studying the ward from this entirely different perspective—the Silvers—as I reached into my other pocket.

To give me momentary reprieve, I flung up my second butterfly charm, the one Nate had given me, and Silver butterflays exploded into the night in a swarm of razor-sharp wings and incredible speed, keeping the area around me relatively clear from shifter and vampire.

Up close, the red mist surrounding the church seemed thicker—but that was probably because it wasn't shifting and moving as fast as real time. It also felt...alive. I couldn't explain why, but I knew I wasn't wrong. It was insanely powerful.

I remembered Ryuu's message from Xuanwu from earlier and found myself repeating it as I stared at the entrance to the church. My church.

"*Abandon all hope, ye who enter here* is a fitting phrase above a locked door," I murmured. And they had been right. This door did deserve such a warning.

My Mask grew warm against my face, latching onto the thought, seeming to massage my temples in hopes of speeding up my brain power. I didn't fight it. I accepted it, recalling the peace I had felt at Xuanwu's home after twelve hours of silence. I tried wrapping that feeling around me, now, meditating with my eyes open.

All Xuanwu's talk of me being the White Rose...how the vines creeped, and they crawled into the most unwanted of places, crumbling everything in their path...

And the haunted look I'd seen on Xuanwu's face while watching Claire and Cain tease each other...at the despair threatening to slip through the numerous cracks in the crumbling walls of his will to live—cured only by watching others laugh. A depression he suffered.

How—as strong as Solomon was—he wasn't stronger than the relentless creeping vines crawling through his body, breaking him apart from within....

And I thought about despair itself. Despair was a mental poison. It seeped through our best defenses, our best days, finding any crack of self-doubt it could expand.

Not entirely understanding what I was doing, I closed my eyes and opened myself up further to the Mask of Despair, allowing it to see my own cracks and weaknesses, my own insecurities and self-doubts. Many I had already vanquished in my trip through the Doors.

But that was the funny thing about confidence.

It could always be broken back down by Despair.

So I shared them all, old and new—not relishing in them, but accepting them fully. That they were the demons in my mind, haunting me and gripping my shoulders, ever-circling me as they waited for their moment to pounce and knock me back down.

But...

They would never keep me down. Because...

I.

Was.

Despair.

I would *always* get back up. Even if it was only to die by my enemy's blade. Because it was worse to die a coward and give in. Even in those darkest moments when the world threatens to gobble you up and there is no hope...

You.

Must.

Stand.

It's the only way to *beat* despair. To lie to yourself with false hopes.

Because guess what?

That's what despair was doing to *you*. Always whispering, always laughing, always mocking you, always planting negative thoughts—whether true or not—in the fields of your mind. Knowing that you could only take so much before giving in and buying the lies.

The only way to combat that was to *lie right back*, counteracting the attacks. Balance the self-doubt with self-confidence. Whether false or not, it didn't matter.

Use their tactics against them. Lie for lie. Self-confidence for self-doubt.

So I did that now. Knowing that no matter what knocked me down, I would *always* stand back up. Always. No matter how many times I had to rebuild my walls. I would always be ready to lay another brick.

And the Mask grew warmer, and warmer, and warmer against my face. I opened my eyes to see that the world had dimmed faintly, as if made of fog.

Despair was like mist, able to slip through the smallest crack in existence, and it could only be defeated by the sun's light—by the concrete knowledge that the sun would always rise again tomorrow and burn it away.

So as invincible as the mist—despair—was...

It was just as invincible as the sunlight—hope—was...

The two battling back and forth for eternity, each fearing the other's seemingly immortal, invincible power, but never ceasing their war.

I glanced down at my hands and smiled maliciously.

I wasn't surprised in the slightest to see that I was now a cloud of mist, no longer flesh.

The dark cloud of Despair laughed as it drifted through the red haze surrounding the church, shifting and realigning its particles to slip past the strongest of wards.

I found myself inside the church within moments and noticed a repetitive chime.

Ding. Ding. Ding.

I felt the Mask of Despair struggling against me as my form solidified again, leaving me to stand inside the church, blinking rapidly. I felt a strange, rattling sensation deep within my soul, and the Mask of Despair evaporated in a puff. I shoved my hand in my pocket eagerly and let out a sigh of relief to find the silver butterfly charm—my Horseman's Mask—resting within. It...seemed exhausted.

Ding. Ding—

The sound cut off abruptly and I spotted a necklace sitting on a nearby pedestal. It was the necklace Alucard had told me about—the one that sensed demons. And...it had just stopped.

I looked up to follow a long red carpet leading to the altar to reveal a table and two men standing before me. Henri and Roland. They looked like they'd just crapped their pants. Maybe that was because I still had my katana on me.

I silently commanded the Silver butterflays outside to guard the door so no red-eyed reinforcements could interrupt our reunion.

My smile turned savage as I drew my katana, harnessing my inner Nate Temple. "Ding, ding, chuckleheads. Don't worry, I'm not here to sell you a vacuum," I said, flicking my chin at the door behind me that I'd just invaded like a soul-slurping salesman. "I see more than enough suckers here already."

Roland stared at me incredulously. "Callie..." he breathed.

I nodded coldly. "Did you miss me?" I asked as I slowly advanced in a fighting stance.

56

I halted six paces away, studying the scene before me. Henri Bellerose was shaking in terror, standing his ground—probably by command from Roland—and hating every single second of it.

Because he was Roland's Renfield, now.

Roland stood before a long, antique wooden table. The table held an old book and a large bowl of blood. Blood painted his mouth—exactly like the milk mustache kids get when chugging milk. It dripped down his chin like a macabre goatee. He wore no shirt or shoes, only fitted silk pants. Strange, haunting symbols painted in blood decorated his chest, and I immediately averted my eyes from them as they seemed to spring to life, making me think of the omegabet I had seen in my mother's laboratory.

Two standing bowls of glowing coals squatted on either side of the table, and dozens of candelabras lined the perimeter of the room as well as the long red carpet, but all the pews had been taken away. The hundreds of tiny flames flickering from the candelabras cast the room in a soothing, spiritual, almost romantic glow. The Silver statue of Nameless stood where it always had, no one daring to attempt moving it since it encased a literal Fallen Angel. Right now, he looked concerned, but that could have been the lighting.

Oh, and there was a huge fucking portal of crimson blood—like a pond but hanging vertical—standing where the altar would have been had this still been a church. It was big enough to drive a car through. I refused to stare into it, afraid of what I might see.

"Callie..." Roland repeated in a breathless whisper, gripping the table with both hands as if it was the only thing keeping him upright. "How..."

I stared at him, my blood pounding in my ears, magic literally screaming and crackling at my fingertips and down the length of my katana, begging to be unleashed—even though Roland held no weapon or magic at the ready.

"Do me one favor, Roland. You owe me," I said, calmly shrugging out of my Darling and Dear jacket and walking away to hang it on the wall. I wouldn't need it. It wouldn't be fair.

He watched me return back to my initial position, now garbed only in my white set of ninja garb with the bloody red cross over my chest. He didn't say a word, his eyes haunted as everything he had done recently seemed to suddenly hit him at once, filling him with despair and shame.

I wasn't even surprised that he knew me. My Horseman's Mask must have stripped away the Demonskin.

"And what is that...Callie?" he whispered, his voice hoarse. He said my name like he personally needed to hear it, a lifeline through the rivers of blood he had unleashed upon my city.

"I want to savor this moment..." I told him.

He nodded slowly, willing to do anything to have me back.

"*You, my father, there on the sad height*," I whispered, not even having to try hard to remember the words of his favorite poem.

He shuddered as if stabbed. Because he'd spoken Dylan Thomas' famous poem out loud before prayer every single night before going to sleep. When he had been a good, pious man.

A single tear rolled down his cheeks.

The power around me manifested more noticeably at his audacity to shed a tear for my judgment when he'd spared none for shedding blood. The magic screamed and whipped, tore and railed against our clothes, the walls... our souls. Henri Bellerose was openly whimpering.

"*Curse, bless, me now with your fierce tears, I pray*," Roland finally whispered.

My rapid breath felt as sharp as razors.

"*Do not go gentle into that good night*," I quoted. But I was also telling him...

Telling him to give it to me as hard as he could. To show me no mercy. I *needed* this. To know I had beaten him, utterly, once and for all. That at least one of us had remembered his lessons, his creed. That I had followed that creed and was here now to punish him for breaking that creed. The ultimate poetic justice.

Pun. Fucking. Intended.

This wasn't him committing suicide. This was a debt between every master and student. That one day, the student learned enough to challenge the master, and on that day, she deserved an honest, all-out confrontation. A *true* win.

Not a participation trophy.

He nodded, another tear spilling down his cheek, making my already tumultuous grip on my magic flare stronger, more violent. He held out his hand and Henri hunched as he tugged Roland's own katana from the wall where it had been mounted. Henri carried it to his master, handing it over with the weapon reverently balanced on the meat of his two hands.

Roland took it, closed his eyes, and nodded to himself. Then he looked up at me, and through his pain, his guilt, his unhappiness, and his shame, I saw a flicker of honor and obligation. Of excitement and respect. Of...anticipation.

This situation was rare and was a tradition to truly cherish.

He knew what I wanted. What I deserved. Even if it never should have been this way...

He *owed* it to me, and to himself, to test his student once and for all, holding nothing back. Because even if he lost, that loss only verified—beyond question—his superiority among all teachers. That he had taught someone so well that they had *beaten* him.

The only one who had anything to lose in that regard was me. And by challenging him like this—with his own poem and the first weapon he'd ever trained me with—I had willingly forfeited any easy way out, claiming that I believed I was the better swordsman.

"*Rage, rage,* Callie, *against the dying of the light!*"

He'd even personalized the ending.

I would do the same. With my blade.

And the church pretty much blew to hell as the master's blade flashed out against his student's blade in an explosion of sparks and sound.

We were both laughing and crying.

Living and dying.

Triumphing and losing.

Hoping and Despairing.

Loving...as only two true warriors could ever understand.

It was a celebration. A wake. A cumulation of our entire existence encompassed in the momentary flash of steel on silver, blade on blade, eye to eye with a true warrior.

57

Roland roared, his fangs glinting in the candlelight. And our blades met again, chiming violently as we both pivoted and danced, spun and swung, lunged and parried...

He kicked over one of the bowls, sending a cascade of coals my way that forced me to hop back—and I barely avoided his sword lunge with a clumsy parry. The coals ignited the carpet, slowly filling the room with smoke.

And still, we danced, both resetting our stances to resume our swordplay.

There was no judgment on *any* chosen form of attack. Roland had taught me to use everything at my disposal—and him kicking over the bowl was a subtle reminder that anything was fair game. This was a battle between master and student—not just in swordplay...

In the art of war.

In response to the maelstrom of magic still crackling down my blade—the magic that I hadn't actually intended to use, Roland flung up his own to counteract the constant wind batting at us from every angle, and it was only a matter of seconds before we were hurling magic even as our blades clashed in a continuous peal that sounded like windchimes in a storm.

Because he hadn't only trained me in blades.

He'd trained me in magic.

So it was a duel on multiple fronts. He hurled jagged bolts of crimson lightning at me, and I flung up traps to catch them—not even sure how I'd done it. His bolts of power would strike the white orbs I flung to hover about the room like magnets, even when he tried throwing them directly at me. They sucked up his lightning, turning them to crimson glass bars that fell and shattered on the floor.

And all the while, we danced, our blades never halting, as we circled the room, knocking over candelabras and stepping over the crimson glass hunks strewn about the floor.

Flame met ice, spirit met water, air met earth in concussive explosions that rocked the attacker as much as the defender.

And soon, we both sported dozens of minor cuts—none debilitating, but each slowly weakening us. Our breaths were heavy and loud, our passion wild and savage.

Our love unbreakable.

Which is why we never slowed. This was our moment. Our greatest achievement.

We didn't *want* to slow down. This moment was as alive as we would *ever feel.*

I harried him, slicing, lunging, spinning, pirouetting with my katana until I neared the lone remaining brazier of coals. I encased my hand in my angelic gauntlet like I'd done when fighting a demon long ago and shoved my hand into the orange embers in an explosion of sparks. Roland gasped, dancing back a step as I lifted my massive gauntlet to reveal a large pile of smoldering coals. I used air to lift and slam the coals together with an explosion of embers and sparks, forming a crucifix as large as a man's torso, and bound together by Silver wire whipping out from my gauntlet like spider silk.

And then I hurled it at Roland with as much power as I could muster, banishing my gauntlet.

It struck his chest and he screamed from the depths of his soul, the crucifix burning into his flesh down the center, literally branding him with a crucifix the size of his body. He flung it away, panting and gasping, almost dropping his sword. The smell of burned flesh filled the room.

But I was already pursuing my weakened, battered, injured prey.

I chased him around the perimeter, ignoring the smoke and burning carpet, the hunks of crimson glass littering the floor, lunging and swinging as he knocked over more candelabras in an attempt to get a single *second* of reprieve so he could turn around and reset his stance.

But I didn't let him.

Just like he wouldn't have let me.

I kicked him in the back, knocking him into the table with the book and bowl of blood. I pivoted with my hips, bringing my entire strength and momentum behind my overhead strike to end this once and for all. In one toe-curling climax.

Roland had spun and, upon seeing my inbound attack, ducked beneath the table, knowing he didn't have time to get his sword up fast enough to parry my strike.

My silver katana sliced entirely through the table, the book, and the bowl of blood, showering him with all of it as the table crashed down—each jagged end of the center of the table trapping an arm to reveal the helpless, wounded, branded man beneath.

He was covered in blood and pages of paper, and the crucifix brand looked ghastly.

And I didn't give him the chance to roll free or use his magic to blast the table away.

I had already lifted my sword from my initial blow, and it was screaming down towards his face before I could have even tried to stop it.

In his eyes...

I saw a glint of relief.

An applause of congratulation.

A lifetime of memories.

A bond of love and respect that...

Welcomed this end.

The *only* end he'd ever wanted.

Not in a fight with some punk monster, but in a battle that truly *meant* something.

A battle of love. A death he could be proud of rather than ashamed of.

And I saw forgiveness. And gratitude. And a million other emotions. I knew it would be the last thing I saw in his eyes before the blank stare of death took its place.

A third silver blade abruptly darted between us, batting my katana clear out of my hand to fly free and stick into the wall.

I don't know who was more shocked. Roland, as he was kicked clear of both me and the portal by his own Renfield...

Or me to see Henri Bellerose no longer hunched and cowering.

Henri stood before me with a confidence even deeper than the first time I'd ever met him.

"Enough, Callie," Henri said in a gentle tone. "Enough. Your mother would be proud."

And the heartfelt smile on his face made absolutely no sense to me. He slowly descended to kneel before me, holding up the sword he'd just used so that it rested on his two open palms. He offered it to me, with his eyes downcast. "Let me explain before you choose to kill me," he said, with absolutely no fear in his voice.

Roland stared at Henri in utter shock, so imagine how *I* felt.

Without replying, I took the blade from his hands and backed up a few steps to reassess the situation, still panting from my prematurely-ended fight. One thing was certain.

Even if the rules had just changed...

I wasn't finished playing yet.

58

Henri slowly climbed to his feet but made no threatening gesture whatsoever.

I blinked at him warily, realizing that I'd been right from the beginning. Even though I didn't know how he'd pulled it off, Henri was no Renfield. He was *not* a broken vampire. His face was still a scarred ruin, but he didn't seem affected by it. And he stood to his full height.

Henri had tricked Roland, using him to...

I avoided looking at the crimson portal behind him.

Dracula's Castle was just beyond it. I knew it for a fact.

And Henri wanted to step through it. I could practically taste his desire to do so.

So...as the seconds stretched on, I wondered why he made no attempt. Hell, why hadn't he hopped through while the master and student were duking it out?

Roland was sprawled on the ground, leaning against the wall, clutching his horribly wounded chest as he stared at Henri in utter disbelief.

Henri finally turned to face me, and I realized the reason for his silence had been to give me the time to catch my breath. Because he'd turned to look at me the *moment* that I'd told myself I had recovered enough from my fight to go another round. He smiled at me—not a sinister, evil overlord smile, but a soul-deep smile of...approval.

Which was *always* worse. About a million fears sprang to mind, but I silenced them all.

Henri closed his eyes, and tendrils of silver and black smoke began to slowly swirl up around him. They spun faster with each passing second until I could no longer see Henri at all.

Then they puffed out and a second man was suddenly standing behind Henri. He was only a few inches shorter at most, and stockier with broad, wide shoulders. He commanded the room with his presence. Henri, on the other hand, collapsed, and I knew without looking that he was dead.

This new man's long, dark hair hung past his shoulders and his face was...beautiful.

Roland cursed, struggling weakly to climb to his feet, but he hissed and groaned, falling back down. Even though vampires healed fairly fast, that crucifix brand didn't look to be getting any better.

Which was why I had thought to try it—a memory from the Doors.

When I'd seen that stained-glass window with a man and a young child staring at a burning cross...

Even with the necklace hanging around his neck—the one that let him step inside churches, touch holy objects, and use the Lord's name—his powers could do nothing about the crucifix branded into his very flesh, from neck to navel, and nipple to nipple.

Just like the one marking my chest.

I was far enough away to notice all this about Roland without ever taking my eyes off of Henri's dead body and this second man. He didn't look familiar, but I suddenly realized my boots were tingling and that they had been ever since he appeared. I gasped, lifting my sword.

"Samael," I breathed, wondering how the hell my boots had failed to warn me any of the other times I'd been near Henri.

Roland, recognizing the name, tried the whole fish on dry land routine again to similar effect. He wheezed as he leaned against the wall, his eyes furious.

Samael lifted a hand casually. "Hear me out before you do anything drastic. Please."

"Give me one good reason, Samael," I snarled, wondering how any of this was possible. There were no demons in Kansas City. Everyone had said it.

He shrugged, tucking both hands behind his back. "Because Roland is innocent, Callie." He paused for a moment. "Well, at least of all major crimes," he admitted.

I blinked, pointing my sword at Roland. "Many have died at his hands."

Samael shook his head. "Indirectly."

"I said give me one good reason, not a pile of lies," I growled at his ridiculous answer. Even Roland looked baffled by it.

"The truth?" he asked, sounding tired and uneasy.

I nodded. "It will feel good to get off your chest before I send you back home," I said, brandishing the Seal of Solomon on my finger.

He sighed, letting out a breath. "I'm your Godfather. Your mother's request."

I laughed loudly. "Right. You. Samael...my Godfather." I laughed harder, even turning to Roland to shake my head instinctively. He had started to smile back before lowering his eyes in shame. I lowered mine for a different reason. Disappointment.

Samael cleared his throat gently. "Check for yourself. I'm sure you learned all about your blood mix..." he said slowly, the words catching my attention. "Maybe you can focus and check our blood bond for yourself. Maybe you already bonded me in an alley..."

I dropped my sword, gasping as the room suddenly flashed with light—not an actual external light, but an internal one—my mind suddenly replaying that moment I had first stepped back into Kansas City. This same man, Samael, *had* approached me. That much was true. I shook my head, refusing to believe the memory. But Cain had been so sure of himself. That it had been Le Bone.

"Why would I have believed a single word from your mouth? We were expecting an attack. I wouldn't have approached a stranger," I argued, glaring at him. "And I definitely would not have disguised myself at your word, let alone wiped my own memory of it all."

Samael nodded with infinite patience. "I approached you and stopped at a distance, announcing my name and that I would submit to you, but I asked that you do one thing for me," Samael said. I tapped my foot, waiting. Roland was watching the two of us as if the candelabras had come to life and were debating the space-time continuum.

"And I suppose I liked your smile so much that I agreed?" I asked sarcastically.

Samael smirked. "Well, it *is* a pretty smile," he said. Sensing I was not amused, he dipped his head—the motion from such a commanding presence was...bizarre. "I asked you to check our blood bond for yourself."

I did that now, taking a second to factually dispute at least one of his ridiculous claims and...

I took an instinctive step back, shaking my head in disbelief, feeling as if I was on the verge of a mental break. Because I saw a black and silver cord of power even thicker than the blood bond that I shared with Claire or Cain...

Whatever was going on, he truly *was* bonded to me. Meant me no harm.

Samael waited patiently for me to look up at him. "I'll admit that it wasn't *that* strong in the alley. You doubted me, for obvious reasons. You required further proof. Made me shake your hand, exchanging our blood in a new blood bond," he explained, circling back to his original claim.

And my memory confirmed it, replaying our conversation almost word-for-word.

He nodded satisfactorily. "Maybe a certain tortoise and dragon talked to you..."

"What?" I whispered.

"An unholy trinity, you could say," he explained. "Your mother's idea. Her test."

Roland gasped, and I spun to see Xuanwu step forward from beside the front of the church, as if he'd been leaning there for the last hour. As did Qinglong, leaning against the wall on the opposite side of the door from his brother. "He speaks the truth," Xuanwu grumbled.

If Xuanwu's advice, his ninjas, his sanctuary, and his personal involvement outside hadn't helped me so much, I would have killed him on the spot. I remembered him telling me Samael had left Kansas City when I first disappeared, and I scowled. It hadn't been a lie.

"Deals with devils are often complicated and far-reaching," Qinglong echoed, his body slithering as he moved. I ignored Roland's panicked breathing, remembering the dark altar I'd seen in my mother's laboratory. How Qinglong had said *Dealing with devils is dangerous*. He'd basically told me right there, glancing at the altar and then my Seal. I had thought him speaking of just my Seal—of the demons inside it.

When I had been looking at the altar that likely summoned Samael to my mother. When she asked him to be my Godfather.

Damn.

If Qinglong hadn't shared a blood bond with me, I might have attacked him on the spot.

"I'm not going to lie," Samael said. "I was beyond impressed that you could pull off that Demonskin spell in less than a minute. It belonged to your mother, by the way. And you did it with only a single glance at the omegabet," he said, shaking his head in awe.

I froze, hearing a ringing sound in my ears. "I...*used* the omegabet?"

He nodded. "Like a pro. *I* won't even touch that stuff. That's *Masters* territory. You think I want anything to do with that? They mean the end of my kind, too. They want to use us up like batteries with their omegabet if we don't fall in line."

No wonder I had recognized it in my mother's laboratory. I'd already *used* it...I'd been remembering it, not *learning* it.

Which lent further proof to Samael's claim. He really did work for my mother...as my Godfather. Every rational part of me wanted to argue and deny, but...if he'd wanted me dead, I would already be dead.

And that bond throbbed between us, stronger than any I had ever seen.

Samael glanced at the crimson portal behind him. "There was a purpose to all of this, and there is very limited time before that window expires," he said meaningfully. "All questions will be answered, I swear it. You can see our blood bond, so even if you do not understand *how*, you can see it is *true*."

I hesitated. "Except everything I have learned has been at your hands," I said, pointing to the three of them. "So this could be a con. No, it *is* a con, either way. I'm just trying to understand your end goal."

Samael pointed a thumb over his shoulder at the rippling portal. "That's the end goal. Or...the first real step to the end goal, anyway."

"If you believe us enemies, execute us," the two gods said in stereo, kneeling before me.

Samael hesitated. "Or maybe just toss me back inside the Seal of Solomon. No need to be hasty," he said, smiling. I stared at him, pointing before me. He sighed, hanging his head, and knelt.

I studied the three of them in silence. Xuanwu or Qinglong could have detached my head before I ever knew they had even moved.

Samael had fought me once in the Doors and had so sorely outclassed me that I traveled the realms searching for power in the hope I would have a *chance* at defeating him.

All three of those kneeling before me could kill me as easy as taking a step.

I let out a breath, shaking my head as I ran a hand through my hair. "What's so fucking special about Dracula. And why get Roland involved?"

Samael looked up sharply, an excited gleam in his eyes. "Does that mean you agree?" he asked anxiously.

I pursed my lips at him. "Maybe if you didn't sound so strangely aroused about it..."

He grimaced at me, slowly climbing to his feet.

Xuanwu hesitantly lifted a claw, smiling at me compassionately. I nodded and his beak tightened as if my approval had made him feel some kind of way. He set the gargantuan claw on my shoulder, using his cane to support his weight.

"None of us liked our roles, but we all understood the reason for them," he explained. I nodded, not necessarily empathizing, but acknowledging what he said. "What I told you about Dracula's Castle is true. The only way to reach him is the way Roland has done." He glanced over at the man in question to find him still staring at us, clutching his chest. The tortoise god waved at him and Roland hesitantly waved back a single time. "Samael—through possessing Henri's body—gave Roland everything he needed to connect the two locations, establishing a bridge between them, and a barrier over both of them," he explained. "The Blood Moon, a vampire tyrant, a flock of blood-bound followers and...a hellbent vampire hunter," he said, looking at me.

I shivered. Although I hated to admit it, I knew he was right. They'd needed to make both places similar. "That's why you made me erase my memory of it," I said softly.

Qinglong nodded. "It was the only way to truly have a chance at entering—and surviving—his Castle. Because Samael knows how to rotate this barrier around Kansas City to put *both* barriers over Dracula's Castle, preventing him from *escaping*."

My eyes widened incredulously. This wasn't some robbery attempt.

This was a fucking *hit*.

Qinglong continued, quivering with excitement so that his flesh-stache bobbed up and down in tentacular glee. "You and Samael have trapped Dracula...A *Master*. And he can't call for reinforcements or escape..."

My knees wobbled and I would have collapsed if Xuanwu hadn't caught me.

"You...want me to kill Vlad Dracul. And he's a *Master*," I whispered in horror.

"It's the perfect opportunity. Kill one of the upper-echelon Masters while they're trapped and vulnerable," Samael said. "We needed to know that you wouldn't waffle. Going up against the Masters could bring you face-to-face with people you once called friends. We had to know you wouldn't waver," he said, glancing at Roland pointedly. "But I never would have let you kill him. He is innocent of any major crimes," Samael said. "Those were all me and Henri. We just made it look like Roland, and then led Roland to believe he had done it."

"How did you convince Roland to even attempt this?" I whispered.

Roland spoke up for the first time. "He promised a way to bring you back. That Dracula had the key to save your soul."

I hissed, slapping Samael in the face. He took it unflinchingly. I hit him again, because I couldn't think of what to say. In a strange way, he had been telling the truth. As he met my eyes, his cheeks red, I knew that's what he was thinking, too. Yet he still let me strike him.

Confident I was done slapping him, Samael shot me an imploring look. "Time is not our ally, here," he said, pointing a thumb at the portal. "And if we don't beat the clock, the bridge and barriers will fall. Guess who will be on the next flight to Kansas City and who he will want to talk to?" he asked, jerking his chin at Roland. I shivered. "He will come to Kansas City like a plague, Callie. He will annihilate this town, because if he shows any weakness, the other Masters will take him out and steal *his* power."

I was silent, considering it as hard as I'd ever considered anything. I had so many questions...how had no one known Samael was in town? Everyone had said Kansas City was demon-free. And what had happened to Phix? Why had Cain been so confident he'd seen Le Bone? And—

I realized that none of that mattered. It was like knowing atoms existed but denying them because you didn't know what color the electron was.

Because that blood bond between Samael and me...

There was absolutely no denying it.

Samael cleared his throat, drawing my attention. He was appraising me from head to toe, glancing pointedly at the wounds from Roland's sword. I hadn't even thought about them, so they must not have been life-threatening. "Unless you're too weak to continue the fight. Or you *want* Dracula to come here..." he taunted.

I grunted, recalling something that I'd learned from my Mask of Despair. That I would always get back to my feet, no matter the odds against me.

"I'd have to be Dracula's sidekick..." I muttered, straightening my shoulders, meeting his gaze. "To be down for the Count." I spit out some blood and nodded at him.

He grinned.

I sighed, shaking off my dozens of questions. "How long is this going to take?"

"That's the spirit!" he crowed excitedly.

59

I told Xuanwu to take Roland, Claire, and Cain to his sanctuary with his ninjas. The Sanguine Council was going to be pissed and would have all sorts of questions when the barrier around Kansas City dropped. I had to know they were safe. Alucard was to be invited but allowed to leave for home if he chose—after he *unfixed* the political system in Kansas City back to the way it was. To some extent, anyway. Events of the past twelve months were still redacted, but no more policemen or politicians in vampire pockets.

Really, the only one not allowed to leave was Roland. He was on house arrest. To that effect, I told Xuanwu about Starlight's *Vampyr* bracelet.

Even as I was telling Xuanwu this, Roland stared at the distant wall, not reacting in any way whatsoever. Xuanwu noticed and nodded comfortingly to appease my fearful thought—to make sure Roland didn't take his own life. That was all Roland was getting from me until I returned. We'd said all that needed to be said with our blades.

Xuanwu cleared his throat pointedly, drawing Roland's attention even though he made it sound like he was only speaking to me. "Roland was manipulated. In a way, Samael's interference saved your old mentor." Roland scoffed, proving he was listening, but Xuanwu went on as if he hadn't heard. "Samael caught wind of how upset Roland was at your disappearance into the Doors. He also caught wind that Henri Bellerose and Haven were meeting in private, planning to break Le Bone from prison and overthrow Roland..." My eyes widened, and there was dead silence from Roland's direction. "Samael chose to possess Henri for this reason—a way to get himself close to Roland while preventing an assassination," Xuanwu explained.

"The devil works in mysterious ways," Samael grunted from across the room, having also been listening. "Three birds, one stone."

Roland made no sound. I wasn't sure if it had helped him in the short-run, but maybe it would in the long run.

"You mentioned he was innocent of all crimes?" I asked loud enough for Roland to hear.

Xuanwu nodded. "He did kill Haven, but even without knowing why, it was justified since Haven had been plotting to murder him. Other than torturing Henri—Samael—he never actually got his hands dirty. Henri would pass on Roland's commands, leaving Roland to focus on the spell to make the bridge and the barriers."

I shook my head in disbelief.

Could it be true?

I couldn't afford an emotional reunion until I solved this Dracula situation. Despite being innocent of the major crimes he'd been accused of, he had still willingly agreed to cross some pretty solid lines in order to 'save me.'

At the indirect expense of a lot of innocent lives. He needed to think about that.

I continued getting my affairs in order for my trip.

Qinglong promised to heal Solomon of the thorn growth he'd given him and to give them some kind of update on what had happened—so that Last Breath didn't do anything reckless and come searching for me. Ringing Dracula's doorbell, for example.

It also meant I didn't need to worry about Alucard failing to heal Solomon.

I turned to find Samael waiting patiently at the portal.

"How long do we have? There is one more thing I need done."

Samael glanced at the portal. "Maybe ten minutes. Better make it five."

I turned back to Xuanwu, choosing him since he'd been present during the fight outside. "I don't want to waste energy stepping back through the ward outside the church, so I need you to make an announcement to everyone for me, and to have that announcement spread far and wide to anyone else in town."

He nodded. "What do you need said?" he asked, closing his eyes to focus.

And I told him. I wasn't a speech writer, and I had a lot I would save for later—if I survived my encounter with Dracula, of course.

But I needed everyone to know that the White Rose had returned, and that she was responsible for breaking the barrier around the city. That Roland was in custody, and certain evidence forced me to look deeper into the allegations of the Red Pastor—that he may have been framed by unknown parties.

Xuanwu smirked at that, the corners of his beak creaking with chipped ice.

Most of all, I wanted the Masters to know my name. That Kansas City was off limits to anyone looking for a throne. I wanted everyone to know I claimed credit for taking down Roland so that the Masters would know who was the deadliest bitch in Kansas City.

So they wouldn't go knocking on doors and hurting people when they wanted answers.

I wanted my name to haunt their nightmares, to ruin their vacations and to make them connect some dots to me when they realized Dracula had missed their last meeting...

I also asked Xuanwu if his ninjas—shinobi—would mind being Kansas City's unofficial police, keeping tabs on any nefarious activity. He'd smiled, nodding instantly.

"And lastly," I told him. "Make it abundantly clear that this is my fucking church, and my fucking city, and my top priority is looking out for the citizens of Kansas City. The Shepherds, and any other authority in town, remain only at my permission. Until an official announcement is heard directly from my lips, no one is to be given the title ally of the White Rose. Except for your ninjas," I added with a smirk. "To that effect, Fabrizio and Arthur may remain at Abundant Angel Catholic Church. All other Shepherds or Vatican men are banished."

Qinglong chuckled. "I like the way you work, Callie."

I nodded. "Get all that Xuanwu?"

He nodded. "Have fun with your godfather," he said, pointing a claw at the portal.

I sighed, gave them each a hug, and walked over to my katana buried in the wall. I yanked it clear and scooped up my Darling and Dear jacket, tugging it on. Then I stood beside Samael, not even bothering to look at Roland in the corner against the wall.

Without further ado, we stepped through the pool of blood together, and into a world of embers and sparks...

60

We stood on a bridge of black crystal. It did not have a Disney princess vibe.

The bridge was much longer than I would have thought, suspended across a vast chasm of gray boulders far, far below. I didn't see a single tree anywhere I looked. Not even a dead one. Embers and sparks whipped through the air like gnats, even though I saw no fire anywhere and felt no wind on my cheeks. I remembered Pandora mentioning a fear of embers and sparks, some place the Temple family had saved her from.

Maybe this was it.

Despite the lack of wind, the biggest thunderstorm I had ever seen warred in the sky above—a storm of silence. No thunder or cracks of lightning struck the ground. Just a riot of light high above.

On the far end of the black crystal bridge stood another portal—identical to the one behind us—that led to Dracula's Castle.

The two of us started to walk, setting our sights on the portal ahead.

Our date with destiny.

"What is this place?" I asked, staring down at the bleakness far below the bridge.

Samael pursed his lips. "Purgatory. Neverwas. The Night Currents." He waved a hand. "For a place no one wants to visit, it has many names."

I shivered. "Why are you doing this, Samael? Why help me pick a fight with the Masters?"

He eyed me thoughtfully. "Your mother asked me to, and I was blood bound to her." He was silent for a few steps. "I admit it wasn't just out of obligation. I want the Masters in control as much as I want a holy spear in my eye." He seemed to stare through me for the briefest of moments, as if eyeing the spear inside my soul. I narrowed my eyes at him. A warning. He relented with an amused smirk. "I never truly wanted it. Your mother wanted it strengthened. That was the whole point of me chasing you into the Doors. Another test," he explained. "To make you stronger. To give you a reason to fight. To confront the Masters, you will need all the tools in your precious Temple—and Temple will need all the precious tools his parents *stole*," he added, shaking his head with a strange look on his face.

I frowned, surprised to hear he knew of Nate. "You knew his parents..." I said, realizing what he'd meant. Of course he had. He'd worked with my mother.

He nodded, smiling wistfully. "You have no idea how much fun that was, working with such vicious sociopaths as Calvin and Makayla..." he whispered nostalgically. "Truly legendary. Like meeting your idols..."

We continued on in silence after that, all too soon standing before the portal.

Samael looked up at me with a devilish grin. "Look at the two of us. Godfather and Goddaughter, going on our first adventure—"

I shoved him through the portal of blood. "Godless, maybe," I muttered, stepping through after him without a moment's hesitation.

We arrived in a courtyard with a thirty-foot-tall door ahead of us and the outer gates to the castle behind us. The wind screamed and ripped at my jacket, the Blood Moon hanging in the twilight sky like a Christmas ornament. The stone walls themselves seemed to groan in protest of our arrival, growling at us to leave, outraged by our invasion.

"Have you ever heard of a Beast before?" Samael asked casually, doing something with the portal behind us. I turned to watch as he grabbed one edge of the portal and pulled it over to the opposite side like he was closing a curtain. The portal winked out with a wet splash of blood that soaked the grass. "There. Both barriers are here, now. Which means we can't leave until we kill this bastard."

I nodded. "What were you saying about a Beast?" I asked, staring up at the foreboding castle before us. I counted at least a dozen towers—only the part of the castle we could currently see—each climbing as tall as any skyscraper I'd ever seen before. Vast structures connected the towers to portray how large the space really was.

This wasn't just a bunch of skinny towers surrounding a small building.

No. This was literally the size of a *city*. We were on somewhat of a rise, overlooking a vast section of the castle-grounds below, since Dracula hadn't bothered to level the grounds before construction. No. He'd just built his castle around the nature of the land itself. I saw at least ten gardens, a maze, a few cemeteries, gardens seemingly filled with only statues and other marble monstrosities, and stairwells that wrapped up around the sides of most of the towers before continuing on in vast swinging or solid bridges to connect some of the loftier heights. I shook my head in awe. It felt like I was parked on one of those point lookouts that stood on a mountain above a city like Hollywood—construction spreading as far as the eye could see.

I realized Samael hadn't answered me, so I turned to look at him expectantly.

He noticed, turning away from the city below to meet my eyes. "A Beast powers Dracula's Castle. The place is quite literally alive, possessed by this Beast. Have you ever heard of something like that?" he asked. Then he shook his head, frowning. "Why am I even asking that? You know the Temple family's Beast, Falco."

I swallowed, nodding. "Yeah. I've heard of Beasts," I said, recalling the one he'd just mentioned. Falco occupied Nate's 17,000 square foot mansion...

Although it was *nothing* compared to the size of this. Falco was an *outhouse* compared to this place.

The thirty-foot-tall door opened on squeaking hinges, ever so slowly, dust falling from the joints. Faint piano music drifted out from within.

As did a rumbling purr of the Beast inviting us into her jaws.

I didn't bother waiting for Samael. I placed one boot before the other until I was walking—even though it felt robotic and awkward. Samael stepped up beside me and let out a breath.

"There's only one way to kill Dracula," he said. "And it is well-guarded. Dracula's Bane lies at the heart of this Beast," he said, gesturing at the doors about to swallow us up.

I nodded. "At least we know where we're going..." I said with hollow cheer.

Samael nodded, his eyes distant. "Into the belly of the Beast..."

Nate was going to be so jealous.

I got a Master first, I got a Master first...

Or he would never hear from me again.

One of the two...

DON'T FORGET! VIP's get early access to all sorts of Temple-Verse goodies, including signed copies, private giveaways, and advance notice of future projects. AND A FREE NOVELLA! Click the image or join here: www.shaynesilvers.com/l/219800

Callie returns in GODLESS... Get your copy online!
http://www.shaynesilvers.com/l/545338

Turn the page to read a sample of ***OBSIDIAN SON*** *- The Nate Temple Series Book 1 - or* ***BUY ONLINE****. Nate Temple is a billionaire wizard from St. Louis. He rides a bloodthirsty unicorn and drinks with the Four Horsemen. He even cow-tipped the Minotaur. Once...*

(Note: Nate's books 1-6 happen prior to UNCHAINED, but they crossover from then on, the two series taking place in the same universe but also able to standalone if you prefer)

Full chronology of all books in the TempleVerse shown on the 'BOOKS BY SHAYNE SILVERS' page.

TRY: OBSIDIAN SON (NATE TEMPLE #1)

There was no room for emotion in a hate crime. I had to be cold. Heartless. This was just another victim. Nothing more. No face, no name.

Frosted blades of grass crunched under my feet, sounding to my ears like the symbolic glass that one would shatter under a napkin at a Jewish wedding. The noise would have threatened to give away my stealthy advance as I stalked through the moonlit field, but I was no novice and had planned accordingly. Being a wizard, I was able to muffle all sensory evidence with a fine cloud of magic—no sounds, and no smells. Nifty. But if I made the spell much stronger, the anomaly would be too obvious to my prey.

I knew the consequences for my dark deed tonight. If caught, jail time or possibly even a gruesome, painful death. But if I succeeded, the look of fear and surprise in my victim's eyes before his world collapsed around him, it was well worth the risk. I simply couldn't help myself; I had to take him down.

I knew the cops had been keeping tabs on my car, but I was confident that they hadn't followed me. I hadn't seen a tail on my way here but seeing as how they frowned on this kind of thing, I had taken a circuitous route just in case. I was safe. I hoped.

Then my phone chirped at me as I received a text.

I practically jumped out of my skin, hissing instinctively. "Motherf—" I cut off abruptly, remembering the whole stealth aspect of my mission. I was off to a stellar start. I had forgotten to silence the damned phone. *Stupid, stupid, stupid!*

My heart felt like it was on the verge of exploding inside my chest with such thunderous violence that I briefly envisioned a mystifying Rorschach blood-blot that would have made coroners and psychologists drool.

My body remained tense as I swept my gaze over the field, fearing that I had been made. Precious seconds ticked by without any change in my surroundings, and my breathing finally began to slow as my pulse returned to normal. Hopefully, my magic had muted the phone and my resulting outburst. I glanced down at the phone to scan the text and then typed back a quick and angry response before I switched the cursed device to vibrate.

Now, where were we?

I continued on, the lining of my coat constricting my breathing. Or maybe it was because I was leaning forward in anticipation. *Breathe*, I chided myself. *He doesn't know you're here*. All this risk for a book. It had better be worth it.

I'm taller than most, and not abnormally handsome, but I knew how to play the genetic cards I had been dealt. I had shaggy, dirty blonde hair—leaning more towards brown with each passing year—and my frame was thick with well-earned muscle, yet I was still lean. I had once been told that my eyes were like twin emeralds pitted against the golden-brown tufts of my hair—a face like a jewelry box. Of course, that was two bottles of wine into a date, so I could have been a little foggy on her quote. Still, I liked to imagine that was how everyone saw me.

But tonight, all that was masked by magic.

I grinned broadly as the outline of the hairy hulk finally came into view. He was blessedly alone—no nearby sentries to give me away. That was always a risk when performing this ancient rite-of-passage. I tried to keep the grin on my face from dissolving into a maniacal cackle.

My skin danced with energy, both natural and unnatural, as I manipulated the threads of magic floating all around me. My victim stood just ahead, oblivious to the world of hurt that I was about to unleash. Even with his millennia of experience, he didn't stand a chance. I had done this so many times that the routine of it was my only enemy. I lost count of how many times I had been told not to do it again; those who knew declared it *cruel, evil, and sadistic*. But what fun wasn't? Regardless, that wasn't enough to stop me from doing it again. And again. And again.

It was an addiction.

The pungent smell of manure filled the air, latching onto my nostril hairs. I took another step, trying to calm my racing pulse. A glint of gold reflected in the silver moonlight, but my victim remained motionless, hopefully unaware or all was lost. I wouldn't make it out alive if he knew I was here. Timing was everything.

I carefully took the last two steps, a lifetime between each, watching the legendary monster's ears, anxious and terrified that I would catch even so much as a twitch in my direction. Seeing nothing, a fierce grin split my unshaven cheeks. My spell had worked! I raised my palms an inch away from their target, firmly planted my feet, and squared my shoulders. I took one silent, calming breath, and then heaved forward with every ounce of physical strength I could muster. As well as a teensy-weensy boost of magic. Enough to goose him good.

"*MOOO!!!*" The sound tore through the cool October night like an unstoppable freight train. *Thud-splat*! The beast collapsed sideways onto the frosted grass; straight into a steaming patty of cow shit, cow dung, or, if you really wanted to church it up, a Meadow Muffin. But to me, shit is, and always will be, shit.

Cow tipping. It doesn't get any better than that in Missouri.

Especially when you're tipping the *Minotaur*. Capital M. I'd tipped plenty of ordinary cows before, but never the legendary variety.

Razor-blade hooves tore at the frozen earth as the beast struggled to stand, his grunts of rage vibrating the air. I raised my arms triumphantly. "Boo-yah! Temple 1, Minotaur 0!" I crowed. Then I very bravely prepared to protect myself. Some people just couldn't take a joke. *Cruel, evil,* and *sadistic* cow tipping may be, but by hell, it was a *rush*. The legendary beast turned his gaze on me after gaining his feet, eyes ablaze as his body...*shifted* from his bull disguise into his notorious, well-known bipedal form. He unfolded to his full height on two tree trunk-thick legs, his hooves having magically transformed into heavily booted feet. The thick, gold ring dangling from his snotty snout quivered as the Minotaur panted, and his dense, corded muscles contracted over his now human-like chest. As I stared up into those brown eyes, I actually felt sorry...for, well, myself.

"I have killed greater men than you for lesser offense," he growled.

His voice sounded like an angry James Earl Jones—like Mufasa talking to Scar.

"You have shit on your shoulder, Asterion." I ignited a roiling ball of fire in my palm in order to see his eyes more clearly. By no means was it a defensive gesture on my part. It was just dark. Under the weight of his glare, I somehow managed to keep my face composed, even though my fraudulent, self-denial had curled up into the fetal position and started whimpering. I hoped using a form of his ancient name would give me brownie points. Or maybe just not-worthy-of-killing points.

The beast grunted, eyes tightening, and I sensed the barest hesitation. "Nate Temple...your name would look splendid on my already long list of slain idiots." Asterion took a threatening step forward, and I thrust out my palm in warning, my roiling flame blue now.

"You lost fair and square, Asterion. Yield or perish." The beast's shoulders sagged slightly. Then he finally nodded to himself in resignation, appraising me with the scrutiny of a worthy adversary. "Your time comes, Temple, but I will grant you this. You've got a pair of stones on you to rival Hercules."

I reflexively glanced in the direction of the myth's own crown jewels before jerking my gaze away. Some things you simply couldn't un-see. "Well, I won't be needing a wheelbarrow any time soon, but overcompensating today keeps future lower-back pain away."

The Minotaur blinked once, and then he bellowed out a deep, contagious, snorting laughter. Realizing I wasn't about to become a murder statistic, I couldn't help but join in. It felt good. It had been a while since I had allowed myself to experience genuine laughter.

In the harsh moonlight, his bulk was even more intimidating as he towered head and shoulders above me. This was the beast that had fed upon human sacrifices for countless years while imprisoned in Daedalus' Labyrinth in Greece. And all that protein had not gone to waste, forming a heavily woven musculature over the beast's body that made even Mr. Olympia look puny.

From the neck up, he was now entirely bull, but the rest of his body more closely resembled a thickly furred man. But, as shown moments ago, he could adapt his form to his environment, never appearing fully human, but able to make his entire form appear as a bull when necessary. For instance, how he had looked just before I tipped him. Maybe he had been scouting the field for heifers before I had so efficiently killed the mood.

His bull face was also covered in thick, coarse hair—he even sported a long, wavy beard of sorts, and his eyes were the deepest brown I had ever seen. Cow-shit brown. His snout jutted out, emphasizing the golden ring dangling from his glistening nostrils, and both glinted in the luminous glow of the moon. The metal was at least an inch thick and etched with runes of a language long forgotten. Wide, aged ivory horns sprouted from each temple, long enough to skewer a wizard with little effort. He was nude except for a massive beaded necklace and a pair of worn leather boots that were big enough to stomp a size twenty-five imprint in my face if he felt so inclined.

I hoped our blossoming friendship wouldn't end that way. I really did.

Because friends didn't let friends wear boots naked...

TRY: WHISKEY GINGER (PHANTOM QUEEN DIARIES BOOK 1)

The pasty guitarist hunched forward, thrust a rolled-up wad of paper deep into one nostril, and snorted a line of blood crystals—frozen hemoglobin that I'd smuggled over in a refrigerated canister—with the uncanny grace of a drug addict. He sat back, fangs gleaming, and pawed at his nose. "That's some bodacious shit. Hey, bros," he said, glancing at his fellow band members, "come hit this shit before it melts."

He fetched one of the backstage passes hanging nearby, pried the plastic badge from its lanyard, and used it to split up the crystals, murmuring something in an accent that reminded me of California. Not *the* California, but you know, Cali-foh-nia—the land of beaches, babes, and bros. I retrieved a toothpick from my pocket and punched it through its thin wrapper. "So," I asked no one in particular, "now that ye have the product, who's payin'?"

Another band member stepped out of the shadows to my left, and I don't mean that figuratively, either—the fucker literally stepped out of the shadows. I scowled at him, but hid my surprise, nonchalantly rolling the toothpick from one side of my mouth to the other.

The rest of the band gathered around the dressing room table, following the guitarist's lead by preparing their own snorting utensils—tattered magazine covers, mostly. Typically, you'd do this sort of thing with a dollar-bill, maybe even a Benjamin if you were flush. But fangers like this lot couldn't touch cash directly—in God We Trust and all that. Of course, I didn't really understand why sucking blood the old-fashioned way had suddenly gone out of style. More of a rush, maybe?

"It lasts longer," the vampire next to me explained, catching my mildly curious expression. "It's especially good for shows and stuff. Makes us look, like, less—"

"Creepy?" I offered, my Irish brogue lilting just enough to make it a question.

"Pale," he finished, frowning.

I shrugged. "Listen, I've got places to be," I said, holding out my hand.

"I'm sure you do," he replied, smiling. "Tell you what, why don't you, like, hang around for a bit? Once that wears off," he dipped his head toward the bloody powder smeared across the table's surface, "we may need a pick-me-up." He rested his hand on my arm and our gazes locked.

I blinked, realized what he was trying to pull, and rolled my eyes. His widened in surprise, then shock as I yanked out my toothpick and shoved it through his hand.

"Motherfuck—"

"I want what we agreed on," I declared. "Now. No tricks."

The rest of the band saw what happened and rose faster than I could blink. They circled me, their grins feral...they might have even seemed intimidating if it weren't for the fact that they each had a case of the sniffles —I had to work extra hard not to think about what it felt like to have someone else's blood dripping down my nasal cavity.

I held up a hand.

"Can I ask ye gentlemen a question before we get started?" I asked. "Do ye even *have* what I asked for?"

Two of the band members exchanged looks and shrugged. The guitarist, however, glanced back towards the dressing room, where a brown paper bag sat next to a case full of makeup. He caught me looking and bared his teeth, his fangs stretching until it looked like it would be uncomfortable for him to close his mouth without piercing his own lip.

"Follow-up question," I said, eyeing the vampire I'd stabbed as he gingerly withdrew the toothpick from his hand and flung it across the room with a snarl. "Do ye do each other's make-up? Since, ye know, ye can't use mirrors?"

I was genuinely curious.

The guitarist grunted. "Mike, we have to go on soon."

"Wait a minute. Mike?" I turned to the snarling vampire with a frown. "What happened to *The Vampire Prospero*?" I glanced at the numerous fliers in the dressing room, most of which depicted the band members wading through blood, with Mike in the lead, each one titled *The Vampire Prospero* in *Rocky Horror Picture Show* font. Come to think of it...Mike did look a little like Tim Curry in all that leather and lace.

I was about to comment on the resemblance when Mike spoke up, "Alright, change of plans, bros. We're gonna drain this bitch before the show. We'll look totally—"

"Creepy?" I offered, again.

"Kill her."

MAKE A DIFFERENCE

Reviews are the most powerful tools in my arsenal when it comes to getting attention for my books. Much as I'd like to, I don't have the financial muscle of a New York publisher.

But I do have something much more powerful and effective than that, and it's something that those publishers would kill to get their hands on.

A committed and loyal bunch of readers.

Honest reviews of my books help bring them to the attention of other readers.

If you've enjoyed this book, I would be very grateful if you could spend just five minutes leaving a review (it can be as short as you like) on my book's Amazon page.

Thank you very much in advance.

ACKNOWLEDGMENTS

First, I would like to thank my beta-readers, TEAM TEMPLE, those individuals who spent hours of their time to read, and re-re-read the TempleVerse stories. Your dark, twisted, cunning sense of humor makes me feel right at home...

I would also like to thank you, the reader. I hope you enjoyed reading *BLACK SHEEP* as much as I enjoyed writing it. Be sure to check out the two crossover series in the TempleVerse: **The Nate Temple Series** and the **Phantom Queen Diaries**.

And last, but definitely not least, I thank my wife, Lexy. Without your support, none of this would have been possible.

ABOUT SHAYNE SILVERS

Shayne is a man of mystery and power, whose power is exceeded only by his mystery...

He currently writes the Amazon Bestselling **Nate Temple** Series, which features a foul-mouthed wizard from St. Louis. He rides a bloodthirsty unicorn, drinks with Achilles, and is pals with the Four Horsemen.

He also writes the Amazon Bestselling **Feathers and Fire** Series—a second series in the TempleVerse. The story follows a rookie spell-slinger named Callie Penrose who works for the Vatican in Kansas City. Her problem? Hell seems to know more about her past than she does.

He coauthors **The Phantom Queen Diaries**—a third series set in The TempleVerse—with Cameron O'Connell. The story follows Quinn MacKenna, a mouthy black magic arms dealer in Boston. All she wants? A round-trip ticket to the Fae realm...and maybe a drink on the house.

He also writes the **Shade of Devil Series**, which tells the story of Sorin Ambrogio—the world's FIRST vampire. He was put into a magical slumber by a Native American Medicine Man when the Americas were first discovered by Europeans. Sorin wakes up after five-hundred years to learn that his protégé, Dracula, stole his reputation and that no one has ever even heard of Sorin Ambrogio. The streets of New York City will run with blood as Sorin reclaims his legend.

Shayne holds two high-ranking black belts, and can be found writing in a coffee shop, cackling madly into his computer screen while pounding shots of espresso. He's hard at work on the newest books in the TempleVerse—You can find updates on new releases or chronological reading order on the next page, his website, or any of his social media accounts. **Follow him online for all sorts of groovy goodies, giveaways, and new release updates:**

Get Down with Shayne Online
www.shaynesilvers.com
info@shaynesilvers.com

facebook.com/shaynesilversfanpage
amazon.com/author/shaynesilvers
bookbub.com/profile/shayne-silvers
instagram.com/shaynesilversofficial
twitter.com/shaynesilvers
goodreads.com/ShayneSilvers

BOOKS BY SHAYNE SILVERS

CHRONOLOGY: All stories in the TempleVerse are shown in chronological order on the following page

FEATHERS AND FIRE SERIES

(Also set in the TempleVerse)

by Shayne Silvers

UNCHAINED

RAGE

WHISPERS

ANGEL'S ROAR

MOTHERLUCKER (Novella #4.5 in the 'LAST CALL' anthology)

SINNER

BLACK SHEEP

GODLESS

ANGHELLIC

NATE TEMPLE SERIES

(Main series in the TempleVerse)

by Shayne Silvers

FAIRY TALE - FREE prequel novella #0 for my subscribers

OBSIDIAN SON

BLOOD DEBTS

GRIMM

SILVER TONGUE

BEAST MASTER

BEERLYMPIAN (Novella #5.5 in the 'LAST CALL' anthology)

TINY GODS

DADDY DUTY (Novella #6.5)

WILD SIDE

WAR HAMMER

NINE SOULS

HORSEMAN

LEGEND

KNIGHTMARE

ASCENSION

CARNAGE

PHANTOM QUEEN DIARIES

(Also set in the TempleVerse)

by Cameron O'Connell & Shayne Silvers

COLLINS (Prequel novella #0 in the 'LAST CALL' anthology)

WHISKEY GINGER

COSMOPOLITAN

MOTHERLUCKER (Novella #2.5 in the 'LAST CALL' anthology)

OLD FASHIONED

DARK AND STORMY

MOSCOW MULE

WITCHES BREW

SALTY DOG

SEA BREEZE

HURRICANE

BRIMSTONE KISS

MOONSHINE

CHRONOLOGICAL ORDER: TEMPLE VERSE

FAIRY TALE (TEMPLE PREQUEL)

OBSIDIAN SON (TEMPLE 1)

BLOOD DEBTS (TEMPLE 2)

GRIMM (TEMPLE 3)

SILVER TONGUE (TEMPLE 4)

BEAST MASTER (TEMPLE 5)

BEERLYMPIAN (TEMPLE 5.5)

TINY GODS (TEMPLE 6)

DADDY DUTY (TEMPLE NOVELLA 6.5)

UNCHAINED (FEATHERS...1)

RAGE (FEATHERS...2)

WILD SIDE (TEMPLE 7)

WAR HAMMER (TEMPLE 8)

WHISPERS (FEATHERS...3)

COLLINS (PHANTOM 0)

WHISKEY GINGER (PHANTOM...1)

NINE SOULS (TEMPLE 9)

COSMOPOLITAN (PHANTOM...2)

ANGEL'S ROAR (FEATHERS...4)

MOTHERLUCKER (FEATHERS 4.5, PHANTOM 2.5)

OLD FASHIONED (PHANTOM...3)

HORSEMAN (TEMPLE 10)

DARK AND STORMY (PHANTOM...4)

MOSCOW MULE (PHANTOM...5)

SINNER (FEATHERS...5)

WITCHES BREW (PHANTOM...6)

LEGEND (TEMPLE...11)

SALTY DOG (PHANTOM...7)

BLACK SHEEP (FEATHERS...6)

GODLESS (FEATHERS...7)

KNIGHTMARE (TEMPLE 12)

ASCENSION (TEMPLE 13)

SEA BREEZE (PHANTOM...8)

HURRICANE (PHANTOM...9)

BRIMSTONE KISS (PHANTOM...10)

ANGHELLIC (FEATHERS...8)

CARNAGE (TEMPLE 14)

MOONSHINE (PHANTOM...11)

SHADE OF DEVIL SERIES

(Not part of the TempleVerse)

by Shayne Silvers

DEVIL'S DREAM

DEVIL'S CRY

DEVIL'S BLOOD

DEVIL'S DUE (*coming 2020...*)

NOTHING TO SEE HERE.

Thanks for reaching the last page of the book, you over-achiever. Sniff the spine. You've earned it. Or sniff your Kindle.

Now this has gotten weird.

Alright. I'm leaving.

Made in United States
North Haven, CT
15 June 2024